T
NEWCASTLE
ECCENTRICS

Frank Bray

Tyne Bridge Publishing

First published in the UK in 2017 by
Tyne Bridge Publishing, City Library,
Newcastle upon Tyne, United Kingdom
www.tynebridgepublishing.org.uk

Design/edit David Hepworth

Special thanks to Mr Howard Gold.

Also by Frank Bray:
Over the Bridge
Village of Dark Secrets

Some of the events and characters described in this novel were real. I have, however, tampered unashamedly with their chronology. And that is not the only liberty I have taken.

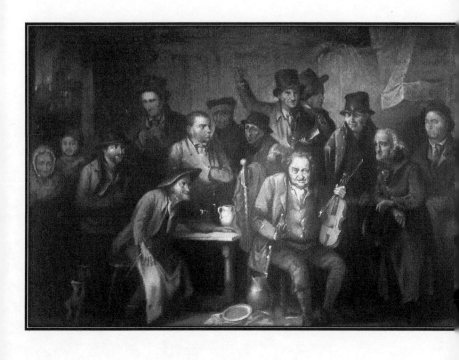

PROLOGUE

Several of us have got parts of our body missing or parts which don't work as they should. Maybe it's a hand or a leg or an eye or something of the kind, the absence or malfunctioning of which is immediately remarkable. Or maybe it's something which cannot be observed directly - something inside the head, for example, a section of the brain that is designed to enable us to remember things or to talk without stammering and stuttering or mixing up our words. Or maybe it's the case that some of us are just a bit out of the ordinary - you know, funny looking or mumchance or, well, not very proficient at communicating with others.

We became acquainted with one another mainly because most of us frequent the town centre or the Keyside. By and large, other Geordies are fairly well-disposed towards us despite our peculiarities. They probably feel sympathetic towards us. They give us what they can and even speak civilly to us on occasion. Exactly as they would do to a normal human being – which, of course, they realise we're not.

There are just a few people whose intentions towards us are no kinder than towards the rest of their fellows. They treat us wickedly, making amusement of our deficiencies or chasing us away, sometimes employing stones or even the contents of their piss-pots to assail us. In good time, they will surely reap the reward which their lack of charity merits. In this world or the next ...

We have even been endowed with a unique appellation. The 'Newcastle Eccentrics'. That is the name with which we have been christened, a name which gives us great pleasure. The Newcastle Eccentrics - I don't quite understand *exactly* what Eccentrics means – as far as I can establish it refers to people

who are a little peculiar, but in a likeable way, if such an explication makes any sense at all. Whatever the word means, I think
it sounds most satisfactory, anyway. And having our own name
makes us feel … well, a bit special, I fancy. Important, even. As
if we've gained some form of official recognition. Perlee Parker,
who regards himself as something of an artist – and rightly so,
I should make absolutely clear – asked us all to turn up one day
in Hell's Kitchen, the taproom of the Flying Horse Tavern in
the Groatmarket (not a problem, as many of us spend quite a
bit of time there anyway) so that he could paint a portrait of us.
At first, some of the Eccentrics were most reluctant to come –
in all probability, they felt embarrassed or were afeard that the
constables or the Town Guards might see it and recognise them
- but eventually they relented. I reckon old Perlee did a canny
job. Perhaps you've seen the painting yourself. If so, I'm sure
you'll agree that we're quite an assortment of characters.

You might have been wondering who we all are and how
we ended up as the Newcastle Eccentrics …

1

The first time I ever clapped eyes on Bold Archy, by which name I came to know him many years later, was on the morning that my parents (God rest their souls) took me to watch a hanging on the Town Moor as a special treat for my tenth birthday, which fell on the last day of November, 1795. The occasion made such an impression on me that even now, after the passage of well over a quarter of a century, I can recall the details with as great a degree of clarity as if it had taken place a mere seven days ago.

I remember that it was a chilly, bright day, the autumn sun low in the sky and a gentle south-westerly breeze rustling what few leaves still remained on the trees bordering the Moor. The air was lightly tainted with sulphurous fumes from the surrounding coal-mines. People had turned out for the spectacle in their thousands – tens of thousands, I should say – as it had been more than six years since the last execution there and the public had been starved of this particular brand of entertainment.

By arriving early, we succeeded in obtaining a vantage point within thirty yards of the gallows and my father lifted me up on to his shoulders to afford me a good sight of the proceedings. After we had waited what seemed to me an age, the sound of a muffled church bell was heard in the distance, prompting a surge of excitement among the crowd and, soon after, a procession came into view, approaching from the direction of the town. As it came nearer, I could make out the leading figure, a cassock-clad clergyman holding what I assumed to be a prayerbook and walking ahead of a cart on which a man whose hands were bound in front of him sat astride a coffin and was flanked by a dozen or so constables from the Town Guard bearing jave-lins. Behind this miserable assemblage came an assortment of individuals whose role and designation I could not, at that point, determine but who, as I was soon to be informed by my parents, included the Town Marshal (the one on horseback wearing a fine red uniform and cocked hat), several Town Ser-jeants, the condemned man's gaoler and the Whipper-and-Hougher, whose grim task it was to carry out the execution. One fellow stood out among the rest – the biggest man I had ever seen, as tall as a gas lamp and as broad as a hogshead – the man who, I was to learn later, bore the name Archibald Henderson. The purpose of his participation in this event was to become clear before long.

The jeers and boos of the spectators, accompanied by vol-leys of rotten fruit, swelled to a climax as the party neared the scaffold where the gallows had been constructed. When it came to a halt at its destination, the gaoler led the prisoner down from the conveyance and delivered him to the clergyman who imme-diately launched into a solemn prayer, beseeching God to have mercy on the soul of the sinner about to be dispatched and then calling upon the sinner himself to seek the Lord's forgiveness and make his final peace with the world from which he would shortly depart. The prisoner, a native of Scotland by the name of William Alexander, appeared to be in surprisingly fine spirits considering the nature of the ceremony at which he was the central figure and responded with a dignified speech which sat-isfied the pastor's injunctions and induced the erstwhile rowdy crowd's mood to alter, albeit briefly, in his favour. Then, in a sweetly melodic tenor voice, accompanied by a respectful and decorous silence among the on-lookers, he sang a verse of the Sinner's Lament:

All Cristen men that walkys me by,
Behold and see this dolefull sight!
Hit happith me noght to call and crye,
For I am dampned a woeful wight.

Afterwards (with some difficulty because of his bonds), the man shook hands with the Whipper-and-Hougher before submitting himself for preparation for the final act. A cord was placed around his neck and he was assisted to climb on to a small bench which, without further ceremony, was kicked away, causing his body to fall with a sudden and violent jerk and drawing a collective gasp from the spectators at the speed with which the deed was performed.

He died quickly and without a great struggle, much to the disappointment of a large section of the crowd – many of them had been waiting for hours to witness the free entertainment - from whom an audible groan issued as the man's twitching and twisting ceased no more than a minute or so after he had taken the drop. (In contrast to what happened on that day, I have since been present on a number of occasions when I have had the misfortune - many would say *good* fortune - to witness some poor creature twist in agony for over thirty minutes before the last breath was strangled out of his body, by which time many spectators had become bored with waiting and repaired to the nearby ale-houses in what is known as Bulman Village.)

When a further half-hour or so had passed in order to allow the corpse to be viewed by the public - and, it is to be affirmed without pleasure, subjected to a considerable amount of contumely and vituperation (which I believed to be due to the man's having deprived spectators of a lengthy period of expiry) - the Whipper-and-Hougher cut down the prisoner and pronounced him to be completely, unmistakeably, irreversibly and officially deceased. At this point, the exceptionally large man about whom I remarked earlier stepped forward, removed the coffin from the cart and placed it on the ground. Then he picked up the prostrate corpse as if it were no heavier than a rag-doll, laid it carefully inside, closed and secured the lid and, in what seemed to my young eyes an astonishing display of strength, picked up the coffin under one arm, swung it over his shoulder and returned it to its previous position on the cart.

When, as an adult, I was old enough to understand the meaning of such matters, I learned that the crime for which William Alexander was put to death involved the forgery of a bill of exchange which he subsequently attempted to negotiate at the Tyne Bank. Had he committed the same offence thirty years later, he would have escaped the death penalty and would instead have been transported on a convict ship to spend the rest of his days on the other side of the world. I learned too that his corpse was taken from the execution site by Archibald Henderson to the Barber-Surgeons' Hall in King's Manor where the colossus was employed as a helper to those whose occupation required them to acquire a thorough knowledge of human anatomy, in order that when it came to operating on live bodies the outcome would be more propitious than if they had been unable to first practise their art through experimentation with cadavers.

I remember too that our family's enjoyment of that event was tarnished somewhat by my father's discovery, on our return home, that his pocket had been picked by a cut-purse who had relieved him of the sum of half-a-guinea. 'Damn that fellow Barrington,' he cursed, in reference to a notorious rogue who was, by chance, arrested within the month in the act of making off with the proceeds of a break-in at the premises on the Side of Thomas Proctor, an elderly cheese-monger and bacon-dealer, and further charged with attempting to steal a watch from the Reverend Hector Warrilow, a Roman Catholic priest.

*

'Hold that lantern steady, will ye?' the short one hissed. 'How d'ye expect me to do this if Aa canna see me hand in front of me face?'

'Get a move on then, Aa'm getting cold here,' the tall one snapped back, his teeth chattering slightly. He didn't like to admit that it was not just the temperature that was affecting him. Despite all the time he had spent in his current enterprise, he was still unnerved by the darkness, especially being in such an eerie location, where every unexplained sound caused him to shudder and to wonder whether some horrible creature was lurking nearby, ready to pounce.

'This 'uns a bit hard to shift,' the short one said.

'Should still be nice and loose,' the tall one countered. 'Only got filled in yesterday morning.' He heard a slight movement in the grass at his feet and his body tensed as he imagined that an adder might be about to coil itself around his ankle and deliver a fatal bite.

The short one said nothing more for a while but continued to shovel the soil out of the hole and on to the canvass sheet laid out alongside. 'This un's canny deep too. Must be a good four foot down.'

'They probably had to pay an extra guinea to the grave-digger for that,' the tall one said.

'And that's on top of the guinea he got from us,' the short one riposted. Once he had removed enough soil to uncover about a third of the top of the coffin, he stood up, put down his spade, stretched his back and cracked his knuckles loudly (although not so loudly that anyone who might happen to pass the churchyard at such an ungodly hour would hear). Then he placed a piece of sacking over the exposed lid of the coffin in order to deaden the sound of the operation he was about to perform. The dim glow from the lantern picked out the beads of perspiration on his forehead and the puff of his breath in the frosty air. 'Pass me the lever,' he said.

The tall one reached over to a neighbouring grave, picked up the long iron crowbar he had leaned against the headstone and handed it to his companion. With surprising strength, the short one rammed the narrow end under the leading edge of the coffin lid until it splintered and then, with an expert twist of his wrist, forced it upwards until the front section broke off with a dull snap, revealing the head, shoulders and upper trunk of its occupant.

For a good five minutes the two men waited in anxious silence, listening for any indication that they might have been overheard. But all they could detect was the faint squeaking of the bats flitting around the churchyard in pursuit of insects, a sound which raised the hairs on the back of the tall one's neck. When they were as sure as they could be that the noise of their breaking into the coffin had not given them away, they set to work to remove the corpse. The tall one carefully balanced the lantern on the adjacent pile of soil so that it would shed enough light to enable them to see what they were doing without being visible from the road. Then, working in tandem, they looped a rope over the corpse's head and under its armpits. When the rope was firmly in position, they dragged the body out of the grave and placed it on the ground a few feet away. With practised ease, they quickly stripped it of all its clothes, pushed them back into the coffin and replaced the broken section of the lid as near to the original position as they could. Reversing their roles, the short one held up the lantern while the tall one shovelled the excavated soil back into the hole and stamped it down until he was satisfied that the grave was restored as nearly as possible to its former state and that no casual observer would detect that it had been disturbed.

'Ye get the feet,' he said when he had finished and the two men lifted up the naked corpse.

'He's a heavy bugger,' the short one said, panting a little at his exertion. 'Certainly never died of malnutrition.'

They carried him in reverential silence to a sheltered spot behind the row of yew trees at the margin of the churchyard. The tall one took up the large sack he had hidden there earlier and spread it out on the ground. Then the two of them manoeuvred the body inside it and the short one used a piece of rope to secure the neck of the sack.

'Aa'll stay here,' said the tall one. He didn't want to go back to the grave and risk a possible encounter with a snake. 'Ye gan and clear up and get the other stuff. Make sure ye dinaa leave nowt behind.'

Ten minutes or so later, the clattering of a horse's hooves and the rumbling of wooden wheels could be heard approaching until a gig came to a halt at the churchyard gate. The tall one waited for a few moments then let out a low whistle, which was returned immediately.

'Let's away,' he said to the short one. He was glad to be out of the place.

2

It would be impossible for me to forget the first time I went down to Sandgate, reputedly the most impoverished, squalid and detestable district in Newcastle. My father was a medical man and visited patients in all parts of the town. On some occasions he used to take me along with him on his rounds, but whenever he had to make a call to somebody in Sandgate he declined to let me accompany him. I had heard numerous tales of how wild and dangerous the place was and, as a naïve and idealistic young boy, I possessed neither the fear nor the commonsense of an adult, so that I longed to be able to see it for myself. I asked him repeatedly to allow me to go to Sandgate with him until at last he gave in.

We left behind the cuddy which he often took with him to reach his appointments, particularly when he had to travel some distance out of town, and went on foot. As we made our way through the chares running down to the riverside, the area was thick with what my father warned me were footpads and coat-snatchers, which, although I did not understand these terms, I assumed were people to be avoided. We were pestered unremittingly by beggars and pimps. What I now know to have been prostitutes, both male and female – as well as many of indeterminate sex – solicited us aggressively. Vagabonds stared at us resentfully and threateningly as if they recognised by our clothes the prosperity of our household relative to their own and were determined to deprive us of our possessions - and perhaps our lives too. There was an almost tangible atmosphere of tension and menace, such that I began to regret my insistence on being brought there. My father brandished his walking staff ostentatiously, presumably trusting that a display of readiness for action might deter potential assailants.

Half a mile or so from the waterfront, we reached an area honeycombed by dog-loups where we soon became disorientated. It was at that point that I began to realise that my father had lost his way. (He confided in me later, somewhat apologetically, that he had not visited that particular patient before and did not know exactly where he lived. This disadvantage was heightened by the fact that the names of the chares were changed frequently.) We found ourselves within a maze of cramped, winding alleys, so narrow that an average-sized man could touch both sides with his arms outstretched and a very fat one would pass only with difficulty. Here, sordid hovels were packed tight together, their inhabitants obviously in the habit of discharging all forms of household and human waste directly into the street outside, so that the ground had become slippery with a creeping tide of rotting filth which polluted the air with a foul, nauseating stench.

Enormous rats scuttled and squealed among the garbage, their bellies obscenely distended by unrestrained gorging on the foetid piles of decay. The air, thick with the sickly-sweet odour of decomposition, swarmed with dark clouds of flies. Tiny, naked urchins, apparently oblivious to their disgusting surroundings, scavenged among the heaps of putrefaction, compelled by the pangs of their hunger to retrieve any edible scraps, however rotten. Older children, clearly inured to the surrounding filth and determined not to let it deter them from enjoying their pastimes, rolled glass penkers along the cundies designed to drain away the fluid waste from the streets.

I had never imagined that human beings could descend to a level of degradation where they could be forced to live in such vile misery, such miasmic squalor. Appalled by the sights and smells that besieged our senses, I wrapped the collar of my coat over my mouth to avoid breathing the nauseous air but could not prevent myself from retching. Unable to find an exit from this hellhole, we became increasingly fearful at the prospect of being trapped in some pestilential labyrinth, perhaps to be ambushed, robbed and murdered, our bodies left to swell the festering contents of the thoroughfare.

As it was, our luck eventually turned. When we rounded the next corner, we happened upon a group of aged crones, all done up in widows' weeds, picking their way through the piles of decay. At first, these hags showed no inclination to respond to my father's request for help in finding our way to his patient's house. Then one of them, apparently acting as the leader of the group and displaying a flair for greed and enterprise, announced that this information could be provided in return for a payment of sixpence. Only when my father had produced his purse and handed over the bribe did she take the stick with which she had been poking the piles of rubbish and draw a rudimentary map in the slime.

Following the direction indicated, we soon reached an alleyway that led away from the worst slums. To our immense relief, the path eventually brought us to an open space where the breeze whipping off the river added a fresher tang to the air. Here, there were rows of shops, taverns and lodging-houses advertising *Beds to Rent* and *Good Beds to Rent*. And, at last, in a lane called Dark Chare, we located the house we were seeking. I say 'house' but it was not much less of a hovel than the others we had recently passed. Its tenant was a surly fellow of average height and stocky build, aged about thirty, broad-faced with a scar on one cheek and with the upper part of his nose looking as though it had once been broken in. He worked as a keelman and was wearing an outfit consisting of a blue jacket and yellow waistcoat, both of which were blackened with coal-dust. His home, so far as I could ascertain without exploring further -

which I certainly had no inclination to do - appeared to consist of two rooms, one a filthy kitchen and the other a filthy bedroom, both hanging with cobwebs, and in which the only item of interest (to me, at least) was a wretched spuggy in a little wooden cage. In the corner of the kitchen, a grubby baby was taking refreshment at the breast of a young, scrawny, half-naked woman who stared bleakly at my father and me during the entire time we spent in her company without uttering a word, or indeed, any other sound.

I remember that the purpose of my father's visit to that place was to administer to the patient, who had suffered a concussion of the brain and a dislocation of the great toe. He claimed that he had sustained these injuries in an accident at work. 'Aa was up-a-height and fell doon off the Winkhamlee staithe,' he muttered.

This account was meaningless to me until my father explained later that Winkhamlee staithe was a large wooden structure projecting into the river from which boats are loaded with coals transported by waggonway from Longbenton colliery. My father examined his patient carefully. The man was covered in cuts and bruises. 'Your pulse is ninety-eight and it's fairly weak, which suggests that you're losing blood,' my father told him. 'So I'm not going to bleed you today. Maybe I'll bring some leeches and do the job tomorrow if your pulse is stronger.' He looked at the man's dislocated toe, which was pointing in a different direction to the others. There was a huge amount of purple swelling on the foot. 'I'll try to put the joint back in for you. Hold on to something. This will be painful but you're a strong man so it shouldn't worry you.'

He grasped the man's heel with one hand and the damaged toe with the other and twisted vigorously for several seconds while the sweat stood out on his brow. The patient's eyes rolled and his face contorted with the pain but he uttered no sound. 'Can't do it,' my father said after several attempts. 'I'll prepare a fomentation for you, instead.'

'What's that?' the keelman asked, suspiciously.

'A hot compress,' my father told him. 'To reduce the luxation. You'll need to keep it on until I see you again.'

'Aa canna pay ye till after the weekend, Doctor.'

'That's alright, my good man,' my father told him. 'It can wait until next time.'

'Thank ye kindly, Doctor. Here…' He handed my father a walnut. 'There's something for the bairn.'

On our way back, my father confided in me that he found the keelman's description of how he sustained his injuries somewhat implausible. 'I suspect that he got them in a fight,' he said. 'The people here are always brawling.' It was certainly my impression of Sandgate that its population seemed uncommonly aggressive and malcontent. I could hardly blame them for being resentful of living in such an awful place and I vowed to avoid it in future.

In the event, however, I did not keep my vow for very long.

*

Just about everyone who lived in or visited the warren streets of Sandgate had heard of Cuckoo Jack Wilson. He acquired his soubriquet as the son of a mender of timepieces who specialised in the repair of cuckoo clocks, although Jack never considered following his father's profession. Instead, he became the best known waterman on the Tyne, hiring out boats at sixpence an hour. He had an intimate knowledge of the peculiarities and characteristics of the river – its tides and currents, shallows, sandbars, the location of submerged wrecks and other hidden hazards. On one occasion, he was confronted by an envious pilot who challenged him to prove his expertise, secretly hoping that Jack would come to harm in the process. Jack responded by wading across the river as far as the Gateshead bank at low tide.

The constabulary made regular use of Cuckoo Jack, enlisting his help to locate and retrieve the bodies of those wretches who had deliberately jumped, accidentally fallen or been cruelly pushed into the river. Jack would inquire as to the exact details of when and where the person had entered the water. Then he would sit in absolute silence for several minutes, a look of intense concentration etched upon his weather-beaten face, mentally calculating the speed and direction of the tide, the influence of the currents, the elapsed time and, no doubt, various other complicating factors. Eventually, when he had reached a conclusion, he would nod his head gravely, pick up his grappling irons and set off in one of his boats for the spot where he expected to find the body. He was rarely wrong and almost invariably collected the fee of ten shillings paid by the Corporation for the recovery of a drowned corpse. And, whenever he was able to rescue from the river someone who was fortunate enough to be still alive, he was content to forego any payment and was happy just to have saved them.

Cuckoo Jack also provided a private service to anyone who had lost something of value in the Tyne and had fashioned a number of ingenious hooks, chains and sundry tools which he used to salvage jewellery, coins, silver tankards and other items, which even included a whole cargo of copper articles and a pig of lead which had sunk near the mouth of the river. While he was renowned for his generosity and kindness, he was also a hard-nosed businessman and expected everyone to act fairly in their dealings with him so that those who tried to double-cross him usually regretted it.

There were many tales of his exploits. He was once approached by a ship's captain, one of whose sailors had fallen overboard and drowned. Having made his normal calculations, he directed the search to a mooring on the river where a number of ships were tied up to a buoy. He instructed the crews to haul in their cables and when they had done so, the sailor's body was found tangled up in the ropes. The grateful ship's captain rewarded Jack with the sum of five pounds.

On another occasion, a Frenchman promised Jack a sovereign if he could recover a valuable watch which had been dropped in the river. When Jack managed to bring it to the surface in no time at all, the Frenchman, surprised at how easily the task had been completed, offered him only a half-sovereign saying, 'This is enough reward for so little work.' Such was Jack's fury at the man's attempted deception that he flung the watch into the river and roared, 'It won't take ye lang to get it yarsel then, will it, mon ami?' It was only when the distraught and suitably contrite Frenchman agreed to pay *two* sovereigns ('handed ower in advance,' Jack insisted) that he got his watch back again.

Cuckoo Jack and his wife had two daughters and three sons, one of whom, Ralph, the spitting image of Jack, became my childhood friend. We first met when my father received an emergency call to attend the younger girl who, having taken an epileptic fit, was in danger of death and managed to treat her successfully with a mixture of rhubarb and magnesia. So grateful was Jack for this service that he rewarded my father with the gift (in place of his normal fee) of a silver tankard which he had recovered from the Tyne and the promise that I could accompany him and his son on a free boat trip whenever I wished.

As a result, attracted by the prospect of an excursion on the river, I dispensed with the pledge I had made to myself on my first visit to Sandgate that I would never return there. Subsequently, Ralph and I spent a great deal of time together and soon became as close as brothers. We used to spend hours on the Shore next to Petrie's-entry, near the spot where Jack kept his boats, observing the traffic passing up and down the Tyne. Our favourite spectacle was the fleet of keels making their way down river at slack water or on the ebb tide with their cargoes of coal to be transferred to the collier brigs waiting inside the sand bar at Shields Harbour. Each boat was manned by a skipper assisted by two crew known as keel-bullies and a peedee, a young boy. On more than one occasion, we followed them down to the mouth of the river and, if there was no sea-fret to spoil the view, watched from our vantage point on the Spanish Battery headland as the keelmen shovelled the coal from their chunky, blunt-nosed boats into the ships' holds. At other times, we waited for them to return on the flood tide to Sandgate Shore where groups of women – the so-called Keel Deeters – welcomed back their sweat-and-dust-covered men folk and set to work sweeping the coal waste from the boats in preparation for their next tide. In between tides, we were content to sit and watch the women standing up to their knees in mid-river, washing clothes. Sometimes, we even managed to catch a few salmon.

On occasion, we had the misfortune to be there when Cuckoo Jack returned from a rescue mission, only to witness him dragging out of his boat the bloated corpse of some poor devil who had ended up with his lungs full of Tyne water. Apart from the hanging on the Town Moor I had watched as a ten-year-old, those were my first experiences of seeing a dead body. In time, I was to see many more.

3

Less than two years after my tenth birthday, the day which proved to be William Alexander's last on this earth, I found myself orphaned by the death of both my parents, victims of the cholera morbus.

The cholera morbus! Time and time again the Common Council announced that the disease had finally been beaten, eliminated, obliterated, wiped out. But they were wrong and it kept coming back. Some said that it could only be explained as a curse of the devil, sent to punish those who were poor – because it was mainly the poor who were infected. It wasn't *just* the poor though. Sometimes it attacked others – traders, chandlers, publicans and businessmen – and, on one occasion, even an alderman of the town. I heard from one person who had heard it from another who had heard it from yet another, spoken in whispered tones at the Holy Jesus Hospital, that the source of the cholera morbus was the bad smell emanating from the open cundies which flowed down through the chares to the riverside. A miasma, they called it.

I remember watching the disease take both my parents from me within a few days. I believe that my father must have caught it from one of his patients. As a doctor he would, of course, have been fully aware of the affliction which had caused his sudden stomach pains and, knowing how infectious it was, ordered me to stay away from his bedside in order to save me from contamination. But how could I leave him in such a state? Ignoring his instructions, which rapidly transformed themselves into imprecations, I attended to him as assiduously as I was able, wiping his cold clammy brow, changing his soiled clothes, washing his aching body and responding to his constant craving for water. By the third day, he was hardly recognisable as my erstwhile hale, sturdy father. His eyes were sunken into their sockets, his breathing had become laboured and noisy and his skin had acquired a strange colour somewhere between grey and blue. By the fifth day, the cholera had taken hold to such an extent that even a generous dose of Dr Radcliffe's Famous Purging Elixir could not save him and he died during the afternoon.

My poor mother had scarcely begun her grieving when the vomiting seized her and it was obvious that she too had become a victim of the disease. Thankfully, her suffering ended much more quickly than my father's, her death occurring a mere two days after the onset of symptoms. By then, her husband had been hurriedly buried (within the stipulated twelve hours) in St Nicholas' Churchyard in a grave covered with quick lime to prevent the spread of infection.

Alone and distraught as I was, I prayed fervently that, as an act of divine mercy, I would be taken in the same way. But, somehow, I was spared. How I managed to escape the same fate as my parents I will never know, although many of those to whom I have recounted my experience attribute my good fortune to the Zimmerman's Stimulating Fluid which a compassionate neighbour, upon learning of my parents' demise, insisted that I should take, brushing aside my juvenile protests at its vile taste and forcing the medication down my throat in an act of kindness not appreciated by me at the time.

Notwithstanding my survival, I was, nevertheless, now deprived of the family home which went with my father's job and instead left to beg for charity on the Keyside. I don't remember exactly how long I spent in that impoverished condition, buying stale food at half-price from pastry shops or stealing from market-stalls, sleeping rough - often freezing cold and drenched to the skin - in the chares leading from the river, dodging the constables, being chased away by fishwives or gangs of ruffians and darting in and out between the dogcarts and gigs which criss-crossed the area. I confess that on more than one occasion, when my hunger pangs had become unbearable, I helped myself to a handful of hay from the nosebag of a horse left unattended in Sandhill while its master had repaired to a nearby hostelry. I guess it must have been two or three months until the miserable fog-laden day on which I was approached by a fine-looking gentleman riding in a fine-looking two-wheeled chaise drawn by a fine-looking chestnut cuddy. He was, I recall, rather stout-made but curiously light-legged, with a remarkably good set of teeth and his hair powdered and clubbed at the back. He descended from his carriage, dressed in a bright blue morning-coat, frilled shirt, waistcoat and breeches, and addressed me kindly.

'Tell me, young man, what is your name?'

'James Maclachlan, sir,' I replied truthfully, despite my apprehension at his interest in me.

'Ah, Maclachlan, you say. I do detect some Scotch blood there,' he ventured.

'So my parents told me, sir,' I replied.

'Ah, yes,' he said, as if pleased to have deduced the information correctly. 'And your parents, Master Maclachlan? Where *are* they, pray?' He looked around, as if expecting them to materialise at any moment from some dark recess.

'Dead, sir,' I replied. 'Both of them. From the cholera.'

'Ah, the cholera. Yes, such a misfortune to be orphaned so young.' He shook his head sadly and a little puff of powder drifted down on to the collar of his coat. 'And how old might you be, Master Maclachlan?' he asked.

'Eleven years, ten months and one week, sir,' I replied precisely.

He seemed very surprised at this news, but pleasantly so. I imagined that his astonishment derived from the fact that I was at the time (and still am) very slight of stature.

'Well, Master Maclachlan,' he said, peering at me through a quizzing glass. 'I think you could pass for a lot younger than that, wouldn't you agree?'

'Certainly, sir.'

'And I imagine you could shin up a tree like a monkey, couldn't you?'

'I don't know about that, sir.'

'And crawl through a hole the width of a firkin, if I'm not mistaken?'

'I'm not sure what a firkin is, sir.'

'Of course. That's not something for a boy of your age to know about.'

I don't believe that I comprehended the purpose of his questioning or the meaning of his remarks but I clearly remember that at some point in the conversation (perhaps, in retrospect, it was more like an examination, although that's not how it felt at the time) he seemed to come to a sudden resolution and motioned to me to climb into the chaise, which instruction I complied with obediently. Off we went, headed towards Westgate-street and quickly reached a row of cottages whose dilapidated condition was in stark contrast to that of the gentleman who took me there. No sooner had we come to a halt than there appeared from a narrow passageway a tall dusty fellow rendered even taller by the dusty top hat perched upon his dusty head which matched his dusty tailed coat and dusty boots. Had it not been for the dust, I would have taken him for an undertaker. Motioning me to alight from the chaise, he looked me up and down carefully, rather in the manner of a prospective buyer inspecting an animal in the marketplace. Then he nodded to the fine-looking gentleman and passed him what I imagined to be a coin – of what denomination I could not say – whereupon the gentleman shook the reins to stir his pony into action and was on his way. The tall dusty fellow guided me into one of the cottages to begin what I soon discovered was to be my first situation, that of an apprentice climbing-boy, indentured as a servant to Jeram Boag, Esquire, Master Sweep.

*

Felix Brandling was a very important person, one of the highest rank and station, as he never tired of telling those who cared to listen to him, as well as those who did not. However, it had to be admitted, even by those who did not share the lofty regard in which he held himself, that Felix Brandling did occupy a significant position in the life of the town. After serving for two years as High Sheriff of Northumberland, he became one of the two Members of Parliament (elected unopposed) for Newcastle-on-Tyne. He resided at his family seat at Gosforth House when in the country and owned estates in the Counties of Northumberland and Durham which contained rich coal deposits where he had established a number of collieries, thereby increasing his already-considerable wealth. He also had major commercial interests and connections in the West Indies. He considered himself to be not only a very important person but also a very astute businessman, never paying a single penny more than he needed to for anything and often paying a lot less than he had promised.

He presided over the Company of Hoastmen, a powerful body of landowners and merchants who controlled the northeast coal fields (the most productive and lucrative in the country). In return for paying modest levies to the Crown, the

Hoastmen had been given the sole rights to sell Tyneside coal, thereby acquiring a monopoly of the commerce between the colliery-owners and shipmasters. They were also able to control the transportation of coal down the river by virtue of the fact that they alone supplied the Tyne keels and employed the Tyne keelmen under annually-renewable bonds to operate them. Because of the importance to the town of the coal trade, the influence of the Hoastmen (or the Kings of Coal, as they were widely known) extended even to municipal life, so that many of their number could be counted among the aldermen and members of the Common Council.

Felix Brandling was not only a very important man (in his own opinion) but he was also a very fat man and as unprepossessing as he was arrogant. His corpulence was due in equal measure to his fondness for the excessive consumption of rich food and port and his indolent refusal to engage in any activity which others could be obligated to perform on his behalf. He grew to such a size that, whenever he rose from his place on the Tory benches of the Palace of Westminster to deliver a rare contribution to a debate, he struggled to get up without assistance from at least two others and his pursiness obliged him to pause and take several deep breaths in between sentences. Then, when he made his way from the Chamber, carrying his vast corporation before him, he could do so only at a snail's pace.

He suffered badly from an involuntary and severe flatulence with the unfortunate consequence that he always seemed to be shrouded in a malodorous haze and was generally unpopular with his associates and singularly lacking in invitations to social gatherings. He possessed a persistent nervous tic which quickly transformed itself into a frequent nervous laugh which in turn caused an uncontrollable ripple to course through his flabby jowls. And whenever he laughed, he was unable to prevent himself from coughing. And whenever he coughed, he was unable to prevent himself from farting. Similarly, whenever he farted, he was unable to prevent himself from laughing. And so, his life was a constant round of laughter, coughs and sulphurous detonations.

It was his repellent custom, on those infrequent occasions when he could be persuaded by his doctor to take a few steps in the open air, never without the assistance of a walking stick, to deposit large and recurring gobs of catarrh upon the pavement or, occasionally, upon some unfortunate who happened at the very moment of discharge to be passing between the expectorator and his intended target.

'We're going to have to do something about those damn keelmen,' he complained loudly to fellow Hoastman Aeneas Snitterby JP, as the two sat opposite one another (a little too close for the latter's comfort, it must be said), in the coffee lounge of the Assembly Rooms, a favourite haunt of those in the town who were wealthy enough not to need to soil their hands in manual labour.

Snitterby cut by far the more elegant figure of the two, being a slender, upright, well-made man of genteel appearance with a fresh complexion and expressive features. 'Damn keelmen,' he parroted. 'Had two of them up before me yesterday in the magistrates' court. Stealing geese.'

'Stealing geese, eh? I trust you came down hard on them, Snitterby. Sent them off to Australia, I mean.' He started to chuckle, then thought better of it, but was too late to prevent himself breaking wind loudly.

'Ha! I did think about it, Brandling.' Snitterby surreptitiously moved his chair further back. 'Then I remembered that we might need them back on the river, so I just sent them off to the House of Correction for six months hard labour.' It was his turn to chuckle.

'It's really no laughing matter, Snitterby,' Brandling retorted, trying desperately not to laugh. 'Things are looking bad. The ship-owners are screaming out for more of our coal because they know it's the best in the country but there's a limit to the amount we can send down the river unless we get the keels to take more than the king's measure.'

'According to the report at our last Company meeting, Brandling, we're making more money than ever.'

'Be that as it may, I can't afford not to take advantage of the chance to increase my profits. We could soon be having to deal with the threat of privateers across the Channel from what I've heard. They say that a lugger was seen off Tynemouth bar a few days since that had the look of one.'

'I agree we can't get too complacent. I remember that only last month a bark carrying coal from Shields to London was chased back from near Whitby by a privateer.'

'Not just that, Snitterby, but I've got other businesses to worry about, you know. And things in the West Indies aren't looking too good. There's even talk in Parliament of outlawing the slave trade, for God's sake.'

'Damned liberals. They're everywhere, these do-gooders.' He paused to light a cigar. 'But surely you can vote against that, can't you?'

'And I certainly will, you can take it from me. Mind you, Snitterby, I'm not very confident that I'll get the support I need from my colleagues. A lot of them are going a bit soft these days. Some of them are even backing the idea of extending the vote to the lower orders.'

'What? You mean that you and Ridley would have to face an *election* to be our Members of Parliament, Brandling?'

'Quite so, Snitterby.'

'And you would no longer be spared the expense of a canvass?'

'Quite so, Snitterby.'

'And the ignorant and criminal classes would be permitted to participate?'

'I know. Can you believe it? It would no longer be permissible to sell House of Commons seats to the highest bidder. Disgraceful isn't it? Shameful.'

'You can say that again. We'll just have to hope that people see sense in time. It would be unthinkable to have someone other than a Brandling and a Ridley representing Newcastle in Parliament. That's the way it's been for as long as I can remember - and long may it continue. Those people who want to mess about with our sacred traditions don't realise what problems they could be letting us in for. Whatever next? Catholics? Quakers?'

'God forbid that *they* should ever be given any place in society. You know, Snitterby, we can't afford just to sit back or we'll get trampled all over. Take these keelmen, for example. We have to take things into our own hands.'

'What have you got in mind, Brandling?'

'We have to make them agree to carry more coal. And if they won't agree, we'll have to think about getting rid of them.'

'Getting rid of the keelmen? Surely that's not possible? We've tried it before and they just go on strike until we give in.'

'Well, it might be,' Brandling said, leaning towards his colleague conspiratorially, while the latter leaned back in the other direction. 'You see, Snitterby - and I tell you this in confidence - I've been consulting a friend of mine, a professor at Oxford University who specialises in marine and mercantile law and has taken a close interest in the coal industry. He's come up with some very interesting suggestions about how we could replace the keelmen. Or, at least, make ourselves all a lot less reliant on them. Break their stranglehold, I mean. I'm going to put his ideas before the next Company meeting.'

4

Mister Boag had three other apprentices, all of whom, being covered in soot from head to toe, looked to me almost identical but could, with a little difficulty, be distinguished by the timbre and pitch of their voices. They were much younger than me but nevertheless about the same size as I was. I soon learned that my Master had taken me on, despite my being of an advanced age for such an occupation, because of my smallness of stature which, he judged, would facilitate my passage along the narrowest of flues. Of my new workmates, two were rather surly and distant, appearing to treat me as an unwelcome intruder into their midst. The third, who spoke in a shrill high-pitched voice which earned him the nickname Squeaky, seemed to be willing - even eager - to associate with me and tell me about the tasks on which I was to be engaged. Like me, he was an orphan, although he never fully explained how he came to find himself in that state and I did not press him for details for fear of opening up a subject which might cause him distress.

Mister Boag, perhaps cognisant of the close friendship which quickly developed between myself and Squeaky, decided that the two of us would work together until I had become sufficiently well acquainted with the trade to be judged competent to practise it on my own. In a word, Squeaky was to act as my mentor, a curious role for a child only eight years old but one which I nevertheless welcomed.

On the first day of my apprenticeship I was issued with a small wooden-handled brush and a metal scraper with which to remove the soot from the inside of flues and the hardened crusts of tar deposited by smoke. In my naivety and ignorance of the hardships involved in their employment, I received these tools of my trade with a sense of pride at possessing them. However,

I readily confess that, at first hearing, I was not enthused by Squeaky's description of the work which was to be my daily occupation (with the exception of the Sabbath, when we were required to attend Sunday School to receive instruction in the Holy Bible).

Although I was initially reassured by the belief that from now on I was to be provided by my Master with food, clothing and shelter, as the fine-looking gentleman who delivered me to Mister Boag had indicated to me during our short journey, I gradually came to the understanding that the real nature of my situation was less alluring. True, I had a roof over my head at night, but we four apprentices were made to sleep in a filthy cellar on a bed made of sacks full of soot and with empty sacks as blankets. We were rarely provided with food or clothing by Mister Boag and instead told to beg for these from the owners of the houses whose chimneys we climbed. I soon came to despise the treatment meted out to us and even dared to suppose that our Master lacked consideration for us. He beat and scolded us regularly for no apparent reason and it was only on those occasions – quite frequent, I readily admit - when he was disguised with liquor that he seemed to lack the will to upbraid us. There were times when I began to wish that I could return to my previous existence as a street urchin begging for my livelihood.

The work was harsh and dangerous. We were woken by the Master at dawn and sent out in all weathers to go into the town touting for business, which we did by walking through the chares and streets calling out at the tops of our voices until our throats were raw:

Soot Sweep, Soot Sweep,
Chimney on fire will make you weep.

Once we had found a willing house owner, the Master would cover their fireplace with a heavy clootie and send us behind it to go up the flue. We would have to use our feet, elbows, knees and back to climb and by the second or third job (we sometimes did as many as ten in a day) the skin had been rubbed away from these parts, although the thick layer of soot on our bodies usually concealed any sign of blood. I would often find that a chimney in which I was working had not been swept for many months, even years, and was consequently clogged with soot which would become suddenly dislodged as I ascended, threatening to choke or suffocate me. Some of the flues were so narrow that I was hardly small enough to pass through and faced the constant danger of becoming lodged inside and unable to move up or down. I heard it told that one of his previous apprentices who became stuck up a chimney was left there to starve to death by Mister Boag, who cursed his luck at having lost such a fine servant. But before the end of the week, the lad, having lost so much weight, slid back down the flue without difficulty and emerged in the fireplace still alive, whereupon Mister Boag beat him severely for having missed several days' employment. I don't know whether this account is entirely reliable but I believe the likelihood that it is a true story to be greater than the possibility that it is not.

*

Ten miles north of the town and situated on a wind-swept spot near the coast stands Seaton Delaval Hall, a fine country mansion in English Baroque style belonging to the Delaval family. It was commissioned by Admiral George Delaval, designed by Sir John Vanbrugh and completed in 1730, replacing a Tudor manor house, on part of the estate which has been in the family since the eleventh century. The Delavals' wealth derives from salt production, coal mining and glass manufacture. Among their extensive assets, the family owns a colliery next to the Seaton estate and the natural harbour of Hartley Pans, from where coal can be transported directly out to sea, and another near Benwell on the River Tyne.

Constructed amid extensive gardens on three sides of a large forecourt, Seaton Delaval Hall consists of a central block and two wings. The main building contains the family residence and state rooms including a magnificent entrance hall and a saloon which regularly serves as a ballroom and banqueting suite. The West Wing houses a huge kitchen and servants' quarters where footmen, coachmen, grooms, gamekeepers, house maids, scullery maids, cooks and housekeepers are lodged. The East Wing is given over to the stables, in which stone-built stalls accommodate a dozen horses, each with the name of its occupant emblazoned above: Zephyrus, Hercules, Abel, Regulus, Admiral, Peacock and so on, as well as several carriages of various types and sizes. The grounds are laid out partly with ornamental gardens and contain a Norman chapel, an orangery and an icehouse used for the storage of perishable foodstuffs. There is also a domed mausoleum constructed of stone, which was commissioned by the present owner of the Hall in memory of his only son who died aged twenty, 'having been kicked in his vital organs by a laundry maid to whom he was paying his addresses,' as the Coroner recorded when announcing his verdict.

Captain Francis Blake Delaval, who inherited the Hall when the Admiral died after falling from his horse while attempting to chase trespassers off his land, was well-known for his love of playing outrageous practical jokes on those who enjoyed his hospitality. There were many occasions on which guests were invited to a theatrical performance followed by a sumptuous dinner (reputedly consisting of thirty-five courses) and liberally indulged with draughts of Holland's gin, ale and port wine, then fell asleep in a drunken stupor only to find upon waking that their heads had been shaved. It is said that after his great friend Prince Edward died, Captain Francis became distraught and attempted to console himself through excessive eating and drinking, becoming grossly overweight and reaching no less than twenty-one stones, a condition which occasioned his demise in 1771 from a headlong tumble down a flight of steps while distracted by a surfeit of alcohol, after which he was succeeded by one of his twelve children, Sir Stanhope Delaval, who inherited the ownership of the Hall together with his father's spendthrift habits.

It was never entirely clear why Sir Stanhope (whose vastness approached that of his father) decided to keep a weighing machine in the entrance lobby of his residence and directed that the weight of each visitor be measured by this contraption and duly recorded by the doorkeeper in a large tome which was dedicated for that purpose and set upon the hall table for all to see. Some speculated that there may perchance have been a slight weakness in the floor or other component of the building and that he therefore wished to guard against a possible catastrophe occasioned by overloading the structure. Another theory, no doubt put about by those envious of the man's fondness for good living, was that Sir Stanhope had become rather proud of his huge bulk and wished to satisfy himself that it exceeded that of each of his visitors.

Whatever the true explanation, it was certainly the case that the recorded weights of all those who entered and exited Seaton Delaval Hall, (including the owner himself whose details were entered in the book each time he passed across the threshold) were open to public gaze and scrutiny. And anybody who cares to peruse the entries listed for 24 June 1797 will come across one which relates to a Mrs. Shaw, housekeeper, who tipped (some may say, crushed) the scales at nineteen stones and nine pounds and, curiously and in sharp contrast, appears to have been accompanied by a Miss Kitty Dace, who is described therein as a dwarf weighing four stones and seven pounds. The inference that can be drawn from this information, namely that a housekeeper of such an enormous size was allowed to work as a domestic servant in Sir Stanhope's employ – not to mention the latter's own dimensions - must surely destroy the supposed possibility of there being a structural defect which left the Hall vulnerable to the presence of bulky occupants. It must also be remarked that the prospect of Sir Stanhope and Mrs Shaw being together in the same room conjures up an extraordinary and perhaps unsettling image, especially to anyone in straitened circumstances who may be unsure of the source of their next meal and therefore understandably envious of those who have clearly consumed several large ones.

Kitty Dace, who is mentioned above, was employed at Seaton Delaval Hall as a scullery maid whose duties consisted mainly of scrubbing the cooking utensils and keeping the working surfaces spotlessly clean. One day, however, Sir Stanhope happened to be walking through the so-called King's Corridor, a passage on the first floor of the West Wing which overlooks the kitchen. He often did so during the late afternoon in order to savour the aromas of food being prepared for the evening which tended to float upwards. Peering down, he noticed a dwarfish woman seated at a table directly below who appeared, to his amazement, to be holding a quill pen over a sheet of paper. Can it really be possible, he asked himself, that we have within our household a scullery maid who is capable of writing? It was a question that he felt could not wait to be answered and, within the hour, he had summoned Mrs Robson, the Head Cook, and put it to her.

'Beggin' yer pardon, sir, but Miss Kitty likes to write down the day's menus for her own amusement,' Mrs Robson explained, clutching the hem of her apron nervously in anticipation of a reprimand. 'I'm sorry, sir, I didn't see no harm in letting her do it. She always works extra time to make up for it. I'll tell her to stop it directly, sir, beggin' yer pardon again.'

Sir Stanhope laughed heartily. 'You misunderstand, madam. I'm not angry about it. Not angry at all. On the contrary, I think it most amusing that one of our scullery maids has acquired such literary skills. In fact, I believe we could find a more fitting role for such a talented young lady. I will give the matter some thought and send for Miss Kitty when I have come to a decision. In the meantime, you must say nothing about this to her.'

Before another day passed, Sir Stanhope checked the entries in the book which recorded the weight of all those who entered his house and came up with an idea of what use he could make of Miss Kitty. He had always had a bizarre sense of humour, no doubt something he had inherited from his father, and he imagined what a comical spectacle it would be for a four-and-a-half-stone dwarf to be seen with a man almost five times her size. Moreover, he quickly realised how he could benefit from her ability to write, since he had always found it tedious having to rely on his own scribbles in order to recall what transpired at the many business meetings he was forced, by dint of his commercial interests, to attend. He therefore determined to get her to accompany him as his scribe and record the proceedings on his behalf. What better way, he thought, to relieve himself of that tiresome responsibility and, at the same time, to amuse his colleagues with a freakish sight. Think of what they'll say, he mused. There they go - the mammoth Sir Stanhope and the minuscule Kitty! What a laugh that would be! It would undoubtedly be the talk of the Assembly Rooms.

'Thank ye kindly, sir,' Kitty Dace replied timidly when she was informed by her master of the new role which he had assigned to her. 'Aa'll do my best for ye, sir.' She was secretly alarmed at the prospect of having to accompany a man of Sir Stanhope's importance to gatherings where she would undoubtedly find herself surrounded by others of similar standing and would feel completely out of place. She knew, however, that she was in no position to refuse his injunction unless she was prepared to risk forfeiting her employment at Seaton Delaval Hall altogether, a consequence that, for the sake of her ailing parents who were wholly reliant on her wages for their survival, she could not countenance.

'I'm sure that you'll do very well, Kitty,' Sir Stanhope said encouragingly to his newly-appointed secretary. 'We'll get along fine together, you mark my words.'

Of course, he hadn't told her the whole story of how he proposed to put his plan into operation. Neither did he mention that he had just ordered his cabinet-maker to construct a wooden box of modest proportions with enough air-holes to ensure that its occupant did not expire through a lack of oxygen.

5

A strange thing occurred after I had been in Mister Boag's employment for well over twelve months, during which period of time neither I nor my workmates had been afforded the opportunity to wash the soot from our bodies or change our clothes. Furthermore, my knees were so badly affected by the cramped postures I was obliged to adopt in carrying out my duties inside narrow flues that my legs had acquired a peculiar curvature which meant that I found myself no longer able to walk without leaving a large gap between my feet – an affliction which would later earn me the nickname of Knacky-Kneed Mack.

I'll recount the event precisely as I remember it.

That day was particularly memorable because we were roused early from our wretched sleeping-place in the expectation of being chased out to seek customers, instead of which the Master's wife, a rotund woman with a very sullen countenance whom we had seen only once or twice before but who had never previously spoken to us, beckoned us into the scullery and presented us with four pots of steaming broth, which we devoured in short time. Soon afterwards, Mister Boag appeared and spoke to us collectively.

'Today, my fine boys, …' he said, using a tone of voice and form of address which radiated affability and which he had never used before, '… a special visitor is coming to see us'.

Of course, we all wondered immediately what manner of special visitor it might be whose impending arrival could generate such a fine breakfast.

'The gentleman will probably ask you some questions,' he explained. 'He is a very *important* gentleman and so we need to make sure that you all give him the correct answers …'

I remember thinking that at this point the Master's expression changed slightly and seemed to be tinged with hint of menace.

'… Otherwise, it could create an unpleasant situation,' he sneered, but with a smile. Then, he surveyed us fiercely before continuing, with added emphasis, 'A *very* unpleasant situation, you understand,' leaving us in no doubt at all that the unpleasantness would be *ours* to experience, rather than his. Meanwhile, Mistress Boag, standing alongside her husband with her hands rested on her fat stomach, nodded her assent at his every phrase.

'Now, my fine boys,' the Master continued, 'if the important gentleman asks what you had today for breakfast, what will you tell him?'

'Broth, sir,' squeaked Squeaky.

'Well done, boy,' said the Master. 'And was it delicious?'

'Most delicious, sir.'

'And nourishing?'

'Most nourishing, sir.'

'And do you eat a delicious and nourishing breakfast each morning?'

'No, sir, this is the fir…' My Master's hand brayed Squeaky's face before the poor lad had time to finish the sentence and he fell to the floor with a cry. The Master dragged him back on to his feet.

'Think carefully now, boy, before you answer again,' he said, then repeated the question. 'Do you eat a delicious and nourishing breakfast each morning?'

'Yes, sir,' snivelled Squeaky through tears. 'Every single morning, sir.'

The Master then addressed the same question to the rest of us one at a time and waited until each had replied in the same way.

'That's good, my fine boys. Very satisfactory. Now, another question …' This time he looked directly at me and I could feel fear in the pit of my stomach. '… How does your Master treat you?'

I answered quickly, knowing that any hint of hesitation could count against me and earn me a beating. 'Very well, sir,' I said with as much conviction as I could muster.

It was clear, however, from the expectant look on Mister Boag's face that he wanted a more lavish commentary on his virtues.

'He's a most generous man, sir. Very caring, sir. He treats me like his own son, sir.' I hoped my reply would satisfy him but, for good measure, I added, 'And his lady wife, Mistress Boag, is a most accommodating woman, sir. Most accommodating, she is, sir.'

He seemed pleased by my words and made my three companions repeat the same formulation, at which juncture he announced that, in anticipation of our visitor's arrival, we were each to take a bath in order to be able to present a tidy appearance in keeping with the respect to be accorded to the important gentleman. Afterwards, we would be given new clothes to put on. 'When I say *new*,' he corrected himself, 'I mean *new to you*. They might not be *brand*-new but they're quite acceptable. Mistress Boag has been up to the Poorhouse to collect the stuff they were going to throw out and she's checked personally that they ain't full of dickies or forkytails. Not *completely* full anyway'. He pointed to a pile of shirts and breeches which had clearly seen a great deal of wear but were nevertheless infinitely superior to our own filthy, soot-caked rags. Then, he directed his wife to place a wooden tub (recently emptied of its customary contents of coal-lumps) in the yard, fill it half-way to the brim with cold water and scrub each boy in turn from head to toe.

I cannot speak for the others, but my discomfiture at being completely naked in the presence of a woman who was not my mother was to a great extent mitigated by the blissful feeling as Mistress Boag washed away the accumulation of months of soot from my skin. When she had finished the task, she handed me a clean sack with which to rub myself dry and summoned Squeaky, the last of us to be bathed (by which time, I must say, the water in the tub was distinctly murky).

Only a few minutes later, those of us who had retired inside to put on our 'new' clothes were assailed by a startled shriek from Mistress Boag, followed by her cry of, 'Jeram, Jeram, get 'ere quick. This 'un's a lass.' We all rushed outside, anxious to discover the cause of the commotion, to find Squeaky standing in the wooden tub, naked but with his hands clasped over his sexual organs in order, presumably, to conceal them, while Mistress Boag was attempting to pull his hands away in order, presumably, to expose them. We were quickly joined by the Master who, being sturdier than his wife, easily managed to wrench Squeaky's arms and raise them above the child's head, at which point we all stared in disbelief at the revelation that Squeaky, far from having covered up his sexual organs, *did not have any*. Well ... none to speak of, anyway.

'You see what I mean, Jeram?' shrieked Mistress Boag again. 'Look! This boy's a lass ... I mean, this 'un ain't a boy at all ... He's a *lass* I tell you!'

The Master looked on, unable to comprehend, paralysed with horror and momentarily dumbfounded. Then the awful implications of the discovery struck him. 'God preserve us,' he yelled, his voice breaking into a howl of anguish. 'This'll cripple me. The constable'll be here within the hour and if he finds I've been employing a lass as a climbing-boy it'll be the Antipodes for me. For the rest of me life.'

My own shock at the discovery that my best friend, as he had become over the months we shared together up chimneys and in the coal-black cellar, was in fact a girl, somehow instilled in me a sudden and overwhelming sympathy and a desire to rescue him – or *her*, I should say - from the wrath of my Master, whose rising anger at the deceit she had visited upon him and his consequent and imminent transportation to a penal colony in Australia was about to lead to a violent attack on Squeaky. Taking advantage of Mister Boag's temporary incapacity, I seized a few items of the poorhouse's hand-me-down clothing, grabbed Squeaky's arms and ran with her out of the yard, along the narrow passageway between the row of cottages and out into Westgate-street, where we paused briefly so that she could dress herself, my eyes averted from her nude body. Then we hurried towards the centre of the town with as much expedition as my bow legs would permit, stopping frequently to check if we were followed and unsure of our destination or what fate awaited us.

*

'If ye dinaa get a move on,' the tall one complained, 'there'll be watchmen here afore we're done.' It had become a matter of great concern to both of them that their enterprise was facing a real threat from the practice recently adopted in some churches of creating a rota of volunteers to carry out nocturnal visits to churchyards in order to ensure that no graves were being disturbed.

'Aa'm ganning as fast as Aa can,' the short one countered breathlessly, with a note of annoyance in his voice to indicate that he felt that *he* was the one doing all the hard work. 'This lid's stuck fast.'

'Are ye certain ye got that crowbar in the reet way?' the tall one asked, impatiently. These places gave him the creeps. Despite all the time he'd spent in churchyards, he had never conquered his fear of being in one at the dead of night and was sometimes almost overwhelmed by a presentiment that the ghosts of the long-dead, angered by the desecration of their resting-places, would rise out of their graves to surround and terrify him. On the other hand, he now consoled himself, surely no volunteer watchman was likely to turn up at *this* hour.

'Course Aa'm certain. How many times have Aa done this before, eh?'

'Well, ye'll just have to hurry it up, that's aal Aa'm saying.' He realised that it was just beginning to rain and that made him feel even more miserable and grumpy.

'Here, give us a hand, will ye? Get hold of that shovel, then if Aa can prise the lid open a bit, jam the blade in hard.'

The tall one picked up the shovel lying on the pile of excavated soil alongside the grave. 'Alreet, Aa'm ready with it. Say when.'

'Got it,' gasped the short one after a few more unsuccessful attempts. 'There … Keep it steady, can't ye? … Hold on now, it's coming.' He fell back on the grass as the lid swung open and took him off balance.

'Jesus, what a stench!' The tall one turned away hurriedly, threw down the shovel and vomited into the darkness.

The short one picked himself up and held the lantern over the open coffin. 'This un's gone bad,' he tutted. 'Judging by the state of her, she's been deed a lot more than four days, Aa'll wager.'

'We must have opened the wrang one,' the tall one said. 'How did that happen, for God's sake?'

'No, it's the reet one. The relatives must have asked the gaffer to put quicklime in. Religious types, no doubt – the ones who think the deed will be resurrected only so lang as their grave ain't been touched.'

'Bastards. Anyway, this 'un ain't fit for the surgeon. He'll never accept a body in that state. Look, it's falling to bits.'

'So that's wor eight guineas doon the drain.'

'Well, we'd better cut wor losses then. We'll just take the teeth. If she's got half a set left in her heed, at least we can flog 'em for a few shillings.'

'Not much to show for a night's work, is it?'

'Better than nowt, Aa suppose. Lucky Aa brought me pliers, ain't it?'

6

I should perhaps pause briefly at this point in my account and retrace a few steps to explain what became of my friend Squeaky and me after our flight from the man (I will not say *gentle*man) who went by the name of Jeram Boag. Our fear of recapture led us to spend several days and nights in hiding, moving between various locations in the vicinity of the Keyside but steering well clear of Sandgate and avoiding any behaviour which might throw suspicion upon ourselves and result in our being apprehended by the Town Guard.

We could not, of course, be certain that our Master was set upon pursuing us or, indeed, whether he was free to do so. Perhaps he had been detained by the constable who, we deduced, must have been the important visitor of whom he spoke and was attending the premises in order to establish whether we apprentices were being treated in accordance with the regulations governing such matters. For all we knew, Mister Boag was already on his way to Australia in a convict ship. However, we felt it wise in the circumstances to assume that we were being hunted as fugitives.

It was our great good fortune - I am not sure how or why, but I think we must have let our guard down briefly in the desperate search for food and ventured out into the open - to come to the notice of Mister Hadwen Bragg. This gentleman was the owner of a large and highly regarded clothing emporium, located in Pilgrim-street and known as *Bragg and Company*, which caters, to this very day, for the sartorial requirements of wealthy male and female clients. Mister Bragg belonged to a group of people who went by the name of the Society of Friends (but others called them Quakers) which was a kind of religious movement whose followers supported charities and other philanthropic causes, abstained from the consumption of alcohol and read passages from the Bible each day. The organisation also encouraged its adherents to follow a righteous path in their business and social dealings. Consequently, Mister Bragg had acquired a reputation – a merited one, as will be demonstrated – as an honest and upright tradesman and a generous benefactor and contributor to charitable works. It was his nightly custom, at the end of the working day in his clothing store, to visit the Keyside in search of those to whom he could give alms – cadgers, trampers, prostitutes and other fallen women who tended to frequent the area, spreading joy and syphilis by making themselves available to sailors, keelmen and, occasionally, an errant man of the cloth. And it was during one such visit that he happened upon Squeaky and me in our sorry state – starving, cold, filthy and frightened – and immediately took pity on us and invited us to return with him to his house where he would accommodate us for so long as was necessary to restore us to a condition where we could fend for ourselves.

Mister Hadwen Bragg who, I estimated, was in his early sixties, cut a curious figure. His head was at once as bald as an egg and as shiny as a polished apple, so shiny in fact that, on a sunny day, it could represent a hazard to the driver of a chaise who, temporarily blinded by the reflected light, might inadvertently guide his nag across the path of an oncoming errand boy, causing the lad considerable damage, if not worse. The lower part of his face was entirely surrounded by a voluminous expanse of snow-white whiskers which started right under his nose (indeed, you might have said *inside* his nose) and extended several inches below his chin and could have been mistaken for a large angora cat but for the pair of bright-blue eyes which twinkled above it. It was said that he never resorted to the trimming scissors except to attend to the hairs of his moustache whenever they began to tickle his nostrils and cause him to have a sneezing fit. The twinkling eyes revealed a cheerful, optimistic disposition on the part of their owner. In truth, he was as gentle and kind a man as you would ever care to meet.

His house, located at Number 264 Spital Tongues on the outskirts of the town, was well-appointed but not ostentatious. He lived there with his wife, Margaret, and their two sons and two daughters, together with a black and white Dalmatian dog called Hamlet, which made a great fuss of us, and a more agreeable family you could not imagine. Mistress Bragg, we soon discovered, was also a prominent member of the Society of Friends and even held the position of a preacher, which struck us (as I am sure it must do you) as a very surprising role for a woman.

I should explain, by the way, so as not to confuse the reader, that Squeaky, now that her true gender had been revealed and she felt no further need to engage in any subterfuge to secure employment, had reverted to using the name of Bella with which her mother had endowed her during the short period between Bella's arrival in this world and her mother's departure from it.

We often used to hear Mister Bragg talking to his wife about the good causes which they both supported. They belonged to a group of people in the town known as the Newcastle Society for Effecting the Abolition of the Slave Trade who protested against the immorality of that enterprise and the terrible conditions endured on ships bringing captives from Africa and in the plantations of the southern states of America and the West Indies. Mistress Bragg regularly wore a medallion depicting a black man bound in chains and bearing the inscription, 'Am I not a man and a brother?' which, she told me, was the emblem of the anti-slavery Society. I remember too that, on occasion, Mister Bragg used to read out passages from a book called *The Interesting Narrative of the Life of Olaudau Equiano*, which was written by someone who had been captured from his home in Africa at the age of ten and taken as a slave to America. I could not help but contrast this poor man's fate with that of myself and Bella who had the great fortune to have been taken into the care of such a kind family. I once overheard Mister Bragg complaining to his wife that he had approached the town's Member of Parliament urging him to persuade the Government to abolish slavery in the colonies but found to his disgust that the very same man profited personally from the trade and, therefore, wanted it to continue.

Another of Mister Bragg's campaigns involved what he regarded as the unconscionably harsh penal code which proclaimed more than two hundred different crimes for which a person could be executed. He found it depraved that someone - even a child - could be hanged in the King's name for cutting down a tree, or poaching, or spending more than a month in the company of gypsies, or stealing from a rabbit warren or stealing an article worth one shilling. (I must confess that, when I heard about this I surmised that, had I been discovered in the petty pilfering from market stalls in which I was engaged during the time I spent living rough on the Keyside after my parents' deaths, I might well have ended up on a slab at the Barber-Surgeons' Hall as a subject for dissection). Mister Bragg had appealed to the mayor and the magistrates of the town to take up his cause but again his approaches were rebuffed on the grounds that the measures were essential in order to maintain public order and to prevent an intolerable increase in the number of the lower classes which might lead to a revolution such as had been suffered across the Channel in recent years.

For how long our new benefactor had intended to provide Bella and me with hospitality under his roof I do not know, but one month at Number 264 Spital Tongues turned into two, two turned into six, six into twelve, and twelve into twenty-four, and still Mister Bragg and his wife showed no sign of wishing us to move out nor any sign of irritation at our continued presence in their home. Indeed they treated us as members of their family and even allowed us to share their dining table on Sundays, a ritual which we found most satisfactory, as well as their daily Bible readings which, although less to our liking, we felt it our duty to bear in reciprocation. There were even a few occasions when Mister Bragg, whose ears news of Cuckoo Jack's good deeds had reached, had the kindness to invite his son, my boyhood friend Ralph, to dine with us at Number 264.

During most afternoons Bella and I also joined the Bragg children in instruction from their mother in reading and writing, which I had not had the opportunity to practise since the death of my own dear parents, who had tutored me in these arts from an early age. Indeed, my father had always encouraged me to attempt to study the columns of the *Newcastle Courant* (which I found difficult) and would regularly recite to me the content of amusing or serious articles from that journal in order, as he told me, to improve my education as well to prepare me for life as an adult in the town by giving me a flavour of the kind of things I might expect to face there when I was older. As a result of this childhood experience, I came to make it my regular habit to take note of those newspaper stories which offered an insight into either the felicitous goings-on in our society or those which revealed it in a less happy light.

In order to try to repay at least a little of our hosts' generosity towards us, Bella and I performed various small tasks to assist them. On most weekday mornings, I accompanied Mister

Bragg to his clothing store in Pilgrim-street where I would occupy myself in the workshop which was located at the rear of the retail area, going up and down between the rows of seamstresses, sweeping up discarded needles, thimbles, threads, buttons and other accessories of the trade and collecting and sorting through the surplus pieces of cloth to identify and put aside any which might be reusable. For her part, Bella helped Mistress Bragg in the kitchen at Number 264, preserving fruit, preparing vegetables, scrubbing pans and collecting the leftover food which was to be given to the poor and needy during Mister Bragg's nocturnal sorties to the Keyside. And the two of us loved nothing more than to take Hamlet for a walk when the weather was fine.

And so we continued to live in comfortable surroundings in Spital Tongues, well looked after, protected from and oblivious to the dreadful activities taking place only a mile or two away.

*

They called Blackie Johnson an occultist but there was, in his own opinion at least, a lot more to his art than merely predicting a person's destiny from the tarot cards. True, he had to ensure, using his amazing powers of prestidigitation, that he drew either the Death card or The Lovers at an early stage in any consultation in order to grab his client's full attention, prompted as they might be by fear and optimism respectively, and then, slowly, to reveal the cards depicting The Devil and The Fool in such a manner as to lead them to an abiding confidence in his powers, sometimes finishing with a flourish as The Hanged Man fluttered magically on to the table. But the real skill which he exercised lay not in reading the cards but in reading the client – that is to say, in understanding the woman's (because the clients were almost always women) motive for consulting him, estimating the extent of her wealth, assessing her level of naivety and her capacity for believing the most outrageous interpretations and predictions and calculating her propensity for being relieved of some of her riches.

He had always possessed some kind of special power. Indeed even his birth was something of a miraculous event. As his mother's seventh son, it was to be expected that he might be different from other children but she had not in her wildest nightmares imagined what she would be faced with when she gave birth to him. Not only did he already have a full head of hair, the colour of jet (which is how he got his name), but his left eye socket was completely devoid of any organ of vision. There was just a blank, gaping hole. It was greatly to the woman's credit that she did not crush the child's head immediately but, instead, invested it with as much love and tenderness as one would with a fully-formed creature.

The upper part of Blackie's face was heavily lined through years of screwing up his solitary eye in order to fix his sight upon those wondrous visions which were indiscernible to those not gifted with his magical powers. Over the course of his calling as a forecaster of fortunes, he developed the ability to make predictions which were as plausible and ambiguous as the utterances of the Python priestess at the Oracle at Delphi. To his credit, Blackie never attempted to mislead or defraud anyone who was impoverished or handicapped, but if a person fitting that description should happen to seek his services he would, to the best of his ability, give an honest account of their fortune, except that he always mitigated any prediction of catastrophe which he envisaged would be visited upon the wretched creature by playing down the worst elements of the calamity signified by their cards.

For many years, he had somehow managed to scrape together a meagre income by charging a small fee for his services — just sufficient to finance his modest lifestyle. He never stopped dreaming, however, that one day he might be fortunate enough to receive a commission from somebody of high status and considerable wealth who would be prepared to pay him a large sum of money to discover what the future held for them.

7

The Mansion House, the residence of the mayor of Newcastle during his year in office, is situated in the Close, a handsome, brick-built building fronted by a wide courtyard and with a terrace down to the river on its southern flank. A visitor would ascend the flight of steps to the imposing entrance, cross the threshold and find himself within an oak-panelled lobby where the regalia of the corporation are displayed, including the large silver mace bearing the inscription, *Made for the corporation of Newcastle-on-Tyne, anno regni Jacobi Secundi, tertio, anno Domini 1687, Nicholas Cole, Esq. mayor; Thomas Pace, Esq. sheriff.* Several doors lead off from the lobby. The second one on the left would take the visitor into the Grand Saloon, a magnificent room whose walls are bedecked with row upon row of firearms, cutlasses, halberds and other weapons, as well as some suits of armour. It also boasts a beautiful carved chimney-piece, above which hangs a splendid painting of the town by Jonathan Richardson the Younger. Next to the Grand Saloon is the Dining-Room, an ample and well-appointed chamber capable of accommodating eighty persons, the activities of whom will be overseen by a number of former dignitaries of the town whose likenesses gaze down from a line of their engraved portraits.

Felix Brandling MP had summoned his fellow Hoastmen to a meeting of the Company at the Mansion House and they now sat before him, a dozen or so of them, at a circumspect distance on the other side of the solid oak table which occupied the centre of the Dining-Room. 'Gentlemen, we have some important matters to discuss and some important decisions to make,' he announced.

'What's more important than increasing our profits?' asked a sandy-haired pipe-smoker with overhanging eyebrows and a large round chin, to general acclaim.

'Nothing, my friend,' Brandling replied, wheezing heavily. 'And we won't be able to continue to do that unless we take action to clip the wings of that ruffian Scuffins and the rest of the keelmen.'

'How are we going to do that without them striking again?' Henry Huddup was still dressed in his mayoral robes, having hurried to the meeting direct from a civic engagement at the Barber-Surgeons' Hall.

'Maybe we won't be able to avoid another strike, Your Worship,' conceded Brandling. 'But we'll have to make damn sure that it's their last.'

'I think we should hear what our chairman has to tell us,' Aeneas Snitterby suggested impatiently to the assembled group. The magistrate, invariably well-turned out, was resplendent in a yellow-and-black striped swansdown waistcoat and olive-coloured velvet pantaloons.

'Thank you, Snitterby. Well, gentlemen …' Brandling coughed loudly and inadvertently released an unpleasant odour into the room. He pretended not to notice and hurried on with his statement, trying in vain to conceal the indiscretion. 'A very good acquaintance of mine, someone you might regard as an expert in the field, has come up with a plan which, I believe, will set us a long way on the path towards reducing our reliance on the keelmen. And maybe even removing it altogether in the long term.'

'Huh! I'd like to hear it,' called out one voice, doubtfully.

'Me too,' called another, ostentatiously fanning the air in front of his nose with a copy of the *Newcastle Courant*.

'Then please allow me to explain, gentlemen.'

The room fell silent with respectful anticipation.

'The first thing we *must* insist upon is an increase from eight chaldrons to ten in the standard load of each keel ...' He broke off as the door of the room was flung open and in waddled Sir Stanhope Delaval, followed by two servants dressed in coachmen's livery who carried a large box between them.

'Sorry not to have arrived earlier, Brandling,' the latecomer said, breezily. 'Hope I haven't missed anything important.'

'I know you've got a big appetite, but there's no need to bring your own lunch, Delaval,' quipped the MP, secretly pleased that *he* was no longer the largest person in the room, as the coachmen placed the box on the table in front of their master. 'Plenty of food available here, you know.'

'It's not my lunch, Brandling,' Delaval said, stepping forward and whipping the lid off the box with a flourish to reveal a female dwarf dressed in a child's smock and a mob-cap and holding a quill and a sheaf of writing paper. There was a collective gasp from the rest of the Hoastmen at the freakish sight.

'If this is supposed to be one of your family's practical jokes,' roared Brandling, puce with outrage, 'I tell you, man, it's not at all funny. We are here to conduct some serious business.'

'He's turning this meeting into a circus,' complained Aeneas Snitterby.

'This is *not* a circus act,' retorted Delaval, angrily. 'This is my secretary. She is here to take a record of proceedings to save me the trouble of doing so.'

'Why didn't you say so in the first place?' said the chairman, slightly placated by Delaval's explanation. 'Very well then, the midget can stay so long as she behaves herself. Any monkey business and she goes straight back in the box, is that understood? And the coachmen can go. Now.'

Once the two had left the room, Brandling said to nobody in particular, 'Now, what were we discussing before that interruption?'

'You were saying we need an increase in loads from eight chaldrons to ten,' the mayor reminded him.

'Ah, yes, Your Worship, the keel loads. It's a scandal that those boats go down the river now only four-fifths full. Just think what a difference it would make with an additional twenty-five per cent on every tide.'

'That's been tried before,' countered an elderly, short-sighted Scotsman who was sitting directly opposite Brandling, his voice slightly muffled by the handkerchief he held over the lower part of his face. 'Problem is, there's a legal agreement preventing us from …'

The chairman quickly interrupted him. 'I know what you're going to say, Strathmore. We can all quote it word for word – *No keel shall be obliged to take more than the king's measure according to statute.* Well, what I have to say to *that* is *this*. The arrangement to which you refer is fifty years old. It's time for progress.' He paused for a few deep breaths before continuing. 'And may I remind you, gentlemen, that nobody in this room was party to it? We can't all be bound by something drawn up by our fathers and our grandfathers. It's out-of-date, I tell you.'

'Hear, hear,' the majority of those present concurred.

'The next thing we need to do, gentlemen,' Brandling declared, 'concerns the staithes.'

'What about them?' asked the sandy-haired man with overhanging eyebrows, his head now wreathed in clouds of pipe smoke, which made Brandling cough again, with inevitable and disagreeable consequences.

'Well, as you know, Ridley, the keelmen are already grumbling about the staithes. They're don't like the fact that when there's a delay in loading at those staithes that are fitted with chutes and a risk of missing the tide, the coal has to be sent direct on to the keels by the spouts rather than shovelled by hand.'

'Why should that concern them?' came a voice from the end of the table which had not been heard before. 'It's much quicker, isn't it?'

'Of course it is, Applegarth, but the keelmen have to pay sixpence to the staithesmen for using the spouts. They'd rather load the cargo by hand and save the money. They won't admit that, though. Instead, they're arguing that the staithes constitute a hazard in the river. A danger to navigation, they claim. It's just an excuse.'

'So what are you suggesting, Brandling?' The Scotsman sounded irritated as he squinted to read the dial of the half-hunter which he had pulled from his vest pocket.

'Firstly, we should instruct the off-putters who supervise the staithes to delay loading as long as possible without jeopardising the tide, so that the spouts *have* to be used.'

'And we should make damn sure that they overload the keels,' Strathmore suggested mischievously and received some cheers of approval. He stood up and shuffled myopically across the room to open a window. In spite of the bitter cold, none of the other Hoastmen complained or tried to stop him.

'Secondly, gentlemen, we should commission an engineer – I know a good one – to devise a way of using the staithes nearest Shields Harbour, the ones that are accessible to some of the collier-brigs, to load the coal by spouts *directly onto the ships.*'

He let that sink in for a few moments while he wheezed a little more, then added melodramatically, 'Then we won't need any keels at all at those staithes.' He sat back in his chair, panting heavily, and enjoyed the moments of shocked silence which met his assertion.

Then, as his audience began to grasp the implications of that statement, spontaneous applause broke out around the room.

'Brilliant stuff, Brandling,' someone shouted, and others murmured their agreement.

'But the brigs can't come far up the river.' Sir Stanhope Delaval pointed out a slight flaw in the proposal. 'And certainly not past the bridge. We'll *have* to use keels for those sites.'

'You're right, of course, Delaval,' Brandling acknowledged. 'But there are other things we can do to put pressure on the keelmen.'

'Such as?'

'Well, at the moment, we pay the skippers twenty pence a tide more than the other crew members. What if we were to dispense with the skippers and persuade the keel-bullies to steer the boats? We could pay them an extra, say, four pence a tide. *They*'d be happy and *we*'d save sixteen pence. We would still charge the ship-masters twenty pence.'

'That's all very well.' Delaval wasn't letting go easily. 'It's a clever idea and I congratulate you on it, Brandling, but let's be realistic. The keelmen aren't going to accept this. Even if they were inclined to agree to any changes they will demand an increase in wages.'

'Of course, I'm not saying that all this will be easy to achieve. If what I have proposed is accepted by the Company – and we will put it to the vote before we leave today - we will have to be absolutely resolute in putting our plans into effect.

We will have to expect resistance, opposition - yes, even threats and violence. And if - or *when* would be more accurate - we are confronted by a strike, we must stand firm and not give in. We must be prepared to call on the magistrates to deal with such lawbreaking …' (At this point, Brandling looked over at Aeneas Snitterby JP, Chairman of the Bench, for a signal that support for the Hoastmen from that source could be relied upon and received a nod of confirmation in reply). '… We must be prepared to summon the military to protect our livelihood, if necessary. We must be prepared to employ substitute workers to replace those who withdraw their labour in breach of the terms of their bonds. We must be prepared to send in the candymen to evict strikers from their homes. We must be prepared to prevent access to charity for them and their families. After all, gentlemen, if their wives and children starve, could it be said that they have anyone to blame but themselves?'

*

Newcastle Courant

40 GUINEAS REWARD

WHEREAS on the night of Wednesday last, the Burial-ground of Ballast Hills was entered and the Corpse of a Male which had been interred during the preceding Afternoon was dug up and removed therefrom by an evil-disposed Person or Persons unknown,

THIS IS TO GIVE NOTICE THAT A REWARD OF FORTY GUINEAS

Will be paid to any Person who shall furnish such Information as may lead to the Conviction of the Offenders, the Newcastle Association for the Prosecution of Felons being determined to use every Exertion to bring to Justice the Party or Parties who have been guilty of an Act so abhorrent to the Feelings of human Nature.

The Reward will be paid on Conviction of any one or more of the Offenders by the Treasurer of the aforesaid Association and an additional **TEN GUINEAS** by the Mayoralty at the Town Clerk's Office, Guild Hall.

8

At least once a month, Mister Bragg made it his business to visit one of the town's poorhouses, taking with him a supply of new clothes to donate for the benefit of the inmates. In the past, I had heard grim tales of these establishments, mainly from the lips of our erstwhile fellow apprentice climbing-boys in the employ of Jeram Boag, Esquire. Stories of the miserable paupers who sought refuge there being treated harshly, humiliated and beaten. Of their being violently stripped naked, shaved and scoured for dickies on arrival. Of their being made to wear a degrading uniform of scratchy, coarse fabric which chafed and blistered the skin. Of families being split up and housed in different parts of the building, with parents and children forbidden to speak to one another even in the communal areas. Of their being fed an unremitting diet of thin gruel, occasionally flavoured with scraps of rancid meat, and given only polluted water to drink. Of their being brutally roped and caned for the most minor misdemeanour. Of the sick and diseased being left to starve and rot to death among those yet to be stricken, then taken out and buried in anonymous pits.

And so, when one afternoon Mister Bragg asked, 'Well, James, would thee care to accompany me to the All Saints' Poorhouse?' I felt obliged to assent but did so with a great deal of apprehension at what I was about to encounter. As things turned out, I need not have worried and was pleasantly surprised at the experience.

All Saints' Poorhouse is situated on the site of the former Augustine Convent near the General Hospital. It is an impressive, substantial building – much bigger than I had imagined it would be – and its lofty position in the town affords a fine view across the river. The rooms were clean and tidy – not at all what

I expected and I surmised that Mister and Mistress Milburn, the master and his wife, might have had prior warning that Mister Bragg would be calling and had made a special effort to make the place respectable for him. They welcomed us warmly and, while the master whisked Mister Bragg off to his office (to talk business, I supposed), his wife insisted on giving me a guided tour of the establishment.

'Come now, Master James,' she said, signalling for me to follow her and then, seeing my hesitation (which in truth was born of nothing more than a natural reluctance to intrude upon the inmates' privacy), took me by the hand. Being fifteen years of age, I did not think the latter gesture altogether necessary or appropriate but I imagine that Mistress Milburn probably thought I was a lot younger. Many people made the same mistake in those days.

She led me into a spacious room, well lit and ventilated by several sash windows high up on the wall and with rows of wooden tables positioned under large banners announcing *God is Good, God is Holy, God is Just* and *God is Love.* 'This is where we eat,' she said. 'Breakfast, lunch and supper'. As if to provide conclusive corroboration of this statement, she pointed to a large notice board on which was displayed the day's Bill of Fare. Far from the offering of thin gruel and suchlike that I had expected to see was a list of meals which almost made my mouth water.

BREAKFAST: Hasty pudding and one gill of milk (Sick and infirm residents will be allowed coffee and tea)
DINNER: Boiled mutton and suet dumplings with potatoes and fresh vegetables from our garden followed by plum pudding
SUPPER: Warm broth and bread with good table-beer

'We put this up for those among our guests who are able to understand it,' she explained and then added, in answer to my unasked question, 'and Mister Milburn reads it out each morning for the benefit of our illiterates and lunatics.'

The dormitory was even larger than the dining area. It must have been a good fifty yards long and contained four lines of beds which stretched from one end to the other. 'We normally cater for seventy, but sometimes we've had to cram in as many as eighty. We'd love to be able to take more but there are usually a number of sick guests who need to be kept separate from the rest to avoid spreading infection.' She pointed to the far side of the room where half a dozen or so beds were occupied. 'They're waiting for a visit from our house surgeon. A wonderful man. Looks after all our sick cases.'

'Where are the rest of the inmates, ma'am?' I asked, perplexed that I could see so few people in such a sizeable building.

'We don't refer to them as inmates,' she said kindly. 'We like to call them our guests. Or sometimes our residents, especially the ones that have been with us for a long time. Calling them inmates would make All Saints' sound like a prison and we want them to think of it as their home. Now, the rest of our guests are either at the Charity School – that's the twelve children who live here – or they are working. The adults, that is. You'll see some of them shortly. She led the way back through dining area and out into a corridor which looked in to a series of smaller rooms. One was occupied by women engaged in various tasks, some sewing, some spinning, some knitting. 'We make new clothes and repair old ones to sell or for our guests to wear,' Mistress Milburn explained, 'and of course we are always delighted when Mister Bragg brings us some from his shop'.

In the next room, the women appeared to be picking at coils of rope. 'What are these ladies doing, ma'am?' I asked.

'Teasing oakum,' Mistress Milburn replied. Seeing my puzzled frown, she elucidated. 'They are unravelling the fibre strands from old hemp rope. We sell baskets-full of the fibres to boat-builders. They soak them in tar to make a waterproof lining for their hulls. The money we get helps to pay for the upkeep of our House'.

She greeted every guest she saw with a friendly smile, addressing each one by their first name and receiving a polite, 'Hello, Mistress Lucy,' in response.

'You're probably wondering why you have seen so few men here, Master James,' she said. 'It's because they have various tasks outside, chopping wood, tending the nursery garden or pumping water. You'll meet some of them soon as their work is nearly finished for the day. Anyway, let's go and find Mister Bragg, shall we? I expect that he and Mister Milburn will have finished their business by now.'

We made our way through the dormitory and the dining-room where we were greeted by the sound of an old man singing and playing a fiddle. 'That's Willie Purvis, our resident musician,' Mistress Milburn told me. 'The others call him Blind Willie, but he doesn't mind. He makes up all his own songs and he loves to entertain the other guests.' The singer looked more than seventy years old but still displayed a shock of white hair above his sightless features. We watched and listened as he performed a ditty in a strong Newcastle dialect, oblivious to our presence, his voice harmonising perfectly with his instrument:

If ye want a buzzem for to sweep yor hoose
Come to me, ma hinny, ye may hae yor choose.
Buy broom buzzems, buy them when they're new
Fine heather bred uns, better never grew.

Up the Butcher Bank and down Byker Chare,
There you'll see the lasses selling brown ware.

By the time the song had ended, the dining–room was beginning to fill up with men returning from their chores outside and women from their workrooms inside. I judged from the disposition of the guests and the manner in which they were dressed that, despite their straitened circumstances, they were generally well-looked after and content with their situation. Most of them appeared to know Mister Bragg well from his regular visits and it was clear from their attitude towards him that they held him in high regard. One poor soul, possibly among the small number of lunatics housed there and unfettered by an appreciation of the requirements of respectful behaviour, even had the temerity to tug at Mister Bragg's whiskers while enfolding him in an exuberant and distinctly over-familiar embrace, the like of which even Mistress Bragg herself would be unlikely to subject her husband to.

One guest who made a particular impression on me was a very short fellow - shorter even than myself - probably in his forties, with neatly-styled hair, wearing a clean shirt, striped waistcoat and knee-breeches adorned with red ribbons. Indeed, so smartly turned out was he that he seemed to me to be completely out of place in such an establishment. Mister Bragg, perhaps observing the look of curiosity on my face, introduced me to him.

'Captain, this here is my young friend James who renders me invaluable assistance in my business and honours me and my good wife with his company in our humble abode.'

The Captain, as Mister Bragg had referred to him, responded with a deep sweeping bow, saying as he did so, 'I'm extremely delighted to make your acquaintance, young sir. *Extremely* delighted indeed. Benjamin Starkey at your service. Benjamin Starkey.' Once he had regained an upright position he offered me his hand, a gesture which I, being still a lad, had never before experienced. I hesitated, wondering how I should react, but seeing Mister Bragg's encouraging nod, I plucked up the courage to shake his hand which, disappointingly, was limp and a little damp. What kind of Captain he was and how he had come to reside in a poorhouse, I could not fathom and determined to ask Mister Bragg as soon as we were out of the place.

When I did so, he replied, 'That's a very good question, James. A very good question indeed. But I'm sorry to say that I can't give thee a very good answer. Or even just a good one. You see, nobody knows – apparently not even Captain Starkey himself – how he became a Captain. I fear that the poor man seems quite unable to recall the circumstances by which he acquired the title but he insists that he really is a Captain and he often recounts in great detail episodes and exploits from his past. That's very strange of course but I have no reason to doubt his word. I suppose that his memory is just not as sound as it should be. He's obviously a well-travelled fellow, as far as I can tell from his descriptions of the far-off shores he's visited. And he's also well-connected, as he often talks about his friends in high places. He seems to know Felix Brandling and Sir Stanhope Delaval, among others.'

He must have spotted the blank look on my face at the mention of these gentlemen, so he said, 'Felix Brandling is the Member of Parliament for Newcastle. Active in the slave trade, I regret to say. Sir Stanhope Delaval is a wealthy businessman.' At the time, these names meant nothing to me but were destined to acquire greater significance later in my life.

Looking back, I guess that the day of my visit to All Saints' Poorhouse was when I was first inspired to think about following in my late father's footsteps and taking up a calling in the field of medicine, a capacity in which I considered that I could afford some service and comfort to those less fortunate than myself. I believe that I may have mentioned this to Mister Bragg on our way back to Number 264 Spital Tongues and I remember him making some remark about it being an honourable calling and saying that he would look out for an opportunity for me to become apprenticed in that profession.

9

Perched above Sandgate, on the northern side of the Shields turnpike and a little to the east of the Town Wall, stands the Keelmen's Hospital, a charitable establishment founded for the benefit of aged and distressed keelmen and their families. It was built about a century ago, financed from payments by the Tyne keelmen of a levy of a halfpenny per chaldron of coal carried down the river, as can be confirmed by the inscription above the entrance which reads: *The Keelmen's Hospital, built at their own Charge, Anno Domini 1701.*

The Hospital, which is constructed somewhat in the style of a monastery or a Cambridge college, contains sixty private apartments on two floors around a quadrangle with cloisters enclosing a central garden area, offices and meeting rooms. Its residents are subject to strict regulations which are rigorously enforced, with fines stipulated for a series of offences ranging from violence to drunkenness, abusing women and falling into debt. A perusal of the pages of the Hospital's Minute Book reveals that Ernest Campbell was fined one shilling for being disguised with liquor on the Sabbath Day, Cuthbert Crissop was fined two shillings and sixpence for abusing the whole society and Francis Alder was fined a shilling for breaking another resident's head.

In the clubroom, a group of eighty or so keelmen, recently returned to Sandgate Shore on the floodtide from Shields Harbour, had gathered to discuss the latest threat to their livelihood.

'Brothers, Aa spoke to the Hoastmen yesterday. Or, Aa should say, they spoke to me. Aa hardly got a word in.' With a scowl, Jasper Scuffins turned his head to one side and spat onto the floor. The others weren't sure whether he was merely clearing his throat or demonstrating his contempt for the cartel of men who controlled the export of coal from Newcastle. Jasper Scuffins was a tough, rough, obstinate character, as the keelmen of the Tyne tended to be. Indeed, while the keelmen were notorious for their uncouth ways, he was even more uncouth than most of his fellows. He was hardened by many years of heaving coal, navigating his unwieldy craft through the treacherous waters and shoals to load his cargo onto the waiting collier brigs and clashing constantly with the wealthy businessmen who owned and licensed the keels and who seemed to imagine they also owned the keelmen. He had become the unofficial (some said, self-appointed) spokesman of those who plied their trade between the upper reaches of the river and the Shields Harbour. His latest encounter with the Company of Hoastmen had prompted him to call an urgent meeting of his fellow-workers to discuss their latest demands.

'What's the crack then, brother?' asked a second keelman.

'They want to raise the weight limit, brother. To ten chaldrons. For no extra fees.'

'Ten chaldrons, ye say, brother! Do they seriously think we can take more than eight chaldrons a tide?' growled a third, the lines on his face marked out with years of ingrained coal-dust.

'Wor boats'll capsize if we load 'em up anymore,' snarled another. 'We'll be drownded and the coal will gan to the bottom of the river. And what good, brothers, will *that* do for them greedy beggars?'

'What did ye tell 'em, brother?'

'Aa told 'em that they canna up the loads,' Scuffins replied. 'The law's plain enough. The king's measure is aal we can take.'

'Ha! What did they say to that, brother?'

'They laughed in my face. Said they divvent read it that way.'

'Aa suppose they can afford their fancy lawyers to swear that black is white.'

'Aye, but we canna let them think we can be tret like cuddies, can we?'

There was a general murmur of consent from the rest of the company to that sentiment, which was expressed by the keelman who appeared to be the oldest among them, a grim-looking, snowy-haired fellow of at least forty-five years.

'What else did they tell ye, brother?'

'They said they wanted wor answer by the first of next month,' Scuffins replied. 'But Aa told 'em they could have it directly, brothers. Aa told 'em we won't load wor boats any heavier. Aa told 'em that the keelmen'll honour the agreement on the king's measure and that, if they were honourable men, they'd do likewise …'

'Well said, brother,' called out several supporting voices.

'Aa thought ye said ye nivvor got a word in,' called out a cynical one, earning an angry glare from Scuffins.

'… And that's not aal. Aa told 'em the staithes are causing a danger on the river and they should be pulled doon. They thought Aa was joking at first, brothers, but they soon realised Aa was deadly serious.' He cast his eyes around the room to ensure he had everyone's attention before adding, in grave tones, 'Mark my words, brothers, those staithes are threatening wor very jobs.'

'Aa've worked on this river, man and boy, for nigh on thirty-five years,' said the grim-looking, snowy-haired man, shaking his head, 'and Aa'm telling ye that for as lang as coal has to be taken downriver to the brigs, there'll aalways be need of yous keelmen.'

'Work it oot for yarsel, old fellow,' Scuffins countered. 'If we dinaa do something about the staithes, one day soon they'll be trying to load the brigs direct from the spouts. Especially the ones downriver that the ships can get to.'

'He's reet,' agreed several keelmen.

'So what's wor next move, then, brother?'

'Aa suggest that we send a petition to the mayor to call a meeting of the Hoastmen and the shipmasters. We'll have to draw up a list of wor demands. And a list of wor grievances.'

'Grievances?' shouted one. 'We've got plenty of them, brothers. For a start, their Can Houses deduct full price from wor wages for a quart of drink and then serve us savage beer instead of the proper ale.'

'And why should we have to accept beer vouchers for wor work, anyway, brothers? They should pay us in cash,' added another. 'We canna buy bread for wor bairns with beer vouchers, can we?'

'And we haven't had a pay rise for years,' said a third. 'The only things that have gone up are the prices of everything in the shops and the coal-owners' profits. Meantime, brothers, we're expected to live on a pittance.'

'Aa say we should accept what Brother Scuffins suggested and put wor case to the gaffers,' a fourth proposed.

'And what if the gaffers don't accept wor demands? Last time we struck all that happened was that wor bairns went hungry for weeks and then we went back to work with nowt.'

'Then we'll have to find a way of changing the gaffers' minds, won't we, brothers?' replied Scuffins.

*

From time to time, Mister Hadwen Bragg used to invite friends and business associates to dine with his family at Number 264 Spital Tongues. On these occasions, he never failed to include Bella and me in the company, as though he harboured no feelings of embarrassment or shame at the presence in his house of a couple of down-and-outs, such as we regarded ourselves (although I must emphasise that Mister Bragg never gave any sign of sharing this opinion).

Among his regular dinner-guests was a gentleman by the name of Abel Grope, a sombre fellow who carried on the profession of undertaker and coffin-maker at premises on High Bridge. Mister Grope cut a rather morose figure, due largely to his painfully thin body (which, I surmised, had been wasted by the consumption), his watery eyes, his pinched grey complexion and his habit of dressing almost entirely in black (with only a frilled white shirt to provide some contrast with the rest of his ensemble). He was invariably accompanied on his visits by his wife, who was as stout as her husband was skinny and scarcely contributed a word to the pre- or post-prandial conversations. Despite his ostensible sullenness, Mister Grope was in truth a most amusing guest, betraying the gravity of his appearance with a light-hearted manner and a facility for entertaining the rest of the company with amusing tales drawn almost exclusively from his long experience of laying out corpses and organising their burial.

It was during one such evening that Mister Grope fixed me with a grey eye and said, 'Well, young fellow, have you thought about what profession you would like to follow?'

At first, I was rather taken aback by being addressed so directly by such a well-respected man of the town. And then I was not a little flattered that he should display such an interest in me - an interest which, to my young ears, sounded completely honest and unaffected.

'I ... I ...' I stuttered, not being accustomed to trading conversation with adults other than Mister and Mistress Bragg. 'I ... would like to do good for others, sir.' I felt embarrassed as this inadequate response left my lips, but Mister Grope was not to be diverted.

'That's a fine thing to hear from a young fellow,' he said approvingly. 'Tell me more.'

'Well, sir, I visited the poorhouse with Mister Bragg.'

At this point, I looked towards my patron, who nodded encouragement and, turning to my inquisitor, added the confirmation, 'All Saints.'

'Yes? And what did you learn there?' asked Mister Grope. Now, even his wife seemed interested in what I might have to say. She leaned forward and held against her temple a peculiar conical instrument which, I was later to be informed by Mister Bragg (after his guests had departed), was a device known as an ear trumpet, reputed to assist those who are hard-of-hearing to follow a conversation.

'Well, sir, although my father was a medical man, he died when I was still too young to understand much about his work. But when we visited All Saints' I spoke to a doctor there who told me how it was his job to help the inmates. The guests, I mean. To help them with their medical problems, help to cure them or comfort them. He said that he found it very rewarding to have it in his power to help people in that way.'

'So you think that *you*'d like to go into the medical profession, is that it?'

'Yes, sir.'

'What exactly do you have in mind, young man?'

'I'm sorry, sir. I don't understand what you mean.'

'I meant, which branch of the medical profession attracts you?'

'I don't know about any of them, sir.'

'Well, maybe you'd like to become a physician. Or perhaps an apothecary. Or you could do an apprenticeship and qualify as a surgeon's assistant. There are plenty to choose from.'

'Thank you, sir. I would like to know more about all of them before I decide.'

'Well said, young man. Very sensible.' His wife nodded vigorously to indicate that she agreed with him, as I assumed. He continued, 'You know, James, I like you. I like the way that you're determined to do good for your fellow-men. It's an admirable trait in a young man – and not too common, I dare say. Well, now, I need a boy in my business. Someone who is keen to learn. Someone I can trust to do a good job. I can afford to pay a small salary and provide you with food and lodgings.' He looked across at Mister Bragg, as if seeking his endorsement for his, as yet, undisclosed proposal and was rewarded with a smile and a bob of the head. 'How would you like to come and work for me?'

'Well, sir … ' I hesitated. I had been presented with a dilemma. 'Thank you, sir… but I help out at Mister Bragg's store on most days, sir. I'm sorry that I wouldn't be able to work for you in the mornings.'

Mister Bragg came to my rescue. 'James,' he said, 'what my friend is suggesting would be a great opportunity for thee. I know a number of young medics who have worked for an undertaker before taking up their apprenticeship. Thee would learn a lot – about the human body and so forth – that's what it's about, after all.'

I blushed at the prospect and the adults laughed, not unkindly, at my discomposure.

'But, sir … ' I addressed myself to Mister Bragg, 'what about my duties in your store?'

'I'd rather that thee grasped the chance of something which will put thee on the ladder to the medical profession. And that, in turn, will open up a vacancy for me to offer to some other deserving lad or lass.'

'Thank you, sir,' I replied, 'but … er … I'm not sure …'

'Is something else troubling thee about this, James?' he interrupted gently.

'Well, sir … ' This time I turned towards Mister Grope. '… I halt a little about my legs, sir. From my days as a climbing-boy. The chimneys have done for my knees.'

Mister Grope looked over at Mister Bragg, who told him reassuringly, 'It doesn't affect the lad badly. He's a good worker, I promise thee.'

Mister Grope nodded his head gravely as though weighing up a difficult problem. 'Could even be an advantage,' he said without further explanation.

And so it was that, at precisely seven o'clock on the following Monday morning, almost three years to the day since I had first crossed the threshold of Number 264 Spital Tongues, I arrived at the premises on High Bridge of Mister Abel Grope, Undertaker and Coffin-Maker, having been kitted out at the emporium of *Bragg and Company* with a new black suit, waistcoat and top hat and carrying the rest of my worldly goods, ready to take up my new employment and move into my new lodgings in the attic room above the business.

10

Sir Stanhope Delaval shared his father's love of overindulgence. Despite the considerable sums he derived from his lucrative, legitimate business interests, his expenditure on entertaining, gambling and womanising obliged him to supplement his income by various illegal activities and other shady practices. Nevertheless, under his stewardship, the family riches which Captain Francis Blake Delaval had looted so profligately continued to dwindle until they reached the point where there was a real prospect that the Hall would have to be sold to pay off mounting debts. Sir Stanhope was also as superstitious as he was spendthrift and when it so happened that news of Blackie Johnson's skill at fortune-telling reached Seaton Delaval Hall, he decided to send for the man in the hope of learning some morsel of information about the future which could be turned to his own financial advantage.

Blackie was deeply flattered to be invited to attend such a distinguished client at such an imposing location and was determined to make a strong impression which, he imagined, might lead to further commissions from among the wealthiest citizens of the County. He planned to achieve this by bringing to light some exceptional event, the revelation of which would both astound Sir Stanhope and convince him that he needed to retain the services of the leading occultist in Newcastle.

The phaeton which Sir Stanhope sent to collect him from the Keyside took him up the Great North Road, then turned off to the east along a broad avenue lined with magnificent lime trees. Blackie had never before been transported in such a conveyance and he enjoyed the experience of feeling just as he imagined an aristocrat would feel. He eagerly grasped the opportunity to wave graciously to the sprinkling of local peasants who stood to attention at the roadside and doffed their caps to him as he passed. At last, the sea came into view and, shortly after, the carriage swung off the highway and through the gates onto the forecourt of Seaton Delaval Hall, coming to a halt in front of the central building. The coachman, who was under strict instructions to treat his passenger with the utmost consideration, helped him down from the carriage, ensuring he did not trip as he clutched what looked like a heavy parcel under his arm, then led the way up the steps to the front door and into the entrance hall with its chequered marble-paved floor. Blackie was transfixed by the splendour which confronted him – the massive Doric columns, the classical carvings, the statues lining the niches in the stone walls.

When Blackie was ushered into his host's presence, Sir Stanhope, despite the turn in his own eye, was rather disconcerted by the man's appearance and could not prevent an inadvertent look of horror from crossing his face. 'Er … I'm so sorry …' he stammered with embarrassment, 'but nobody told me … er, … you know.' Blackie, who had encountered the same reaction on numerous occasions and was heartily sick of it, did not bother to try to alleviate the man's discomfiture but faced him brazenly, deliberately fixing him with his sightless eye socket. At last, Sir Stanhope managed to compose himself and held out his hand in welcome. Blackie shook it unenthusiastically.

Sir Stanhope shepherded him from the entrance hall into a side room lined with dark wooden panelling on which were hung various family portraits of fearsome-looking men and women who scowled down from their vantage points, each displaying the strabismus and Mediterranean features which marked every generation of the Delaval line. 'This is what we call the Mahogany Parlour,' he announced proudly. When this evoked no reaction from his visitor, he said, 'Well then, Mister Johnson, shall we get to work?'

'Aa divvent suppose ye'd have anything in the way of a drink to wet me whistle, would ye, my lord? Me throat's as dry as a pit-yakker's crotch from the journey, ye knaa.'

'Oh … yes, of course. I'll call for some wine right away, if that would suit you.' He pressed a small bell-push situated next to the door and a manservant appeared within seconds to take the order. 'And by the way, Mister Johnson, you mustn't address me as *my lord*.'

The wine arrived almost as quickly as the manservant had done and Blackie polished off a half-pint in no time at all. Then they sat down at the large mahogany table which dominated the centre of the room and Blackie drew a pack of tarot cards from his pocket and held them out in front of him. 'Will ye take three from here, my lord? From anywhere ye like.'

'I've told you, I'm not a lord. Just call me Sir Stanhope.' He contemplated his strategy for a few minutes before carefully selecting three cards, one from the middle of the pack and then two from near the bottom. He handed them gingerly to Blackie, who, with exaggerated ceremony, slowly turned the cards one at a time face up onto the table between them and gazed at them, deep in thought for what to Sir Stanhope, waiting anxiously for the verdict, seemed an age. A look of extreme puzzlement cast a shadow over Blackie's bleak features. Then he picked up the cards and turned them face down again, sighed deeply and reached for the large tome which he had brought with him.

'Aa need to consult *De occulta philosophia*,' he explained to his bemused host.

'What?' Sir Stanhope asked.

'*De occulta philosophia*,' Blackie repeated.

'What?' Sir Stanhope, none the wiser, asked again.

'It's my bible, Aa suppose ye could say. Written by the world's greatest ever magus, Heinrich Agrippa. Heinrich Cornelius Agrippa von Nettesheim, to be precise,' Blackie explained. 'A German, my lord,' he added unnecessarily.

'Oh,' Sir Stanhope said. 'Can't say I've heard of him. And it's *Sir Stanhope*, not *my lord*.'

'A very clever man. A master of the hidden arts,' Blackie continued. Then he opened the book. 'Excuse me while Aa check with the great man. Aa believe Aa have the answer to yer enquiry, my lord, but a second opinion from Heinrich Agrippa which coincides with mine would make for absolute certainty.'

'Yes, of course. I suppose it would,' Sir Stanhope said doubtfully, having given up as a lost cause his attempt to establish his correct nomenclature.

Eventually, Blackie looked up from the book and closed it with a snap. 'Aa thought so,' he declared gravely. Then he picked up the three cards and said,' Let's look at the ones ye selected, my lord.' He flung down the first melodramatically and let Sir Stanhope scrutinize it for a few moments. It showed a hand emerging from what looked like a cloud and holding aloft a branch from which sprouted a few leaves. 'It's The Ace of Wands,' Blackie stated.

'What does it mean?' Sir Stanhope asked.

'Aa'll tell ye that in a while, my lord,' Blackie replied. 'When we've seen the others.' He flung down the second card in the same manner as the first and Sir Stanhope could see that it depicted the head of a goat, a five-pointed star and what appeared to be a lighted candle. The images unnerved him.

'Is it bad?' he asked, his voice shaking a little.

'It's The Devil's card,' Blackie told him. 'The goat-headed figure is called Baphomet. It's an ancient representation of Satan. The inverted star is a pentagram.'

'What's the significance of that?'

'Wait until we've seen the last one. We have to consider them aal together as a set, not just individually.'

The third card contained a picture of a cylindrical building from which flames were shooting out in several places, with streaks of lightning striking the top of the structure. 'That's called The Tower,' Blackie said and turned to look at Sir Stanhope as if expecting him to detect the thread which linked the three cards. 'Well, my lord, can you see any connection?'

'Connection? Er … no … you'll have to tell me. That's what you're here for, isn't it, Mister Johnson?'

'Right enough, my lord. Aa'll explain what these are telling me. This card here…' – he picked up the first one - '… The Ace of Wands, is the highest of the Wands suit in the Minor Arcana. The Wands represent three signs of the zodiac, Aries the ram, Sagittarius the archer and Leo the lion. Do they mean anything to ye?'

'I can't say they do,' Sir Stanhope shook his head. 'I've heard of them, of course, but beyond that … no, they don't mean anything specific to me.'

'They're fire signs. They relate to things or people that can flare up quickly or have sudden flashes of illumination.' He let that thought sink in for a few moments then picked up the second card. 'The Devil's card is a trump card, one of the Major Arcana. As ye might imagine, it's usually an indication of some form of evil. It conveys a sense of danger, particularly as the pentagram, which is normally the sign of harmony between the elements, is inverted. So it suggests *dis*harmony.'

Sir Stanhope had gone quite pale. 'What do you mean … danger?' he asked. 'Am I in danger?'

Blackie chose not to answer the question directly, but instead continued his analysis. 'The interesting thing about The Devil's card …,' he said, pointing to the image above the goat's head, '… is this candle. Ye can see that it's burning.'

'Is that a link to the fire sign, then?' Sir Stanhope had suddenly spotted a connection between the first two cards.

'Correct,' Blackie confirmed. 'Then we come to The Tower.' He held it up. 'Another trump card.'

'That shows a fire too, doesn't it? Is that it, then? Something to do with a fire?'

'Aa believe so, my lord,' he replaced the card on the table. 'Aa couldn't help noticing, as soon as Aa stepped out of that carriage that yer lordship kindly sent to pick me up, that this building - Aa mean the middle section of the Hall – has a tower that looks very much like the one pictured on the card.'

Sir Stanhope grabbed the card and looked at it as if he was seeing a ghost. 'Oh my God,' he yelled. 'We're all going to be burnt alive in our beds, is that it?'

'No, no, my lord. There's going to be a fire but Aa don't think anybody's ganning to get hurt.'

'How so?'

'Well, my lord, what these cards are telling me is that one day, not this week, not this month, not this year, but in maybe a year or two or maybe even more, the Hall will be severely damaged by a fire that starts when ye and yer family are away …'

'Are you quite sure about that?' Sir Stanhope enquired anxiously.

'… Please divvent interrupt,' Blackie snapped angrily. 'Aa need complete quiet to help me think this through. Ye can ask me questions when Aa've finished.' He closed his good eye in a look of intense concentration, bowed his head and clenched his fists so tightly that his knuckles whitened. After at least a minute in this posture he said, 'Yes, Aa can picture it now. Aa can see a bright glow in the main building ... the roof is well on fire now, melted lead is running down the walls ... the night sky is lit up with flames and sparks ... there is a mighty crash as the roof caves in ... people are running into the east and west wings ... they canna get near the main building because of the heat ... they are trying to save things from other parts of the Hall from being burnt ... the stable doors have been thrown open and the horses are running around the forecourt in terror ...' He fell silent.

'Go on,' urged Sir Stanhope.

'That's aal,' Blackie said, sounding exhausted by his exertions.

'Well, what happens in the end?' Sir Stanhope.

'No one is killed, as Aa told ye before, my lord. There's not much left of the Hall though. Just the kitchen block and the stables. The rest's destroyed.'

'How is it that nobody dies in the fire?'

'Aa told ye. Ye and the rest of yer family are away at the time. Aa canna tell exactly where ye are, but it's somewhere over the sea. France probably.'

Sir Stanhope was experiencing a hotchpotch of emotions. He was, of course, shocked by Blackie's description of the conflagration which was to destroy much of his family home, albeit without harming any family members. But there was an uncanny resemblance between the events which Blackie had described and his own speculative ideas on how he might, if the worst came to the worst, bolster his finances by perpetrating a fraud, taking out an insurance policy on Seaton Delaval Hall with a greatly inflated valuation and then setting fire to the place. He had of course told nobody of this. Was it possible that Blackie, being blessed with supernatural powers of clairvoyance, had become privy to his secret, most innermost thoughts? Or was it nothing more than an amazing coincidence that the man's prediction accorded so closely with his own scheme?

'I don't suppose you have any idea of how the fire started?' he ventured tentatively.

'Aa canna be certain, yer lordship. The cards are a bit un-clear on that point. It could be one of two things. Aa've got a plan of the building in my mind that Aa need ye to help me with. When ye gan through the entrance hall, do ye find yarsel in some kind of wide room?'

'Yes, the saloon. Sometimes we use it as a ballroom.'

'Is there a fireplace there?'

'There are two.'

'Well now, let me see … The one on the right as ye enter the saloon. Aa believe it has a flue leading up to a chimney in the roof which passes close to a wooden rafter.'

'What of it?'

'Ye see, my lord, one explanation is that when the chimney was not being used - it must have been a warm springtime when a fire was not lit – a pair of jackdaws built a nest inside and blocked the flue. Then, when the fire was eventually lit – prob-ably in the following autumn – the flames couldn't escape and caught onto the rafter, then spread to the roof.'

Sir Stanhope was secretly delighted to have a plausible ac-count which he felt would easily pass muster with the insurance assessors at Lloyd's of London. 'What's the other possible cause of the fire?' he asked, hoping to hear another innocent explana-tion.

'Arson.'

'Arson? You mean it's been started deliberately?'

'Well, that's what arson means, ye knaa.'

'Who on earth would do such a thing?'

'Who d'ye think, yer lordship?' Blackie seemed to be teasing him. Or was it his guilty imagination playing tricks?

'Someone with a grudge against the Delaval family?' he suggested cautiously.

'No, Aa divvent think that's very likely. Far more likely to be done by somebody who wants the insurance money.'

Blackie could tell by the look on Sir Stanhope's face - a mixture of guilt, embarrassment and fear of exposure - that he'd scored a bull's-eye with that remark. It confirmed what he had already deduced from the cards.

11

I was introduced to my two new workmates, who were much older than me and were called Belcher (the tall one) and Jago (the short one). They never did bother to tell me whether they had any other names, nor did Mister Grope inform me, nor did I ever find out from anyone else, nor did I consider it necessary to enquire myself. They were the first to christen me, on account of the injury occasioned by my days spent inside chimney flues, Knacky-kneed Mack, a moniker by which I was to be known for the rest of my life (well, up to now, at least). There was something slightly unpleasant about them, something I couldn't quite put my finger on but which made me uncomfortable in their company, just as I had once been made to feel unwelcome by two of the other apprentices in Mister Boag's employ. They often spoke together in whispers, so as not to include me in their conversation, and when Mister Grope was away from the premises on business, as frequently happened, they referred to him - rather discourteously in my view - as 'the gaffer'.

For the first few weeks, things went well from my point of view and Mister Grope expressed himself content with my progress in mastering the basics of my role. I learned how to lead a funeral cortege by walking before the hearse and the mourning coaches at exactly the correct pace, somewhere between the speed of a stroll and a saunter. 'Don't try to disguise that limp of yours,' Mister Grope instructed. 'It helps to emphasise the wretchedness of the occasion.'

I learned to look suitably solemn and sorrowful at our clients' bereavements and to feign sympathy for the accompanying mourners, although these were not skills which came to me easily. 'I'm not sure I can do that, sir,' I explained to Mister

Grope when he had asked me to demonstrate how I would simulate a display of tears.

'Nonsense!' he roared. 'It's quite straightforward. You merely need to imagine that it's your poor mother lying in that coffin.'

At this, the tears welled up immediately in my eyes and he clapped me on the back, saying, 'That's it, my boy. Well done, very convincing.'

When I had been in his employ for some three or four months, Mister Grope suggested that I might like to broaden my experience by assisting in the laying out of the bodies, a task normally assigned to Belcher and Jago, whose other duties included the arrangement of the deceased in the coffin and the securing of the fastenings. Laying out was a responsibility which I baulked at initially but, after a little practice, I came to espouse, especially as I still had my sights on the medical profession, in which, it was obvious, I would have to encounter fellow human beings in a state of extreme distress – even mortality. My employer was a kind and patient tutor and demonstrated the method a number of times before allowing me to help him directly.

We would first strip the body and then I would be given the task of biting hard on the joint of the great toe in order to make absolutely certain that we were dealing with a dead person. Fortunately, there never an occasion when this produced any reaction which would have led us to think otherwise. As Mister Grope put it, not without a modicum of humour, 'We have to be sure that the departed really *has* departed'.

Then we would wash the corpse thoroughly with soap and warm water. Sometimes, if there had been a delay on the relatives' part in informing us of the death, the rigor mortis may have set in, in which case I learned how to break down the stiffness by gently massaging and flexing the joints and moving the head carefully from side to side several times until the muscles of the neck relaxed and the deceased could be placed in a straight position. This had to done before washing could begin. Then, we would block up the intimate orifices with cloth (I think that is sufficient detail on that point) and dress the body, make sure the eyelids were closed (this had to be done very carefully to avoid damage to the fragile tissue) and do our best to make the face look as near as possible in death to how it had looked in life. This was usually the most difficult part of the procedure, particularly if the death had been as a result of a violent blow to the head or the deceased had no teeth, in which case it was necessary to stuff the mouth with cotton wool to prevent the face caving in. A touch of rouge powder was often rubbed on to the cheeks to reduce the pallor. Unless Mister Grope had received instructions that the corpse was to 'lie to attention' in its coffin, which often happened if the deceased had been a soldier, we would cross the arms over the chest. Finally, it was important, in order to deter blowflies from laying their eggs in the nostrils, a favourite breeding place for maggots, to cover the face with a heavy cloth in between the times when mourners would visit to pay their respects.

Meanwhile, although I was enjoying my new occupation, my relations with Belcher and Jago continued to be difficult. When the three of us were together, I could not help feeling that I was intruding on their company and that they would rather I had not been there. It became a regular occurrence, particularly on cold mornings when they were to act as pall-bearers, for Belcher and Jago to drink gin before donning their funeral garb, a practice which I considered to be both a reprehensible misuse of our employer's time and one which might lead to drunkenness on duty.

Once, when the tall one had been yawning all morning and it appeared that he might doze off at any moment, I enquired of him – politely, or so I thought - whether he'd had a disturbed night's sleep. This seemed to annoy him greatly for he turned on me as if I had offered him a great insult and bellowed, 'Exactly what do you mean to imply by that remark?' So taken aback was I with his reaction that all I could do was to stutter an apology for having distressed him and try to assure him that I meant no mischief by my question.

I could tell that my association with Belcher and Jago was unlikely to end agreeably.

*

Kitty Dace could remember very clearly the one and only time she had entered the icehouse which stood in the grounds of Seaton Delaval Hall, just at the rear of the east wing. Because of the strange character of the place, it was always considered a special treat among the kitchen staff to be allowed to accompany Mrs Robson, the Head Cook, on one of her regular trips there, not in order to perform any specific task but solely to look inside while Mrs Robson collected whatever provisions she needed for the day's menu.

'It's your turn today, Kitty,' Mrs Robson said, one frosty morning. 'Go and wrap up nice and warm and come with me. You can help by reading out the list for me. But don't you go messing about with anything or the Master will be furious, d'you understand? He's very precious about his icehouse, you know. He's even got his own special area inside where no-one else is allowed to go.'

Kitty felt that it was quite a privilege to be allowed into the mysterious building with its dome-shaped roof topped by a thick layer of clay and soil and was intrigued to learn what she would find inside. During the depths of winter, she had often seen the menservants cutting the layers of ice from the garden ponds and carrying them into the icehouse together with piles of snow. At other times she had watched them taking in large sacks, presumably filled with the carcasses of pigs, sheep, deer and other foodstuffs. Now she was about to discover for herself the secrets of the icehouse.

Mrs Robson took a large iron key from her apron and unlocked the wooden door set in the arched entrance wall. 'Now, Kitty,' she instructed, 'go in straightaway. No tarrying. We don't want to let out the cold, do we?' Once inside, they were confronted by a leather door which Mrs Robson pushed open. Then a second one. Then a third. The deeper they advanced inside, the colder the air became. They reached a narrow passage lined with small straw bales, which then widened into a chamber and at the far end there was a well which disappeared down into the darkness. 'That's where they store the ice,' Mrs Robson explained, pointing into the void. 'In a good year, the ice that goes in there in the winter will last us until October. As it melts, the water drains down underneath and back into the ponds.' The rest of the chamber was divided by more straw bales into compartments crammed with crates and other containers. Pulling aside a couple of bales, Mrs Robson handed Kitty a sheet of paper listing the various provisions which she required for the evening's banquet. 'You read that out, Kitty,' she said, 'and I'll pick up what we need.'

By the time they had retrieved a saddle of mutton, five brace of rabbits, several ducks and fowl, half a dozen pigeons and a side of venison, they had completed four trips to and fro, alternating between the cold of the icehouse and the warmth of the kitchen. On their final visit, Kitty waited inside the chamber while Mrs Robson rummaged inside one of the compartments for the last few items. Overcome with curiosity, she momentarily forgot the Head Cook's directive and tentatively began to pull aside a straw bale covering an adjacent compartment. As she did so, Mrs Robson, emerging from her search, shrieked at the top of her voice, 'Stop, Kitty. What do you think you're doing? That's the Master's private area.'

'I'm sorry, Mrs Robson,' Kitty replied meekly. 'I was just …'

She did not have the opportunity to finish her explanation before Mrs Robson's hand slapped her hard across the face. 'How dare you? I thought I could trust you, Kitty, but it's obvious I was wrong.'

As she returned to the kitchen, a figurative cloud hanging over her head because of the disobedience which had so infuriated Mrs Robson, Kitty reflected on what she had just observed. She could not be absolutely certain, of course, since she had only the merest glimpse of what lay behind the straw bale. And, in any case, her imagination often seemed to play tricks on her. Nevertheless, she had the faintest impression that, in that split second, she had seen what looked like a human foot protruding from one of the sacks.

12

The word had spread quickly through Sandgate that important news was about to break and over four hundred keelmen were packed into the club room at the Keelmen's Hospital to hear Jasper Scuffins' report of what had transpired during his meeting with the Hoastmen and the ship-owners. But as he rose to address them, they could tell from his scowl that what he had to impart would not be to their liking.

'The ship-owners nivvor even turned up, brothers,' he said. 'Aa was sitting there at the Mansion House, in the Mayor's Parlour, with just a few of the Hoastmen. Brandling was there, of course, and Snitterby and Delaval and a couple of others who Aa divvent knaa. That's aal. It was like they dinaa think it was worth coming.'

'Why are ye surprised, brother?' a voice called out from the crowd. 'They've aalways tret us like scum.' Several others murmured their agreement with the sentiment.

'Anyway,' Scuffins continued, 'Aa put wor case to 'em. Aa told 'em about everything yous asked me to tell 'em about. Aa told 'em the way the prices of food have gone up without us having an increase in wor wages. Aa told 'em how the spouts are creating a danger on the river. Aa told 'em how we divvent like the way they serve us savage beer at the same cost as the proper stuff. Aa told 'em the lot. Aa said we needed at least another two shillings a tide for each keel. A man with a family canna feed his bairns with less than two pounds a week. Aa told 'em they had to stop using the staithes otherwise they were ganna cause a wreck and block up the channels even worse than they are now.'

'And what did the gaffers have to say to that, brother?' an impatient listener demanded to know.

'What they told me was that they thought it would be an infringement of their property. They said it would be a violation of their legal right to organise their things in the best way to maximise their profits.'

A burst of scornful laughter went round in the room.

'Aa told 'em, brothers that if they wanted to prove they were decent folk they could give a charity payment. Aa suggested sixpence a keel for the upkeep of wor Hospital.'

'Ye should have said a shilling,' suggested someone.

'Perhaps, but no matter. In any case, they reacted as if Aa'd asked them to cut off their ain hands. They said it was out of the question.'

'What else did ye tell 'em?' asked another.

'Aa said we wanted no brigs heading for London to be loaded at the staithes but to wait for the keels at the bar at Shields.'

'And did ye get anywhere with 'em on that demand, brother?' asked yet another.

'Just hear me out, will yous?' Scuffins replied curtly. 'When Aa finished saying my piece they told me they'd consider everything Aa'd put to 'em. They aal went off to the dining room and left me sitting around outside for about an hour. Aa divvent think they even talked about what Aa'd said. Aal Aa could hear was them laughing and clinking glasses and stuffing their mouths with scran. Then Snitterby came out at last, stinking of wine, red in the face and slurring his words. Told me he was there as their spokesman to give me their response. Tried to sound apologetic. Said he was terribly sorry. Said the Hoastmen couldn't agree to any of wor demands. Not a single one. Could hardly hide the smirk on his face, as if they were aal regarding the whole thing as a big joke and treating us with contempt.'

Silence.

Then, 'So what do we do now, brother?'

'If they wanna treat us like rats, perhaps we should start to behave like 'em,' Scuffins growled.

'What d'ye mean, brother?'

'It's war. That's what Aa mean. War.'

'War?'

'Aa mean it, brothers. Just think about it seriously, will ye? It's no good us threatening to strike and just saying we're not using wor boats. If we do that, the gaffers will bring in blackleg labour, Aa'll wager. We need to gan further than that. Much further.'

'What are ye suggesting, brother?'

'This time it mustn't be a matter of just wor sels striking, brothers. We'll have to get the mariners and the pit-yakkers to support us by striking too. Because if no coal moves on the Tyne, the gaffers won't make a penny piece. That should bring 'em to their senses.'

'And what if it doesn't?'

'Then, we destroy the spouts, we wreck the staithes, we target the Hoastmen, attack 'em, attack their homes, make them afeared. There's nowt we should rule out. If we find any scabs taking ower wor jobs, taking wor coal doon the river, we'll sink 'em, we'll let 'em drownd.'

The shocked silence that followed Scuffins' passionate call to arms was at last broken only by one keelman's misguided attempt to lighten the dismal mood which pervaded the room.

'If we let 'em drownd there'll at least be one boat on the river. Cuckoo Jack'll be out there with his grappling irons, dragging out the bodies and collecting his ten shillings from the Corporation.'

Scuffins was angered by the comment and glared aggressively at the man responsible for making it, disgusted that one of his fellow keelman should try to make a joke out of such a serious matter as their livelihood. 'You're not fit to call yarsel wor brother,' he roared at him. He was angered too by the mention of Cuckoo Jack, whom, like everyone else in Sandgate, he knew. In fact, he probably knew about him better than most, as his own wife Martha was a friend of Jack's wife and often regaled him with tales of the man's heroic exploits. It was not in Jasper Scuffins' nature to enjoy hearing praise being heaped by his wife on another man and, in consequence, he disliked him intensely. 'From what Aa've heard about Cuckoo Jack,' he said, 'he's often in the habit of hoying bairns into the river. And leaving 'em to drownd 'cos he gets more for a deed one than a live one.' Even before the words had left his lips he knew them to be untrue, but nevertheless hoped that the lie might be received as credible and thereby remove some of the gloss from the man's good reputation.

'Think about it, brothers,' he continued, returning to the offensive he had been urging before the interruption. 'It's either the gaffers' profits or wor livelihood that were talking about here. The Company of Hoastmen, the magistrates, the aldermen and the rest – they're aal in it together to run this toon how *they* want. They're corrupt. They divvent care a bagie for the likes of us watermen. We canna afford to lose this fight. If we do, they'll wipe us out.'

Several voices were raised in agreement with these sentiments.

'Aa'm for the war against the gaffers,' yelled one man.

'Me too,' yelled another and soon the whole room seemed to be filled with keelmen shouting and raising their fists in support.

'This is what Aa think we should do, brothers,' Scuffins said, once order had been restored. 'We need a group of us to organise things. To come up with ideas of how we can hurt the gaffers. To delegate the plans to others to carry out. To work out how we get people on wor side. Not just the pit-yakkers and the sailors – we need them, of course - but the ordinary people of the toon, I mean. And the keelmen on the Wear as well. Who's willing to be part of that group? Part of wor Action Committee?'

Virtually every hand in the room shot up.

'Right, brothers. We've got plenty of volunteers here. Wor fight starts now.'

*

As far as I can remember, it must have been some time after I moved out of Number 264 Spital Tongues that I took to visiting a number of public houses and eventually settled on the Flying Horse Tavern as my favourite watering hole. During my stay at the home of Mister and Mistress Bragg, I had, out of respect for my hosts' strict teetotalism imposed by their religious beliefs and lifestyle, abstained from any contact with alcoholic beverages or the locations in which they were dispensed. And, initially at least, I had continued this abstention even after I had left behind the Braggs' hospitality and passed into the employ of Mister Grope, Undertaker and Coffin-maker.

I was pleasantly surprised one morning when, despite the apparent hostility previously demonstrated towards me, Belcher and Jago invited me to accompany them at midday to the White Hart Inn. At first, I was reluctant to absent myself from my duties during working hours but, as Belcher explained, 'Wor gaffer won't be back until tomorrow and he won't mind us taking ye along for a little celebration,' and eventually I was persuaded to accept the invitation. Precisely what they were celebrating, I was yet to learn.

The location of the White Hart Inn is officially named Meal Street but has come to be christened by the locals as the Groatmarket since the Common Council decided to restrict the activities of vendors of groats to that small part of the town. It is a bustling thoroughfare, on the south side of which are several taverns, eating houses and tearooms as well as a row of shops and small businesses, including a cheese-monger, bacon dealer, book-binder, buckle-maker, salmon-pickler and even a dancing school. On the north side, near where the street joins Pudding Chare, stand the Post-house and the Town Hall.

The White Hart, a commodious and well-conducted Inn, is undoubtedly the grandest drinking-house in the Groatmarket and, to my young eyes, its clientele (excepting ourselves) seemed to be drawn from the most respectable sections of Newcastle citizenry. I wondered why my colleagues had chosen this particular venue for their celebration, but I confess that I was greatly excited by the vibrancy of the place. After we had each consumed at least a quart of ale, the strength of which and my unfamiliarity with it caused my head to swoon, Belcher and Jago ordered more drinks. I declined and opted instead to deposit myself in a vacant corner seat in order to recover from the effects of the alcohol. Meanwhile, my colleagues fell into conversation with an enormous, cock-eyed gentleman with dark features who sported a Roman nose and a red-spotted silk handkerchief, a conversation which at first appeared secretive, then became animated and eventually reached a point where I wondered whether the three were about to come to blows.

After the gentleman had left, his parting from the others being patently less than amicable, Belcher and Jago ordered and consumed even more ale and then revealed that the purpose of our visit to the White Hart Inn had been to celebrate my recent appointment as an assistant to Mister Grope (to whom they referred once again as 'the gaffer') and that, in keeping with tradition, it was I who was to settle the bill. I felt then that I had been comprehensively duped. However, I was forced to admit to myself that it would be churlish to protest at having to meet the cost of a jollification held in my honour even though it made a sizeable hole in my meagre salary.

That was, to my relief, the only occasion on which Belcher and Jago invited me to join them at one of their drinking sessions. Indeed, from that day on, they resumed their erstwhile animosity towards me. Nevertheless, my fascination for the comings and goings of the Groatmarket had been aroused and, on one evening not long after, I ventured there again and found the place just as lively as it had been on my previous visit. On this occasion, however, being on my own, I baulked at the thought of entering the White Hart Inn and instead deliberated on whether I should try one of the other public houses in the street. There was certainly no lack of choice. On the south side, the Spread Eagle, the King's Head, the Black Boy, the Fighting Cocks and the Dog and Duck, all elegant enough in their individual ways, competed alongside one another for the drinking man's custom. But it was an establishment situated on the north side, a short distance from the Town Hall and below the junction with Pudding Chare, which caught my eye. The Flying Horse Tavern looked less pretentious and intimidating than its neighbours. This was the drinking-house of which I was to be a regular patron for many years to come.

At first acquaintance, it looked like a confusing muddle of several separate rooms set in a rectangular building around a central yard. But, as the frequency of my visits increased and I became more familiar with the geography of the place, not only was I able to find my way around quite easily but I learned to recognise and distinguish the unique characteristics of each of the Tavern's rooms, its clientele and the regulations prescribed by the publican which were to be observed under pain of expulsion or humiliation.

13

Newcastle Courant

A ROBBERY

Sir Stanhope Delaval of Seaton Delaval Hall, in the County of Northumberland, was travelling between his Residence and Bulman Village early last Saturday Evening when he was stopped near the Seven Mile Bridge by four Footpads who violently seized from him 28 Guineas in Gold, 38 Pounds in Banknotes and 2 Drafts, Values together 18 pounds, his Horse and Carriage, Saddles, Bridle, Bags, 2 great Coats and 1 close Coat, a Pocket Book and several other Articles.

His Amanuensis, a Miss Kitty Dace, also resident at Seaton Delaval Hall, who was travelling with him at the Time, is missing and is presumed to have been forcibly kidnapped by the Villains responsible for the Robbery.

Sir Stanhope is a prominent Member of the Company of Hoastmen, which Association is currently in a Dispute with the Brotherhood of the Keelmen on the Tyne over a Number of the latter Group's alleged Grievances. He is understood to have been on his Way to visit Mister Felix Brandling MP at the Time of the Incident.

It is hereby declared that a handsome Reward will be paid for the Discovery or Apprehension of the Offenders, and the Restoration of the Property, and for the Discovery of the Whereabouts and the Restoration of the aforementioned missing Person, on the Conviction of such Offenders, by Application to the Mayor's Chamber, where Information is requested to be communicated.

*

Martha Scuffins could stand it no longer. She had had quite enough of living with her husband. She had been married to Jasper for ten years, had borne him six children (two of whom had survived childbirth, the younger now barely a week old) and, for the past four years, had been the vicarious target of his anger at the treatment meted out to him and his colleagues by Felix Brandling and the rest of the Company of Hoastmen. He had beaten her frequently – almost weekly – forced his unwanted attentions on her when he returned from the Can House and set his bull terrier on her on those occasions when he was too palatic to carry out the violence personally. She was fed up of constantly having to invent some plausible domestic mishap to try to explain away to her concerned and disbelieving neighbours the bruised arms, keggy eyes, bloodied nose and swollen cheeks. Now, she longed to get away from the hovel in Sandgate's labyrinth of dark chares which had been their marital home for many years. More than that, she longed to get away from her husband. But, most of all, she longed to receive news that he had been drowned in one of the regular accidents which

beset the Tyne keelmen, so that she could join what she regarded as the envied ranks of the so-called 'keel-widows'.

The opportunity that she craved came on the day of what
the *Newcastle Courant* was to describe as 'the storm of the century' (although, since the new century was scarcely three years
old, this description may have been somewhat premature). The
newspaper reported that in Westgate-street many houses were
damaged, several chimney stacks fell, and the woodwork of the
Vicar's Pump was torn away. The bark-mill near St Andrew's
church was struck by lightning and set on fire and a dozen cattle
and horses on the Cowhill were scorched. The river was said to
have come rolling down like a sea, swelling every brook and riv-
ulet to an alarming height and inundating the houses at the
Stock Bridge to a depth of three or four feet.

Jasper had set off before dawn in order to load up a cargo
of coal at the staithes opposite Stella colliery (the farthest upriver) and transport it fourteen miles down to Shields. The rain
started to fall around mid-morning and increased steadily in intensity until by noon it had become a torrential downpour, accompanied by gale force winds, thunder and lightning. Martha
realised that her husband was probably on his way downriver
on the ebb tide and she harboured the wicked but sincere hope
that he had been caught in the storm and was in difficulties in
the dangerous and unpredictable currents of the river. She also
knew that even if he managed to cope with the conditions he
would be unable to reach Shields and unload his cargo in time
to catch the next flow tide, so that his return to Sandgate would
be delayed at least until the following morning.

When the storm eased off towards evening, she seized her
chance. Breaking open the wooden chest in which her husband
stored his personal possessions, she found a purse containing
several gold sovereigns, wrapped it in her skirts, gathered up a

few necessities, entrusted her two children to the custody of Cuckoo Jack's wife, who lived in the adjoining chare and was well aware of the aggressions which Jasper had visited upon Martha, and headed across the bridge towards St Mary's Church at Pipewellgate on the Gateshead bank of the Tyne.

Unlike the unfortunate occupants of two other keels out on the Tyne during that dreadful storm, Jasper Scuffins did manage to return safely to Sandgate with his crew, but not before being forced to remain idle overnight awaiting a favourable flow tide to bring them back upriver. He was furious when he discovered that his wife had deserted the family home and left him to fend for himself. He was even more furious when he realised that she had taken the purse containing his gold sovereigns. He determined that he should not incur further expense through her doing and so, on the following Saturday, the *Newcastle Courant* carried an advertisement placed by him under the heading GENERAL HUE AND CRY: CAUTION (presumably drafted by a clerk in the newspaper office who possessed a greater degree of literacy than its signatory).

Whereas my wife Martha Scuffins hath eloped from me without any just cause: This is therefore to give public notice that I will not from the Date hereof be accountable for any Debts she may contract in my Name. As Witness my Hand this 30th day of January 1803. J SCUFFINS

When he had received no word from his wife or on her behalf after a further fortnight, Jasper Scuffins' fury at her flight and theft of his sovereigns had become so great that he vowed to seek her out and bring her back. Then he was determined to teach her a lesson and make a public humiliation of her. Realising that the cost of a divorce was well beyond his paltry financial means, he devised a plan which, he believed, would achieve both of these aims and, at the same time, enable him to get rid of her for good and to recoup at least some of the money she had stolen from him. But first, he had to discover her whereabouts.

*

To enter the Flying Horse Tavern from the Groatmarket, you go through a dark passageway that leads on to a rectangular yard around three sides of which are located three bar-rooms, each of them separated from the others but accessible by its own dedicated door. On my first visit there I decided, for no better reason than that it was the most adjacent, to try the one whose plate declared it to be the Printers' Room. I made my way to the bar through a crowd of customers somewhat apprehensively, never before having been in such an establishment on my own (and, of course, only once before in the company of my workmates, Belcher and Jago) and, in what must have sounded a very timid voice, asked for a quart of ale.

'A *quart* you say, young man?' the barman replied, looking askance. Then he continued in a voice which, most incongruously, was as pleasant and gentle as the message it delivered was severe. 'Not in here you can't. Pints only in the Printers' Room. That's the rule and don't you forget it or you won't come in here again.' He pointed to a faded sign displayed on the wall beside the bar which read: *IMPORTANT NOTICE TO OUR ESTEEMED CUSTOMERS The volume of ale which may be purchased and imbibed by each customer at any one time shall not exceed or be less than one pint. For the avoidance of doubt, one pint is to be defined as the eighth division of one gallon.*

That was my first encounter with the perplexing assortment of regulations which obtained in the various rooms of the Flying Horse Tavern, as well as my first acquaintance with the publican. He was, as I later learned, a gentleman by the name of Mister Elias Tobin, also known to his clientele as His Satanic Majesty, due to the harsh treatment which he meted out to transgressors, but somebody whom, with the passage of time, I grew to know well and greatly admire. I apologised to him meekly for my inadvertent breach of the no-quarts rule and took my pint of ale to a corner seat from where I could observe the comings and goings of the Printers' Room. I could not help noticing that many of the customers were smartly dressed, rather in the manner of those who patronise the performing arts, as I speculated. My hunch was quickly confirmed as, without intending to eavesdrop, I was nevertheless unable to avoid overhearing a number of conversations conducted at unnecessarily high volumes on the subject of that evening's concert at the Theatre Royal. Reconstructing the various snippets which I gleaned from these exchanges, I was able to work out that the entertainment had consisted of a musical piece called The Smuggler and the Mermaid followed by a dance by a Madame Solange (probably a pseudonym, I imagined), renditions of A Sailor's Song by a Mister Brown (probably his real name since, had he chosen a pseudonym, it would surely have been more exotic) and Silly Sally by a Mrs Haddock (ditto) and, to conclude the evening, a play entitled The History of a Young Lady. But what I remember particularly, since it was such a curious thing to hear, was that during the play one of the actresses had been involved in an accident with a stage prop occasioning a serious injury which shocked the audience and brought the entertainment to a premature conclusion.

I did not learn the nature of the mishap until the following weekend, when by chance I spotted an article in the *Newcastle Courant* which revealed exactly what had happened at the Theatre Royal. (I was, however, still no nearer discovering why that part of the Flying Horse Tavern was called the Printers' Room.)

A MOST UNFORTUNATE OCCURENCE

A fatal Accident was narrowly avoided last Wednesday Evening, in the Theatre Royal in Mosley-street, during a Performance of the romantic Drama The History of a Young Lady, based upon the substantial epistolary Novel by Samuel Richardson. Mrs Gladys Trenton, in the Character of Clarissa Harlowe, had (through a curious Oversight by the Stage Manager) been provided with a genuine Dagger; with which, not realising the Character of the Implement, she wounded herself; but inadvertently – or, perhaps, through a lucky Mistake on her Part - happened to aim her Thrust at an oblique Angle, so that she was fortunate enough to procure only a minor Injury to the Chest.

One is led to conjecture gravely about the Grounds on which it could be considered necessary or even advisable to allow such dangerous Instruments in the Vicinity of an Establishment where, by its very Nature, illusory Events are liable to occur with Regularity.

14

The keelmen who had been assigned the task of waylaying and robbing Sir Stanhope Delaval on his way to meet his fellow hoastman Felix Brandling MP were shocked when they opened the wooden box which they had taken from their victim's phaeton. They had expected to find more items of value inside, perhaps gold or silver bowls and goblets from the banqueting hall at Seaton Delaval House or oil-paintings which could fetch a good price. Instead, they discovered the cowering figure of a tiny woman dressed in child's clothing. The wretched creature was terrified at the sight of two hefty men, their faces blackened by coal-dust, and she screamed aloud as she was lifted out from her hiding place into the daylight. But the men did not intend her any harm and tried to soothe her with kind words. She eventually calmed down a little and was able to explain how she came to be concealed in such a strange way.

'Aa thought the master just wanted me to gan with him to his meetings and write down what happened,' she sobbed. 'But wherever we went, Aa was made to travel in this little box like an animal. He really just wanted to use me to make people laugh, to make fun of me. Aa wish Aa'd never agreed to be his secretary – that's what he called me. My friends at the Hall treated me well and accepted me for what Aa am. But the master thinks that Aa'm a grotesque, misshapen creature – some kind of freak, not even a human being.'

'We'll look after ye, miss,' one of the keelmen assured her. 'We'll take ye to the Keelmen's Hospital and find ye somewhere to stay.'

'Thank ye, sir,' said Kitty. 'Aa'm pleased that you ambushed the master. He deserved it.'

'He's not your gaffer anymore, miss. Ye divvent have to gan back to Delaval if ye dinaa want to.'

*

'Now, just you listen to me, Belcher,' said Donald Stickler angrily, poking his finger into the tall one's chest to emphasise the importance of his point and the strength of his feeling. 'You two are going to have to get your act together. I've had only one body from you in the last three weeks. That's nowhere near good enough.'

'Wor job's getting a lot tougher these days, Doctor,' the short one replied, seeing his companion stuck for words. 'Churches have started forming watch committees to look out for the likes of us who's just trying to earn an honest night's living and …'

'I know all about that,' the doctor interrupted impatiently, mopping his brow with a large handkerchief.

'… and ye should see what other things they get up to. It's scandalous. Aa've seen shards of glass atop churchyard walls, iron gratings ower the coffins, quicklime on the …'

Again, the doctor stopped him. 'I'm not interested in your excuses, Jago. Not interested in the slightest. I've got my students to worry about. Things have now got to the point where they're having to share one cadaver between six! One between six, d'you hear? Intolerable. They're never going to learn enough to qualify in a hundred years at that rate.'

Belcher spoke up at last. 'But ye knaa how much the number of executions has dropped off lately, Doctor. And because of that, there's a lot more competition now for bodies and sometimes other gangs get them afore us. They even take wor ain clients, the ones we buried wor sels.'

The doctor was paying no heed to these attempts at justification. 'And then there's my own private research, of course,' he said. 'I'm on the verge of a great discovery but *I need bodies* ...'

He spoke the last phrase so loudly that all three men looked around anxiously as if worried that the topic of their exchange had been discovered. When they saw with relief that there was nobody else within earshot, they resumed the conversation in lowered tones.

'Aa'm confident we'll do what we can for ye to the best of wor ability, Doctor,' Belcher assured him, taking care to avoid any specific commitment.

'Well, you'd better make sure that you do. I want at least one body a week. At least one a week, d'you hear? Otherwise, I shall be forced to take my custom elsewhere. There are plenty of others in your line of business who would jump at the chance to earn eight or ten guineas for a couple of hours work.'

'Ye'll get yer one body a week, Doctor, Aa promise ye,' Jago pledged, much to Belcher's consternation, before adding, to the latter's even greater consternation, 'Maybe even two some weeks.'

'That's a guarantee then, is it?' the Doctor asked cautiously, looking Belcher (who, as the taller of the two, he assumed to be the senior partner) straight in the eye.

'Er ... er ... well, Aa suppose it is, then,' he stuttered, glancing at Jago irately.

'And make sure they're fresh,' the Doctor said. 'I can't stress that enough. Fresh, d'you hear? Fresh, I say.'

'As fresh as a field of lilies,' replied Jago, receiving another black look.

'And another thing. That last one you brought me. He was still wearing one of his stockings.'

'Well, we try to strip 'em but we canna always see what's ganning on in the pitch-dark,' Jago said. 'Must have just owerlooked it.'

'Don't you idiots realise what kind of trouble you could have got us all into with that mistake?' Stickler raised his voice once more and, again, the three looked up to check that they had not been overheard.

'What, just for one stocking, d'ye mean?' Belcher asked incredulously, picking up the conversation where it had left off for a few seconds.

'Yes, I do,' Stickler said angrily, not bothering to speak softly. 'Taking a body is not necessarily something that the law regards as a criminal offence because technically it's not property and it doesn't belong to anybody. But take just one piece of clothing or a ring or some other item with it - and *that* is robbery. You could both hang for that, you know.'

'Aa'm sure we'll be more careful in future, Doctor.' Belcher was beginning to think that their job was going to be a lot more difficult with all these restrictions.

'You'd better be, otherwise it'll be the last bit of work you two do for me. This is your final chance. A minimum of one cadaver a week, you understand, with no accessories left on the body. And remember ... fresh. It must be fresh.'

After the doctor had left, the short one said, 'Did you notice how he kept talking about making sure the bodies are *fresh*?'

'Aye, Aa did that. He mentioned it a few times,' the tall one replied.

'Well then, d'ye knaa what Aa'm thinking he *really* meant by that?'

'Ye knaa, Aa think Aa'm thinking the same as ye.'

*

On my return to the Flying Horse Tavern, I decided not to go back into the Printers' Room, among whose patrons I had felt decidedly ill at ease on my previous visit, but to explore instead the rest of the facilities. I followed the dark passage from the Groatmarket into the central yard and headed towards the adjoining bar-room, only to be confronted by a sign affixed to the entrance which announced: *Old Men' Room. No-one under forty years old allowed in. Absolutely no women whatsoever. No smoking after four of the afternoon.*

It was clear that there was no point in my daring to set foot inside without a serious chance of rebuff. There was nothing for it but to try my luck in the third bar-room, the entrance of which displayed a sign saying no more than *Taproom. Divvent clash the door on yer way in or oot.*

Crossing the threshold, I found myself in a cavernous space redolent with the smoke from a coal fire burning in a huge fireplace mingling with the fumes from customers' pipes and cigars. Decorating the walls on all sides were several hand-written signs, many of them scarcely legible, warning against various misdemeanours and threatening dire sanctions against transgressors. It was difficult to tell exactly which were meant to be taken seriously and which were displayed as some kind of practical joke or light-hearted diversion.

The place was full of a strange assortment of characters, several down-and-outs, some rough-looking sorts and, so far as I could make out through the thick stale gloom, all men with the exception of a sturdy-looking woman with a weather-beaten face and a briar pipe clenched between her teeth, who was leaning against a glass case containing a stuffed badger, next to a little girl and an elderly crone hunched almost double over a walking stick and accompanied by a scruffy little dog which barked noisily at a sign warning that *Unattended children will be dispatched to the Poorhouse at their parents' expense.*

I dared to ask for a quart and the same man who had previously refused to serve me with a drink of that volume in the Printers' Room now gave me a smile of acknowledgment, as though greeting me merrily as an old friend, despite only having spoken to me before on a single occasion. I will always remember what he said: 'Welcome to Hell's Kitchen'. He was a moderately tall man of about forty, with an oval visage of cheerful appearance, grey eyes, brown hair inclining to curl and a pair of thin spectacles perched on the end of his thin nose.

Looking around, I guessed that the majority of my fellow customers in Hell's Kitchen would not have felt at home – or even been permitted - in the Printers' Room. Many of them were certainly of an age to enable them to gain admission to the Old Men's Room – I speculated that they may have disqualified themselves because they wished to be allowed to smoke after four of the afternoon. Finding myself a space to stand in the midst of the heaving throng I supped my ale, constantly at risk of having it spilled by the swipe of some careless arm and surrounded by a good-natured hullabaloo, my ears besieged by odd snatches of conversation which, disembodied as they were from their context, meant little or nothing to me.

'His boy's very poorly with the dropsy …'

'The place was overrun with rats before they sent for Bogie …'

'Wor lass says it's best to avoid a full moon if yer ganning anywhere near Javil Groop with yer sweetheart …'

'He's been tapped twice by the physicians and they got nearly twenty quarts of water out of him …'

'Reckons he's caught over eighty in his traps in one neet …'

Despite the crush of the crowd, I managed to finish my ale without mishap and was on the point of setting off to return to my lodgings in order to prepare for the following day's lecture when I spotted a familiar face. It was the military man to whom Mister Hadwen Bragg had introduced me in the All Saints' Poorhouse. He was standing below two fading signs, one of which read, *The poker may not be unchained from the fireplace without the express permission of the Management* and the other, *No rioting during Lent.*

As I approached him he showed no sign of recognising me. 'Good evening, sir,' I said.

'And a very good evening to you, sir,' he returned civilly, bowing deeply. 'A very good evening indeed. Benjamin Starkey at your service.'

'Yes, I know who you are, Captain Starkey,' I said. 'We've met before, haven't we? I'm James Maclachlan.'

'I'm pleased to make your acquaintance, Master Maclachlan. Very pleased indeed. Extremely pleased, in fact.' He bowed again, this time even more deeply, and still with no indication that he recalled our previous encounter.

'Don't you remember that I was introduced to you by Mister Hadwen Bragg?' I pressed him. Then I threw in a further prompt. 'It was in All Saints.'

'All Saints, you say?' He looked around as if to ensure that no-one else was listening to our conversation. A frown crossed his face as he added, 'You mean All Saints' Poorhouse?'

'Yes. You *do* remember then.'

'Certainly not.' He shook his head vigorously, a little *too* vigorously, I thought. 'Never been to the place. Never in my life. Never.'

'It was definitely you,' I insisted.

'Not me. Couldn't have been. I'm staying at the Turf Hotel. I usually stay at Gosforth House with Felix Brandling, but when he's in the West Indies on business, I take a suite at the Turf Hotel.'

I decided not to pursue the matter further, but I could not resist saying, 'Well, it's good to see you again, anyway, Captain Starkey.'

'I expect I'll have to be off to fight the Frenchies soon,' he said, unexpectedly. 'I was with the 5th Dragoon Guards when we defeated those Irish rebels and their craven French supporters at the Battle of Vinegar Hill in County Wexford, you know.'

'Oh, really?' I said, not knowing anything about the events he described but aware from various remarks I had heard that there were threats to our country from across the Channel as well as the Irish Sea.

Then Captain Starkey launched into an astonishing monologue which seemed to me to owe more to self-delusion than reality. 'I thought the peace would hold but it doesn't look like it to me. Can't trust them, you know. They only agreed to the treaty to give themselves a chance to get their breath back before they have another go at us. I should know, I was over there for years, fighting against that Bonaparte fellow. From Corsica, they say, wherever that is. Thought he could beat us English, he did. Bad mistake. *Very* bad mistake.'

At this stage, he seemed to be talking to himself, oblivious to my presence, so I grasped the opportunity to take my leave and headed for the door by which I had entered, learning as I did so that *Rioters will be dealt with by the use of the poker.*

I should state that, since that day, I have often spoken to Captain Starkey in Hell's Kitchen and, on each occasion, he has believed me to be a complete stranger, introducing himself as if for the very first time in his accustomed manner. 'Captain Benjamin Starkey at your service. I'm pleased to make your acquaintance. Very pleased indeed. Extremely pleased, in fact.' He has also given me several different accounts of his place of residence, which have included references to the Mansion House, the White Hart Inn, the Grand Hotel and Seaton Delaval Hall.

15

When the news reached the ears of Jasper Scuffins that, in re-lieving Sir Stanhope Delaval of a share of the man's personal possessions, his colleagues on the keelmen's Action Committee had also liberated a female dwarf who could write, he was very interested indeed.

'Aa think Aa knaa who ye mean,' he told them. 'Aa've seen the little lass with the Hoastmen in the Mayor's Parlour. They were aal laughing and teasing her like she was there for their entertainment. And Delaval was laughing as much as the rest of 'em. Aa'd like ye to bring her to me. Aa've got things to ask her.'

'Do ye remember me?' Jasper Scuffins said, when the keel-men who had found Kitty Dace brought her to see him.

'Aye, sir,' she replied. 'Aa saw you when the master took me to the Mansion House.'

'And what did the master and his friends have to say about me?'

She shook her head nervously and stammered, 'Er … noth-ing, sir, …er … nothing that Aa can recall, sir.'

'Come now, ye divvent have nowt to fear from 'em any-more. Ye can tell me what they said.'

'Well, sir …' she was still reluctant to repeat the cruel things she had heard the Hoastmen say but, when she looked up at the men who had rescued her from Sir Stanhope, she felt a huge burden of debt to them and, suddenly, the truth came pouring out. 'They said ye were a troublemaker, sir. They said they weren't going to agree to anything ye asked for. They said that if the keelmen gan on strike they'll call in the military. They said they will let yer families starve.'

Jasper Scuffins said nothing for several minutes, as if con-templating the implications of what he had just heard, while

Kitty Dace wondered anxiously whether she had done the correct thing by being so forthright. Then, very quietly, he muttered, 'Thank you, miss, that's very interesting,' and sunk back once again into silence.

After a little while, he asked, 'It's true that ye can read and write, is it?'

'Aye, sir,' she replied. 'That's why the master chose me to work for him. As his secretary, Aa mean. Aa was a scullery maid before that, and very happy too.'

'Aa want ye to do something for us,' he told her. 'We need to tell people about wor fratch with the coal owners. Tell 'em what we're asking for. Tell 'em how wor jobs are at risk. And wor wives and bairns. Tell 'em how the gaffers have been grinding us doon for years and now it's time to stop 'em. Time to fight back. Get the people on wor side.'

'What can Aa do about that?' Kitty did not understand how she could help in such matters. In fact, she was a little scared of getting involved at all.

'Aa just want ye to write a handbill for us. We'll get it printed and sent round the toon. Then there's a fair chance the papers will reprint it and everyone will knaa about wor cause. Come back here tomorrow and Aa'll tell ye what to write.'

*

My digression into my sojourn as guest of Mister Hadwen Bragg and his good lady and, latterly, as a servant of Mister Abel Grope has taken me away from my original theme for rather longer than I intended, so I must now give an account of my discovery of an opportunity for employment as an apprentice in the medical profession, a position which interested me greatly.

It was by entirely by chance that I saw the advertisement which had been placed in the previous Saturday's edition of the *Newcastle Courant*. The newspaper had been discarded in an alleyway from where I picked it up, intending to use it to ignite a fire to warm my room, the recent weather having been unseasonably cold – down to fourteen degrees below freezing point, according to the press article read aloud earlier that evening by Mister Elias Tobin, publican of the Flying Horse Tavern, whom I overheard holding forth to a small gathering of his regular customers in the bar-room of that same establishment which is known as Hell's Kitchen. He even went so far in his homily as to caution ladies whose dresses were composed of muslin or other combustible fabrics to be very careful of approaching too near a fire in case a spark flying out or a current of air drawn towards the chimney, carrying an apron or gown to the grate, might set them ablaze.

WANTED IMMEDIATELY

An apprentice assistant to a Surgeon. Enquire of the printer, Ed. Walker of Pilgrim-street.

I think it must have been the word *apprentice* which caught my eye at once, determined as I then was to obtain another situation as soon as possible, one which I hoped would be more agreeable than my time in the employ of Jeram Boag Esquire, Master Sweep, and more like my experiences with Messrs Bragg and Grope. And when I spotted that the advertised position would put me on the first step to a calling in the medical profession, I knew there was not a moment to lose.

Very early the next morning, while a bleak grey fog hung low over the river, I hirpled round to Pilgrim-street as fast as my damaged knees permitted, clutching the advertisement and the letter of recommendation which Mister Grope had kindly consented to write. I waited outside the printing shop for a good two hours in the freezing cold before Mister Walker arrived to open up the premises and ushered me, shivering, inside. Less than twenty-four hours later I was sitting opposite Mister William Ingham, Surgeon, in a room at the Newcastle Infirmary on Forth Bank.

'Well now, my boy, so you want to be a surgeon's assistant, is that right?' As he posed the question, Mister Ingham fixed me with a steady green eye and gently rubbed a thumb through his bushy sideburns. He was, I guessed, in his late thirties, a tall, well-dressed man with long, sleek, clean fingers as befitted someone in his profession.

'No, sir. Not exactly a surgeon's assistant, sir. Not straightaway anyway. I want an apprenticeship, sir. To *become* a surgeon's assistant, sir. So I can prove myself a good worker, sir. And learn the ways of medicine, sir. Then maybe if I work hard and study hard, I can better myself, sir.'

'Well said, young fellow. After all, no point in expecting to become a surgeon's assistant overnight. I like a lad who's willing to learn and work and study hard.'

'Yes, sir. Thank you, sir.'

'Well, tell me now, my boy. Do you think you could face up to cutting open a human corpse?'

'I'm willing to try, sir …' I replied hesitantly, gulping back my discomfiture, '… if that's what's required.'

'Are you now?' He had spotted my nervousness at this subject and sounded unconvinced. 'Well, I wonder about that … Have you ever seen a body, my lad?'

'A *dead* one, do you mean, sir?'

'Well, I assume you've seen plenty of live ones,' he smiled.

'Oh yes, sir, and dozens of dead ones, too'

'Dozens? Really?' he exclaimed with a mixture of incredulity and admiration.

'Yes, sir. The first time was when I saw a man hung to death on the Town Moor.'

'Very good.' He nodded approvingly.

'He was a criminal, sir,' I added - probably unnecessarily, as I realised almost immediately.

'Glad to hear it,' he said, scarcely able to conceal another smile. 'One of ours, no doubt.'

I inferred from this remark that he and his assistants must have taken in the man's body for dissection.

'And I've seen a fair few drownded bodies dragged out of the Tyne, sir. Mostly by Cuckoo Jack Wilson, sir ...'

He nodded again, as though he knew of the man and his reputation for retrieving the corpses of those who ended up in the river.

I was anxious, in order to try to dispel any doubt of my suitability, to give him as much proof as possible of my lack of squeamishness and so I continued, '... And I watched both my mother and my father dying, sir. I watched them both dying until they was both dead. Of the cholera morbus, sir.'

'Ah, yes, the cholera morbus.' He put an avuncular arm round my shoulders. 'A terrible thing, You poor boy. How old were you at the time?'

'Nearly twelve years old, sir.'

'You poor boy,' he repeated.

'And I've been working for Mister Abel Grope for the last year.'

'Mister Grope the undertaker?'

'Undertaker *and* coffin-maker, sir.'

'Yes, quite. Mustn't forget the coffin-maker bit. Well, you must have come across quite a few cadavers in *that* line of business,' he asserted.

'Quite a few, sir,' I agreed.

I wasn't sure whether it was the fact that I had seen a number of corpses which clinched my indentureship as an apprentice at the Barber-Surgeons' Hall or whether he merely felt sorry for me and decided to take me on out of sympathy, but it was this last bit of information which appeared to help him make up his mind.

*

It was through a combination of chance and deception that Jasper Scuffins recovered his wife from the place of refuge to which she had fled from their family home in Sandgate. He knew that Cuckoo Jack Wilson's wife was a good friend of Martha's and guessed that she probably had a good idea of the fugitive's whereabouts but was most unlikely to share the information with the very person who was the cause of her flight. So, when he spotted Cuckoo Jack's son, Ralph, on the shore next to Petrie's-entry where the young man often sat to observe the boats passing up and down the river, he decided to engage him in conversation.

'Still like watching the keels, Master Ralph?'

Ralph looked round to see who had addressed him and was confronted by a figure, decked out in his Sunday best in a shag hat decorated with tassels, a short blue jacket, slate-coloured trousers and yellow waistcoat, whom he knew to be Mister Scuffins, a near neighbour, a keel skipper and an important figure among the fraternity which manoeuvred the boats through the treacherous reaches of the Tyne, but one who had never spoken to him before. He experienced feelings of flattery and awe in equal measure.

'Yes, sir,' he replied.

'Aa'd wager ye'd like the chance to gan doon the Tyne in a keel, wouldn't ye, young man?'

'Yes, sir, I'd love to.' Although Ralph had ventured out on the river many times in one of his father's hire boats, it had always been an ambition of his since he was five years old to experience what it was like to be one of the crew of a keel.

'Maybe Aa could take ye in my boat one day. When the weather's faired up.'

'Thank you, sir.'

'Aa trust yer father is well, young man?'

'Yes, sir, thank you, sir. He's helping the constable today at Walls End.'

'And your mam?'

'Very well too, thank you, sir. And busy looking after your children, sir.'

Jasper Scuffins was quite taken aback by this information. So, Martha had left the bairns with Cuckoo Jack's wife! He certainly wasn't expecting that. He'd assumed that she'd taken them with her to wherever she'd gone. He tried not to show his surprise at the news and hoped that the young man did not realise that he had inadvertently betrayed a confidence. He decided to venture a tentative enquiry to see whether he could glean any more details. 'It's very kind of yer mam to look after the bairns while my lass is away visiting her sister.'

'Yes, sir, thank you, sir. Does her sister live in Pipewellgate then, sir?'

'Pipewellgate? What makes ye think that, young man?'

'Well, sir, it's just that I heard my mother say that Mrs Scuffins had gone to St Mary's, sir.'

So, at last, he had learned that his wife was at St Mary's Church in Pipewellgate. It was well-known that the rector of that parish, a Reverend Collinson, was willing to shelter women who had been abandoned or subjected to violence by their husbands. He was surprised that he hadn't thought of that before. 'Ye're a good chap for keeping yer ears open. Aa like a fellow who's got his wits about him. Someone who can be relied on. In fact, just the sort of person Aa need for my crew. So let me think about bringing ye on a tide with us before long. What d'ye say to that, young man?'

'Thank you, sir. I'd be most grateful to you for that, sir.'

'Well then, let's keep that as wor secret, shall we? We won't even mention to anyone that we've had this chat. Shall we make that wor gentlemen's agreement?' He proffered a horny hand.

'Yes, sir. Thank you, sir.' Ralph shook it cautiously.

16

The end of my period of employment with Mister Abel Grope, Undertaker and Coffin-maker, was particularly memorable, not because of the lengthy and sincere farewell that he bade me but on account of the calamitous events which took place on the day.

I had spent the previous afternoon laying out a Mrs Emilia Sly (deceased). Whereas I would normally have removed all items of jewellery before handing over the body for my colleagues to arrange in the coffin, I was on that occasion under strict orders from the lady's widower that she was to be buried wearing her gold wedding ring. However, just when the funeral cortege was about to set off for the cemetery, Mister Sly arrived at our premises on High Bridge, in a state of panic and consternation. He managed through a series of breathless and disjointed sentences to convey to us that, only a matter of an hour ago, he had discovered Mrs Sly's last will and testament which directed that her wedding ring should be removed from her body before burial and given to the couple's only daughter. Consequently, he felt that he had no choice but to beseech Mister Grope to allow him to comply with his wife's dying wish. After demurring for several minutes, Mister Grope at last consented reluctantly and instructed Belcher to open the coffin. At this, the latter flew into a fury and refused point-blank to obey his employer's order, accusing him of, 'Being about to commit a terrible blasphemy and a disgraceful and contemptible crime which will bring down the wrath of God upon every one of us.'

Eventually, Mister Grope, faced with Belcher's surly insubordination and Mister Sly's frantic entreaties, decided to carry out the act himself and, with some difficulty, and in spite of the former's continued imprecations, delivered in increasingly pro-fane language, he unscrewed the brass fittings securing the lid and lifted it off, only to discover to his uncomprehending hor-ror that not only was there no wedding ring inside the coffin but that there was no corpse either. In fact, it contained nothing more than a collection of dusty bricks.

'What in Heaven's name is the meaning of this?' roared Mister Grope in the direction of Belcher and Jago while, almost simultaneously, Mister Sly roared the identical question in the direction of Mister Grope.

Belcher and Jago exchanged looks of desperation and, as if the solution to their predicament had been communicated wordlessly between them, they both suddenly turned tail and bolted from the premises, an incongruous sight as they raced headlong in full mourning attire across High Bridge towards the Keyside, never to return to the scene of their appalling deed.

The wretched woman's body was never recovered. In retro-spect, I imagine that at the precise time we were preparing to escort her coffin to its final resting-place, its supposed contents must have been occupying a slab in one of the dissecting rooms of the Barber-Surgeons' Hall. The solitary but small consolation for Mister Sly was that his late wife's wedding ring was recov-ered from one of the many pawnshops on the Side to which my employer sent me in search of it that afternoon, albeit on reim-bursement of the five guineas which the pawnbroker stated that he had paid to the pair, one tall and one short, who had depos-ited the item with him the previous evening.

I do not doubt that the incident did immense harm to the reputation of Mister Grope's business, a thought which made me very sad, particularly bearing in mind the great kindness he had shown to me. On the few occasions that I saw him again, he looked even more morose and thin, as if overwhelmed by the events of that fateful day.

*

Kitty Dace had carefully written out the statement on behalf of the keelmen which Jasper Scuffins had dictated, doing her best to reproduce his words as correctly as possible, although there were a number of them which she had never heard before and had to guess at the spelling. When she had finished, Scuffins pronounced himself satisfied with the result (although, being almost illiterate, he was hardly in a position to judge) and took himself off to the town in order to get it printed and circulated, confident that the keelmen's grievances would soon receive a wide circulation, particularly if their pamphlet came to the notice of the *Newcastle Courant*.

His first call took him to the premises of Burdus Lawson, Printer, Vine-entry Fleshmarket. The man's wife was busy working at a wooden hand-press and, looking up to greet her visitor, who was the only customer of the day so far, was somewhat unsettled by his daunting appearance. 'Good day to ye, ma'am,' he said, politely enough. 'Aa'll come straight to the point. Aa'd like ye to print me fifty of these, as quick as ye can. Aa'm willing to pay ye in advance.' He handed over a grubby sheet of paper. Mrs Lawson took it and read through, not without some difficulty, and then began to cough nervously. 'What's the trouble, ma'am?' Scuffins asked, sensing her discomfort. 'There's some part of it that ye canna understand, is that it?

'Er... no, sir,' she replied. 'It's er ... just ... that ... er ... Aa daren't print that paper here, sir.'

'What? *Daren't*, ye say?' roared Scuffins. 'Why ever not, woman? My money's not good enough for ye, is that it?'

'No, sir, it's not that.' By now, she was almost in tears. 'It's because if Aa were to print it, the constables will close me down. They'll say that Aa'm encouraging the strikers, sir, and that striking breaks men's contracts and that breaking men's contracts is illegal and so if Aa encourage it then Aa'm doing something illegal too and …'

'So ye think we should just do what wor gaffers tell us, do ye?' he interrupted. 'We should let them get away with their overmeasures and their savage beer, should we, while wor bairns gan without bread in their mouths?'

'No, sir, Aa sympathise with you good men, truly Aa do. But Aa canna get involved in any trouble, sir. My husband hopes to buy a better printing machine and if they close us down we won't be able to afford it. Aa'm sorry, sir, Aa really am.'

'Ye can keep yer sympathy, woman, Aa divvent want it,' Scuffins shouted as he stormed out, convinced that, in the absence of her husband, he would make no headway with her.

He received a similar response at the premises of Angus Thomas, Printer, eastside of St Nicholas-churchyard, and at the premises of Beilby and Bewick, Engravers and Printers, Amencorner, and at the premises of Thomas Saint, Printer and Bookseller, Pilgrim-street and at the premises of Solomon Hodgson, Printing Office, Groatmarket and finally at the premises of William Temple, Printer, Burnt-house entry, the Side, where he learnt what he had gradually begun to realise, namely, that every printing-house in the town had been threatened with closure by the Corporation should they do anything to support or publicise the strike of the keelmen.

'I've heard all about these kind of people, James,' Ralph said, when I had described to him the episode which marked my last day with Mister Grope, Undertaker and Coffin-maker. (I should explain that Ralph has never referred to me as Knacky-Kneed Mack and besides, my nickname had not, by that time, gained general currency.) 'Resurrectionists, that's what they're called. And sometimes, body-snatchers. Or sack-em-up men. Or grave-robbers. Different names, but they're all doing the same thing really. Stealing bodies and selling them to medical students or surgeons so they can practise cutting them up.'

'I never imagined that such things went on,' I responded, reflecting on how much more worldly-wise Ralph was than me.

'It's more common than you think,' he continued. 'You wouldn't believe the tricks some of them play in order to get their hands on a fresh corpse. They get an accomplice to watch churchyards during the day to find out whether any funerals are taking place. They send women along to the funerals to act as mourners, or to pretend that they are visiting a nearby grave. Sometimes they don't even need to do that because instead they bribe undertakers or gravediggers to pass on the information to them to save them the trouble. Even men of the cloth aren't above being bought if the price if right.'

I was astonished at this last revelation. 'Do you really mean to say that a priest would go against his Holy Orders, knowing exactly what would happen to a newly-buried parishioner?'

'I assure you, James, that in some parts of the town the priest is the greatest friend of the resurrectionists. And once he tips them off about a new grave, they turn up in the middle of the night, dig up the body and cart it off.'

For the first time, I began to dawn on me why Belcher had appeared tired one day at work and had reacted so aggressively when I asked him if he hadn't slept well the previous night. He had obviously spent it stealing a body from a grave.

'Of course, sometimes they don't even wait until after the funeral but they try to get hold of the body before it's buried. Makes their job a lot easier … For example, they visit a hospital mortuary. They say that they are relatives of a patient who has just died and claim their body. Simple isn't it?'

'Or they steal it from the undertaker's,' I suggested, referring to my own recent experience.

'Exactly. I wonder how many of the people that Mister Grope thought he had buried either weren't in their coffin when it was lowered into the grave or, if they were, were soon removed from their resting-place?'

'Well, as far as I know, Belcher and Jago had been working for him for several years.'

'Then they would have had plenty of opportunity to make a lot of money by stealing bodies.'

I was still struggling to come to terms with the ghastly notion that the dead could be violated in this way in order to satisfy someone's greed. 'How much do they get paid for a corpse?' I asked.

'It varies. It's a matter of supply and demand. And the more demand there is from medical establishments, the higher the price goes up. Could fetch up to ten guineas for a good, undamaged, fresh one. It's a lucrative business. From what I've been told, it used to be just individuals or pairs of resurrectionists stealing and selling corpses but now there are professional gangs at work. Sometimes fights break out in graveyards between two gangs over a body they both think they're entitled to. There was even a case of a body-snatcher being killed by a rival. He had his skull smashed against a headstone.'

'How ironic it would be if *his* body was sold to a surgeon,' I ventured.

'You know, James,' Ralph said, ignoring my inappropriate attempt at humour, 'when I think about how many bodies my father fishes out of the river, I reckon he would have made a fortune if he had sold them to the surgeons. He could probably get not far off eight guineas for each one. But he refuses to hand them over to the wrong people. He always does the right thing, because he sees it as performing a public service. He takes them to the Corporation and gets his ten shillings.'

'But I can't imagine everyone being as honest as your father. It must be tempting to use the illegal route, especially as it's so profitable.'

'You're right. In fact, it's so profitable that some gangs are now resorting to even more extreme methods to get hold of a corpse.'

'What do you mean by that?' I asked.

To my astonishment, Ralph replied, 'Well, if they can't find a dead person, they abduct a live one and kill them.'

'Murder? Are you serious?'

'Yes, I am, James. There's many a lass in Sandgate afeard for her life. Afeard of being murdered by body-snatchers who can't get enough corpses to satisfy the demands of their customers.'

17

On his frequent visits to the Dun Lion in the Fleshmarket, Jasper Scuffins had often observed the livestock sales which took place in front of the tavern. He admired the skill with which the auctioneer teased and cajoled potential buyers into outbidding one another so as to obtain the best possible price for the seller (and, no doubt, the highest commission for himself). Consequently, it was only natural that when *he* had goods to sell, Jasper Scuffins should approach the very same auctioneer to conduct the sale on his behalf.

'My fee is five guineas,' the man told him.

'Five guineas, ye say?'

'That's my fee. Five guineas.'

'Aa canna pay ye that amount up front.'

'Then you'll have to auction your goods elsewhere, my friend.' The man had a touch of the gypsy about him. 'Try Hexham market. You might find someone prepared to take you on for four guineas on a quiet day.'

'Hexham? That's ower twenty miles away. Too far to take her.'

'*Her*, you say? *Her*? What d'you mean by that?'

'My lass. That's who Aa'm selling.'

'You're selling your *wife*? Is that what you're telling me?'

'Why shouldn't Aa? Aa've got no further use for the woman. Aa want rid of her.'

The auctioneer pondered for while on what he had just been told. It was certainly an odd thing for a man to sell his wife, he mused. Odd, surely, but not outrageous. Anyway, why shouldn't a man sell his wife, he asked himself. After all, wasn't she his property, just like his house or his furniture or his dog? And, if a man has no further use for his wife or needs to raise some money for some important reason, it would seem to be a sound financial strategy. Yes, on reflection, it was quite a sensible proposition. But it *was* a very unusual thing to do, nonetheless. Of course, he had never personally experienced any such thing during his professional life and he felt somewhat apprehensive at the prospect of taking on the task. On the other hand, it would do no harm for him to oversee the sale of a man's wife. The event was bound to arouse a lot of interest in the town. Indeed, it could do his reputation as an auctioneer a great deal of good.

'Maybe we could come to some arrangement about my fee,' he suggested.

'Arrangement? What sort of arrangement?'

'Well, you say you can't afford to pay me five guineas up front.'

'Aa canna afford to pay ye even one guinea up front,' Scuffins affirmed. 'My lass stole all my money.'

'In that case, I'll make you an offer. I'll auction your wife as you ask and I'll take a cut of the sale price. Twenty-five percent commission. How does that sound?'

'Twenty-five percent, ye say?' After all his experience of negotiating wage rates with the Hoastmen, Jasper Scuffins was clever at his sums. It didn't take him long to do some arithmetic. 'So ye'll aim to get twenty guineas for my lass, will ye? Then ye'll get your five and Aa'll get fifteen. Is that it?'

'Precisely, my friend. I'll get five, you'll get fifteen and we'll both be happy.'

'Well, Aa suppose so. Mind ye, Aa wouldn't take less than that for her.'

'And if she makes forty, you'll get thirty and I'll get ten.'

'D'ye think she will fetch that much?'

'I couldn't tell you, my friend. I don't know what the going rate is for wives. I've never auctioned one before.'

*

The Barber-Surgeons' Hall, where I was to begin my apprenticeship as a surgeon's assistant, stands on King's Manor, adjacent to Carliol-croft. It is an impressive edifice, built in what is known as the Georgian style, as I have been informed, its frontage distinguished by an arched doorway and a series of arched windows at ground level and rectangular ones on the upper floor. Above the entrance is the coat of arms of the Company of Barber-Surgeons (or, as it is more correctly entitled, the Worshipful Company of Barber-Surgeons, Wax and Tallow Chandlers of Newcastle-on-Tyne), which bears the motto, presumably written in the Latin language, *De Prescientia Dei*.

An inscription on the wall inside the main door states that the Company was founded on the tenth day of October in the year of 1442, although how anyone can be so precise about an event which took place over three hundred and fifty years ago must be a matter of some speculation. Originally, the Company was a craft guild, established for the mutual benefit of its members but which also carried out charitable works by aiding injured soldiers and sailors as well as anyone else who needed their help. You may consider that barbers and surgeons make strange bedfellows, but their curious alliance is explained by one story, the truth of which I cannot vouch for but which is fascinating nonetheless, that it originated in the abbeys and monasteries of the so-called Dark Ages. The monks who inhabited such places espoused an interest in the cure of diseases and treatment of injuries but were forbidden by the teachings of their religion to practice surgery. However, they passed on their medical learning, such as it was, to their servants, whose duties included the shaving of their masters' beards and tonsures. Consequently, the servants, having acquired skills in both disciplines, were acknowledged as barber-surgeons. Over the years, members of their guild no doubt came to specialise in one branch of learning. Later on, for no good reason which I can divine, chandlers were admitted to the guild.

In front of the Hall is a spacious square with four lawned areas divided by gravel paths, each of which is adorned with a statue on a raised plinth, depicting a figure connected to the practice of medicine. Galen of Pergamon was a Greek surgeon, Hippocrates of Kos is known as the Father of Medicine and Paracelsus was a Swiss physician. Asclepius was the Greek god of healing (and therefore, I assume, the only one of the four who is not a real person). The space at the rear of the Hall is given over to a garden where herbs are cultivated for their medicinal qualities.

Just inside the entrance is a glass-fronted case containing a selection of surgical instruments, including saws, needles, cautery-irons, rougines, scalpels, trephines and forceps. In time, I came to observe and familiarise myself with the beneficial uses to which these could be put in skilled hands but, on first sight, they looked like nothing more than tools of torture.

Mister William Ingham, Head of the College, was gracious enough to welcome me personally, show me to the place in the dormitory which I was to share with other students (most of whom were apprentice *surgeons*, whereas I was a mere apprentice surgeon's *assistant*) and familiarise me with some of the rules which governed our service.

'You are to be bound to Doctor Donald Stickler for five years, James,' he explained, 'and I trust you will find him a considerate and sympathetic master. Don't fret if, at first, you find him a little difficult to understand. He has a Scotch way of speaking and a tendency towards sesquipedalianism in his discourse.' Seeing my bemusement at this description of my tutor, Mister Ingham hurried to explain himself. 'I meant that Doctor Stickler likes to use long words. Also, I should make it plain that you will not automatically be guaranteed employment at the conclusion of your apprenticeship but, if you have proved yourself to be an industrious and loyal pupil, you can be assured that your candidacy would be looked upon favourably should a suitable vacancy exist within the Barber-Surgeons' Hall. I must emphasise too, James, that there is no place in this College for anyone who fails to uphold the highest standards of personal conduct and medical practice, but I am sure that you will not let me down. You and the others will be supervised and examined by the Searchers. These men, whom you will see shortly, are responsible for discipline and for dealing with some of the outsiders who unfortunately tend to cause us trouble at times.'

'Who might they be, sir?' I inquired boldly.

'Quacks.'

'Quacks, sir?' I was unfamiliar with the term.

'Yes, quacks. Charlatans, you might say. Or mountebanks. Most of them are apothecaries from the Dispensary, trying to peddle their fake potions and pills and their phoney cures. You must beware of them, James. They will approach you with stories of how fantastically effective their medications are. They will even show you letters purporting to be from people whom they claim to have restored to health from some awful disease which the surgeons have been unable to treat. You must not fall for their yarns. Just report them to the Searchers straightaway. Is that understood?'

During my first few days at the Barber-Surgeons' Hall, I gradually became acquainted with the strict code of conduct to which apprentices were subject. We had to be on our best behaviour at all times in order to avoid incurring a fine, the amount of which would be deducted from the small allowance we were paid to cover our basic requirements. At the bottom of the scale, it was against the rules to insult any of our fellow students, to utter an oath or to wash, dress or trim our hair on a Sunday, on pain of forfeiting two shillings for each offence. It was also strictly prohibited to remove a corpse from a graveyard or an undertaker's premises or to purchase one from a body-snatcher or similar brand of tradesman, even for the purpose of dissecting it in the interests of medical science. And on no account could an organ be pilfered from a corpse during a post-mortem examination for private use or personal gain. But the most heinous breach of all - one which would invariably lead to immediate expulsion - was to enter into the state of matrimony without the express prior consent of the Head of the College (which, I was reliably informed by our dormitory Searcher, was never given).

As I recall, it must have been the beginning of my second week there before I spotted Archibald Henderson. Not that he was difficult to spot. Quite the contrary, in fact, since he was the giant I had first seen all those years ago at the execution on the Town Moor when he demonstrated his enormous strength by picking up with one hand the coffin containing the corpse of the man who had been hanged. It so happened that our paths crossed one morning when I called into the lecture theatre and found him setting out tables, chairs and various pieces of equipment in preparation for a public demonstration of some sort.

'Bold Archy,' said a fellow student, seeing my look of puzzlement as I tried to work out how I knew the man. 'That's what we call him. He might not look it, but he's harmless, you know. Very inoffensive. And dim-witted. In fact, he'll do anything you ask him, however stupid it is. There are people here who try to cause him trouble by sending him on foolish errands, which I think is cruel.'

I was to discover in the fullness of time that there was somebody at the Barber-Surgeons' Hall who had plans for Bold Archy which involved far greater cruelty than merely sending him on a foolish errand.

*

Although she was relieved and grateful to have escaped from Sir Stanhope and the constant humiliations which he had visited upon her, and was now accommodated in the Keelmen's Hospital in an apartment which she shared with the Widow Henderson and her son, there were nevertheless times when Kitty felt that she had done no more than exchange one tyrant for another. Every Saturday, Jasper Scuffins insisted upon her scouring the columns of the *Newcastle Courant* and reading aloud to him anything – even an isolated sentence - which related to the keelmen and their strike. There were numerous words in the articles which she had great difficulty in deciphering, much to Scuffins' irritation, which was further increased by the tenor of the reports, most of which were unsympathetic towards the keelmen and highly critical of their actions. Sometimes, he would curse and shout at her and make her cry, as though she was personally responsible for having written the offending pieces.

Newcastle Courant

It is with the utmost Disappointment that we are obliged to inform our Readers that, following a Conference held by the Keelmen on the Tyne, a Strike of Working has been announced by the aforesaid Group, to commence forthwith.

The Cause of their Dissatisfaction cannot be verified absolutely, however our Understanding of their Grounds for Complaint is that they are twofold. The first Ground is that they are being required by the Coal-owners, contrary to prior Commitments and Guarantees, to increase the Load of Coal transported on their Boats, a Requirement which has the Effect of benefiting the Shipmasters and Coal-owners (or 'Hoastmen') without any Advantage accruing to the Keelmen themselves.

The second Ground concerns the increasing Use of the Spouts erected at the Staithes which mark the Termination of the Rail-ways connecting the Collieries with the River, the Operation of which bypasses the Need for Transportation of Coals by Keels, thereby threatening the continued Employment of the Keelmen.

While we understand and appreciate the Apprehension of the Keelmen at this perceived Threat to their Livelihood, we declare that it is wholly incompatible with the fundamental Laws of Economics and the Principle of free Trade to attempt to restrict the Rights of the Coal-owners to seek to use the cheapest possible Method for conducting their Business.

In receiving the News of the Keelmen's Intentions and anticipating that their Action – or rather, we should say, Inaction – can only damage the Prosperity of our beloved Town, we are forced to conclude that the Minds of these normally honest and hardworking Men must have been infected and influenced by the Advice of treacherous Counsellors, and dearly hope that more rational Judgements will prevail before it is too late.

18

Not long after the start of my apprenticeship as a surgeon's assistant, Mister William Ingham suggested that I might find it instructive to join the group of medical trainees who were to be addressed by one of the doctors employed at the Barber-Surgeons' Hall to tutor the students – as it happened, the man to whom I had been bound by my indentures but had yet to encounter. As I entered the lecture theatre, I felt rather out of place among the well-dressed young men who aspired to become professional doctors and whose dormitory I was sharing, while I was aiming to become a mere junior, subordinate to them.

Doctor Donald Stickler – for that was his name, as he informed us in a strong Scotch accent – cast a somewhat forbidding figure, being in excess of six feet tall with a mop of ginger hair and a bushy ginger beard which rivalled that of Mister Hadwen Bragg in its luxuriance.

'As new recruits to the medical profession,' he boomed, 'you are no doubt aware that, in order to familiarise yourselves with the particular components of the human anatomy upon whose living owners you will be expected to operate, it will be necessary in the first instance for you to examine those of the dead. This may to some of you appear a distasteful notion but, I assure you, it is an absolutely indispensable preparation for your callings, if you are to make a success of them.'

I could see several heads among Doctor Stickler's audience nodding in agreement.

'There is, however, another aspect to this element of your training which I must bring forcefully to your attention at this early juncture in your programme of study.' He paused meaningfully, as if to invest his words with added gravity and gazed around with a stern expression etched upon his features, fixing a number of the trainees with an unblinking eye. Heads were no longer nodding and I sensed a strong feeling of discomfort pervading the room.

'We at the Barber-Surgeons' Hall …' he continued, knowing that he had his audience's complete attention, '… rely upon being able to avail ourselves of a sufficient number of cadavers in order that our students - by which I refer, of course, to yourselves – can gain the practical experience of dissecting the human body which is so crucial to their advancement in the medical profession. As you know, virtually the only means we currently have of obtaining a cadaver is following the execution of a criminal, when the law deems it to be a fitting additional punishment for that person's body to be dissected. I say 'virtually' because occasionally – and it is only on rare occasions – we are fortunate in that some public-spirited member of our society will bequeath their corpse to the Barber-Surgeons' Hall in their will.'

At this point, one of the trainees raised his hand to ask a question but upon seeing Doctor Stickler's angry glare, quickly lowered it, realising that the speaker was not in the mood to be interrupted.

'However, the disgraceful and increasing reluctance of our Courts – I should say the jurors, since it is the grand juries at whose feet the blame is to be more accurately laid - to condemn criminals to death means that in recent years the supply of cadavers has been very sparse. Strong representations have been made by the Company of Surgeons to try to persuade the Government to allow us to obtain cadavers from other sources, for example from hospitals and poorhouses, but so far without success. I have even taken it upon myself to approach our eminent Member of Parliament, Mister Felix Brandling, on this matter and, while he is absolutely committed to our cause, he cannot, at the moment anyway, get his colleagues in the House of Commons to support it.'

There were several murmurs of disapproval from the audience at this illustration of the lack of understanding among our legislators of the difficulties faced by the medical profession and Doctor Stickler looked pleased with this reaction.

'I am sure that some of you may have heard stories of cadavers being removed by so-called body-snatchers from the premises of undertakers and even from graveyards for the purposes of anatomical research. Indeed, some of you may yourselves have considered becoming involved in such activities.' He paused for dramatic effect. There was absolute silence in the room. 'If that is so – and I do not doubt your sincerity, albeit misguided, in seeking to advance your medical knowledge in this way - then I say to you most earnestly that you must disabuse yourselves of any such proposition. I trust, gentlemen, that I make myself absolutely and unequivocally clear on this matter. But if, despite my solemn entreaty, any one of you here is still of a mind to engage in the practice to which I refer, then I would beseech that person to remember this: There is no law in our kingdom which can touch anyone who removes a cadaver *and nothing more*. But, should that person also remove, even inadvertently, a single stitch of clothing, then they are guilty of the felonious offence of robbery and thereby render themselves liable to capital punishment upon the scaffold, following which their own cadaver may itself be transported to the dissecting room.'

As we filed out of the lecture theatre, having been dismissed by Doctor Stickler at the conclusion of his discourse, I could not help reflecting upon the events of my last day in the employment of Mister Abel Grope and the removal of the body of Mrs Emilia Sly from her coffin. And the more I thought about what Doctor Stickler had said, the more I was sure that he had intended his words not as a reprimand to prospective body-snatchers but as a gentle encouragement as to how they might go about their business without falling foul of the law.

*

Newcastle Courant

The Keelmen on the Tyne last Week struck Work for an Increase in Wages and other Demands. Apprehensions were entertained in the Town of a Riot taking place among them. Inflammatory and seditious Handbills have been distributed throughout the Town by the Strikers and their Accomplices and posted up at Shields and even outside the Guild Hall. Despite this appalling and treasonous Conduct, it is hoped that this Business will be amicably settled by the good Offices of the Magistrates and that the Men will soon return to their Employment.

---

*

As always, Ralph was keen to hear my latest news and lent me a patient ear as I described my introduction to life at the Barber-Surgeons' Hall. He was particularly fascinated by my mention of the man known as Bold Archy and was able to appraise me of some of Archy's personal history which had led eventually to his present employment there.

'He was a good friend of my father's. Well, he still is, I suppose, although he probably doesn't realise it now. Once upon a time, my father told me, Bold Archy was the finest keelman on the Tyne. He could judge the tides almost by instinct, he knew every eddy and current of the river, he could calculate the effect on the sandbars of the winds and the speed of the ebbs and flows. He was so strong that he could fill a collier-brig with his boat's eight chaldrons in half the time it took others. He treated his keel-bullies and his peedee well and even shared out his beer and bait with them. He often used to come to the aid of other keelmen in distress and he saved the lives of many whose boats had capsized in the terrible storm of 1780. Everyone in Sandgate hailed him as a hero but, despite that, he felt guilty that he couldn't rescue the others who drowned that night.'

'So, what happened to him?' I asked.

'One day, there was an accident in Shields Harbour. The collier that Archy and his crew were loading coal into suddenly broke away from its mooring and he was caught between the two boats. Crushed his head. And, since then, his brains have never worked properly. He's lost none of his physical power, he's still as strong as ever, but well … as for the rest … He could never steer a keel again or calculate the tides or anything like that. He finds it an effort to speak more than a word or two. He can't think for himself. He needs to be told everything and then he just does it, whatever it is. If you told him to jump off the Spanish Battery he'd do it because all he can manage is to follow instructions. He's never violent or truculent or insubordinate in any way, but he needs to be looked after virtually the whole time. He lives in the Keelmen's Hospital with his mother, the Widow Henderson, who cares for him as if he were a baby. A sixty-year-old baby with massive strength. And now he works at the Barber-Surgeons' Hall as a porter, fetching and carrying for the doctors and doing anything for which they need a strong, submissive man. Which includes sending him to hangings to prevent anyone being able to steal the cadaver of the executed criminal to which the Barber-Surgeons' Hall alone is entitled.'

*

Newcastle Courant

We regret to confirm that the Keelmen of Tyne have not yet returned to Work. Indeed, the State of Affairs appears to be worsening. The Spouts on the Staithes serving a Number of Collieries, including Brandling's Main, Walker, Walls End and Unsworth Main, were reported to have been demolished by Gangs of Ruffians, supposedly connected to the Strikers, who also attempted to intimidate Pitmen into stopping Work in support of them. Several Keelmen who, despite the Strike, were continuing to work at Shields were attacked by Men who destroyed their Huddocks and smashed Tools and other Equipment.

The Mayor of Newcastle has commanded the Keelmen to return with immediate Effect to their Masters' Bidding in accordance with the Bonds to which they have previously committed on Christmas Day last, failing which a Warrant shall be issued and executed for their Apprehension by the Town Constables leading to their possible Incarceration and Penalty.

19

Jasper Scuffins waited in the shadows of the bridge which connects Sandgate on the north bank of the Tyne with Pipewellgate on the south bank. It would be at least another hour before the sun came up and the light from the watery moon was scarcely enough to disperse the early-morning mizzle which mingled with the smoke drifting from the nearby roperies and glassworks. His accomplice, he guessed, must by now have reached St Mary's Church and would be delivering to Martha Scuffins the awful news that her two children had been smitten with the cholera and were dangerously close to death. Soon, she would be rushing back to Sandgate, overwhelmed with grief and terrified out of her mind that she would arrive too late to see them alive.

And, indeed, not long after that he heard the patter of urgent footsteps accompanied by the sound of plaintive sobbing. When his wife reached the Newcastle side of the bridge, he jumped out from his hiding place and blocked her way. A scream escaped from her lips and she cried out. 'Please, sir, divvent stop me. Aa must gan to my bairns directly.'

'Have ye been away so long that ye dinaa even recognise yer own husband?' Jasper laughed, pulling his cloak aside to reveal his face.

'Jasper!' She recoiled with shock. 'What are ye doing here? Divvent ye knaa wor bairns are dying?'

'Calm yarsel, hinny,' he smirked. 'The bairns are both fine. It was just a canny trick to get ye to come back.'

It took Martha several seconds to absorb the meaning of what her husband had just told her. At first, she felt a great surge of relief at the knowledge that the story of her children's imminent demise was a fabrication. This was quickly followed by a sense of disbelief that her husband could be so cruel and spiteful as to use this lie as a means of enticing her from her refuge in St Mary's Church.

'Where are my gold sovereigns, ye thieving bitch?' he demanded.

'Oh Jasper, Aa've left 'em behind. Aa forgot aal about 'em. Aa was so afeared about the bairns that Aa had to rush back. '

'Well, now ye are here, Aa've got a little surprise for ye,' he sneered. 'Aa've decided to put ye up for sale.'

'Put me up for sale?' She could not believe what she was hearing. 'Are ye serious, Jasper?'

'It's all aal arranged. Aa'm taking ye to the Fleshmarket directly.'

The previous day, being confident of the success of his planned stratagem, he had taken the precaution of alerting the town bellman to the fact that an extraordinary auction was due to take place on the morrow. He calculated that the news would be spread throughout the town and would attract a host of prospective buyers, thereby raising the likelihood that a good price would be obtained for his wife. And, sure enough, when he arrived at the Fleshmarket and led Martha into the pen normally reserved for cattle, a halter of rope round her neck and another round her waist, a large crowd were waiting for the auction to begin. Such was the interest generated by the sale that the entertainer occupying a nearby pitch who, not half-an-hour earlier, had a sizeable audience for his Punch and Judy show, was now performing to an empty gallery. Many of those gathered there in the Fleshmarket had turned up because of their eagerness to observe such a rare event, others intended to put in a bid if they liked the look of the woman on offer and several small factions of various religious persuasions had come to protest at what they saw as a degrading affair. Even before proceedings began, these groups attempted to prevent the auction going ahead by rushing at the cattle pen, threatening to overwhelm Jasper Scuffins and release his wife from his custody. At this, others in the crowd, jeering at the possibility that their chance of an entertaining spectacle was about to be snatched away from them, started to pelt the protesters with pieces of fruit and lumps of meat taken from nearby stalls. It took the intervention of a posse of constables, assisted by the market supervisors, to restore order.

The auctioneer whom Jasper Scuffins had engaged took up his position on a bench alongside the cattle pen. 'Ladies and Gentlemen …' he announced (although in truth there were, apart from the one for sale, very few members of the female sex in the vicinity), '… we have one item for sale today. Lot One is the woman you see before you …'

He paused to allow the swell of whistles and whoops which rose from the spectators' throats to subside before embarking on a description of Lot One.

'Not much more than thirty years old,' he asserted vaguely. 'Weighed this morning at seven stones and eight pounds. Fine looking, as you can see. Buxom enough for her height …'

Jasper Scuffins, standing nearby and catching every word, was becoming distinctly irritated at the compliments being paid to his wife, a woman he had for some time regarded as singularly lacking in uxorial virtues. He began to feel that he was being betrayed by the man whose services he had hired, even though he had to admit to himself that, since she had been away from home for several days, Martha's appearance (without its usual quota of bruises and blood) had improved somewhat. Then he grasped the truth that the auctioneer was deliberately exaggerating her attributes in order to boost her value.

'… a very fertile woman, still has many of her teeth, almost completely free of dickies. For sale as seen. Overall, Ladies and Gentlemen, I'm sure you would agree, nothing too much the matter with her. I invite any serious bidders among you to come closer and inspect the wares. Feel these fine haunches, check them for yourselves.'

A number of men stepped forward and did as suggested, some perhaps planning to participate in the auction, others with no intention of putting in a bid for the goods on offer but availing themselves of the opportunity for some titillation by running their hands over Lot One.

'Right then, Ladies and Gentlemen,' the auctioneer announced when the preliminaries were over, 'let's get on with the business. Shall we start at ten guineas?' he proposed confidently.

If he had expected a flood of bids at this point, he was disappointed. And so was Jasper Scuffins. Not a single voice was raised in response to the auctioneer's proposition. He waited for a good minute, hoping to tease out a bid from some person who was perhaps too nervous or embarrassed to make the first move. But he waited in vain.

'How about eight guineas?' Less confidently this time. Again he waited, hoping that somebody might be tempted by the lower figure into opening the bidding. But, again, he waited in vain. He became uncomfortably aware of Jasper Scuffins' aggressive glare.

'Six guineas, then?' Desperation crept into his voice. 'Come along now, Ladies and Gentlemen, six guineas for this bonny lass is an absolute bargain.'

Still no bid.

'Six guineas?' he repeated.

Still nothing.

'Six *pounds* then?' he almost pleaded. 'I can't go any lower than that.'

Jasper Scuffins' expression was one of barely-contained fury as he faced up to the unhappy conclusion that he was not going to receive anything approaching the amount he had expected his wife to fetch. The auctioneer looked towards his client as if seeking guidance on whether he should indeed be prepared to accept an even lower bid and received a shrug of the shoulders in response.

'Very well then, Ladies and Gentlemen. I'll throw it open to offers. Who will make me a decent proposal?' He cast his eyes over the sea of faces before him, silently imploring someone to come to his aid. But, despite the apparent presence of a number of prospective buyers, it was as if they despised the idea that a man should sell his wife and had conspired to reach a tacit but firm understanding that no bid would be made for the wretched woman.

It so happened, however, that Aeneas Snitterby, a member of the Company of Hoastmen, was passing through the Flesh-market on his way to an engagement at the Guild Hall and had his curiosity aroused by the large but now almost silent crowd surrounding the cattle-pen. Pushing his way through the throng, he recognised Jasper Scuffins and, after watching the proceedings for a few minutes, summed up what was taking place, realised that no one was bidding and took pity on the woman. Seeing an opportunity to affect a Christian act of kind-ness and at the same time - and more importantly - to spite the hated keelman with whom he had done battle on many occa-sions, he called out a bid of four shillings.

'Four shillings?' gasped the auctioneer, astonished at the meagreness of the bid and the sheer audacity of the bidder.

'Four shillings!' rasped Jasper Scuffins, shocked at the insultingly low bid and the insolence of the bidder, who was concealed from his view by a number of the spectators.

'Are there any other bids?' the auctioneer asked forlornly.

When nobody responded, Aeneas Snitterby called out, 'Do I take it, then, that I am to be declared the winner?'

'In the absence of any more bidders, I suppose you are, sir,' the auctioneer replied grudgingly.

Jasper Scuffins was outraged at the thought that his net earnings from his carefully-laid plan would be a mere three shillings, scarcely more than he would receive for his work as a keelman on a single tide. His first thought was to refuse to allow his wife to be handed over to the purchaser for such a niggardly sum. Then, on brief reflection, he realised that if she were not sold, he would be obliged to continue to incur the expense of keeping her and the children. For her part, Martha had already reconciled herself to her anticipated fate, consoling herself with the distinct probability that it would be better to be sold to another man than to have to remain with Jasper. She was, however, determined not to be separated permanently from her children. She had remained silent throughout the course of the proceedings but now tearfully addressed her new owner, 'Aa thank ye for yer kindness in releasing me from my husband, sir, but Aa canna leave my bairns. If ye want to take me, sir, Aa beg of ye to take my little ones too.'

Aeneas Snitterby, still standing among the onlookers, replied magnanimously, 'I would not separate a mother from her children. You can bring them with you, madam, and I will settle you all in a good home.'

Jasper Scuffins, sensing the chance to increase his tiny profit from the sale, called out to the unseen buyer, 'The bairns weren't part of the deal. If ye want to take them, ye'll have to pay more.'

'I'll gladly do so,' the voice from the crowd came back. 'As well as the four shillings, I'll give you a pint of gin.'

Jasper was about to protest when the auctioneer, who had had quite enough of the farce being played out before him and had wasted the best part of a morning for the sake of one shilling in fees (and, it now seemed, a quarter pint of gin), decided to call an end to the proceedings. Bringing down his gavel, he declared, 'Lot One and accessories sold to the gentleman in the velvet Spencer for four shillings and a pint of gin.'

Aeneas Snitterby stepped forward and, for the first time, Jasper Scuffins learned the identity of the successful bidder. He knew then that he had been made a fool of.

'Aa'll not hand the hinny ower to that man,' he roared.

'I'm afraid you have no choice, Mister Scuffins,' the auctioneer told him. 'The deal has been done. The gentleman has a contract for the goods and is now their legal owner.' He removed the halters from Martha's neck and waist and handed her over to Aeneas Snitterby who guided her through the applauding crowd and summoned a carriage to collect her two children from the house in Sandgate where they were still in the care of Cuckoo Jack Wilson's wife.

20

The Newcastle Society for Effecting the Abolition of the Slave Trade was comprised mainly of Quakers, including its Chairman, Mister Hadwen Bragg, together with a few Anglican clergymen. It was natural that members of the Quaker fraternity should gravitate to the support of such a cause, since it is a fundamental tenet of their belief that all men are created equal in the image of God and that one person cannot, therefore, be regarded as subservient to another. But, as non-conformists and, consequently, excluded from the right to hold public office, they were regarded by many – and, in particular, those who invested in or profited from the slave trade – as dangerous fanatics who espoused an attitude which, if supported, would have a substantial deleterious effect upon the wealth and commercial interests of the town.

The Society's aim was to increase the public's awareness of the cruel and inhumane treatment meted out to slaves and to campaign for a new law putting an end to the Transatlantic trade. They published pamphlets describing the appalling conditions suffered by those transported from Africa to plantations in the Americas, held lectures and conducted public meetings and rallies to try to garner support for their cause.

In their attempts to spread their message, they were often met with fierce resistance and obstruction. At the instigation of some of the leading figures in the town's business community, which exercised great influence over the activities of the Common Council, the Society was refused the use of public venues including the Guild Hall and the Assembly Rooms for their meetings, as a result of which they were forced to hold them in open areas such as the Groatmarket and Sandhill where gangs of thugs, hired or encouraged by the abolitionists' opponents, menaced and intimidated anyone who dared to attend. Eventually, the Society were given sanctuary by the Reverend William Moises, Vicar of St Andrew's Church, nigh to Newgate, who offered to host their meetings in the chantry of the Holy Trinity.

It was a very solemn Hadwen Bragg who rose to deliver his report to the two score or so members of the Society gathered in that ancient and hallowed building.

'Gentlemen,' he began (there being no ladies present since, although the Society did number several representatives of the fair sex among its membership, it was on that occasion a particularly inclement evening). 'It is my sad duty to bring news of the terrible deaths – murders, I should say - of over one hundred and thirty wretches, who were deliberately cast overboard into the sea from the slave ship *Zong* on the orders of the captain …'

He waited until the gasps of dismay had subsided before continuing.

'I understand the circumstances to be as follows. The *Zong* was on its way from the Gold Coast to Jamaica with a consignment of over four hundred abducted Africans on behalf of a syndicate of Liverpool slave traders. Because of various navigational errors made by its inexperienced crew, the ship was first becalmed for several days in the Doldrums and later steered the wrong course, during which its supplies of drinking water fell dangerously low and sickness broke out among those on board. The captain, conscious that the company which employed him would not be compensated for any slaves who died during the journey from so-called natural causes such as thirst, malnutrition or disease, decided to jettison those who were sick or dying. He knew that the ship-owners would be able to claim compensation from their insurers for the loss of those thrown over-board on the grounds that they had been sacrificed in order to save the healthy remainder and had, of course, not died from natural causes …'

He paused, his voice cracking with emotion, and sought to regain his composure. Meanwhile, his audience sat in horrified silence. Had there been any women present they would un-doubtedly have been reduced to tears by this sorry tale.

Before Hadwen Bragg could resume, somebody shouted, 'This is outrageous.'

'A massacre,' someone else added.

'We must express our deepest concern to the Government, Hadwen,' Reverend Moises said. 'It is completely unconscion-able that fellow human beings are treated in this way – traded as goods and chattels and expendable at the whim of an owner, who thinks nothing of killing them as he would kill a chicken. The Government *must* legislate to outlaw this appalling busi-ness.'

There was general approbation among the others for this sentiment and Hadwen Bragg could judge from the atmos-phere of gloom cast over the assembled members by the report they had just heard that nobody had the stomach for a lengthy debate on the matter that evening.

'Very well, gentlemen. On behalf of the Society, I will take up the matter with our Member of Parliament,' he said, pri-vately doubting that he would gain any encouragement or sup-port from that quarter.

Newcastle Courant

It is with the utmost Regret that we are obliged to report that a grave Commotion occurred Yesterday Afternoon, at Shields. The Mayor of Newcastle, with the avowed Intention of unblocking the Obstacle to River Traffic occasioned by the treacherous and unlawful Conduct of the Keelmen, had proceeded down the Tyne in his official Barge, accompanied by the Boats of His Majesty's Ships. On reaching the Harbour at Shields, the Mayor was besieged by a large unruly Mob which immediately commenced an Assault with Stones, Bricks and divers other Missiles, injuring several of those in his Entourage and putting them in Fear of their Boats being capsized.

After some Time, the Crews were obliged, in order to defend themselves against the mortal Threat, to open Fire, with the result that one of those on the Shore was rumoured to have been shot. This Rumour inflamed the Mob, leading them to vent their Fury upon the Low Light Tavern, to which Hostelry the Mayor was believed to have repaired, and which in Consequence suffered considerable structural Damage.

We are happy to report that the Mayor managed to escape without Injury, after which the arrival of a Detachment of the 6th Dragoon Guards ensured the Dispersal of the Rioters and the Restoration of Tranquillity.

*

There was a distinct mood of excitement and tension in the air in anticipation of the exhibition to be conducted by Doctor Stickler. Mister William Ingham once again suggested that, since I was now several months into my apprenticeship but had still not witnessed a dissection at first hand, I should attend for the benefit of my education. I felt obliged to acquiesce but, experiencing a combination of dread and exhilaration at the prospect of seeing a body being cut up, I chose to sit at a discreet distance from the table at the centre of the Anatomy Room where the naked corpse of the adult male was laid out in readiness for the demonstration.

Doctor Stickler, to his credit, treated the whole event in a businesslike way, without too much melodrama or appeal to the baser emotions of his audience, almost as if it was a procedure which he performed daily as a matter of routine. 'Listen carefully and take full notes,' he instructed. 'Remember this, gentlemen. Each of you is likely to be anatomising a cadaver within the year. So pay close attention, otherwise you run the risk of wasting an opportunity to advance your knowledge and of wasting a corpse too. And, at this time of scarcity, that would be unforgivable.'

He surveyed the room to ensure that everyone was settled in their seats and was focused on his words.

'Now,' he said, 'the first thing to do before commencing the dissection is to establish that your subject is in fact … dead.'

A little laughter broke out, something which he had obviously anticipated, based no doubt on the normal reaction to the identical opening remarks he had used on previous occasions. He waited until it subsided, then continued. 'In order to be absolutely certain about that, I would normally introduce one of these (he held up the long needle which his assistant had just handed to him) through the coats of my subject's eyes so that I can detect whether the iris is stimulated. If it is not, then I can be certain that the man is dead. Today, however, I will dispense with this part of the procedure as he has already been examined and certified as dead by Mister William Ingham, the esteemed Head of our College, in whose judgement I have the utmost confidence.'

I deduced from the expressions on the faces of those around me that, like me, they were quite relieved not to have to witness the puncturing of the cadaver's eyeballs. Doctor Stickler moved over to the side of the dissecting table where he had deposited his surgical instruments and carefully selected a large scalpel which he held up to allow his audience to see it clearly. 'It is important to use a knife with which you feel comfortable,' he explained. 'One which fits easily into the hand. Hold it firmly but not too tightly. You need to be relaxed, otherwise you could damage your subject. Then you lay the sharp edge of your blade to the part of the cadaver where you intend to begin and cut it with a deliberate, uniform action …'

Up to this point, Doctor Stickler had made no attempt to touch the cadaver and I imagine that the audience, myself included, may have been lulled into focusing more upon the theory of anatomisation than the practice. I am sure that he did this deliberately in order that his next move would have more impact, because as he spoke these words he stepped forward to the body and, in one movement, made an incision from the sternum to the pubis. There was a collective gasp from the onlookers as the man's chest gaped open.

'So, you can see what I have done here,' he said. 'I have cut the cadaver in such a way that enables me now to explore each of its cavities.' Then he directed a question to his students. 'My subject today is a male. How do you think I would have proceeded had it been a female?'

Various opinions were offered.

'Sir, you would cover the body with a cloth for the sake of modesty.'

'Sir, you would remove the breasts before making an incision from the sternum.'

'Sir, you would first check whether the subject is pregnant.'

Doctor Stickler nodded slowly as if pleased with the responses. 'Well, gentlemen, these are all good answers. It is certainly the case that females are to be treated with a greater degree of decorum. But what I wanted you to understand is that it is important to open up a woman differently in order to expose her reproductive organs. So I would make the incision like this at the navel …' – he drew a triangular shape in the air with his index finger – ' … leaving a flap of skin which I would fold back over the pubis.'

I will spare the reader a detailed description of the remainder of the dissection and an explication of how Doctor Stickler proceeded to open each cavity of the body in turn, removing, displaying and examining the germane organ while giving a contemporaneous commentary on the various inferences which he was able to draw from its condition. Throughout the process, the assistant passed him various surgical instruments, wiped them clean after use, mopped up body fluids, and swabbed the perspiration from the Doctor's face. I must confess that I paid as much attention to the activities of the assistant (in whose role I hoped to become proficient in the course of my apprenticeship) as I did to those of his master.

There were two aspects in particular about that morning's event which left me somewhat perplexed and which led me to reflect about what happened on my last day in the employment of Mister Abel Grope. It was my certain knowledge that, whenever an executed criminal was given up for dissection, the anatomisation was always conducted in an open forum to which members of the public had unfettered access, which normally made for a boisterous affair, often disrupted by applause, barracking and all kinds of disorder. And yet, on this occasion, admission to Doctor Stickler's exhibition had been restricted to those who frequented the Barber-Surgeons' Hall. I wondered, therefore, firstly, why the public had been excluded and, secondly, what the provenance of the cadaver might be, since the answer to neither question had been revealed.

Could it be that the man whose corpse I watched being dissected did not die on the scaffold and that somewhere nearby a black-clad widow was grieving at the supposed grave of her late husband in which was buried a coffin containing only a collection of dusty bricks?

21

Newcastle Courant

WINNER

Mister Felix Brandling MP, resident at Gosforth House near Bulman Village, is said to have won 1,000 guineas on his filly, Hoastman, at the Newcastle race meeting.

Sir Stanhope Delaval sighed despondently as he put aside his copy of the newspaper. He seemed to lose almost as much on the horses as Felix Brandling won. His funds were becoming precariously low and, as always, he was anxious to find some means – whether lawful or otherwise, he did not care unduly so long as it produced the desired result – of bolstering his dwindling finances.

His latest scheme, which outshone his earlier stratagems in its degree of deviousness, occurred to him in the wake of the splendid banquet held at Seaton Delaval Hall to mark the official birthday of His Majesty King George. Among the guests that evening was a certain woman of advanced years and even more advanced infirmity whom Sir Stanhope had not previously encountered. Indeed, he was unsure of how she had managed to secure an invitation to the event, not being among his circle of acquaintances, let alone how she had managed to summon up the energy to attend. On enquiry, he established that she was Lady Isabell Paulet, aged seventy-nine, a very superstitious woman whose late husband made his huge fortune in the

West Indies, a fortune which he foolishly failed to exhaust before his untimely death and which therefore passed in its entirety to his widow. Lady Paulet now resided in the Borders in what Sir Stanhope's informant described as 'a fairly small castle' where, according to the gossip of those in her employ, she eked out a solitary and abstemious existence, grieving for the loss of her husband and yearning for the company of a man who could replace him, a man with whom she could share her remaining days as well as her sizeable inheritance. What's more, she had been advised by her doctor that, because of the numerous ailments from which she suffered, she had only three months to live, six at the most.

Sir Stanhope identified two obstacles to his goal of gaining access to Lady Paulet's wealth. The first lay in the fact that when he had introduced himself to the woman at the conclusion of the banquet she showed no desire to get to know him better but had instead exhibited an overt and singular revulsion at his obesity, his comportment and his inebriated condition. The second related to his own status, in that he was already married to Rhoda - a woman whose assets included youth, exquisite beauty and sophistication - and was not, therefore, currently at liberty to enter into another conjugal relationship without falling foul of the Bigamy Act of 1603. Such trivial impediments, however, were not going to deter a man in the desperate financial straits in which Sir Stanhope found himself and he resolved to activate Phase One of his plan immediately.

It was something of a stroke of genius that he decided to call once again upon the services of Blackie Johnson who, despite his forbidding appearance, had the knack of enchanting the superstitious women whose fortunes he foretold into investing their complete trust in his predictions and recommendations. Lady Paulet was easily lured back to Seaton Delaval Hall by the promise of a dinner, a more intimate affair than the banquet which she had attended previously, at which a world-famous clairvoyant (Sir Stanhope saw no reason why he should not permit himself a little hyperbole in a good cause) would be available, on request, to tell the fortunes of the guests.

In response to Sir Stanhope's entreaty, Blackie agreed to wear a patch over his empty eye-socket in order to appear less intimidating to Lady Paulet and, at the conclusion of the meal, he led her into the Mahogany Parlour where Sir Stanhope had entertained him some months before. As he drew the pack of tarot cards from his pocket in order to embark upon the hoax which his paymaster had instructed him to perpetrate, he almost felt a tinge of compassion for the wizened old crone (as Sir Stanhope had ungallantly described her) but, remembering the large reward he had been offered for his collusion, quickly put aside any feeling of sympathy for his victim or shame at his own part in duping her.

Following his normal procedure, he asked Lady Paulet to choose three cards from the pack and hand them to him face down. She did so hesitantly, changing her mind three or four times before settling upon her final selection. Blackie laid the cards on the table just as she had given them to him and stared at them for some time as if summoning up some supernatural power which would enable him to unravel the mysteries of the paranormal. Meanwhile, Lady Paulet sat with her hands clutched tightly in her lap, nervously waiting to learn her fate.

He turned over the first card slowly, almost reverently. Lady Paulet gasped as she saw that it depicted a skeleton riding on a horse. The figure was holding a black standard in one hand and a sickle in the other and was surrounded by a number of bodies which the horse had trampled underfoot.

'Death,' Blackie declared, unceremoniously.

'What does it mean?' Lady Paulet asked, anxiously.

Blackie held up his hand to silence her. 'Wait until Aa've seen aal the cards,' he said. 'Aa must consider them aal together. Then Aa can divine their meaning.' He turned over the second card. It showed a six-spoked wheel inscribed with strange characters and surrounded by winged creatures perched on clouds. Lady Paulet leaned forward quickly and was about to speak again when she saw the warning look in Blackie's eye and settled back into her chair, her hands clasped even more tightly.

The images on the third card were of two naked figures, a male and a female, in a garden. This time, she could not contain herself and blurted out, 'It's Adam and Eve in the Garden of Eden, isn't it, Mister Johnson?'

Blackie glared at her. 'Aa canna concentrate if ye interrupt me, hinny.'

Lady Paulet was not used to being spoken to in such an indecorous manner and was about to protest when she thought better of it and lapsed back into a grudging silence. Meanwhile, Blackie had started to arrange and rearrange the three cards on the table in front of him in an apparent attempt to make sense of their message. At length, he turned to Lady Paulet and said, 'Ye've got a strange lot here. Aa dinaa knaa what to make of 'em.' Not being used to consorting with the lower orders, particularly those who spoke with the Newcastle accent, she struggled to comprehend what he was telling her, but heard enough to guess that he found it difficult to interpret the cards she had chosen. 'Ye see,' he told her, holding up the Death card, 'this one signifies the end of something. It could be the end of yer life, of course, which seems likely seeing as how ye're a canny age, beggin' yer pardon. Or it could be the end of one phase of yer life and the start of a new one.'

'A new one?' she said, sounding excited.

'Divvent get yer hopes up. Aa haven't finished yet,' Blackie replied, anxious to dampen down any note of optimism until he had delivered his final judgment. Next, he picked up the card which depicted the two figures in a garden. 'Ye were right about them. That's Adam and Eve and the card is called The Lovers. It usually signifies a point at which ye have to make an important decision about a relationship. At the moment, Aa'm not sure what it means in yer case. Tell ye the truth, it seems an odd one for an auld wife like ye to choose. Anyway, Aa need to think about aal yer cards together. This third one …' he said, pointing to the card with the strangely-inscribed wheel, '… this one's The Wheel of Fortune. It shows that things gan round in cycles. There will be good times and there will be bad times.'

'Will mine be good or bad?' Lady Paulet asked anxiously.

'Just be silent now, will ye? Aa have to focus.' He closed his eye, bowed his head and appeared to go into some kind of trance, rotating his hands continuously as if holding an invisible round object and humming quietly to himself. After several minutes of this, he jumped up with a start, opened his eye and looked around the room as if momentarily he could not remember where he was. Then, turning to Lady Paulet, he said, 'No wonder Aa'm finding this so difficult. It's because yer cards are contradicting themselves.'

Lady Paulet was beginning to get rather impatient at Blackie's histrionics and demanded to know whether he had finally come up with a prediction for her. He avoided answering her directly and instead launched into an explanation of the contradiction to which he had referred. 'Aa've told ye the significance of each of the cards individually. But the way they work together is the most important thing and, if Aa look at their combined meaning, they point in two directions. The first interpretation Aa can put on them is that ye will spend yer remaining days in great pain and misery without the companionship or affection of anybody and ye will die a lonely, agonising death in the very near future.'

At this, Lady Paulet burst into tears and sobbed loudly and uncontrollably for several minutes. Blackie tried his best to affect a look of compassion while he waited for her weeping to subside. Then, adopting what he imagined might sound like a cheerful tone, he continued by outlining the alternative meaning which he could read in the cards. 'Remember what Aa said about The Wheel of Fortune. It gans round in cycles, good times and bad times. And the Death card can signify the start of something new in yer life. So my second interpretation is that ye are about to experience a complete change for the better ...'

Lady Paulet was suddenly looking very sanguine. She called out excitedly, 'Oh, what do you think is going to happen, Mister Johnson?'

'If ye'd just shut up, woman, Aa'm about to tell ye,' Blackie retorted, feigning anger at the interruption. 'Yer health is ganna improve, ye will meet a man who becomes yer ... er, ... bedfellow, Aa suppose ye could call him. And ye will live to be a hundred.'

'A *bedfellow*? Me? At my age? Oh, how exciting. And living to be a hundred! I can hardly believe it.' There was no sign of any tears now as she contemplated Blackie's latest revelation. Then, as she remembered that this was only one of two diametrically opposed forecasts of what lay ahead, her enthusiasm subsided as quickly as it had risen. 'Which of your predictions do you think is the correct one, Mister Johnson?' she asked timidly.

'Aa divvent knaa. There's only one way to settle it.' He picked up the pack and proffered it in her direction. 'Here, choose another card,' he instructed, and she did as he said.

Turning the card over very slowly, he took a long look at it before placing it face up on the table with a melodramatic sweep of his arm, as though the gesture were invested with some mystical significance. Lady Paulet could see that it portrayed a large man dressed in flowing robes and wearing a crown, sitting on a golden throne and holding a double-edged sword. 'Ye've chosen The Kings of Swords,' Blackie said.

'What does it mean?'

He did not reply immediately but re-enacted the earlier routine of closing his eye, bowing his head and adopting a trance-like state, this time humming louder than before. Then he suddenly jerked his face up, rousing himself and nodding vigorously to signify that all was now crystal clear. 'That settles it, aal reet,' he said, decisively. 'The King of Swords is the key to this puzzle. He holds the power to determine which one of these predictions will prove to be true.

'Who is this King of Swords?'

'Aa think ye will knaa soon enough. The King of Swords on this card represents a man who is also very important and influential. A man who ye may at first find repulsive and disgusting. Obnoxious even. But Aa counsel ye not to rebuff this man, because if ye do, ye will soon die a miserable and painful death. If, on the other hand ye do as he asks, ye will be pleasantly surprised to learn that he is not at aal as ye initially believed him to be but is, in fact, a charming, witty and intelligent person who transforms yer fortunes so that ye enjoy a long, happy and healthy life.'

'But who is this man that has so much power over my life?'

'Aa canna tell ye anymore than Aa have done, except to say that ye won't have long to wait before ye find out. Now Aa suggest that ye gan back and join the other dinner guests as fast as ye can.'

22

Ever since commencing my apprenticeship, I had made it my daily practice, whenever the weather so permitted, to set off from the Barber-Surgeons' Hall at midday or thereabouts and to head out in a westerly direction towards the more salubrious parts of the town, upwind of the furnaces and factories, in order to reenergise my constitution in preparation for the afternoon's study. I also hoped that regular exercise of this nature might help to restore my knees to the condition in which they were before my spell as a climbing-boy which had left me with a conspicuous and painful limp. Sometimes, I would see a familiar face and exchange a cursory greeting with its owner. On other days, unkind children – or even adults – would laugh at my affliction, call me names or throw stones at me. Very occasionally, I might pass an hour without encountering a soul whom I recognised and would therefore spend the time in solitary and happy contemplation.

It was a year or more after my first day as an apprentice that I somehow fell into conversation during my customary perambulation with a ragged-headed gadgie who approached me and hailed me as a fellow practitioner of medical science. 'If I'm not very much mistaken, young sir, you are an alumnus of that fine establishment, the Barber-Surgeons' Hall, are you not?' he asked in a whining timbre. He was an oily man and his eyes did not look at mine as he spoke. I must admit that I took an instant dislike to him.

I explained that I was merely an apprentice to an assistant surgeon and a recently-engaged one at that, having only just commenced the second of my five year tutelage.

'Ha!' he said. 'A medical man like me, then. I thought as much. I'm sure that we have a great deal in common.' He slapped me on the back in the manner of a lifelong friend, a gesture which made me dislike him even more.

'Grymm.' He thrust out a limp hand which I felt it would be churlish to refuse, so I clasped it tentatively, almost simultaneously realising that he was formally introducing himself. 'Grymm,' he repeated. 'Grymm by name, but not Grymm by nature.'

'Maclachlan, sir. James Maclachlan,' I returned reluctantly, wondering how often he had employed that aphorism.

I hoped that this exchange of names would be the end of the conversation but it soon became obvious that he meant to accompany me at least a little further on my walk. After a few inconsequential pleasantries, delivered with practised insincerity, he turned to more serious business and I began to form a strong impression that he had deliberately targeted me in order to engage me in a discussion to his own advantage.

'Since you are a medical man like me, James,' he said, discomfiting me somewhat with his overfamiliar use of my Christian name, 'I imagine that the welfare of your patients must be at the forefront of your aspirations.'

I could hardly disagree with such sentiments but forbore to reply directly, instead indicating with a casual nod of my head that I assumed his words to be in the nature of a rhetorical statement.

'And, no doubt therefore, James,' he continued, 'you would be most interested to avail yourself of any medication which proved efficacious in relieving disagreeable symptoms and easing the distress of your patients.'

Again, I was unable to deny the validity of his assertion and although I would, at that point, have dearly loved to terminate our association, I felt constrained by my sense of civility to continue to listen to what my interlocutor had to say.

'I suppose that, as a medical man, James, you must be familiar with the Cordial Balm of Gilead?' he enquired in an innocent tone.

I could not recall having come across any mention during Doctor Stickler's lectures and demonstrations of whatever substance bore that name and I told Grymm so.

'Aha!' he ejaculated triumphantly. 'Then you may come to regard this chance meeting as a most auspicious occurrence. A blessing, indeed, my dear James. Because, you see, I am willing to confide in you, as my very good friend, and to share the secrets of the amazing curative properties of this medication.' He withdrew a paper from his waistcoat pocket and proceeded to unfold it carefully. Then, reading from it, he embarked on a recital of commendations designed to confirm the truth of his claim. 'The first person I treated with Cordial Balm of Gilead,' he explained, 'was a woman who had been afflicted for a considerable time with a desperate venereal disease which occasioned unbearable pains in her head, a large tumour in her breast, a loud singing in her ears and a complaint of a serious nature. She had attempted several cures of various kinds, all without success. She spent many days in the Infirmary but even being salivated for her disorders produced no benefit whatsoever. Her family came to me, begging for my intervention, to which I duly assented and, with her approval, I administered several drops (patient confidentiality and commercial sensitivity prevent my disclosing the precise number) of Cordial Balm of Gilead. The medication was immediately effective, dissipating her headache and eradicating the worst symptoms of her disability, creating in their place a pleasing vivacity, comfort and strength.'

At this point, Grymm paused to allow me to express my astonishment at the miracle he had just recounted and I must admit that I did so out of politeness, but without the excessive enthusiasm which he might have anticipated. He was, however, still not finished with his eulogy.

'I believe that this elixir, if I may describe it as such,' he continued, 'is particularly efficacious in treating the weaknesses which are peculiar to the fair sex. In fact, James, there are many ladies of respectability and fashion to whom I have administered who now count the Cordial Balm of Gilead among the favourite appendages to their toilette.'

By now, I was becoming aware that the time available to me before the start of my next class was rapidly expiring and that I needed, therefore, to extricate myself courteously but decisively from the conversation in which I had become uncomfortably ensconced. A church bell proclaiming the hour at which I was due to present myself for Doctor Stickler's afternoon lecture gave me the opportunity to offer my excuse to Mister Grymm (he had not informed me of his Christian name) and I hurried off (if I can apply that term to my pathetic attempt to hirple quickly) in the direction of the Barber-Surgeons' Hall.

I hoped fervently that this would be the last time that I would ever see or hear from that man. I was to be bitterly disappointed in that regard.

*

Newcastle Courant

At the Northumberland Assizes yesterday, Noel Barlow, a Keel Skipper, resident in Sandgate, was found guilty of sallying upon, assaulting, bruising and wounding Tobias Rudge, who was employed as

---

an Off-putter at the Benwell Staithes, to the Effusion of his Blood and Danger of his Life. In his Defence, Barlow stated that Rudge and other Staithesmen at Benwell and at various Locations on the Tyne had colluded with the Hoastmen to overload his Keel in return for Bribes. The Magistrates, in the certain Knowledge that several such Attacks had been perpetrated by Watermen in recent Days, in the Course of promoting their illegal and tumultuous Strike of Work, rejected the Accused's Grounds of Defence and sentenced Barlow to Imprisonment in the House of Correction at Newgate.

*

Sir Stanhope was conversing with the other dinner guests over port when Lady Paulet returned from her consultation with Blackie Johnson. As soon as Blackie indicated through a pre-arranged signal that Phase One of their scheme had been completed successfully, Sir Stanhope summoned his butler and issued him with instructions.

Lady Paulet had only just entered the drawing-room and, having settled into one of the leather-clad Gainsborough armchairs, was beginning to reflect on the events of the past half-hour when she looked up to see a tall, mousy-haired man standing over her. She could tell immediately from the uniform he was wearing and the self-confident but deferential way in which he held a silver salver topped with a domed cover that he was a butler.

'Aa 'umbly beg yer pardon, Yer Ladyship,' he said, in the manner of a member of the working class attempting to disguise his Newcastle dialect. With a theatrical flourish, he lifted the domed cover to reveal an envelope lying on the platter. 'With the compliments of Sir Stanhope Delaval,' he added, in unctuous tones.

'Oh, that horrid man!' Lady Paulet reacted instinctively, reaching for the paper. The butler remained motionless in front of her, as if waiting for further instructions (or, more likely, she fancied, a gratuity). 'That will be all,' she barked and he slunk off, less self-confidently than he had arrived.

Opening the envelope, she withdrew a sheet of paper headed with the Delaval family crest and motto (*Quid tibi fieri non vis alteri ne feceris*) and surveyed the neat, effeminately written message, which read:

> *My dearest Lady Paulet*
> *I have been most taken by your wit, charm and elegance, in consequence of which I would consider it a great honour if you would do me the favour of accepting my heartfelt proposal of marriage in order that we may spend the rest of our lives together in conjugal harmony.*
> *Yours adoringly, Stanhope Delaval*
> *RSVP.*

At about the same time that Lady Paulet was reading this, the butler was delivering a second missive (also presented on a silver platter and bearing the Delaval family crest and motto, as befitting a communication of such import) to Sir Stanhope's current spouse, Lady Rhoda. It consisted of a notification, written in a neat, effeminate script and couched in formal, unemotional language, that Sir Stanhope would be serving official divorce papers on her on the morrow, subject only to his prior receipt from a third party of that person's acceptance of a proposed alternative contractual arrangement.

*

Newcastle Courant

PUBLIC NOTICE

In Consideration of the Fact that the Tyne Keelmen show no Indication that they intend to desist from their outrageous and insulting Behaviour in projecting Missiles against the Crew of His Majesty's Boats, who are carrying out their Duty by offering Protection to those worthy Watermen willing to work; the Civil Authorities are obliged to issue this Caution to those who wish to go peaceably about their Business.

In order to avoid inadvertent Injuries or Death to innocent Civilians, we warn those Inhabitants, and Women, and Children, to remain secure within the Confines of their Homes during the Passage of the Keels down River to Shields, as the Marines are under strict Orders to open Fire on anyone daring to throw a Stone at the said Keels.

23

In my rush to get away from Mister Grymm, I had not thought to enquire of him in which establishment he practised medicine nor, in all honesty, was it a matter of any great interest to me. However, reflecting later on my encounter with the man, I wondered whether he could be one of the so-called quacks about whom Mister Ingham had warned me. Charlatans and mountebanks, he also called them, if my memory served me right. Full of fantastic stories about their phoney cures. We were to report them to the Searchers if they approached us, he said. After much deliberation, I decided that since the episode took place well outside the confines of the Barber-Surgeons' Hall it did not fall within the purview of that injunction. Consequently, I mentioned it to no-one.

Indeed, I thought no more about Mister Grymm until, one day a week or so later as I was setting off for my regular constitutional after a morning's intensive studying, the janitor hailed me and handed me a small parcel which he said had been left for me by a person or persons unknown. I found upon opening it a small bottle labelled Cordial Balm of Gilead and a note written in a spidery scrawl which read, *To my very good friend Master James Maclachlan from your very good friend Septimus Grymm (Grymm by name, but not Grymm by nature).*

This immediately put me into something of a quandary. After all, assuming that Mister Grymm was a so-called quack, my receipt of such an item would, I judged, clearly fall within the definition of those circumstances which I was required to bring to the attention of the Searchers. However, if I now did so, I would undoubtedly be interrogated about the circumstances which led to my being sent the said item and would then inevitably be held to account for having failed to report the original encounter - with what dire consequences for my continued employment I dared not guess at. In the event, and once again after much deliberation, I decided to follow the advice which I had, as a child, often heard my dear father proffer, namely, that discretion is the better part of valour, a principle which, rightly or wrongly in this situation, I took to mean that I should remain silent.

When I had made a good distance away from the Barber-Surgeons' Hall and had almost reached the Forth Walks, I deemed it safe at last to examine my gift more closely. I unscrewed the cap carefully and sniffed the contents of the bottle. They smelt strongly of something resembling brandy with a hint of rosemary - quite a pleasant aroma, in fact. I wondered if I should try a sip but quickly decided against. After all, if Cordial Balm of Gilead really *did* have the amazing properties ascribed to it by Mister Grymm (or Mister *Septimus* Grymm, as I now knew him), it would be quite wasteful for me to treat it as a casual beverage rather than to use it to relieve the suffering of some poor soul.

That evening, I was careful to conceal the bottle among my meagre belongings so that the Searchers would not be led to learn of my violation of the regulations. The following day, I decided that I had to risk taking it with me into the lecture theatre in case the dormitory might be searched in my absence and my secret unearthed. However, so anxious was I about carrying the forbidden item with me that I began to imagine every other person looking with suspicion at my satchel as though they could see through its leather cover and observe what was hidden inside. Indeed, I could hardly concentrate at all during Doctor Stickler's presentation that morning because of my dread at the possibility of discovery and my guilt at transgressing the rules of the establishment. Consequently, I made up my mind to dispose of the bottle as soon as possible, anticipating that the opportunity to do so would arise during my midday walk.

I feared immediately that my plan had been scuppered as I passed through the arched doorway out into the courtyard and headed toward the gate, where there lurked none other than Mister Septimus Grymm.

'Well, Master Maclachlan, what an absolute stroke of luck it is bumping into you completely by chance like this,' he said in a deceitful yammer. 'I happened to be on my way to deliver a potion to a patient in Westgate-street and, just as I was passing by the Hall, I thought to myself, well, if that isn't my young friend Master Maclachlan coming out of the gate. I could hardly believe what an amazing coincidence it was that our paths should cross for a second time in this way.'

'It's a great pleasure to see you, sir,' I rejoined, disingenuously.

'And did you, I wonder, receive the little token of our acquaintance which I had delivered to you?' he enquired, almost casually, as though it was something of an afterthought.

'You mean the bottle of … er … medication?' I asked, not being able to think of a more appropriate way to describe the contents.

'I certainly do,' he asserted. 'Cordial Balm of Gilead. Wonderful stuff.'

'Yes, I received it,' I confirmed, lamely. 'Thank you very much, sir.'

'I am delighted that you were so pleased with my gift,' he declared, ignoring the fact that he had no evidence for such an assumption and adopting a tone of voice which intimated that, by having given me some concoction that I should not have in my possession, he somehow had me in his thrall as a result. Before I could protest at the implication, he asked, 'Have you mentioned it to anybody, by chance?'

I replied that I had not done so and he said, 'That's very sensible of you. Let's just keep it to ourselves, shall we? Our little secret.'

This suggestion made me feel most uncomfortable but I had no choice but to assent and Mister Grymm nodded contentedly before asking, 'And where might you be making for now, Master Maclachlan, if I may so enquire?'

I had, of course, intended to head west towards my favoured midday haunts of Spital Field and Forth Walks but, on the spur of the moment, I fabricated an account of an errand which furnished me with a destination in a direction opposite to that to be followed by Mister Grymm.

'Oh,' he said, briefly feigning disappointment, then added, this time in a faintly conspiratorial tone, 'That's a pity, because I would have liked to walk a little way with you.'

Fortunately, Mister Grymm did not press me to accompany him to his appointment in Westgate-street nor did he offer to accompany me to my supposed appointment on the other side of town. However, as he headed off towards Westgate-street, he left me wondering whether I had misinterpreted the meaning behind some of his comments, which placed me in a state of some confusion and not a little apprehension about his intentions. I was, of course, still anxious to rid myself of my bottle of Cordial Balm of Gilead and I followed the road down to the Keyside, where I imagined I would be able to dispose of it in the river. This I did, dropping it unobserved from the centre of the bridge into the Tyne where the floodtide happened to be in spate and watched it splash then disappear beneath the water. It emerged a few seconds later and bobbed along the surface, propelled by the current towards Benwell, or even as far as Wylam, from where (unless impeded by one of the countless obstacles which populate the river) it would be returned to Shields on the ebb tide and then vanish into the open sea, along with any prospect of discovery by the Searchers of my misdemeanour.

*

Newcastle Courant

MP CONDEMNS VIOLENCE BY THE KEELMEN

We regret to state once again, as we have on many previous Occasions of late, that the Keelmen of Tyne have not yet returned to Work. Indeed, the Strike has shown clear Signs of spreading in that the Seamen of Shields have, in the past Days, ventured up River in Boats and persuaded Crews on Ships being loaded at the Staithes to desist from their Labours. Fortunately, the Corporation responded to this Outrage with great Alacrity and swore in and dispatched several Posses of special Constables. Thirty-two of the Rioters were arrested and detained in Premises between Clifford's Fort and the Low Light overlooking the Pow Gut. Meanwhile, the good People of South Shields were forced to observe a disgraceful Spectacle when a Dozen or so Men who had broken the Strike were paraded through the main Street with their Faces blackened and their Jackets turned inside out.

Felix Brandling, the Member of Parliament for Newcastle-on-Tyne and himself one of the Company of Hoastmen against whom the Strike is directed, speaking yesterday during a Debate in the House of Commons, condemned the Actions of the Tyne Keelmen. He denounced them as Traitors, accusing them of gravely disrupting the Commerce of the Town, terrifying the Populace and jeopardising the King's Peace at a Time when the Country was already imperilled because of the outrageous Conduct of our Enemies on the other Side of the Channel.

We understand that Quietude has now returned to Shields. However, we consider that, unless more vigorous Action is taken urgently by the Civil Authorities, it is likely that Insubordination and Contempt amongst those in the Coal Trade is to lead to Riot and Rebellion, with a grave deleterious Impact on the Prosperity of the Town.

When Jasper Scuffins learned that the *Newcastle Courant* contained a lengthy article about the strike he insisted that Kitty Dace read it out to him. She did so reluctantly, knowing that should there be any criticism or adverse comment about the keelmen in the article, he would fly into a rage and scold her for being the purveyor of bad news. It was therefore with increasing anxiety that she started on the second paragraph, the content of which was bound to inflame him. She recited it in a whisper, hoping that he might not be paying sufficient attention to her words at that point and that the report of Felix Brandling's comments would go unnoticed. Unfortunately, however, he detected her attempt at concealment, stopped her in mid-sentence and demanded that she read the whole thing to him again.

'And Aa mean every single word, hinny, else there'll be trouble for ye, ' he roared.

He roared even louder when he heard what the MP had called the keelmen.

'Aa'll not be called a traitor, not by anyone, and certainly not by that flabby gobshite,' he bellowed, his face twisted in a grimace of incandescent fury.

Instead of telling Kitty to read out the rest of the piece, he said, 'Bring yer pencil and paper, lass. Aa'm ganna send that Brandling a letter that'll give him a fright that's he's nivvor had in aal his life.' He spent the next half-hour dictating his message, changing his mind several times and making Kitty cross out and rewrite several sentences until he was reasonably pleased with the result. 'Read it back to me,' he ordered and Kitty did so:

Felix Brandling if ye divvent give the keelmen a rise of four shillings a tide as sure as hell is hot but o a plague about your house for that o and worse than that before the year is done ye must be deed o ye and yer friends have been the worst gaffers to us that have ever came here and we will take care of some more ye may depend on it

Scuffins pronounced himself satisfied with the result.

'Beggin' yer pardon, sir,' Kitty stuttered, horrified at the prospect of having to send it to the MP and the possible consequence of doing so. 'But ... but ... Aa'm much afeard of sending this, sir. It's a felony, sir, to threaten a man in this way.'

'Nonsense. Divvent concern yarsel with it. Aa'll get one of my keel-bullies to deliver it.'

'If ye say so, sir,' Kitty replied, far from reassured by his words. 'Beggin' yer pardon, sir, shall Aa sign it from Mister Jasper Scuffins or just plain Mister Scuffins then?'

'Are ye mad, hinny? Aa'll not have my name on it. Aa want to keep the contemptible hoit guessing.'

24

The theme of the day's lecture, according to the notice posted at the entrance of the Barber-Surgeons' Hall, was to be *Doctor Donald Stickler's research into THE FELONIOUS PARTICLE*. No doubt most of those who turned up to hear him speak were as ignorant of the meaning of this subject matter as I was.

At precisely twelve noon, Doctor Stickler entered the lecture-theatre to take his place at the lectern. He was followed by Bold Archy who carried an armful of rolled-up charts and placed them on an adjoining table before occupying a seat next to the raised platform at the front of the room. Meanwhile, Doctor Stickler spread out a bundle of papers on the lectern, cleared his throat several times and then, when he was satisfied that the audience had fallen completely silent, glared at them contemptuously as if he considered that they did not deserve the privilege, which he was about to accord them, of hearing him speak.

After what must have seemed to many there like an uncomfortably long interval, he launched into his lecture. 'Gentlemen,' he said, ignoring the presence of the handful of women who had been pressed into attending with their husbands, 'I have been a surgeon now for almost one half of my years upon this earth and, during all that time, I have been driven by a passionate desire to accomplish something which will greatly enhance the lives of my fellow men and women. Something which will remove from our daily experience the fear and dread which we all feel about the possibility (I could even say *probability*, bearing in mind the troubled times in which we live) that we might, quite undeservedly and randomly, fall victim to someone who wishes to do us harm. In short, gentlemen, I have determined to make it my objective in life to discover the source of the evil which lurks within the body of the criminal and which leads that person to commit atrocities. And, when I have discovered this source, I will make it my further objective to find a way of destroying it so that the law-abiding among us will be spared having to suffer the terror to which I alluded earlier.'

There were several calls of, 'Hear, hear,' and various other indications of approbation which, far from being well-received, caused Doctor Stickler to replicate the glare he had adopted earlier, suggesting that he was irritated by the interruptions.

'I remember, some years ago,' he continued, after again waiting for silence, 'passing a preacher who was declaiming to a small crowd at Amen Corner. I tarried a little and overheard part of his sermon on the redemption of sinners. *We are all guilty of sin*, the man ranted, brandishing a bible above his head while several among his audience jeered and booed. *And there is but one way in which a wrong-doer can be acquitted of his sins...* *Hanging*, yelled some of the bystanders in riposte. *Flogging*, shouted others. *No, my friends*, the preacher insisted, unflustered by the hostile reaction. *Prayer is the answer. Prayer is the only means by which the sinner can be cleansed.*

'For some reason, the words of that preacher set me thinking. Thinking that there must be a more effective way than prayer to prevent a man resorting to crime. Applying my scientific turn of mind to the problem, it occurred to me that, in order to cure a sinner, you first have to establish the cause of his sinning. And that cause, I firmly believed, can be discovered somewhere in the person's physical make-up.'

At this point, Doctor Stickler paused, produced a small flask from his pocket and took a drink out of it. Then he resumed his oration.

'During the years while I was studying for my medical examinations, I became more and more interested – obsessed, you might say - by the notion that it would be a major contribution to the well-being of our society for me to establish which part of a person's anatomy was responsible for his propensity to commit crime. The hypothesis which I developed is that once the Felonious Particle, as I have rather aptly named this elusive speck (and rather cleverly too, you may think), has been located, it would be possible to predict which of those among us were destined to become a threat to their fellow citizens. Those responsible for our government and lawmaking could then decide whether such people should be removed from our midst - perhaps by execution or transportation to the colonies – or whether we should attempt to cure them of their criminality by removing the culpable constituent of their bodies before they had a chance to offend.'

This last remark produced quite a reaction among the audience and Doctor Stickler took advantage of their distraction by seizing the opportunity for another nip from his flask.

'Of course,' he continued, 'the ideal way to proceed with this mission - or so it seemed to me in my enthusiastic naivety at the start of my programme of research - was to obtain the cadavers of hanged criminals (who are, by definition, those culpable of the most heinous acts) and to analyse them in such precise detail as to enable me to unearth some abnormality or atypical constituent in their anatomical make-up, some deviation from that of ordinary, peaceable members of the populace, which could then be safely ascertained to be the Felonious Particle, as your humble servant has termed it.

'You may, gentlemen, have already spotted a flaw in the logic of my method. Because - as I came to realise quite soon after embarking on this project - it was not sufficient for me merely to examine the body of a *criminal* in order to achieve my objective. I also have to compare and contrast the criminal's body with that of a *law-abiding person* to enable me to establish what is different about the former's anatomy and thereby to isolate and identify this celebrated Felonious Particle of mine.

'In the course of my work, I began to develop my ideas further by hypothesising that the criminal's motivation for offending and his choice of deviant behaviour must be related to his mental processes. Consequently, I judged that the location of the Felonious Particle must lie somewhere within the organ of the body which supplies that precise function, namely, the brain.

'Now, gentlemen, I would like to show you some diagrams of that organ ...'

He nodded to Bold Archy and the giant picked up the charts which he had brought in and proceeded to fix them to a large wooden board at the side of the platform.

Doctor Stickler walked rather unsteadily over to the board and pointed at it with a long stick. 'Each of these four charts contains a diagram of a brain which I have removed from a subject in one of the dissecting rooms right here in the Barber-Surgeons' Hall.' Moving from left to right, he explained, 'This one was extracted from the cadaver of a highway robber executed at the scaffold. The second one belonged to a young pickpocket and the third to a man who was convicted of the rather unusual felony of being seen on the King's highway with a sooty face ...'

This last remark produced a wave of laughter among the audience which afforded the speaker the chance to quench his thirst once more. Then, pointing to the diagram on the far right, he continued, 'The fourth is from a body bequeathed to the Barber-Surgeons' Hall in the interests of the advancement of medical science. In life, it belonged to a man of the cloth – a person who was virtuous beyond reproach and quite definitely, therefore, deficient in the Felonious Particle. Not the one I heard preaching at Amen Corner, I should add. As far as I'm aware, *that* fellow is still alive and probably continuing to spread his dubious message.' He paused to allow the contrast between this and the other three subjects to be well remarked then said gravely, 'Now, gentlemen, let us examine these vital organs and deduce whether we can locate the elusive element which we seek.'

He turned towards his audience, hoping to witness a sea of faces gazing at him admiringly and in rapt anticipation of the revelation of the nature and identity of his precious Felonious Particle. Instead, he saw only looks of bemusement and confusion. Shaking his head in a show of disappointment, he said, 'I had rather expected that an audience of this composition would have been better able to comprehend the perfectly clear terms in which I have been expounding the subject of my research. I can, however, tell that I am going to have to address you in somewhat simpler language. Or, perhaps, like children, you would profit from an explanation in pictures rather than words. So let us use these illustrations to identify the differences between the criminal brain and the virtuous brain.'

He walked across to the diagram of the brain which once belonged to the man of the cloth. 'If you look closely at this one,' he said (although he must have known perfectly well that it was almost impossible for those at the back of the room to have anything more than a long-distance view of it), you will be able to distinguish the external components which are typical of all human brains. We can compare them with those of the other diagrams showing the brains of the criminals.'

Again, he used the long stick as a pointer. 'The outer layer covering the brain is the cerebral cortex. We have the two halves or hemispheres and each of these contains four separate sections or lobes. Here at the back of the brain is the parietal lobe which looks identical in all four subjects. Below it is the occipital lobe, all of which are also identical. At the side of each hemisphere we have the temporal lobe, again the same in each subject. And finally, the anterior section on top of the brain is the frontal lobe, *and this where the difference appears to be.*' He paused to allow the audience an opportunity to spot the feature which differentiated the brains and several spectators leaned forward in their seats in a vain attempt to do so. Meanwhile, he moved back behind the lectern and helped himself to a small refreshment.

Returning to his position in front of the charts, he continued, 'My preliminary hypothesis on the basis of a comparison between this brain - the good brain, as I like to refer to it - and the three bad brains - those belonging to the criminals - is that the distinguishing feature can be found *here* in the pre-frontal cortex which covers the forward part of the frontal lobe. Under examination through a microscope in my laboratory, I detected that the bad brains all display a slight protuberance which is absent in the good brain. Now, gentlemen, there may be those among you - perhaps the majority - who consider that what I have demonstrated here today provides fairly conclusive proof of the existence and identity of the Felonious Particle. However, any theory predicated on a comparison between what we may call a trio of sinners and a single saint, does not allow me, as an eminent scientist (if I may humbly describe myself thus), to assert with any degree of confidence that I have solved the riddle. The size of my sample is quite inadequate to draw such a firm conclusion. It is a promising start, let us say. But what my research requires is a considerably greater number of subjects on which to test my hypothesis. After all, gentlemen, as my students have heard me say a dozen or more times, science cannot prove anything with absolute certainty. It can only *dis*prove something. And so I intend to continue my quest for more corroboration of the evidence before you today, using as many more subjects as it is my fortune to be blessed with, either from the gallows or from the noble and altruistic donations of those who are prepared to offer themselves after death for the benefit of future generations.

'I cannot let this opportunity pass without an earnest appeal to all of you here to consider making your own contribution to medical science by bequeathing your bodies to the College for research. We have a register of names of our future donors which I have arranged to be made available to you on your exit from this lecture-theatre so that you may sign up. I urge you to do so. I appreciate, of course, that many of you are, at this moment, in the best of health and at the peak of your powers. In the prime of your life, one might say, and many years away from leaving this earth. Nevertheless, your donations will be of great benefit to future generations of doctors here at the Barber-Surgeons' Hall. And, although we may forbear to countenance the possibility in our own case, there is always the phenomenon of premature death to consider. Further to that, many of you may have sick or elderly relatives whose names you could usefully add to the register - today if possible, obviously the sooner the better - in the fairly certain knowledge that their contribution to the advancement of medical knowledge will soon be made a reality. In return for such generosity they will receive an honourable mention in the roll of patrons of the Worshipful Company of Barber-Surgeons, Wax and Tallow Chandlers of Newcastle-on-Tyne. In addition, the expenses will be paid for by the College to give them a modest funeral once we have no further use for their bodies.

'If after, shall we say, a score of further experiments on cadavers I have been unable to *dis*prove my hypothesis then it may be that the world of medicine will come to accept the probability - rather than the absolute certainty - that what I have termed the Felonious Particle resides in the frontal section of the brain and, if excised, will prevent its owner from lapsing into a life of crime. Indeed,' he continued with mock humility, 'perhaps in years to come men of medicine with an even greater level of skill and knowledge than I possess will generously christen my contribution to science as the Stickler Phenomenon.'

Picking up the bundle of papers strewn across the lectern, he declared, 'That concludes today's lecture.' Then he bowed histrionically to the audience and waited in vain for the rapturous applause which he considered that his oration had merited.

25

During those next few months, it became my custom on a Saturday night (and on other days too, I readily acknowledge) to visit the Flying Horse Tavern in the Groatmarket. There, a regular and agreeable routine took place whereby the publican, Mister Elias Tobin (also known as His Satanic Majesty), made it his practice to recite to the assembled company in Hell's Kitchen several passages from that week's edition of the Courant, which he had purchased the same morning for the sum of sixpence. He possessed a sweet melodious voice which, through constant practice and the pursuit of elocution lessons, was hardly tainted by the Newcastle way of speaking and therefore acquired an air of erudition and articulation that was unmatched even in the parlours and drawing-rooms of Bulman Village. Indeed, I used to imagine that his declamations would be well-received and, almost certainly, comprehended in any part of England to which he cared to venture.

However, I remember distinctly the occasion on which Mister Tobin came unstuck, which led to an insalubrious episode with unfortunate consequences for him, as well as for some of his customers. It took place a few days after I happened to overhear a conversation in that place which was prompted by a comment from one of the regulars, who had noticed that Mister Tobin seemed unusually distracted.

'His Satanic Majesty is all of a jitters tonight,' the man remarked.

'Why's that?' asked his friend.

'He's expecting a visit from the ale-conners any day now,' said the first.

'The ale-conners?' rejoined his friend.

'You know, the ones from the Mayor's Office. They're coming to check the beer to make sure it's up to the legal standards.'

'Why should he be worried about that?'

'I'm sure that we shall soon discover the reason.'

The following Saturday night, having read several pieces from the latest Courant for the delectation of his audience, Mister Tobin interrupted his discourse in order to dispense refreshments to a number of his patrons whose thirst had been stimulated by the reports of which they had been appraised. Meanwhile, he left the paper - perhaps inadvertently, but certainly ill-advisedly, as events turned out - in full view. One of those present, an educated fellow, well versed in reading, with an eye for a possible scandal and, assuredly, a hint of devilment in his heart, seized the opportunity to take his own turn at proclaiming the news and, picking up the journal, recited from it the report of a decision of the magistrates' court which did not stand to the credit of the publican.

It went as follows (I hope I have recorded it correctly): *Mr Elias Tobin, publican of the Flying Horse Tavern in the Groatmarket, was fined 20 guineas for using camomile flowers instead of hops for the purpose of embittering his beer. The Act of Queen Anne in respect of malt liquor directs that a fine of 20 guineas shall be applied for using broom, wormwood or another ingredient as a substitute for hops.*

There was immediate uproar in the place. Those who had patronised the establishment regularly (of whom there were a considerable number), upon hearing that the ale which they had consumed at the price of thrupence a pint was in fact a simulation, were outraged. They turned upon the publican, loudly demanding the return of their money. For his part, Mister Tobin, not only furious that his role as lector-in-chief had been usurped but, worse still, humiliated that word of his misdemeanour had gained an even wider readership than the newspaper's normal circulation would have achieved, at first flushed deeply with mortification then, regaining himself, declared sternly that the Flying Horse Tavern was henceforth out-of-bounds to all those present, threatening to summon the Town Guard to arrest them unless the premises were evacuated within five minutes. However, most customers stood their ground, averring that they had been tricked into purchasing a drink which purported to be prepared with hops but which, they now learned, was in fact a concoction containing a much inferior ingredient.

In fairness, it must be admitted that many of the protestors had on several previous occasions professed – even boasted - to be connoisseurs of any alcoholic beverage which was put in front of them and were now themselves deeply embarrassed to be exposed as charlatans. In fact, I heard it whispered later by at least one such person that the illegal product possessed a much more agreeable taste than its legal counterpart and was to be commended. It was, he said, the deceit perpetrated by His Satanic Majesty which was to be condemned.

Nevertheless, the publican carried out his threat and sent his son to call for assistance. Within a few minutes, the lad had come across a patrol of watchmen, accompanied by a constable, who were walking their beat along the Keyside in anticipation of possible disturbances caused by drunks or prostitutes or on the lookout for young boys trundling their hoops and thereby creating a serious risk of injury to the shins of other pedestrians. The constable, perhaps hoping for the offer of refreshment in the Flying Horse Tavern, immediately ordered his men into action in response to young Master Tobin's request, 'To rescue His Satanic Majesty from the mob which is threatening a riot,' as he put it, rather hysterically.

*

The short one was becoming increasingly anxious. He had been waiting in the White Hart Inn for well over an hour and the tall one had still not returned from his rendezvous with Doctor Stickler. Now he was beginning to feel a little light-headed on account of all the ale he had consumed. He hoped that nothing had gone wrong with their business arrangement. They had already lost one of their customers when that fat, pompous boor from Seaton Delaval who supplied some of the medical students with the bodies which they sold to him recently announced that he had found what he described as 'an alternative source' and no longer required their services. A rival gang, presumably. They could not afford to lose another key customer. That was why they had spent the last two nights working long hours in graveyards in filthy weather and were feeling quite exhausted. He was pretty certain that Doctor Stickler would be delighted with the four cadavers they had obtained for him at eight guineas apiece. After all, he had told them that they only had to guarantee one a week (although, admittedly, they had then rather foolishly indicated that they might be able to provide twice that number).

The tall one arrived at last, breathless and dishevelled. The short one didn't need to ask if the news was bad. His companion's face said it all.

'He's double-crossed us,' he snarled.

'What?'

'Doctor Stickler's double-crossed us.'

'But we've got him four stiffs.'

'It divvent matter. He wouldn't take 'em. Said he canna rely on us any more. Said that we'd missed out last week so he's breaking off wor contract.' It was true that they had failed to provide Doctor Stickler with a cadaver the previous week.

'What we ganna do with 'em? We canna put 'em back.'

'Have to let 'em rot, unless we can find someone else to take 'em off wor hands.'

'We could try that Delaval again …'

'Ha! Ye knaa what Aa think… Aa think that Stickler's got a new supplier… And Aa think the new supplier is Delaval.'

'So we've been set up by both of 'em, is that what ye're saying?'

'Aa asked Stickler straight out about Delaval. He denied it but Aa could tell he was lying.'

'So we've lost wor thirty-two guineas and we've got four cadavers we divvent want.'

'Exactly.'

'What we ganna do about it? We canna just leave it.'

'We'll take wor revenge on him.'

'Revenge? What d'ye mean?'

'Aa'll tell ye what Aa mean. Aa reckon that there'll be someone at the Barber-Surgeons' Hall who will be very interested to know what Doctor Stickler's been getting up to, divvent ye think?'

*

During my first few months of my apprenticeship, Doctor Stickler spent many hours in the Anatomy Room with his cadavers and forbade me admittance except on particular occasions when he wished to impart some important piece of information or demonstrate some technique relevant to my study. He often railed against the apothecaries who occupied the Dispensary in Low Friar Chare and reminded me sternly of the prohibition on apprentices having any dealings with them, on pain of expulsion from the Barber-Surgeons' Hall.

It therefore caused me great concern when I was informed by the janitor one morning that another package had been left for me. Guessing at what sort of thing it might contain, I waited until I was good distance away from the building before daring to open it. Inside was a tiny round box with a label which read *Essential Botanical Cerate Pills* and two sheets of paper. The smaller sheet had a printed heading *The Dispensary, St John's Lodge, Low Friar Chare, Newcastle-on-Tyne* and, below it, a message written in a familiar spidery scrawl. *Another humble offering to my very good friend Master James Maclachlan from your very good friend Septimus Grymm (Grymm by name, but not Grymm by nature).* The larger sheet contained what was described as a commendation from Doctor Augustus Granby of Harley-street, London, and written in a different, more orderly, script which read as follows: *This formulation is greatly worthy of the attention of the afflicted. It is uncommonly effective against all venereal complaints, especially onanism and gonorrhoea. Proven to ease the pain of scorbutic eruptions and very speedily heal them. Reduces madness and soothes overpowered nerves. Universally esteemed for its extraordinary efficacy in palsies and gouty affections as well as complaints of the liver, the green sickness and disorders incident to young females.*

I spent the whole night unable to sleep, desperately worried at the possibility that my relationship with the oily apothecary would be exposed to the scrutiny of the authorities in the Barber-Surgeons' Hall and wracked with indecision as to whether it would be preferable to report my involvement to the Searchers in the hope that an acknowledgement of guilt would secure me a lesser punishment than expulsion from the College. After I had passed many hours listening only to the snoring of my fellow students and the half-hourly cries of the patrolling night-watch Charlies proclaiming the time and the weather, the first light of dawn found me exhausted by both my anxiety and my lack of sleep. By then, I had reached the conclusion that a voluntary confession on my part represented too much of a risk in view of the fact that my discussions with the man Grymm and my acceptance of his gifts might be adjudged by the powers-that-be to constitute four breaches of the regulations - a degree of transgression which could hardly be treated leniently.

Consequently, I devoted my next midday perambulation to the disposal of the contents of this second package and managed to rid myself of them in the same manner and at the same location as I had done the first. As I stood on the bridge, looking down at the swirling waters of the River Tyne, I vowed there and then to have no further dealings with Mister Grymm.

26

'At our last meeting, it was my sad duty to bring news of the terrible deaths of those on the slave ship *Zong*,' Mister Hadwen Bragg said, although in reality the assembled members of the Newcastle Society for Effecting the Abolition of the Slave Trade needed no reminding. 'On that occasion, we agreed that I would take up the matter with our Member of Parliament, Felix Brandling, with the hope that he would impress upon the Government the need for urgent action to address these continuing outrages. I carried out thy wishes expeditiously, but I regret to report that my representations and protests to Mister Brandling were rejected. Indeed, he received them not merely with a deaf ear but even with outright hostility to the idea that the trade in human cargo could in any way be considered unethical or reprehensible ...'

At these words, the meeting erupted with a torrent of remonstrations.

'Shocking ...'

'The man is an absolute disgrace ...'

'Scandalous ...'

'He's not fit to sit in Parliament ...'

Hadwen Bragg waited until the uproar had subsided. 'Now, it is with equal regret that I have to inform thee that I have received word from the Plymouth chapter of our Society of yet another scandal concerning our African brothers and sisters who were being transported in the *Brooks*, another Liverpool slave ship.' He picked up a pile of leaflets from the table beside him, handed them to a man sitting in the front row and said, 'I would be obliged if thee would distribute these to our colleagues, Reverend.' Then he resumed his address.

'If there were ever any lingering doubts about the appalling conditions endured by those incarcerated on slave ships, this diagram should dispel them once and for all. Before thee is a plan of the method by which slaves are stowed on the decks of the *Brooks* when they are taken from Africa to the West Indies. The image increases in its horror when it is realised that the arrangement it portrays is in accordance with the Regulated Slave Trade Act passed by Parliament less than twenty years ago. In the case of the *Brooks*, the Act permits the owners to carry a maximum of four hundred and fifty slaves, whereas previously the ship used to carry six hundred.

'We have heard accounts of how as many as one in five of what the ship-owners refer to as their *live cargo* fail to survive the crossing of the Atlantic. This figure, while shameful, is hardly surprising when one considers the conditions in which the slaves are transported. Indeed, one may wonder by what miracle so many manage to cling on to their lives in the face of such inhumanity. As thee observe in this diagram, the wretched souls are packed tight with barely the space to move their limbs, their feet bound together and their arms chained to their neighbour's. There they lie in the suffocating atmosphere, surrounded by a loathsome stench, bathed in perspiration from the daytime heat and shivering from the night chill, gulping air which is unfit to breathe while, all around, the shrieks of women, the cries of children and the groans of the sick and dying add to their torments. If this was not enough to endure, they also suffer regular whippings for refusing to eat the meagre fare they are offered, or for begging for more food or for no better reason than the mere entertainment of their captors. And during the two and a half months of the voyage, dysentery and disease becomes rife throughout this miserable congregation …'

'It is clear to me,' Reverend Moises commented, 'that an Act designed to regulate the number of slaves which can be transported on any particular ship merely confers the status of legality upon this hideous business and gives succour to those who would defend its perpetuation.'

'Hear, hear,' shouted another. 'The only way forward is to outlaw it completely.'

'We must ensure that the thousands who have died have not done so in vain,' said a third.

'Thousands?' a fourth riposted. 'Tens or hundreds of thousands, I'll vouch.'

'We must make this a turning point for our cause,' Hadwen Bragg declared, seizing the mood of the meeting. 'I see no advantage in approaching our MP again or merely expressing our disgust at this trade which so debauches men's souls. We need to demonstrate such a magnitude of opposition to it that our Government is no longer able to ignore the groundswell of public opinion and is compelled to legislate to abolish the trade in slaves and to restore some vestige of Christian values and decency to our kingdom's commercial life.'

And so it was that the Newcastle Society for Effecting the Abolition of the Slave Trade, in collaboration with like-minded organisations throughout the length and breadth of the country, initiated a nationwide campaign to collect the signatures of as many of its citizens as shared a desire to see an end to the trafficking of human beings with a view to presenting to Parliament a petition, the size of which its Members could not disregard.

*

Naturally, Aeneas Snitterby never had the slightest intention of honouring the promise he made to Martha Scuffins to settle her and her children in a good home. The primary reason that he had bid for, and won, her in the auction was to spite and humiliate her husband Jasper, the chief spokesman and troublemaker of the keelmen whose ridiculous demands were threatening the commerce on the Tyne and the profits of the Hoastmen.

Once he had taken the wretched woman to collect her two children from the stinking chares of Sandgate, he deposited them in one of his cottages which had recently been vacated by a pitman consequent upon the latter's fatal injuries sustained in the winding gear of a shaft at Snitterby's Wylam Moor colliery. The cottage was in an advanced state of dilapidation but Martha did not complain about its condition, having been assured by her supposed patron that her stay there was strictly temporary, by which she assumed he meant that the family would shortly be transferred to more salubrious accommodation. Within a few days, however, the temporary nature of her residence became evident when Aeneas Snitterby dispatched one of his agents to inform Martha that the cottage was now required for a new employee who had been taken on as a replacement at the colliery and that she and her children would have to leave by the weekend.

Poor Martha was at her wits' end. She faced the imminent prospect of being thrown out onto the street with a two-year-old and a virtually newborn baby, without food, money or warm clothing and in a part of town with which she was totally unfamiliar, a prey to all kind of villains, scoundrels and rogues. (Such types, of course, also abounded in Sandgate but, when she lived there, Martha enjoyed the protection of being the wife of Jasper Scuffins so that nobody dared to harm a hair of her head.) She knew that they would not be welcome at the church in Pipewellgate to which she had fled the previous week as its doors were open only to single women and the rector's wife had no affection at all for children, Martha having heard her ranting several times, 'Aa'll not have any bairns here, with their pissing and shitting aal ower the place.'

The Keelmen's Hospital would be the place where she would normally have expected to live once her husband, through death, infirmity or old age was no longer able to support her. But she realised, of course, that this option was now completely out of the question. She was sure that Jasper would use his considerable powers of intimidation and bullying to prevent the warden admitting her to that establishment. And even in the unlikely event that she *was* allowed in, she would have to face the probability of coming into regular contact with her husband (or her *ex*-husband as she now preferred to think of him).

The only other alternative which offered some degree of shelter was the Poorhouse. However, Martha knew that no woman who had enjoyed the status of the wife of a Tyne keelman (regardless of how loathsome and insufferable that keelman might be) could possibly countenance the absolute shame of throwing herself upon the mercy of such an institution. Such a fall from grace would be unthinkable, regardless of how blameless the woman was. What if Cuckoo Jack and his wife should discover that she and the children had ended up in such an appalling place? She was sure that if that happened, she would have to kill herself, rather than endure the ignominy. No, she decided, although she had very little to call her own, she *did* still have her self-esteem. So she could not possibly go to the Poorhouse. Instead, she would have to find a way to rent somewhere for them to live, however primitive it might be.

She possessed only one item of value which she could perhaps use to raise some money. Beyond that, the only other way she could see of easing her family's lot was something which she could not bear to contemplate.

*

Newcastle Courant

GENERAL HUE AND CRY

Whereas an anonymous Letter with Contents of an outrageous and minatory Nature was put under the Door of Mister Felix Brandling MP of Gosforth House, near Bulman Village, where the same was found on the Morning of the 14th instant,

His Majesty King George, for the better apprehending and bringing to Justice the Person or Persons concerned in writing and sending the aforesaid Letter, is hereby pleased to promise his most gracious Pardon to any one of them (excepting the Person or Persons who actually wrote the same) who shall discover his or their Accomplice or Accomplices therein, so that he, she or they may be apprehended and convicted thereof.

And, as further Encouragement, a Reward of ONE HUNDRED GUINEAS is hereby offered by the said Mister Felix Brandling MP to any Person making such Discovery as aforesaid (excepting as is before excepted) to be paid on the Conviction of one or more of the Offenders.

---

*

Walter Humble, Pawnbroker, occupied premises near the head of Fenkell-street. For some weeks, business had been very slack and his social life was no better. He had never managed to persuade a woman to be his wife nor even to share his bed and now at the age of forty-five he was well past his best and still unmarried. He badly needed a change of luck.

He was at the back of the shop counting out the morning's meagre takings and reviewing the collection of pledges he had received and which he doubted would attract many buyers when the tinkling of the bell signalled the arrival of a customer. A woman entered, someone Walter Humble had not seen before so far as he could recall, around about thirty years old, he guessed, not a great beauty but handsome enough to stir the loins of a man like himself in search of a wife but without any major aspirations. She appeared to be very nervous and he deduced (quite correctly, as it turned out) that she was unaccustomed to having any dealings with a business such as his and was a person whose self-esteem militated against the concept of loaning one's property to a stranger for a return which was so inordinately small as to be humiliating.

She handed him a tiny pill-box. 'It's gold,' she said.

He opened the box and found a ring nestling inside.

'It's my wedding ring,' she said eagerly, cognisant of the fact that it was the only thing of value which her husband had ever given her.

The pawnbroker picked up the ring and examined it, then turned to the woman and, not wishing to distress her but mindful of his own straitened circumstances, explained gently, 'I'm very sorry, madam, but it's not gold.' He looked at the sadness in her eyes and added, 'I can let you have a guinea for it.'

'A guinea? Is that all?' Her tears welled up with disappointment at the miserly sum which the wedding ring would fetch and realisation of the deceit which her husband had visited upon her by lying about its provenance.

She returned two days later, this time with her hood pulled down across her face and her voice disguised, not wanting to be recognised as a previous customer. Rather than seeking to reclaim the pledge which she had pawned on her last visit, she deposited a bundle of clothes on the counter and asked to be informed of the loan which they would attract. Walter Humble unwrapped the bundle and inspected the contents carefully, observing that the clothes, although not new, were well-maintained, clean and presentable. Accordingly, he announced that he would be prepared to advance her the sum of fifteen shillings on the goods.

'Thanking ye nicely, sir,' the woman said, 'but Aa canna let them gan for that.'

The pawnbroker watched as she repacked the bundle of clothes with great precision as if to emphasise the value of the items, perhaps hoping to persuade Walter Humble to increase his offer. Receiving no further proposition, she called out, 'Aa'll be on me way, then,' and left the shop.

Hardly a minute passed before the doorbell rang again and the woman returned. 'Aa've had a long think about what ye said ye'd pay me,' she announced. 'Aa've decided to accept yer kind offer.' She placed the bundle on the counter, took the money and left once again, apparently in a great hurry.

Walter Humble picked up the bundle, intending to take it into the storeroom at the rear of the shop, when he heard a strange noise emanating from it, a sound rather like the mewing of a kitten. He found this a most surprising occurrence, particularly considering how carefully he had examined the bundle only a short while ago. Unwrapping the outer layers of clothing, just as he had done previously but this time with even greater assiduousness, he was astonished to discover the presence of a tiny infant which beamed coyly up at him. It took him a few moments before he realised that the woman had performed a hoax upon him in order to relieve herself of guardianship of the child by preparing two apparently identical bundles of clothes and then substituting one for the other during her brief absence from his premises. He rushed to the door and looked up and down the street but there was no sign of her.

27

'I don't mind telling you, Snitterby, but that letter has fair put the wind up me.' Felix Brandling's nervous tic was working overtime as he continued his rant. 'As if I haven't got enough trouble already having to deal with that damn Hadwen Bragg and his gang of slavery abolitionists protesting at every opportunity and calling me immoral. Doesn't a man have the right in this day and age to carry on a perfectly harmless business without being subjected to that kind of criticism? And now, along comes an anonymous threat to kill me. I've never been the target of that kind of intimidation before, not even from the slaves when I'm on a tour of inspection of my estates in the West Indies.'

'I shouldn't take it too seriously, Brandling. It's probably just been sent by one of the keelmen who's drunk too much of that savage beer they've complained about and thinks he can scare the Member of Parliament for Newcastle into giving in to their ridiculous demands.'

'All very well for you to sound so unconcerned about it. I bet you've never been threatened with your life, have you, Snitterby?'

'On the contrary, it happens all the time in the courts, my flatulent friend,' Snitterby replied unwisely, causing Brandling to cough, leading in turn to a volley of mephitic emanations and their concomitant sound effects. The magistrate pretended not to notice and continued with his anecdote. 'I've come to expect that whenever I send some convicted criminal off to Newgate Gaol or on a trip to Botany Bay, I'll receive a string of abuse and a promise that I'll end up in some filthy alley with my throat cut and my innards spilt in the dust. Anyway, have the constables come up with an idea of who's responsible? It certainly isn't a professor of English, is it?'

'Ha! They say that it was not done by a man's hand. They think it's a woman that wrote the letter. And what's more, they think that it was written by the same person who wrote the handbills that the keelmen have been distributing throughout the town.'

'Very interesting. A woman, eh? Very interesting indeed. Even more reason for you not to worry about it then. You're not frightened of a woman, are you, Brandling?'

'Be that as it may,' Brandling said, studiously avoiding the question, 'I think it's high time we put an end to this strike, don't you? All this violence sickens me. And every day that it continues is losing us money.'

'Well, we're going to have to make some concessions to get the men back to work, you know.'

'What have you got in mind, Snitterby ?

'Nothing too generous. Just enough to make them realise that there is nothing more to be gained by continuing to bring the whole of the coal trade on the Tyne to a standstill. We know that a lot of the keelmen are being pressed by their families to start bringing home some money again. They're beginning to realise that there's a limit to how long an adherence to their principles will feed their bellies.'

'Of course, you could always issue arrest warrants for any men who refuse the mayor's instruction to return to work.'

'Yes, I could. But the problem, Brandling, is this. Who would execute the warrants? The constables couldn't cope with those numbers and we certainly can't rely on the town militia – they're an undisciplined rabble. We'd have to ask the Government to call out the troops again and there's no knowing where that would all end. And, anyway, where are we going to incarcerate eight hundred keelmen? No, we need a settlement to the dispute.'

'Perhaps we could offer a small increase in pay. One shilling a tide, let's say.'

'A shilling for each man, you mean?'

'No, no. I haven't taken leave of my senses. A shilling a tide for each keel. And maybe a lump sum for their charity – the Keelmen's Hospital. Two hundred and fifty pounds sounds like a munificent donation, don't you think?'

'I can't imagine that they'll be very happy with that, if you want my opinion. But I've got something else in mind that might persuade our friend Scuffins to agree a deal.'

'Oh, what's that, Snitterby?'

But Snitterby did not reply. Instead he held a finger to his lips as if to indicate that he dare not breathe a word of his plan to anyone.

*

She had gone only two or three hundred yards from the pawnbroker's in Fenkell-street when the enormity of what she had just done suddenly overwhelmed her and she collapsed onto the ground in a flood of tears. There were several pedestrians in the vicinity as well as drivers of pony shays and street vendors transporting their wares to the market-places in dogcarts, but nobody came to Martha Scuffins' aid nor, indeed, deigned to take any notice of the wretched woman. She lay in the dust, a despondent figure, contemplating whether, in order to bring an end to her miserable existence, she should throw herself into the river or under the post coach. Eventually, she decided upon the former, picked herself up and headed along Westgate-street in the direction of the Keyside, where she planned to meet her maker. When she reached the junction with Pilgrim-street she became confused, perhaps because of the despair into which she had been plunged and, despite the fact that she knew the area well, she mistakenly turned north instead of south.

Her error proved to be a providential one, for she had walked for scarcely another two minutes before she came upon a large clothing emporium, in the entrance of which an elderly gentleman who sported a shiny bald head, voluminous white whiskers and friendly, twinkling eyes stood under a sign which bore the words *Bragg and Company*.

He addressed Martha in a voice replete with compassion, concern and kindness. 'Madam, I see that thee are in a state of great distress. Pray, permit me to assist thee in any way I can.'

'Ye canna help me, sir. Aa've done a terrible thing,' Martha replied, her words interspersed with convulsions of sobbing.

'Come, come now, madam. I'm sure that thee have done nothing which cannot be put right.'

'Aa'm doomed to Hell for what Aa've done,' she wailed pitifully.

'The Lord forgives everything, madam. And everyone of his flock. Thee will not go to Hell if thee repent.'

'He'll not forgive *me*, sir. Not for what Aa've done.' She seemed inconsolable.

'What *have* thee done, madam? Give me the chance to help thee, won't thou?'

'Aa've abandoned my bairn, that's what Aa've done, sir. My poor little bairn. Aa've abandoned him.'

'Please, madam,' he coaxed her gently. 'Why don't thee come inside and tell me what has happened?'

'Aa've done a terrible thing,' Martha repeated, shaking her head violently and releasing a shower of tears on to Hadwen

Bragg's waistcoat. But she allowed him to take her hand, guide her inside the shop and lead her to a chair where she sat weeping uncontrollably for several minutes.

At last she began to regain a little of her composure, enough at least for her to describe in halting tones, interrupted by frequent outbursts of howling, the terrible thing it was that she had done. And so, bit by bit, Hadwen Bragg was able to piece together the account of how the woman was due to be evicted from the place at which she was staying with her two children. Realising that she no longer had the means to care or provide for them or to protect them from the inevitability of destitution, she had left the older one there and taken the younger one, who was only a few weeks old, to the pawnbroker, whom she had tricked into taking the baby by concealing him inside a bundle of clothes.

'How long ago was it that thee left the pawnbroker's shop?' Hadwen Bragg asked, a plan already forming in his mind.

'Maybe a half-hour or more, sir,' Martha replied.

'Come, madam, let us hasten there. We may yet be in time,' he urged and the two hurried back down Pilgrim-street, along Westgate-street and arrived, both breathless from their exertions, at the premises of Walter Humble in Fenkell-street.

'Please wait here one moment, madam, while I speak with my friend, Mister Humble, to appraise him of thy circumstances,' Hadwen Bragg said. 'I'm sure that he will be most understanding.' He pushed open the door, causing the bell to ring and the pawnbroker, alerted by the sound, came to the front of the shop, still carrying the squawking bundle.

'Good day to thee, Mister Humble,' Hadwen Bragg greeted him. 'I believe that a most unexpected pledge has recently come into thy possession.'

'How on earth do you know that?' Mister Humble replied, astonished at his visitor's insightfulness, whereupon Hadwen Bragg described his encounter with Martha Scuffins and the woman's tale of woe.

'She has suffered greatly and is most distraught at her behaviour in having given up her baby through a deception. She wishes to redeem the articles left in thy care and I will reimburse what she owes thee. I beg thee, Mister Humble, to treat her with consideration.'

Mister Humble was at heart a kind man and his sympathy for the plight of the poor woman was almost as great as the relief he felt at his discovery that he would not, after all, be left as the sole guardian of a tiny infant. He nodded to indicate his acquiescence to Hadwen Bragg's request.

'Splendid,' Hadwen Bragg said. He opened the door, setting off the bell again, and beckoned to Martha to step inside. She entered apprehensively at first, her face tense with anxiety, but when she saw the baby she rushed forward and took it from the pawnbroker's outstretched arms, bursting into tears (this time, of joy) as she did so, then smothering the tiny child with kisses. 'I have asked Mister Humble to return thy pledges and he has kindly consented to do so without payment from thee,' Hadwen Bragg told her.

'Thank ye, sir. Most generous, sir,' Martha said to the pawnbroker, wiping away tears. 'And Aa'm truly sorry for aal the trouble Aa've caused ye, sir.'

'I assure you, madam, it was no trouble,' Mister Humble replied, graciously. 'No trouble at all.' He placed the wedding ring and the bundle of clothes on the counter and said, 'If I may, madam, I have a suggestion to make. A proposal, you might call it. One which will enable us to put this to use.' He pointed to the ring.

'Aa dinaa understand, sir, ' Martha said, gently rocking the baby, which was now fast asleep in her arms.

'Well, madam, it occurs to me that *you* are a lady with two young children but no husband or home to call your own. And it also occurs to me that *I* am a man with a house and a humble business (he often employed that play on his name) but no wife or children to call my own.' He let that sink in for a few moments before posing his question. 'How convenient and to our mutual benefit might it be if we should agree to combine forces, as it were?'

Martha was not immediately sure that she had correctly discerned the implications of the pawnbroker's analysis. 'Ye mean that ye're offering to marry me?' she said, shocked at the man's frankness.

'On the contrary, madam,' he replied. '*I* am asking *you* to marry *me*.'

Her mind was a whirl. Barely an hour had passed since she was on her way to commit suicide and liberate herself once and for all from her misery. Now, here she was on the verge of matrimony, with the prospect of a life of reasonable comfort for herself and her children, shared with a man who, so far as she could ascertain on the basis of such a brief acquaintance, seemed to be passably adequate as a prospective husband. She decided that she had better agree to his proposal before she woke up and found it was all a dream.

'Well, Aa suppose Aa will accept,' she said at last. Then, remembering the need for formalities, added, 'My name's Martha, by the way.'

'And I'm Walter. Walter Humble,' said the pawnbroker unnecessarily, since Martha had seen his name emblazoned above the entrance on each of the three occasions she had visited the premises.

'Well, then, congratulations to thee both,' Hadwen Bragg exclaimed, surprised and delighted in equal measure at the gratifying outcome of the couple's encounter and the speed with which it was achieved. 'And, if the two of thee would care to call in to my store in Pilgrim-street at thy convenience, it will be my pleasure to ensure that thee are suitably fitted out for thy nuptials.'

28

After Jasper Scuffins received a message, read out by Kitty Dace, inviting him to another meeting with the Hoastmen, he arrived at the Mansion House expecting to be confronted with the same dozen or so smug-looking, wealthy coal-owners who had attended on each of the previous occasions. Instead, he found Aeneas Snitterby sitting alone in the Mayor's Parlour in one of the large red leather-clad armchairs, toasting his feet in front of a roaring fire.

'A very good day to you, Mister Scuffins.' The magistrate greeted his guest in a jovial manner which immediately raised the latter's misgivings. 'Please help yourself to a seat. I've ordered coffee for the two of us.'

'Two?' Scuffins said, guardedly. 'Where's aal the others?'

'I thought it might be a little more, er …' – he grasped for the apposite word and selected it carefully – '… *constructive,* if it's just you and I today, Mister Scuffins. I believe we can make a bit more progress without involving the rest of the Company.'

Scuffins eyed him suspiciously. 'Aa divvent knaa what ye mean by that, Mister Snitterby. We've made wor demands and we stick by 'em. Nowt more, nowt less.'

'I understand your position completely, Mister Scuffins. Completely. And I'm sure that you understand ours. Some of the things that you keelmen are asking for are quite out of the question. If we were to agree to them, we'd be out of business by the end of the year. And, consequently, you keelmen would be out of your jobs too. So what, pray, would be the sense in that, eh?'

'Aa haven't come here for a lecture, Mister Snitterby. If that's aal ye have to say to me, Aa'd best be ganning on me way directly.'

'Come, come, Mister Scuffins. It's not my wish to lecture you, I assure you. I'm here to make you a fair offer.'

'An offer, you say?'

They were interrupted briefly by the arrival of a blushing maid carrying a tray of coffee, which she deposited on a side table before curtseying to Snitterby, glancing across at Scuffins with a puzzled frown (not having seen his like before in such a setting) and hurrying from the room.

'Well now, Mister Scuffins …' Snitterby cleared his throat loudly before picking up the thread of the conversation. '… On behalf of the Company of Hoastmen, I am prepared to make you a proposal of an increase of a shilling per tide for each keel, to be distributed among the crew as the skipper thinks fit.' He could tell from Scuffins' expression that the man was unimpressed, so he added, 'That means, of course, that as skipper of a keel you could keep the full shilling for yourself.' Then, in response to Scuffins' look of utter disdain, he concluded meekly, 'Or you could always share it with the others, if you prefer.'

'That's only fourpence a man,' Scuffins snarled. 'And nowt for the peedee. Aa'll wager ye would spend that in a half-hour, Mister Snitterby.'

'That's not our only offer,' Snitterby hurried to assure him. 'We're also willing to donate the sum of two hundred and fifty pounds for the upkeep of the Keelmen's Hospital …' He repeated the figure, this time more slowly, hoping that the emphasis he put on each of the words would enhance its value in Scuffins' estimation.

Scuffins sat mumchance for some time, his face creased in a scowl. At length he spoke, rising slowly from his chair. 'Aa think that Aa've been wasting me time coming here today, Mister Snitterby. Aa've heard nowt that would persuade us to get back to wor work.'

Snitterby could see that the keelman was on the point of leaving so he said quickly, 'Wait, Mister Scuffins, you haven't heard the third part of my offer yet. I think that you'll be very satisfied by it. Very satisfied indeed.'

By now, Scuffins was halfway out of the room and in the process of putting on his hat. At Snitterby's words, he hesitated slightly, turned round and growled, 'What's the third part of the offer?'

'Please, come and sit down and let me explain,' Snitterby said gently.

With some reluctance, Scuffins did as he was bade, staring at Snitterby with a mixture of contempt and cynicism.

'Now, please, hear me out, Mister Scuffins, because what I have to say to you is something to which I, personally, have given serious consideration in an attempt to restore good relations between us. Do you understand what I am saying?'

'Since ye bought me lass and wor bairns at the auction in the Fleshmarket, ye mean?'

'Well, I suppose so, but there's more to it than that, as I will shortly explain to you.'

'Ye better make yarsel plain, Mister Snitterby.'

'Yes, of course. Now let me ask you this. What is your opinion of the off-putters who work for us on the staithes?'

'What do Aa think of 'em, ye say? That's a rum question.'

'Nevertheless, I'd like to hear your opinion.'

'Well, then, ye can have me opinion but Aa dinaa expect ye to like it.' He took a swig of coffee and wiped his mouth with the back of his hand. 'Aa hate 'em. They cheat us keelmen. They deliberately delay the loading so they can charge us extra for using the spouts. Otherwise, we'll miss the tide. Then they cheat us again by overmeasuring so we end up with a canny bit more than eight chaldrons in wor keel. We divvent get extra money for that but the off-putters get a pay-off from the shipmasters. That's why we hate 'em. And while we keelmen are breaking wor backs, the off-putters divvent even have to pick up a shovel. They just stand there with their ticket-book, issuing orders to their staithesmen, watching us sweat and grind. And there's other fiddles ganning on too. Sometimes they forge the tickets to show that the coal comes from the best quality seams so they can charge the shipmasters a higher price. And ye Hoastmen … ye are on the fiddle as well. Aa knaa aal about that, ye divvent need to deny it.'

Snitterby gave the slightest of nods, just sufficient to acknowledge Scuffins' last comment but not enough to appear to agree with it. 'So, what you're telling me, Mister Scuffins, is that the off-putters have got an easy life and make a lot of extra money that they're not entitled to.'

'That's what Aa said.'

'Can I ask how old you are, Mister Scuffins?'

'Aa divvent knaa why that's yer business but Aa'm not ashamed to say that Aa'm coming round to my fortieth before the summer's out.'

'The reason I'm asking you is this. I know that the work of a keelman is tough. Very tough. There aren't many of you that make it much past forty without finding that it's too difficult to continue. That's why the Keelmen's Hospital is pretty nearly full to capacity.'

'Where's aal this leading to, Mister Snitterby?'

'Let me come straight to the point, Mister Scuffins.'

'It's about time ye did.'

'Well, now, one of my off-putters, the fellow at the Benwell staithes, had an accident recently. A most unfortunate accident. You might have heard about it? …' He broke off to give Scuffins a look full of meaning. '… He isn't going to recover very soon. Maybe he never will. So there's a vacancy. A vacancy for a man who knows the river, a man who can command others to do his bidding, a man who would like a job which doesn't require much manual labour, a job which doesn't involve working fourteen or fifteen hours a day, a job he could probably do until he's well into his fifties, a job which would provide him with a decent wage and the chance to make some … well … bonuses, shall we say. In other words, Mister Scuffins – Jasper, may I call you? – I'm on the lookout for a man I could trust.' He stared directly at Scuffins and fixed him with a conspiratorial smile. 'Do I make myself plain?'

'So you're offering me employment as an off-putter on the Benwell staithes. Is that it, Mister Snitterby?' Scuffins said after a long pause.

'That's it exactly, Jasper. What do you say?'

'There's gotta be a catch somewhere.'

'There's no catch. I just want you to use your influence to convince your keelmen colleagues that our proposals for the rise in pay and the donation to your charity are fair and reasonable and that they should accept them and return to work.'

'Ha! So that's it! Ye want me to get the men to give up wor strike. And if they do, Aa'll get me new job.'

'Seems a fair deal, doesn't it?'

'And what if they refuse? Do Aa still get the job?'

'I'm sure I can rely on you, Jasper, to make them see sense. After all, they've had no wages for over a month now. And what's the point of putting the families through even more privation when there's extra money on offer as soon as they're back on the river?'

'So ye think that ye can bribe me to do yer dirty work for ye, Mister Snitterby? Bribe me to betray me fellow watermen? Is that it? How's that ganna gan down in Sandgate?'

'Bribe is a harsh word, Jasper. A very harsh word. I'm merely offering you an opportunity – a *golden* opportunity – to improve your life with a more pleasant, better-paid job. And you won't need to worry about living in Sandgate anymore. I have some properties in Elswick, one of which a single man such as yourself would, I'm sure, find extremely congenial. And what's more, it's quite near to where your children currently reside, as it so happens, should you wish to resume your acquaintance with them.'

'Near the bairns, ye say?'

'Less than a half-mile away.'

'And their mam?'

'I believe that Mrs Scuffins – the former Mrs Scuffins, I should say - lives with the children and has recently found herself a new husband. Quite bigamously, of course, but that's hardly any of my business, is it?'

Scuffins looked shocked at this news, but quickly recovered to enquire, 'So does that mean that if she was reported to the Justices – such as yarsel, Mister Snitterby – she could hang for bigamy?' The possibility appeared to have cheered him up considerably.

'That very much depends on the circumstances. As long as a woman has been absent from her husband for seven years and then remarries, the courts would not consider it a capital felony. But if, let us just suppose for the sake of illustration, her first husband had sold her to another man, then I think it most unlikely that the law would look upon her as deserving of further punishment, however much - or little - time had passed.' Seeing the expression on Scuffins' face that indicated the man's exasperation at this response, Snitterby added, 'Sorry to disappoint you, old chap.'

The keelman lowered his chin on to his chest and lapsed into silence for a while, as if caught in a terrible dilemma and contemplating the best way to extricate himself from it. At length, Snitterby leaned forward until the two men's faces were just inches apart and whispered, 'Well, Jasper, what do you say to my proposal?'

Scuffins jerked his head up quickly and said, 'How do Aa know Aa can trust ye? What's to stop ye ganning back on yer word?'

'I am an honourable man, Mister Scuffins. How dare you doubt me,' Snitterby bellowed, with affected indignation. 'If you do as I ask, I will keep to my side of the bargain. Once the men are back to work, we'll wait a few weeks so that it doesn't look too suspicious and then you can move to Elswick and take up your new position. My word is my bond.' He let that sink in for a few seconds, then pressed Scuffins again for an answer.

'Aa divvent knaa what to say right now,' he said. 'Aal this has caught me unawares. Aa need to think about it.'

'By all means think about it. But don't take too long, will you?' Snitterby's voice took on a harsher edge. 'I might change my mind in a day or two.'

Naturally, he never had the slightest intention of honouring the promise he had just made to Jasper Scuffins.

29

By sheer chance, I came into some money later that month. It so happened that I found myself to be in the right place at the right time.

The fratch between Mister Elias Tobin, the publican of the Flying Horse Tavern, and his customers did not outlast his remorse at the steep drop in business and theirs at the loss of the regular Saturday evening's entertainment afforded by his reading of the main news items in the *Newcastle Courant*. Indeed, within a fortnight of the unfortunate events about which I reported in an earlier chapter, the establishment was restored to its former state, accompanied by undertakings on one side to reduce the price of a quart of ale by one half-penny and on the other to refrain from referring to the unfortunate blunder in its production which had come to their attention through the medium of the newspaper's columns.

For my part, I had – thanks to the assistance rendered to me by Mister Tobin – become a favoured customer to the extent that, once his recital had finished, he would allow me to occupy a corner seat in Hell's Kitchen and read the rest of the newspaper, my literacy having improved rapidly through such opportunities to practice the skill.

On one such occasion, I noticed a dark, sturdy fellow enter the room, purchase a quart of ale at the bar and take a seat within my earshot, where he fell into conversation with one of the regulars. I was certain that, despite my frequent attendance in the Flying Horse Tavern, I had never seen him before and therefore assumed that he must be a newcomer. But, strangely, there was something about him that seemed very familiar. His face was scarred and pox-marked and had a miserable, haunted expression which rendered his appearance additionally forbidding. I guessed that he might have attempted to join the respectable customers who occupied the Printers' Room and had been refused entry, so that he ended up in Hell's Kitchen. Without intending to eavesdrop, I could not help overhearing him as he spoke in loud tones, seemingly having been already oiling his wig in other public houses and now, being a little the worse for the drink, not caring to lower his voice to a moderate level.

'Aa've bin at the market in Hexham,' he slurred. 'A canny hike from here, so Aa've got a grand thirst on me now.'

'The market, did you say?' his neighbour enquired. 'Buying or selling were you?'

'Today, Aa was selling. Selling cattle. That's what Aa do for me living, ye knaa. Buying and selling cattle.' He supped some ale and spilt a bit down his chin, which he wiped with his sleeve before continuing. 'Today Aa was selling. Next week Aa'll likely be buying. Up in the Borders. There's good cattle on yon Borders, ye knaa. That's why so many of them gets lifted.'

'Lifted?'

'Rustled,' he explained. 'By the Scotch.'

It was his habit of gripping his chin in a peculiar way that finally alerted me to the reason for his familiarity. *Discovers his jaw very much when he speaks.* I had read that description only an hour before – I was sure of it!

Turning back through the pages of the *Newcastle Courant* as casually as I could in order not to draw attention to myself or arouse suspicion, I retraced my way among its columns until I reached the announcements listed within the General Hue and Cry section of the paper. And there it was! Under the heading *FELONY: A REWARD OF TWENTY GUINEAS.*

> Whereas Claude Shivers of Newcastle-on-Tyne, aged about 45 years, 5 Feet 7 or 8 Inches high, stout made, dark Complexion, broad Face with a Scar on one Side, a little marked with the Small-Pox and a very sullen Countenance, short dark Hair turning grey, speaks the Newcastle Dialect and discovers his Jaw very much when he speaks, stands charged with the Suspicion of Felony: Whosoever will apprehend and secure the said Claude Shivers in any of His Majesty's Gaols shall receive a Reward of **TWENTY GUINEAS**, upon application to the Town Clerk's Office, over and above any other Rewards that may be payable upon his Conviction. The said Claude Shivers frequently attends Fairs and other Markets, and pretends to deal in Cattle.

I reread the paragraph carefully several times, surreptitiously glancing up as I scanned the man's description to check its accuracy until I was as certain as I could be that Claude Shivers and the fellow sitting less than ten feet away from me were one and the same person. I was overcome with excitement at the prospect of meriting a reward of twenty guineas, mixed with apprehension at the idea of confronting a dangerous fugitive from the law. I sat there, transfixed for many seconds, and at last came to a decision as to how I should proceed. Picking up the newspaper, I approached the bar, caught the eye of Mister Elias Tobin and whispered that I had urgent information to impart to him. He ushered me quickly into a private cubicle, where I showed him the newspaper article, explained my discovery and, through a gap overlooking the taproom, pointed out the man whom I deemed to be Claude Shivers. I assured Mister Tobin that since I had received the loan of his copy of the Courant, without which I would never have recognised the felon, I planned to give him an equal share of my expected reward and asked for his help in summoning a member of the Town Guard to execute the arrest.

He summed up the situation in a trice, almost as though such an event was a common occurrence and, calling his young son, sent the boy off to find a constable. And then, in an act of genius, he dispensed a quart of ale, approached the fellow I had identified as Claude Shivers and presented it to him. 'I believe you are a new customer, sir,' he said. 'I would like to welcome you to my establishment and will be most grateful if you would accept this drink on the house.' The intention of this gesture of apparent hospitality was, of course, to detain Mister Shivers on the premises for a little longer than he might otherwise have stayed, in the hope that a constable would arrive to apprehend the fellow before he sought to depart.

And it worked a treat. The rogue was still sitting there, supping his complimentary ale and oblivious to the trap that had been set for him, when not one but *four* constables burst through the door, were immediately directed to the suspected felon by the waiting publican and had the handcuffs on Claude Shivers (at least, I hoped it really *was* Claude Shivers) before he realised what was happening. Then they hauled him unceremoniously off the premises while the rest of the customers watched with a mixture of bemusement and relief that they might just have been rescued from what they imagined was a violent criminal, and perhaps even a vicious murderer.

Very early the following morning, Elias Tobin and I presented ourselves at the Town Clerk's Office in the Guild Hall to collect the reward of twenty guineas. I had never before set foot in such a distinguished establishment and was at first over-awed by the grandeur of the building whose very walls seemed to exude an aura of importance and to demand a reverential hush from those who entered. By contrast, Mister Tobin appeared completely unruffled and acted as if he felt quite at ease in such a place. He bustled past the formidable-looking woman who was guarding the entrance with the aid of a large stick, collared the doorman and demanded that he should immediately summon the Town Clerk and inform him that Messrs Maclachlan and Tobin were in attendance to receive their reward for apprehending a dangerous criminal.

However, whatsoever might have been Mister Tobin's imagined standing in the corridors of power, his demand signally failed to produce the instant appearance of the Town Clerk. Instead, we were eventually ushered into a waiting room on the ground floor. 'I'm sorry that the Town Clerk is not available to receive you this morning, gentlemen,' the doorman explained politely and with the merest trace of a smirk. 'But if you would care to wait here, somebody will be with you shortly.'

The doorman's courtesy failed to appease Mister Tobin, who boomed, '*Some*body? *Some*body?'

The surly underling who was eventually assigned to deal with our claim was unwilling to release the money without an extensively-conducted process of verification which necessitated a wait of over two hours while he checked with his superiors, during which time Mister Tobin grumbled loudly and effusively. Finally, when the fellow had exhausted his enquiries and was unable to conjure up any further excuse to deny us our due deserts, he reluctantly and begrudgingly handed over the cash, which Mister Tobin demanded he should count out three times before declaring himself satisfied with the transaction.

Twenty sparkling gold coins! I had never seen so much money in my life, let alone possessed half of it.

*

The meeting which took place at the Keelmen's Hospital was an animated, bad-tempered affair and many of those present expressed their outrage and incredulity at Jasper Scuffins' recommendation that they should accept the Hoastmen's offer as being the best that could be achieved. Several questioned how it was possible for a man who had, but two days before, urged them to stand firm until every single one of their demands had been met to the full, to have experienced such a Damascene conversion (although they may have employed other terms to describe the change in Scuffins' attitude) that his present counsel now seemed to be diametrically opposite to that which he had previously avowed.

One of them, a rowdy fellow troubled by the scurvy and with his right hand marked with the letters IP, made an impassioned speech condemning the suggestion that the keelmen should give up their struggle on such poor terms. 'Ye are a damnable traitor, Scuffins, and a disgrace to yer blue jacket,' he ranted, to the boisterous approbation of many of his colleagues. 'Aa'll nivvor call ye brother again even when Aa see ye in hell. Aa hope the cholera bursts yer guts and the spuggies peck oot yer eyes.'

In the end, it was probably the pressure from the keelwives that won the day and, on a show of hands, resulted in a narrow majority in favour of ending the strike. But the decision caused a great deal of bad feeling among the keelmen and bitter resentment between those who voted in support of a return to work and those who voted against.

By contrast, the editorial column in the following week-end's issue of the *Newcastle Courant* struck a wholly positive note concerning the outcome.

Newcastle Courant

It is with the utmost Gratification that we are at last able to inform our esteemed Readers that the unfortunate Difference of Opinion which has recently obtained between the Tyne Keelmen and the Coal-owners (or 'Hoastmen') who employ them has been brought to a happy Conclusion.

We salute the firm Resolve which typified the Conduct of the Gentlemen of the Coal Trade during the difficult Course of the Dispute. We salute the Determination with which they rightly rejected the outrageous and tumultuous Claims of the Keelmen which sought to undermine and even abolish the sacred Principles on which our valued Freedoms are based. We are delighted that Nothing that has been agreed between the Parties in order to achieve an immediate Resumption of Working implies any Interference with the most cherished and important of our constitutional Rights – the free Enjoyment of private Property and Entitlement to conduct one's Business in the most efficient Manner.

It is also extremely gratifying to note that, with the gracious Approval of the Mayor of our Town, the Corporation have expressed itself willing to offer Employment to any Keelman who has been displaced by the Efficiencies introduced by the

---

Hoastmen and wishes to work in another Capacity, so long as that Person is not among those who, during the recent Events, engaged in riotous Behaviour.

30

The first occasion on which I came across Perlee Parker was during one of the regular weekend trips that Ralph and I used to take - for old times sake, I suppose – to the Shields, where we would sit on the Spanish Battery and watch the collier-brigs being loaded, just as we did when we were youngsters. It must have been during a spell of slack water, that brief period between the departure of the ebb tide and the arrival of the flood tide when the keelmen (who had recently ended their strike) had nothing to do but wait for the current which would take them back upstream to Sandgate. They were in the habit of filling this interval by drinking and playing cards so that the taverns were, for an hour or so, teeming with thirsty, boisterous customers.

It was outside the hostelry known as the Low Lights Tavern that we happened to observe a young gentleman, not much older than ourselves, a slender, upright fellow with a fresh complexion and fair hair frizzed at the sides and tied behind, wearing a striped waistcoat, nankeen trousers and a cambric neckcloth. He was holding a sketchbook in which he was working on a drawing of a group of keelmen who, engrossed in their ale and their games of Pope Joan, seemed not to notice him. We approached the artist cautiously, not wishing to disturb his concentration, and were astonished to remark how closely the image on the paper began to resemble the living scene before us. We watched at a discreet distance as the faithful likeness emerged from the lines of the gentleman's pencil.

Eventually, the reversal of the tidal stream was complete, the keelmen returned to their boats and set off upriver and Ralph and I were left alone in the company of the artist. We were on the point of apologising for our discourtesy in observing his labour uninvited when he addressed us amicably and, having put down his sketching implements and taken a small package from his kitbag, asked whether we would care to share his luncheon with him. Thus, we quickly fell into conversation, in the course of which we learned that Perlee Parker (for that was his name, as he informed us, curious though it was, at least to my ears), had come to Newcastle from his home in the south of the country in order to visit his aunt and had liked the place so much that he had decided to try his fortune here. And indeed, far from considering our interest in his work as an intrusion, he seemed genuinely pleased to have made our acquaintance, from which I inferred that as a relative newcomer in our town he may not yet have had the opportunity to cultivate a circle of friends. Consequently, I took it upon myself - rather presumptuously, you might think – to suggest to him (imagining that it would be too much of a coincidence were he to be, like my former patron Mister Hadwen Bragg, a member of the Society of Friends and, therefore, an abstainer from alcohol) that he might like to accompany us, at a date and time to suit his convenience, on a visit to the Flying Horse Tavern. To my relief, he received the suggestion most enthusiastically and responded by proposing in return that Ralph and I should visit his studio, where we could, if we so wished, inspect the portraits which he had created.

As we were to discover on a later occasion, the 'studio' was an unwarrantedly grand name which Perlee Parker applied to a cramped garret in a lodging-house opposite Execution Dock in the Darn Crook for which he paid four shillings a week and from which he planned to move to more commodious premises as soon as he had sold enough of his paintings to produce a decent income. He was fond of repeating a quote which he attributed to somebody called Leonardo di ser Piero da Vinci that 'An artist's studio should be a small space because such rooms discipline the mind while large ones distract it'. Then he would always tell us about his own ambition, saying, 'If I manage to make a success as a portrait painter, I intend to take a respectable apartment in Pilgrim-street'.

*

Newcastle Courant

IMPORTANT ANNOUNCEMENT

THE ANATOMICAL DEMONSTRATIONS, at the Barber-Surgeons' Hall, to be given by Doctor Donald Stickler, will be continued every Day, commencing precisely at Noon (Sundays excepted) until the Conclusion of the Course.

The Medical Profession at large, and their Pupils, will have free Admission; but, for the Sake of preserving Order, and defraying the necessary Expenses, all those not of the Profession who may wish to attend will be required to present a Ticket of Admission.

Ticket for the Course 10s. 6d.; Single Lecture 2s. 6d. Tickets to be had at the Hall.
The Surplus to be given towards the Support of All Saints' Poorhouse.

The lecture theatre was packed full for the afternoon's demonstration. Looking around me, I estimated that at least half of its occupants were people whom I recognised as being from among the medical profession or in ancillary capacities such as my own. The rest, I speculated, were ordinary members of the public whose financial situation was comfortable enough for them to afford the cost of admission and whose curiosity may perhaps have been activated by the notice posted at the entrance of the Barber-Surgeons' Hall which announced that *Today's Lecture by Doctor Donald Stickler will be on the subject of RAISING THE DEAD.*

By the time that St Mary's Church in Pipewellgate could be heard ringing out the noontime Angelus bell across the river, virtually every place was taken and the red-headed speaker, wearing a black academic gown and accompanied by Bold Archy, entered to a smattering of applause from his closest medical colleagues and his most deferential students, which he acknowledged with a slight bow. At the side of the lectern stood a large mechanical contraption consisting of several glass globes, pulleys, metal wheels and handles. In front, there was a table similar to the one on which I had seen him conducting a dissection in the Anatomy Room. On the table was an object covered by a sheet which, judging from the shape of its outline, was a cadaver.

'As you may know, I have just returned from a visit to the Continent,' Doctor Stickler began, without taking the trouble to introduce himself or welcome his audience, the vast majority of whom would not have been privy to information about his recent travel arrangements. 'During my sojourn in the fine city of Bologna, it was my privilege – and, indeed, my pleasure too – to meet a fellow medical man, the renowned Professor Luigi

Galvani, from whom I learned a great deal about the phenomenon he calls animal electricity, the effect of which I intend to show you this afternoon.'

He cast a long, disdainful look around the room before continuing. 'I should make it clear that this demonstration is of a nature which some of you in the audience may find extremely disturbing, shocking even. I would therefore advise all females present and any others of a nervous disposition to leave before I begin.' He paused to allow his advice to be acted upon. Many did as he suggested but there remained a few women (presumably hardy - or, more likely, *fool*hardy - souls) in the lecture theatre.

'For the benefit of those who are not familiar with the device which you see before you and which my helper Mister Henderson will operate for me shortly, I should explain that it is known as an electrostatic machine. It is capable of generating animal electricity through the process of friction, created by the action of these belts rubbing against the glass spheres.' He looked around the audience again with the same disdainful expression as before and with his customary hauteur sneered, 'I trust that my explanation is not too far above the heads of most of you.' Then, he nodded in the direction of Bold Archy who obediently removed the sheet covering the object on the table to reveal the body of man clothed in some kind of garment which left the head, arms and legs exposed.

'This fellow,' Doctor Stickler said, giving him a prod with a wooden stick, 'was formerly a highway robber. But, unfortunately for him, he robbed one traveller too many, was overwhelmed by his putative victim and was then handed over to the authorities, who put him to death at the scaffold on the Town Moor nearly a week ago. So you can be assured that he is now completely lifeless. His soul, if he ever had one, is probably burning in the everlasting hellfire.' He nodded again to Bold Archy who walked across to the electrostatic machine, grasped the handle in his huge fist and started to turn one of the metal wheels, which in turn caused a number of the glass globes to rotate with increasing velocity. It took several minutes for anything to happen and the audience was beginning to show signs of restlessness when, at last, a slight crackling sound could be heard emanating from the device.

'What you can hear now is the animal electricity being produced by the friction, but we'll wait until it gets a bit stronger,' Doctor Stickler announced, at which his helper increased his efforts, the wheel flew round faster and the crackling became more like a roar. Soon the sound was accompanied by the sight of a shower of sparks and Doctor Stickler held up his hand to indicate that Bold Archy could stop. Then he pulled on a pair of stout leather gauntlets which reached up to his elbow, picked up a wire which was attached to the machine and carried it gingerly over to the corpse. He raised his head slowly and melodramatically towards the spectators and said in grave tones, 'Remember what I told you just a few minutes ago. This man was executed nearly a week ago. Is there anyone present who imagines that I can raise him from the dead?'

A profound hush fell over the room. An evil smile flitted across Doctor Stickler's face as he held the wire in front of him and touched the end of it against the right foot of the corpse. Immediately, the man's leg kicked out and continued to jerk in spasms. A collective gasp, intermingled with a few wild shrieks, issued from the throats of the spectators and at least half of the women who had remained in defiance of the earlier warning fainted from shock.

Doctor Stickler's smug expression suggested that he was thoroughly enjoying the audience's discomfort, which seemed to spur him on to cause them further distress. He again applied the wire, this time to the corpse's right arm and the effect was even more startling as the man appeared to raise his hand, clenching and unclenching his fist as though in protest at the treatment being meted out to him. At this point a number of spectators stood up from their seats and rushed towards the door, a ghostly pallor etched upon their faces. However, far from being discouraged from spreading any more alarm, Doctor Stickler moved the wire up to the head of the corpse and held it against the man's chin. At once, the jaw started to shake violently as though its owner was attempting to chew a particularly tough piece of gristle, the muscles of the cheeks quivered and became ghoulishly contorted and, as if these reactions were not ghastly enough, one eye began to open and shut in the most chillingly macabre manner.

This last episode was too much to bear for many of those watching and the sound of several people retching could be heard clearly throughout the auditorium.

Perhaps, at that point, Doctor Stickler realised that he had gone too far in testing the sensibilities of his audience. Or, perhaps, he had concluded the demonstration which he intended to give. Whatever the reason, he put down the wire, removed his gauntlets and replaced the sheet over the corpse. Then he stood at the lectern waiting patiently for the worst of the panic to subside before embarking on an explication of the phenomenon which had just been observed.

'You may have thought, when you saw those limbs and facial features moving, that I had by some miracle of science managed to extricate our robber friend here from his deserved place in the depths of Hell and bring him back to life. How else could it be explained that a man who had apparently been dead for several days was suddenly able to move his hands and feet, exercise his jaw and open his eyes – well, one of them, anyway? Surely the evidence before us today must mean that he has indeed been resuscitated?'

He let his bemused audience absorb those words for a while before continuing.

'Of course, gentlemen,' he said, ignoring the small number of women who had remained in the room and were currently being administered to with smelling salts in order to revive them from their swoons, 'that cannot be so. Nobody has yet discovered a method of restoring life to those who have died. The truth is simpler. What you have seen this afternoon is a demonstration of how animal electricity can stimulate muscle tissue, whether it resides in a living or deceased body. As I learned from my esteemed colleague Professor Galvani when I was in Italy recently, a muscle contracts when it is stimulated by an electric current such as is produced by this machine, giving the impression – only an impression, I repeat – that its owner is moving parts of his body of his own volition.'

It was only when, at the end of Doctor Stickler's lecture, members of the audience were filing out of the room in a gloomy silence born of the depressing subject matter of the lecture and the shocking events we had witnessed, that I glanced across and happened to notice the oily fellow whom I knew as Mister Septimus Grymm. Unfortunately, he had already spotted me and was waving towards me in an animated fashion which suggested that he wished to speak to me urgently, so that it was impossible for me to escape further dialogue without treating him with extreme discourtesy (which, despite my aversion to the fellow, I could not bring myself to accord him).

Had I known then what trouble would ensue from our sub-sequent conversation, I would surely have chosen the path of incivility and shunned his company.

31

'A very interesting demonstration, wouldn't you agree, Master James?' Mister Grymm asked when we had walked beyond the perimeter wall of the Barber-Surgeons' Hall. Without waiting for my answer, he continued, 'You know, I think that some of the audience really did believe at first that Doctor Stickler had raised that man from the dead. Do you imagine that it might be possible to bring a corpse back to life?'

'I do not believe it to be possible, sir,' I replied. 'If it is, that would truly be beyond my comprehension.'

'Well now,' he countered, 'let me show you something which may persuade you to change your mind.' Reaching inside his surtout he took out a tiny bottle of brown glass. 'Look at this,' he said, handing it to me. I saw that the label described the contents as *Reanimating Tincture*.

'What is it?' I asked.

'It's a mixture created by an eminent apothecary by the name of Anders Bergstrom. I have it on the best possible authority that it restores life in the event of violent death.'

I was astounded by this information. After some moments, I said,' Do you really mean that it is capable of raising the dead, sir?'

'Indeed I do - that is to say, as far as I am able to trust the words of those who have witnessed its effects.'

'So you have never actually seen it work yourself?'

'Not yet, Master James. But I believe that we will soon have the evidence of our own eyes.'

'Our own eyes, sir?' I repeated, somewhat alarmed by the direction which the conversation had taken.

'Master James,' he said, 'in the short time we have known one another we have become very close friends and it has been my pleasure to honour you with one or two modest tokens of my generosity. I trust that you have maintained our little secret and have not brought these gifts to the notice of the authorities in the Barber-Surgeons' Hall?'

I confirmed that I had not.

'That's good. Because I do not imagine that the Searchers would look too favourably on your conduct, would they now?' For the first time since I had met Mister Grymm his voice, no longer exhibiting that habitual whine, carried a distinct hint of menace.

'My conduct, sir?' I asked, my throat dry with fear.

'Yes, James, I refer to your conduct – or should I call it *mis*-conduct? – in consorting with me and even accepting samples of medications from somebody whom you know to be an apothecary employed at the Dispensary.'

This statement rattled me to my core. Mister Grymm, the man who had approached me and initiated a discussion on that first day we met and who had since sought to foster what he described as our friendship (a one-sided view, in my opinion) now appeared to be turning the tables on me, so to speak, and accusing me of wrongdoing. It was not an association which I had ever sought or valued and I had tolerated him only because of the innate sense of courtesy with which my parents (God rest their souls) had endowed me.

Sensing my alarm, an emotion that must have been obvious from the horrified look which crossed my face, he affected a sympathetic tone. 'You need have no concerns, Master James, that I may inadvertently let it be known to these brutal Searchers what has transpired between us. I will, as always, be the absolute soul of discretion. However, in view of our great friendship and in return for the immense generosity I have exhibited towards you, I would be most grateful if you, in turn, would now be kind enough to vouchsafe one small favour to me.'

I realised then – far too late, of course – the trap which Mister Grymm had set for me. He must have been well aware from the start of the College's injunctions against contact with those whom Mister Ingham had termed quacks, charlatans and mountebanks and the fact that formulations such as the ones he had given to me played no part in the type of medical science being taught there. In providing me with these so-called gifts, he never expected me to make use of them in the course of my study but instead had employed them as a means of luring me into committing a breach of discipline which he now intended to exploit by blackmailing me into carrying out some act at his request, afraid as I was lest he should otherwise report me to the College and thereby engineer my expulsion.

'What kind of favour, sir?' I asked timidly, aware that I had little option but to accede to whatever demand he was to make of me.

'Well, James, let us see now. I believe that I am correct in stating that Doctor Stickler, being the fine fellow that he is as well as a distinguished anatomist and surgeon, has access to as many cadavers as are supplied to him from the gallows. These cadavers are, no doubt, stored in secure and appropriate conditions within the periphery of the Barber-Surgeons' Hall?'

'Yes, sir,' I confirmed. 'They are normally stored in the cold chamber of the Anatomy Room or laid out on the dissecting table until Doctor Stickler has finished his work on them and then they are passed on to an undertaker for burial.'

'Ah! Just as I thought. And no doubt *you*, Master James, as the good Doctor's pupil, also have access to the Anatomy Room?'

'Not on my own, sir. I am allowed there only under strict supervision by Doctor Stickler himself. At all other times, I am forbidden to enter. Only Mister Henderson whom you saw assisting Doctor Stickler at today's demonstration has permission to go there on his own as he regularly carries cadavers and equipment in and out of the room.'

'I see. So the room is not normally locked, then?'

'No, sir. Not to my knowledge.'

'That's good, Master James. Very good indeed. Splendid, in fact. So let me tell you now about the small favour which I would like you to do for me, in return for all the generosity I have shown you. It is all in the interests of medical science, you understand. Something to which we are both committed, are we not? So listen carefully while I explain.'

As he described what he wanted me to carry out on his behalf, I grew increasingly alarmed both at the nature of the deed and the awful consequences of my being discovered in the act. I protested vehemently but to no avail, as each protest merely drew forth from Mister Grymm a further reminder of what would happen to me should the Searchers somehow learn of my misdemeanours.

*

It is a commonly-held view among observers of the human condition that those of meagre means nevertheless contrive to subsist and remain reasonably content with their lot, whereas many of those blessed with considerable riches are never satisfied with what they have and constantly seek to increase the extent of their wealth. In Felix Brandling MP we find the epitome of the latter category.

Here is a man who owns Gosforth House, a grand mansion near Bulmer Village, and receives income from estates and coal-mines in Northumberland and Durham, sugar plantations in Jamaica and a shipping business which profits from the trans-portation of slaves from west Africa to the Caribbean, as well as winnings earned by his string of racehorses. And yet, despite his being among the richest men in Newcastle, his avarice knows no bounds. Nor does his contempt for the law or his fellow men. For many years now he has, with the assistance or conniv-ance of his partner-in-crime Alderman Applegarth, a fellow-member of the Company of Hoastmen, been in the habit of removing works of art and other valuable objects from public buildings in the town, including the Guild Hall and the Man-sion House. Some of this contraband has found its way into Gosforth House. Some has been sold at Sotheby's in London and the proceeds (after the subtraction of the auction house's eye-wateringly large commission) shared with Alderman Apple-garth. Should anybody happen to detect the absence of any of the purloined items, their disappearance is explained by Felix Brandling's assertion that they have been placed on temporary loan to a university or sent away for repair or restoration. In truth, most members of the Common Council who frequent these buildings are decrepit, senile, insane (and, had they not occupied positions of importance, would indubitably have been committed to the madhouse) or so ignorant of the artistic merit of their contents that they are hardly likely to notice anything amiss.

There was, however, one person who had observed the thievery being conducted under her nose and who was chroni-cling the exploits of Brandling and Applegarth in anticipation of their day of reckoning which, she was quite confident, would eventually arrive.

*

The Anatomy Room consisted of a large area with a dissecting table at the centre and rows of seating to accommodate the medical staff, students and other observers who attended public demonstrations. The desk at which Doctor Stickler sat while writing up his notes was situated next to a window overlooking the courtyard at the front of the building. On the opposite side was a curtained-off area designated for the storage of coffins which were empty except when used to house cadavers newly-arrived from the scaffold on the Town Moor or at Newgate Gaol.

Doctor Stickler was in the habit of visiting the Infirmary in The Forth for several hours each Wednesday morning and so, knowing that an execution had taken place the previous day, I chose that time to let myself into the Anatomy Room in order to carry out the shocking task which Mister Grymm had instructed me to perform on his behalf in return for his silence on the matter of my breaches of College rules.

Carefully pulling aside the heavy black curtain and peering through the darkness I could just about make out the shapes of three coffins, one of which appeared to be big enough for at least two bodies. Once my eyes had become accustomed to the gloom, I steeled myself to confront the macabre spectacle of a corpse badly disfigured by a violent end and lifted the lid of one of the smaller coffins only to find that it was packed full of charts, blackboards and other paraphernalia used by Doctor Stickler in connection with his lectures. I opened the second with the same apprehension and the same result. Turning to the largest coffin, I found its lid much heavier and raised it only with some difficulty. Peering inside, I saw that it contained the body of a man, his lower half covered with rough sacking, his neck displaying the dark ligature mark made by the Whipper-and-Hougher's noose and his countenance contorted in a gruesome rictus which suggested that his death had been slow and agonising. I calculated that if I leaned right over the side of the coffin, I could just about reach the man's face. I removed my neckerchief, holding it against my nose and mouth to stifle my urge to retch and cautiously tested out his cold, clammy jaw with my fingers. I was relieved to find that rigor mortis had passed and the muscles had returned to a relaxed state, allowing me to open the mouth and expose the tongue, which was enlarged as a result of the method by which its owner had met his end.

I reached inside my pocket, extracted the bottle of Reanimating Tincture and unscrewed the cap.

32

Ever since Mister Grymm had described to me the supposed properties of the Reanimating Tincture I had considered his claims to be completely beyond belief. To my mind, it was inconceivable that the victim of a violent death or, indeed, any other form of death, could be restored to life. Doctor Stickler had confirmed as much at the conclusion of his demonstration of the effect of animal electricity on the muscles of a cadaver and I had no reason to doubt my tutor's words. On the contrary, I had the greatest respect for, and total confidence in, his judgement.

However, it was at the point where I was about to apply a few drops of the liquid to the corpse's tongue to test its efficacy in accordance with Mister Grymm's instructions that I was suddenly seized with panic at the irrational notion that the Tincture might actually work as claimed and bring the man back to life. A series of terrifying thoughts raced through my tormented mind. Would the man immediately open his eyes? Would he assume, as soon as he saw me, that I was his killer? Would he rise up out of his coffin to attack me? Could I, encumbered as I was by my crippled knees, escape from a man who looked so much bigger and stronger than me?

I had already decided to abandon my mission and flee from the room when I heard voices, one of which possessed a strong Scotch accent, and I knew that, contrary to my expectations, Doctor Stickler had returned early from his visit to the Infirmary. Even in the state of mental turmoil in which I found myself, I realised that it was impossible for me to get out of the Anatomy Room without being seen and that, in order to avoid discovery, I would have to conceal myself immediately. There was only one place which offered any sort of refuge. Almost without thinking, I dragged my legs over the side of the coffin, wincing at the pain in my knees, tumbled inside and closed the lid. Whether through good fortune or absent-mindedness, I had inadvertently left my neckerchief on the edge of the coffin which meant that the lid was prevented from closing completely and left a small crack which afforded me a clear view of the area around Doctor Stickler's desk where he and his visitor had settled themselves. Since I was in darkness and they were in the light, the likelihood of their observing me was negligible.

The visitor was someone I had not seen before at the Barber-Surgeons' Hall but I recognised him immediately from his huge dimensions, cock-eye and aquiline nose as the man with whom Belcher and Jago had argued in the White Hart Inn on the occasion when they had tricked me (as I perceived it) into paying for their ale. I could also hear every word of the conversation, which they conducted in normal tones in the mistaken belief that they were speaking with complete privacy.

'You must let me into the secret of that weighing machine of yours, Delaval,' Doctor Stickler urged.

'Secret? What makes you imagine that there is a secret?'

'Come now. You're not going to convince me that you record your visitors' weights in the interests of scientific research.'

'No, of course not. If you must know, Stickler – and I trust you to ensure that this goes no further – it's all about catching thieves.'

'Catching thieves? Whatever do you mean, Delaval?'

'It's quite simple. Weigh everyone on the way in and again on the way out. Then compare the difference. If they've gained six pounds or less, it's because they've had a good dinner. More than six pounds probably means that they've stolen something. *Probably*, I say. We can't be quite certain until the gateman has done his duty. He has clear instructions to search anyone who is over the six pound limit. And you'd be surprised at how much of the family silver finds its way into guests' pockets. Quite accidentally, of course – or so they claim.'

'Well, then, Delaval, perhaps you shouldn't consort with so many thieves.'

'Maybe you're right, Stickler, but I'm sure you haven't invited me here today to enquire about my weighing machine. What's the real reason for the invitation?'

'The truth is, Delaval, that I need your help,' Doctor Stickler said. 'My own research into the Felonious Particle is at a stage where it is essential for me to obtain at least one fresh cadaver every fortnight.' As always, he was proud of having invented the term *Felonious Particle* and could never pass up an opportunity to mention it in order to impress whomsoever he was speaking to. 'And that's quite apart from those I require for my students to work with.'

'Ah, fresh cadavers,' Delaval reflected wistfully. 'They're not so easy to get hold of these days, I'm afraid. And even more difficult since your two friends lost their positions in Mister Grope's employment. A most unfortunate business, that was. Most unfortunate. Anyway, Stickler, why can't your students get their own cadavers? That's what they do at the Royal College in London, so I'm told.'

'I'm well aware of that. I've given them more than enough hints without instructing them directly to do a bit of grave-robbing, but they don't show any initiative in finding their own bodies.' He sighed regretfully. 'They seem to think it's the responsibility of their tutors to supply them.'

'Yes, yes, I quite understand your problem. Well, I may be able to assist you. You see, I've managed to persuade a couple of my domestic staff to do a little moonlighting for me, if you follow my meaning. So I could perhaps provide you with enough cadavers for your own research and a few extra for your students.'

'That's sounds very satisfactory. Very satisfactory.'

'You'll need to arrange for them to be collected from Seaton Delaval Hall. I should be able to keep them in a decent condition for a few days in the icehouse. But I can't risk having to transport them into the town in one of my carriages. Can you imagine, Stickler, what kind of scandal it would cause if I were to be stopped on the road? I've got my good reputation to think of, you know.'

'Your good reputation?' Stickler said, with a hint of irony that went unnoticed by Delaval. 'Yes, quite. Anyway, collecting them wouldn't be a problem. A body being carried in one of the Barber-Surgeons' Hall's carriages would be unlikely to arouse suspicion.'

'Good. That's agreed then,' Delaval nodded lopsidedly. 'Of course, you understand that this arrangement will have to attract an increased fee.' It was a statement, not a question.

'Increased fee? What do you mean? I've always paid you handsomely, haven't I?'

'It's a matter of supply and demand, Stickler. And I've got my expenses to cover, you know. So, in future, it'll be another guinea per cadaver.'

Doctor Stickler was about to protest when the discussion was interrupted by the entrance of Bold Archy, who was carrying a large object which I could not see clearly but, from my limited view, I took to be a box of some kind. He deposited it on the other side of the room and left without speaking a word.

'Thank you, Archy,' Doctor Stickler called out after him and, turning to his visitor, explained, 'That's Archibald Henderson. He does everything I tell him except think for himself.'

'Ha! A fine figure of a man. Wouldn't he make a splendid subject for a dissection, Stickler? A body of such proportions would be a prize indeed. You'd be willing to pay eleven guineas for his cadaver, I'll wager.'

'As a matter of fact, Delaval. I'll get it for nothing.'

'Nothing? What on earth makes you say that?'

Doctor Stickler laughed, leaned forward to open a drawer in his desk and withdrew a scroll which he unrolled and handed to Delaval. The latter lifted his monocle, applied it to his good eye, surveyed the paper through a squint and returned it.

'You crafty old devil,' he chuckled. 'You've persuaded the fellow to sign over his body for your exclusive use.'

'Not only that. He's also agreed to allow me to operate on him while he's still alive.'

'While he's still alive, you say? How on earth did you get his consent to that?'

'I didn't need to. I told you, he does whatever I tell him. All I had to do was to draw up the document and get him to put his mark on it. He can manage to do that. But he doesn't understand or even know what it means.'

'So you tricked him into it, Stickler. That's really what you're saying, isn't it?'

'I don't like the word *tricked*, Delaval. It's all done in the interests of the advancement of medical science. And before you start getting too judgemental, don't forget that your own activities are not exactly beyond reproach.'

'I'm a businessman, Stickler, not a moralist. I deal in commerce, not ethics. Anyway, I just hope you won't have to wait too long for him to die before you get to work on his cadaver.'

'Strictly between us, Delaval, I don't believe that I can afford to wait that long.'

'I'm not sure that I follow you.'

'Well, you know that through my research into the Felonious Particle…' - he was pleased to have been able to mention that again – '… I aim to discover which part of the brain produces in the human creature the propensity to commit crime so that it can then be removed or destroyed. Archy is a prime example of the kind of docile being into which I would like to transform every potential criminal. The reason he behaves in the way he does is because of an injury to his brain. He used to be a keelman until he got his head bashed in. An accident on the river. Now the man is nothing more than a simpleton. He lives in the Keelmen's Hospital - looked after by his mother, so they say. Well now, suppose I was able to find out which part of Archy's brain was damaged in the accident? Once I had established that information I would use it to operate on some of the inmates in Newgate prison. I would replicate in *their* brains the injury suffered by Archy in the expectation that it would thereby change them into the kind of meek, submissive members of our society that we would prefer them to be.'

'Fascinating idea, Stickler. You obviously enjoy playing God. The only problem I can see with that is that the operation would kill them.'

'Not so, Delaval,' Stickler contradicted him emphatically. '… Not necessarily, anyway.' Less emphatic this time, but still compelling. 'That's the beauty of it. After all, Archy is still alive with whatever brain injury he sustained, isn't he? So what I'm planning to do is to operate on him as soon as possible to learn the secret of his personality. I don't need to wait until he dies.'

'You're seriously suggesting that while that big fellow's still alive you're going to unscrew the top of his head, or whatever it is that you surgeons do?'

'Not *unscrew*, Delaval. The process is called trepanning. We use a special instrument called a perforating trepan to bore a hole in the patient's skull and then we cut a circular piece of the bone with a saw and remove it with forceps so that we can get to the brain. When we've finished doing whatever it is we need to do to the brain, we replace the bone. It's a very simple procedure. I've carried it out countless times.'

'Ha! Sounds pretty fatal to me, Stickler, I must say.'

'Not at all. The patient sometimes survives,' Stickler insisted, reassuringly. 'Mind you,' he added, 'I must confess to having had an outsize coffin made ready for him. Just in case things don't go quite as well as I'd hoped, you understand. It's over there, as a matter of fact.'

He waved a hand in my direction and I thought for a moment that he might bring his colleague over for a closer look and discover me. Fortunately, however, the colleague distracted him by asking, 'And how's our friend Archy going to feel about that, I wonder?'

'Ha! He won't feel anything after a few mouthfuls of gin. Have faith in us surgeons, Delaval. You might need our services one day, you know.'

'I'd rather die first than trust your scalpel, Stickler.'

'You probably will,' Stickler replied gravely. 'You probably will.'

33

I passed yet another restless night, the silence punctuated by the harsh snoring of those of my colleagues fortunate enough to have succumbed to the power of the god Hypnos and the regular announcements by patrolling Charlies about the time and the weather. Despite the unseasonably cold temperature, I lay awake bathed in perspiration, reliving the events of the previous morning and thinking back on the conversation I had overheard between Doctor Stickler and his guest (whom I now knew to be a scoundrel called Delaval, a name which seemed vaguely familiar to me) as I was pressed up against the cadaver which stank of decay and decomposition, almost ready to give myself up and accept the consequences rather than spend a minute longer in the company of a rotting corpse and in agony from the pain in my cramped and crippled knees.

After the two of them had left the Anatomy Room, I waited for what seemed a good half hour before daring to move from my hiding place. Then, when I judged that the coast was probably clear, I climbed cautiously out of the coffin and made my way to safety as quickly as my poor legs would permit. I was too scared by having been so close to detection and too upset by the nature of what had passed between the two men to think of completing the ghastly task which had been assigned to me by Mister Grymm. I did not realise until later that, in my hurry to escape before Doctor Stickler returned, I had left behind the bottle of Reanimating Tincture.

As I waited in my bed for the morning to come, I was wracked both by fear of the retribution which Mister Grymm was likely to visit upon me for my failure to do his bidding and by indecision as to whether I should inform the authorities – by which, I suppose, I meant Mister Ingham - of Doctor Stickler's appalling intentions in respect of Bold Archy.

I was not to know that the concerns with which I was confronted were soon to be resolved in a most unexpected way.

*

William Ingham had just returned from one of those tedious, tiresome, seemingly interminable meetings which, as Head of the College, he was obliged to attend and he was looking forward to his regular afternoon nap. He sunk deep into the enormous leather chair which he had coveted ever since he first saw it in his predecessor's study, a room which he now occupied in his own right. He closed his eyes and took several deep breaths, a routine which, he had learned through years of experimentation, was likely to ensure that he could be sound asleep within five minutes. He had descended almost into unconsciousness when a loud knock at the door startled him so much that he was instantly wide awake.

'Who is it?' he called out, irritated at the interruption.

'Beggin' yer pardon, sir,' replied a voice which Ingham recognised as belonging to his housekeeper.

'What is it, Mrs McColl?' he asked angrily.

'Beggin' yer pardon, sir, there's two gentlemen to see ye, sir.'

'Tell them to go away.'

'Beggin' yer pardon, sir, but the two gentlemen says it's urgent, sir.'

'I don't care. I'm having my nap. Tell them to go away.'

'Beggin' yer pardon, sir, but the two gentlemen says it's *very* urgent, sir. Very urgent indeed, they say, sir.'

'I said, tell them to go away, Mrs McColl. That's my last word on the matter.'

'Beggin' yer pardon, sir, the two gentlemen says it's about Doctor Stickler, sir.'

'Doctor Stickler? What about him?

'Beggin' yer pardon, sir, but the two gentlemen says it's most important that they speak to you about Doctor Stickler now, sir. In strictest confidence, sir.'

'Who are these gentlemen?'

'There's a Mister Belcher and a Mister Jago, sir.'

'I've never heard of either of them.'

'Beggin' yer pardon, sir, but they say it's a very delicate matter concerning Doctor Stickler, sir. Very delicate and very urgent, sir. They're most insistent, sir.'

'Alright, Mrs McColl. I suppose you'd better send them in.'

'Yes, sir, beggin' yer pardon, sir.'

*

'I like to paint *characters*,' Perlee Parker said, as Ralph and I gazed in admiration at the portraits displayed in what he liked to call his studio. '*Characters*,' he repeated. 'You know what I mean. People who look as though they've got something special about them. They're not necessarily handsome or wealthy or even likeable. They might even be a little sinister or evil-looking. But they look as if they might live an interesting life or follow some intriguing occupation or have some fascinating or mysterious side to their personality. I just paint them as I see them. I don't try to make them look any better than they really are. Nor any worse for that matter. I try to imagine what they're like as people, whether they're miserable or contented, for example, whether they're reserved or rowdy, whether they're charitable or mean-spirited, and so on. Because if I feel that I have some insight into their personality I am more likely to portray them true to life. That's why it's easier for me to paint people whom I know well ...'

'Surely you didn't know those keelmen we saw you drawing at Shields?' Ralph interrupted.

'No, of course, it's not always possible,' Perlee replied. 'I'd never seen them before and I don't suppose I'll ever see them again. Nor those smugglers.' He pointed to a painting of a group of a dozen or so men resting in a cave. 'Nor those spate gatherers at Cullercoats,' he added, indicating one depicting women scouring the rocks at low tide for items left behind by the sea. 'But occasionally, somebody will ask me to do a portrait of them. When they act as my model, I can find out more about their character than if I just happen to spot them at random and sketch them. I can study them for longer and in much more detail. Where the shadows fall on their face, whether or not their features are symmetrical, how they hold themselves. Those kind of things make all the difference when it comes to making an accurate portrait which conveys the subject's personality.'

'How long does it take for you to complete a portrait?' I enquired, imagining that such a task would require numerous hours of study and execution by the artist and an equal number of hours of patience - or even endurance - by the subject.

'That all depends on the model and the length of time they're prepared to sit still,' said Perlee. 'Some people find it impossible not to fidget. The quickest one I have completed took me less than a week. But I've heard it said that Leonardo di ser Piero da Vinci, who was a much better artist than I will ever be, spent over four years before he was satisfied with his portrait of a young woman who was the wife of a wealthy silk merchant in Florence.'

'Perhaps this Leonardo fellow was being paid by the hour,' Ralph quipped.

'No,' Perlee disagreed, feigning annoyance at the joke at the expense of the man he regarded as his idol. 'I imagine that he was such a perfectionist that he refused to regard his portrait as finished until it was an exact representation of his subject.'

He led us across to the other side of the studio (a very short step) to where a framed picture stood against the wall. 'Here's one I've only just completed,' he said, proudly. 'I painted it from a scene I came across quite by chance in the Fleshmarket, where a man was auctioning his wife. There was such a huge crowd that I had to stand on a wall in order to get a proper view. But it was such a rare thing to witness that I felt I just had to sketch it.'

'I recognise that man,' exclaimed Ralph. 'I'll be damned if it's not Jasper Scuffins. He was talking to me only recently. Asking me about his wife …' His voice trailed off and I could tell that he was wondering whether his encounter with Jasper Scuffins was linked in any way to the event captured in Perlee's painting and whether he had somehow been innocently complicit in Mrs Scuffins' tribulations.

I recognised my friend's discomfiture and sought to change the subject in order to spare him further embarrassment. 'How do you convert one of your sketches into a something like this?' I asked, intrigued at how something which started off as a simple pencil drawing could become such a lifelike representation in oils.

Perlee seemed pleased at my interest and keen to explain his method. 'Well, if I see a subject which takes my fancy, I make a sketch and note down any significant colours – eyes, hair, clothes, for example. The rest I can normally remember – I'm good at carrying colours in my head. Then when I get back to my studio, I copy the sketch as precisely as possible on to a canvass with charcoal, usually to a bigger scale than the original one. I make my own wooden framework and stretch and fix the canvass over it. It's important to use a thick, high-quality canvass. Once I'm satisfied with my drawing, I seal it with a layer of shellac and then I can use it as my template for the painting.'

'If you're looking for interesting characters, as you call them,' Ralph said, having regained his composure, 'you'll see plenty of them in the Flying Horse Tavern. Especially in Hell's Kitchen. You're likely to meet the strangest assortment of people in Newcastle there.'

'Hell's Kitchen?' asked Perlee. 'What's that?'

'It's the name they call the taproom,' I interjected before Ralph could reply. 'Ralph's right. It has a weird selection of characters, I can assure you.'

'In that case,' said Perlee, 'I'm inclined to take up the kind offer you made to me the first time we met and accompany you there, my friends.'

*

Some devastating news today at the Barber-Surgeons' Hall.

The story must have spread like wildfire among the medical students and it reached my ears almost as soon as I arrived in time for what should have been an address by Doctor Stickler on the topic of *The Human Brain*, only to be confronted by a notice on the door of the Anatomy Room which baldly announced that *Today's lecture is cancelled due to unforeseen circumstances*. According to the information enthusiastically supplied by a number of those milling around the courtyard at the front of the building, Doctor Stickler had been arrested that morning by a posse of constables and taken away to be interrogated in connection with a scandalous business involving illegally obtained cadavers. He was currently incarcerated in Newgate Gaol, it was said, although I rather suspected that, in this regard, my informant had embellished the tale beyond the boundaries of his knowledge.

Within the hour, I had received an instruction to attend Mister Ingham's study and I duly presented myself to the Head of the College, oblivious as to the purpose of the summons. It was soon to be revealed. In fairness to the man, I declare that he dealt with the matter in hand very compassionately, but his humanity scarcely lessened the impact of what he had to convey to me.

'I regret that I have some unwelcome news for you, James,' he said gently. 'I received a visit recently from two gentlemen who gave me some extremely disturbing information about certain, er, … activities which have apparently been taking place within the College. When I heard what they had to tell me, I felt it my clear duty – a most unpleasant duty as it happens, but my clear duty nonetheless - to report the matter immediately to the Authorities. As a result, your master, Doctor Stickler, has unfortunately been …' - he searched for a phrase devoid of prejudice and eventually chose one which he no doubt intended to be anodyne but which struck me as unduly euphemistic – '… called away. He will probably be unavailable to his pupils for some considerable time.'

He paused, apparently expecting me to appreciate the implication of what he had told me. Then, seeing that I had not done so, he asked, 'Do you understand what this means for you, James?'

'Well, sir,' I replied, 'I suppose it means that I will have to be apprenticed to another master in the meantime.'

Mister Ingham shook his head sadly. 'No, James, I'm afraid that won't be possible. I'm very sorry to have to inform you that in view of Doctor Stickler's ... er, indisposition,' - another euphemism, I thought - 'I shall be obliged to cancel your indenture. However, before you leave I will, of course, be pleased to furnish you with a written commendation which you may submit to any prospective new employer.'

I was overwhelmed at the news. Despite my attempts to control my emotions, the tears welled up in my eyes and I began to sob like a child.

Seeing my discomfiture, Mister Ingham attempted to console me by kind words but I hardly took in whatever it was that he said to me. I do, however, remember that at the end of the interview he told me, 'If it would make things a little easier for you, James, I am prepared to extend your allowance and to let you to stay on in the dormitory until the last day of the month to give you a chance to find some other lodgings for yourself.'

That is how my apprenticeship came to an unexpected and premature close and how I ended up occupying a settle in Perlee Parker's so-called studio in the Darn Crook.

34

Perlee Parker was intrigued by many of the things which went on in Newcastle – things which he had never encountered before or even heard of in the southern town where he had previously lived – and he found that these often provided him with new ideas for his painting.

'Look at this,' he said to me one morning, pointing to an advertisement in the *Newcastle Courant* which read as follows:

TO BE FOUGHT FOR AT EMANUEL MORDUE'S PIT IN THE HIGH BRIDGE

On Monday next, 24 February, 50 pounds by Cocks,
Stags and Blenkards of weight not exceeding 3 lb. 11 oz.
Tuesday, 50 pounds. .. .. 3 lb. 14 oz.
Wednesday, 50 pounds. .. .. 4 lb. 1 oz.
Thursday, 50 pounds. .. .. 4 lb. 4 oz.
Friday, 50 pounds. .. .. 4 lb. 7 oz.
Saturday, 100 pounds. .. .. 4 lb. 12 oz.

'What about it?' I asked, never having been particularly interested in such contests which, as I was well aware, took place with great frequency at several venues in the town and were enthusiastically attended by devotees of all classes and status.

'Well, don't you see?' he rejoined. 'There are bound to be *characters* there, aren't there? They'll make good subjects for me, I'll be damned if they won't.'

I couldn't disagree with his analysis and after much urging I eventually agreed to accompany him to the cock-pit, not from any keenness on my part but as a means of returning a favour to somebody who had kindly offered me a roof over my head following my eviction from the dormitory at the Barber-Surgeons' Hall. And so it was that, at ten in the morning on the following Saturday, Perlee and I found ourselves paying one shilling each to gain admission to Emanuel Mordue's pit and a further sixpence to purchase a cock-list showing details of the birds entered for the contests and the names of their owners, the so-called 'Masters of the Match'. The place was already thronging with rowdy groups of men - from all walks of life, so it seemed – many of whom were placing bets with the bookmakers whose stalls were set up all around the cock-pit which occupied the centre of the room. We were fortunate enough to locate two vacant seats in the spectators' gallery, which afforded a splendid view of the proceedings.

At ten-thirty prompt, the opening match was announced by the Teller of the Law, a rotund fellow with a rugose visage and dirty leather breeches who acted as ringmaster and referee. This was to take place between the two cocks which had been established as the lightest at the weigh-in held earlier and would be followed by a succession of fights culminating in the final between the two heaviest. Two pitmen, the owners of the first contestants, took up their places opposite one another at the side of the cock-pit. Then their Feeders appeared, each carrying the game-cock which it was their responsibility to train and nourish with grain (normally soaked in port wine) in order to improve the bird's strength. They handed the cocks to the Official Setters-on who placed them beak to beak in the centre of the pit, whereupon the fight began, continuing until one was killed or beaten into unconsciousness, at which point the Teller of the Law declared the other to be the victor. Meanwhile, the onlookers either cheered or jeered depending on the performance of the bird on which they had placed their bet. Those gamblers who had backed the winner went gleefully to collect their reward. The losers waited miserably for the next contest and the chance to recoup their losses. The Teller of the Law signalled to an assistant to rake the feathers and gore to the side of the arena, another pair of owners and cocks were brought on and the grisly proceedings started all over again. During all this time, Perlee was completing several sketches, apparently paying less attention to the spectacle than to the spectators, no doubt hoping to seek out some *characters*.

And so the noble sport continued into the afternoon until, at nearly three o'clock, it was time for the main event of the day with a prize of one hundred pounds to be competed for, as the Teller of the Law declared, his voice scarcely audible above the hubbub of the crowd, by fighting cocks owned by Alderman Applegarth and Mister Felix Brandling MP, respectively.

I thought that the second name seemed vaguely familiar to me and, shortly after, I recalled that it was Felix Brandling who, on the occasion of our visit to All Saints' Poorhouse, Mister Hadwen Bragg had mentioned to me as being an acquaintance of Captain Starkey. A path opened up in the huddle of punters clustered around the bookmakers' stalls as the two Masters of the Match made their grand entrance, attended by loud applause. One was a lumbering, grossly overweight man, with shuddering jowls, the other an upright, slender-made fellow of a more active appearance. They reacted to their reception as if well accustomed to receiving the plaudits of lesser beings and took their places on either side of the cock-pit, the seat originally earmarked for the former having been hastily replaced with a large bench, the better to accommodate the extent of his buttocks. As he did so, the surrounding group of spectators cleared a wide space around him, possibly out of respect for his elevated station in the community or, perhaps, on account of some other reason which I could not divine.

The Feeders entered with their respective birds, which were then paraded in the pit at a good distance from one another. They were freakishly large and muscular, but exquisitely beautiful too. Their burnished plumage showed off a striking array of colours - gold, orange, black, red and green. As they strutted arrogantly around the arena, both having had their crests removed in order to deprive their opponent of a beak-hold, a narrow blade, the size of a man's little finger, could be seen glinting on the right heel of each. At the sight of such magnificent specimens, many punters rushed to the bookmakers' stalls and another rash of betting ensued in anticipation of the contest.

When the flow of bets had ceased, the Teller of the Law clapped his hands to signal that the combat could begin and the cocks were placed beak to beak by the Official Setters-on. As soon as the birds were released, each sprang forward in attack. The fight was breathtakingly fast and shocking in its ferocity. In a blur of feathers, the combatants cut and tore with their beaks, talons and lethal blades, shredding flesh and slashing eyes, to an accompaniment of blood-curdling shrieks. After a minute or so of this, both birds became exhausted and appeared to call a temporary truce, each retreating to the perimeter of the pit while cautiously watching its opponent, at which point the Teller of the Law began to count down from the number forty. As soon as he had reached zero, the Official Setters-on picked up the cocks, both of which had by then recovered somewhat, and returned them to the centre of the pit, placing them beak to beak to begin Round Two.

Again, the battle was brutal and ferocious, lasting even longer than the initial encounter, until both birds backed away from the tussle for another respite. This time, the countdown started at twenty, following which the Official Setters-on placed the birds once more together so that the fight could resume. However, at this juncture, one bird (which the Official Setter-on had great difficulty in keeping hold of, judging from the commotion which ensued when he picked it up) appeared to be completely disoriented as if unable to see or locate the other so that it was at its adversary's mercy, powerless to attack or even to defend itself. Consequently, the fight was over very quickly. The vanquished cock lay motionless in the dirt, around it a bloodstained patch, spreading wider. The victor, itself grievously injured and close to death, barely moved. Its Feeder reached into the pit, picked it up, quickly inspected the extent of the damage and, with a shrug of his shoulders, looked towards the owner who was still sitting on the bench at the side. Mister Felix Brandling MP signalled his consent with a nod of the head and the Feeder unceremoniously rung the bird's neck. Meanwhile on the opposite side of the pit, Alderman Applegarth looked dejected at the loss of both his champion gamecock and the prize of one hundred pounds.

I turned to tell Perlee how sickening I had found the spectacle only to discover that the seat next to mine was empty. In the tumult which had accompanied the last contest, I had not realised that he must have left the room and, presumably, gone elsewhere in search of *characters*. I made my way through the throng of punters, a mixture of the jubilant and disconsolate according to which birds they had backed, and soon came across Perlee waiting outside on High Bridge. I recounted to him the story of the last cock-fight and the curious way in which it had ended, with one of the birds suffering an injury which eventually turned the contest into a one-sided affair and the winner itself having been so severely wounded that its owner immediately did away with it.

'I didn't see any of it,' he said, brandishing a hefty sketch pad as if to signify the reason for his exit. 'I came outside well before it started. And I believe that I overheard a conspiracy in the process of being hatched.' I found this statement particularly intriguing and ask my friend to elucidate. He did so. 'I had positioned myself behind a carriage waiting near the entrance, for no other reason than to obtain the best perspective of the horseman whom I intended to draw. He was quite a character, you see. However, I inadvertently intruded upon what was presumably intended to be a private, or should I say secret, conversation between a gentleman - in retrospect, I hesitate to assign that description to him - and a member of the lower classes, as I would judge by his Newcastle way of speaking, if I may beg your pardon, James …'

'What was this conversation about?' I interrupted him, impatient to discover the nature of this conspiracy and not in the least affronted by his assignment to me of responsibility for speaking with the local accent.

'It was about influencing the result of the prize fight,' Perlee rejoined. 'One man offered to pay five guineas to the other if he would blind his opponent's bird. The second man replied that he would do it for ten guineas. The first agreed, then handed over five guineas and promised to pay the rest once the deed was done. Then they both went inside, unaware of my presence.'

'That explains why the fight ended as it did,' I said. 'Can you remember what these men looked like?'

'I don't need to remember,' Perlee said, smiling. He opened his sketch pad to reveal a drawing of the two men. There was no mistaking who they were. I found myself gazing at perfect likenesses of Mister Felix Brandling MP and one of the Official Setters-on, the man who had picked up Alderman Applegarth's bird with such apparent difficulty and placed it in the centre of the pit to resume the fight.

At that very moment, the door behind us opened and a disconsolate Alderman Applegarth emerged, accompanied by his Feeder, and made for the waiting carriage. Instinctively, I rushed towards him and, without paying him the courtesy of introducing myself, I blurted out the words, 'I beg your pardon, sir, but I fear that you've been cheated.'

He stopped in his tracks, looked me up and down and then asked, 'Cheated? Whatever do you mean?'

By then, I had realised my indiscretion in addressing the man in the first place, but having done so, felt obliged to give him an answer. 'Mister Brandling bribed the Setter-on to blind your bird, sir. That's why you lost the prize.'

It took him a few moments to take in what I had told him. A look of incredulity, mixed with anger, shadowed his features. 'Brandling?' he said, his voice heavy with disbelief. 'Brandling cheated me, you say?'

'Yes, sir. This gentleman overheard their conversation.' I pointed to Perlee Parker, who stood a few feet away, looking embarrassed as though he wished I had not mentioned anything to Alderman Applegarth about his involvement.

'I wasn't eavesdropping,' Perlee hastened to explain. 'I just happened to hear what they were discussing.'

'And what *were* they discussing?' asked Alderman Applegarth and Perlee repeated what he had told me.

'He's made a drawing of them,' I added, hoping to bolster the strength of the evidence, at which I received an irate look from Perlee who, in consequence of my remark, was then required to present his sketch for inspection.

This seemed to confirm to Alderman Applegarth's complete satisfaction the truth of what I had alleged. 'I congratulate you on your artistry,' he said to Perlee. 'There is not a man worthy to be called a Geordie who would not immediately recognise our beloved Member of Parliament in this picture.' I could not be sure whether this description of the culprit was intended to be ironic or whether those who are accustomed to tread the corridors of power instinctively attach such epithets to their peers.

'I find this business most distressing,' Alderman Applegarth continued, 'but I am grateful to you two gentlemen for the information. I shall be obliged if you would do me the honour of calling upon me at the Guild Hall on Wednesday next at your convenience so that I may be permitted to return your kindness.'

Had I been aware of the consequences of my impetuosity in disclosing to Alderman Applegarth the duplicity effected by Felix Brandling that day, I might well have decided to keep that information to myself.

35

He had been deprived of the savings which his wife had stolen and which he had been unable to recover, denied the handsome sum which he expected her to fetch at auction and had been without wages during the whole period for which the keelmen had struck work. Consequently, Jasper Scuffins was desperate to bolster his meagre funds pending the commencement of the new employment promised to him by Aeneas Snitterby. The idea of how he might do so occurred to him when Kitty Dace, imagining a particular newspaper article to relate to the activities of the keelmen, due to an ambiguous headline, read out a report which greatly appealed to his dishonest way of thinking.

MISSING SAILOR SOUGHT

LOST, STOLEN or STRAYED from Charlotte-square, Newcastle, between the Afternoon of Tuesday, and the Morning of Wednesday last, a light-brown coloured DOG, of the Terrier Kind, which answers to the Name of SAILOR, not of a furious or fierce Nature nor constituting a Menace to any Member of the Public who bears it no Harm.

Any Person who conveys the said Dog to its rightful Owner, Mister Aloysius Salmond, at his Residence in Charlotte-square, shall receive a generous Reward; and whosoever detains the said Dog after the Promulgation of this public Notice, will be subject to Prosecution. If the said Dog has in Actuality been feloniously taken, any Person or Persons giving Information of such an Act, as may

---

be the Means of convicting the Felon or Felons responsible, shall receive a **REWARD of FIVE GUINEAS.**

The following morning he made his way out of Sandgate, eschewing his keelman's uniform in favour of some less conspicuous apparel, and headed to the affluent suburb of Spital Tongues, on the lookout for a docile dog which he could persuade to accompany him back to his house. He had not gone far past the St Mary Magdalene Hospital when he noticed, some twenty yards ahead of him, a woman who had stopped to give alms to a beggar. She had with her a large black and white spotted dog of a type with which Jasper Scuffins was unfamiliar. Certainly, he had never seen such a creature in Sandgate and imagined that it might be a rare and valuable breed and, therefore, ideal for his purpose. As he came nearer, he saw that the woman, who by now was in deep conversation with the beggar, had let go of the dog's harness and, seeing his opportunity, he grabbed hold of the leather strap and ran off, with the animal racing along behind him as if it were enjoying a game of chase. By the time the woman had turned around and realised that her dog was missing, Scuffins was out of sight.

As he headed back towards Sandgate he could just about catch the sound of her distressed cries of, 'Hamlet! Hamlet! Hamlet! Where are you, Hamlet?'

*

It had not been long since Mister Elias Tobin and I had presented ourselves at the Guild Hall in order to collect our reward of twenty guineas from the Town Clerk's Office for our part in securing the arrest of one Claude Shivers. Now I had returned at the invitation of Alderman Applegarth, this time with Perlee Parker, who proudly clutched his sketch pad in case his handiwork should again be the subject of appreciation. We both felt a sense of anticipation - elation even - at the prospect of receiving some token of gratitude for having reported to the Alderman the gross deceit to which he had been subjected by Felix Brandling MP at Emanuel Mordue's cock-pit.

There was a slight commotion in progress outside the Guild Hall caused by the presence of some unruly urchins and hobbledehoys, the girls skipping with ropes and the boys playing leap-frog and rolling hoops without regard to the importance of the location. The delinquents were, however, quickly dispersed thanks to the efforts of the stick-wielding old woman whom I had seen when last here and who chased them off with a host of curses and imprecations. Much to my surprise, Perlee doffed his cap to her, addressed her by name and wished her a good day, his salutation being immediately reciprocated.

As we proceeded inside, I recognised the doorman as being the same person who had received us on my previous visit but he showed no sign of remembering me - an indication, so I assumed, of the large number of strangers who passed across his threshold, some of whom he was attending to while we waited in the lobby for our turn to come. For some reason (which escaped me at the time but which I had good cause to recall much later), I could not help noticing a large rectangular mark on the wall which suggested that a painting had once been hanging there and was recently removed. I was to learn in the fullness of time that this spot had been the resting-place of a portrait by the renowned artist Thomas Gainsborough which had subsequently been sold at auction for five hundred guineas by Sotheby's of London.

'This way, gentlemen,' the doorman said when we announced our business there. 'Alderman Applegarth is expecting you. He's waiting for you in the Robing Room.' He led us up a wide winding staircase to the upper floor, past a large and unflattering statue of King Charles II, then along an oak-panelled corridor lined with a plush red carpet and into a cavernous chamber which boasted a hammerbeam ceiling decorated with gargoyles and shields of the elite guilds of the town, a floor of patterned marble slabs and a brass plate stating *Company of Merchant Adventurers of Newcastle-on-Tyne: Deus Sit Noster Amicus*. Our guide informed us that this was the Jacobean Great Hall. He approached a door at the far end and knocked loudly.

'Yes?' enquired a voice and the doorman responded, 'Your two gentlemen visitors, sir.'

'Come,' the voice called and the doorman beckoned us to go inside.

To say that Perlee and I were both completely taken aback at the sight which confronted us would be no exaggeration. At the far end of the room, Alderman Applegarth was perched on the edge of a deep-buttoned leather-bound sofa in front of which a low table held a tray of cups and a coffee-jug. A few feet away, next to the inglenook and before a roaring coal-fire, the unmistakeable figure of Felix Brandling was seated in a matching armchair engulfed in a rank aroma, a smug expression etched upon his flabby face.

It was Perlee who regained his composure first. 'What's *he* doing here?' he demanded angrily, pointing pointedly at the pungent politician.

The question was addressed to Alderman Applegarth but it was Felix Brandling himself who replied. 'You two have got some explaining to do,' he said in a voice full of menace. 'You can't just go round telling lies about important people, you know.'

'What are you talking about?' Perlee retorted curtly and Brandling bridled, clearly unused to being spoken to in such a manner.

'I explained to Mister Brandling what you two gentlemen alleged to have taken place at the cock-pit last Saturday,' said Alderman Applegarth, reaching for his coffee and taking a mouthful in order to create a meaningful pause in his statement. 'But Mister Brandling has assured me quite categorically that no such thing occurred. Therefore, you were clearly mistaken.'

Perlee was not to be put off so easily. 'I was *not* mistaken,' he said calmly. 'I quite clearly heard this man …' – he pointed again at Felix Brandling, this time disdainfully – '… plotting with his fellow conspirator to win the prize fight by blinding your bird. I saw him hand over five guineas. I was only a matter of feet away.'

'How dare you gainsay me, sir,' roared Felix Brandling, his jowls rippling and his cheeks reddening. 'I'll have you know that I am an important person. A very important person. I can tell by your accent, sir, that you are not a native of these parts and you may, therefore, not realise that I am no lesser a person than the Member of Parliament for Newcastle-on-Tyne.'

'All I know about you, sir,' said Perlee calmly, 'is that, unless you have an identical twin, you are a liar and a charlatan.' I confess to having been somewhat alarmed - and not a little impressed - by Perlee's pluck at standing up to a man of Felix Brandling's power and influence.

The MP looked ready to burst. 'You should know, sir, that if I so wished I could summon the mayor this minute and have you arrested by the constables for your damned insolence. How does a month in Newgate Gaol appeal to you?'

'Do you suppose that this scene is a figment of my imagination too, sir?' Perlee opened his sketchpad, took out the page which contained the drawing of the MP handing money to the Official Setter-on and held it up for inspection.

Brandling's eyes bulged at this revelation. 'Where on earth did you get that, sir?' he asked in astonishment.

'I drew it myself, sir. I was watching you both.'

'I don't believe you. I saw nobody else there.'

'I was standing out of sight behind a horse and carriage, sir, while the two of you were hatching your plot.'

'You were spying on us, were you? Listening in on a private conversation, is that it? You have the impertinence of a blackguard, sir.'

'Ah! So you admit it then, do you, sir? You admit having the conversation!'

'I mean … I mean … I've never had a conversation with this other man, whoever he is. I've never seen him before.' Brandling was temporarily flustered by his inadvertent slip, but soon recovered and was back on the attack. 'So it seems to me, sir, that not only do you dare to spread a calumny against my good character - which, I'll have you know, has never been called into question before - but you have also had the temerity to create a portrait of me without my consent.'

Brandling's bluster may have temporarily distracted my friend because, at that very moment, Alderman Applegarth leapt out of his chair like a man half his age, snatched the sketch from Perlee's grasp, dashed across to the fireplace and threw it into the coals. I was completely startled by the unforeseen destruction of this crucial piece of evidence and, at the same time, amazed at Perlee's apparent self-control at the sight of his precious drawing being consumed by the flames.

'There!' exclaimed the Alderman. 'That's put an end to this nonsense once and for all. Now get out of here, you two.'

'By the way, Brandling,' Perlee said, as we were about to take our leave. 'A word of advice if I may.'

'What's that, sir?' the other asked, guardedly.

'You might try Doctor Smellome's Worm Lozenges, sir. I've read that they have proved the greatest efficacy in restoring the constitutions of those who, either because of a debauched lifestyle or through mere ill-fortune, are enervated by flatulence.'

'Debauched, you say? How dare you, sir. There's not a word of truth in any of the scurrilous rumours which may have reached your ears.'

'Then I must grant you the benefit of doubt to which you are entitled, sir, and conclude that in your case the condition is purely a consequence of ill-fortune. I wish you well at the Dispensary.'

'Damn your insolence. I assure you, sir, that any more of your impudence and I will have you thrown into the House of Correction. A long spell in there will teach you not to test the patience of a man as important as myself.'

As we went out through the door, Perlee turned and uttered what sounded to me like to be an ill-considered threat - and, indubitably, an idle one. 'And I assure *you*, Mister Felix Brandling, Member of Parliament for Newcastle-on-Tyne, that before this year is out, sir, I will see you hang. That is my solemn promise.'

*

Newcastle Courant

A GRUESOME DISCOVERY

On the Evening of Friday last, a gruesome Discovery was made by a courting Couple on the south Side of St Bartholomew's Church-yard. Four bodies, two belonging to female Persons and two belonging to Males, were found wrapped in coarse Sackcloth and partially concealed a few Inches below the Surface of the Soil. The Pair who happened upon this harrowing Scene and whose Identity at the present Juncture remains unknown, at least to this Newspaper, were greatly distressed by their unanticipated Encounter with the Quartet of Cadavers and required the Assistance of several Passers-by, together with the timely Administration of smelling Salts, to restore their Equanimity.

It is understood that, upon Questioning by the Captain of the Watch which was on duty that Night, the Sexton of St Bartholomew's Church recalled having observed two Gentlemen, one tall and one short, loitering outside the Church-yard during the previous Afternoon. Upon approaching the Gentlemen in Question and enquiring as to the Nature of their Business, the Sexton received a curt and imprecise Response which gave rise to a Feeling of Insecurity on his Part and led to his summarily terminating the Discourse.

The Matter has been reported to the Mayor who in turn has instructed the Town Constables to investigate these curious Circumstances further and, in particular, to attempt to ascertain the Identity of the Cadavers and of the two Gentlemen referred to above and, if possible, to detain the latter with due Dispatch.

36

I could not understand why, after Alderman Applegarth had destroyed his sketch and then sent us packing from the Guild Hall, Perlee Parker spent most of our journey back to his room chuckling away to himself.

'How can you be so cheerful after that obnoxious man burnt your work?' I asked.

'You'll soon find out,' he replied enigmatically. He halted at the public pant situated at the corner of the Darn Crook and plunged his head into the cold water while I watched, flabbergasted. 'I do that every day,' he told me, once he had shaken the excess drops from his hair. 'It's supposed to improve my eyesight, you know. Or, at least, stop it from deteriorating. Leonardo di ser Piero da Vinci said that it is essential for a painter to maintain a keen eye.'

I followed him up the creaking staircase leading to the garret at the top of his lodging house. 'Here,' he said. 'Come and look at this, James.' With a flourish, he whipped off a large cloth that covered the easel standing in the centre of the cramped room to reveal a canvass on which was a drawing of Felix Brandling in the act of surreptitiously passing his accomplice a handful of coins while whispering conspiratorially in the latter's ear. Perlee laughed aloud at the astonishment which my face must have betrayed. 'There!' he said. 'Didn't I explain to you how I always copy my sketches on to a canvass and seal them with shellac as the foundation for my paintings?'

'So that's why you weren't livid when Alderman Applegarth got hold of your drawing and threw it in the fire.'

'Exactly. I had no further use for it except to show Brandling the proof of what I had witnessed outside Emanuel Mordue's cockpit.'

'So you are going to finish the painting, then?' I asked, somewhat disingenuously.

'I certainly am. And I will hang it somewhere. Just as I promised Brandling that I would …'

For the second time in quick succession, the truth dawned on me, as I recalled Perlee's parting remark to Brandling – a promise to see him hang - which I had assumed to be some empty threat on his life, spoken out of petulance but with no serious intent.

'… And do you remember,' Perlee added, 'that I told you how important it is for me to get to know as much as I can about someone if I am to produce a really lifelike image which captures their personality as well as their physical appearance?'

'Yes. What of it?'

'Well, the time we spent this morning in the company of Mister Felix Brandling MP was invaluable to me in that respect. I was able to make a proper assessment of the man.'

'And what did you learn about him during that brief encounter?'

'Quite a lot, James. For example, I ascertained that he is arrogant, full of self-importance, condescending, scheming and mendacious.' I nodded my assent and Perlee continued, 'I will do my best to incorporate as many as possible of these … er, … qualities, if I may call them that, in my portrait. My objective is to ensure that anyone viewing the finished product will not only see a picture of a man whose physical characteristics are immediately recognisable but will also be readily able to detect the kind of person who lurks within.'

'And where do you plan to display it, Perlee?' I asked.

'I have yet to decide that. I have a few ideas but I must allow them to gestate. However, James, I want to show you something else,' he said, searching through several framed canvasses which were stacked in covers against the wall. He selected one and carried it over to the window, through which the watery sun was casting its rays. 'One of the advantages of living in an attic,' he remarked. 'More natural daylight than in the rest of the building.' Then he took the cover off the canvass, held it up in front of me and asked, 'Well, do you recognise this one?'

It was a portrait of an old woman wearing a white bonnet on her head and an embroidered shawl around her shoulders. Her hands were clasped in front of her around the top of a wooden staff. Her expression conveyed the impression of a person with a strong determination to do what she believed to be right and to challenge anyone or anything which she regarded as unjust. The accuracy of the image was such that even though I had, to my knowledge, seen this person only twice in my life – the last time, admittedly, quite recently – I could not fail to recognise her.

'It's the woman at the entrance to the Guild Hall. The one who was running after the children.'

'Auld Judy,' Perlee confirmed. 'Judy Dowling, to be precise. Keeper of the Town Hutch.' Observing my puzzlement, he elucidated. 'She has a number of jobs at the Guild Hall. She acts as the messenger for the Council Chamber and the Mansion House. Runs errands for the mayor and other councillors. Chases away children who try to get into the building or loiter in the vicinity – that's why she carries a stick. She doesn't need it for walking, she can run like a hare even though she must be all of fifty years old. Everyone calls her Auld Judy, but her official title is, as I've said, Keeper of the Town Hutch …'

'What's the Town Hutch?' I interrupted.

'It's a large oak chest, probably three hundred years old or more, which in days gone by used to hold the Corporation's documents, books and money. Now, it's kept inside the Council Chamber at the Guild Hall. To secure the contents, it has nine locks each requiring a different key. There used to be eight Chamberlains, elected every year, and each one had a separate key, with the mayor holding the ninth. Consequently, the chest could be opened only in the presence – or, maybe, with the collusion - of all nine people.'

'So Auld Judy is now the person in charge of it, is she?' I asked, slightly bemused.

'Oh. no. The Hutch is no longer used, it's preserved as a relic of the past, I suppose. And Judy's title is just symbolic. I imagine they just wanted to call her something that sounded notable to reward her for all the good work she does there.'

'You seem very well-informed about all this,' I couldn't help observing.

'Of course,' Perlee replied. 'Auld Judy told me all this while I was making my sketch of her. A good way of passing an hour.' He began to chuckle, just as he did earlier on our return from the Guild Hall.

'What is it that so amuses you now?' I asked.

'Well, James, that's not all she told me,' he said with a mischievous smile. 'She's in a good position to see what Applegarth and Brandling get up to there. She had some very interesting information to recount about their outrageous thievery. Information which I am sure we can put to our advantage in our dealings with these scoundrels.'

*

Things had gone seriously wrong with what Sir Stanhope Delaval had fervently believed to be his well-laid schemes.

According to his previous calculations, he would have expected by now to be at the head of a thriving business supplying cadavers to the Barber-Surgeons' Hall. After all, had he not displayed immense commercial acumen in spotting the opportunity to meet a burgeoning demand for something for which the students and staff there were willing to pay considerable sums of money? And what's more, he reminded himself, it was money which was mercifully free of that damnable income tax introduced not long ago by that rascal Pitt in order to pay for the Government's expenses in fighting that scoundrel Napoleon. However, it was Sir Stanhope's dreadful misfortune that, shortly after he had launched this new enterprise, his main customer for the purchase of cadavers, Doctor Donald Stickler of the Barber-Surgeons' Hall, was initially incarcerated in Newgate Gaol and subsequently sent back in disgrace to Scotland where he had, no doubt, already found some way to continue his nefarious activities in partnership with some grubby resurrectionists operating in the Presbyterian graveyards of Glasgow.

Finding other customers to fill the gap left by Doctor Stickler had proved extremely difficult. William Ingham, the Head of the Barber-Surgeons' Hall, had made it his personal mission to stamp down hard on the practice of receiving cadavers from unlicensed sources. Furthermore, there was now even talk of an attempt being made by Felix Brandling and other Members of Parliament to introduce a law intended to make it easier for surgeons to acquire cadavers by providing that the bodies of hospital patients and residents of poorhouses could be used for dissection unless their relatives objected. Sir Stanhope, realising that the wider availability of corpses which this legislation was likely to produce would seriously undermine the current illicit trade, had taken Brandling to task about this on many occasions, trying to persuade him to desist from his ill-conceived crusade, but without success.

'That old busybody,' Sir Stanhope had muttered to himself during meetings of the Company of Hoastmen, while Brandling pontificated from the chair about the evils perpetrated by the keelmen. 'Why can't the man just stick to worthy causes like opposing the abolition of the slave trade instead of poking his nose into matters which should be no concern of his?'

Of course, the approaching failure of his corpse-supplying enterprise was of nothing in comparison to the failure of the plan he had contrived with Blackie Johnson. Had *that* plan succeeded, he would by now be the rich widower of the late Lady Paulet. But it had all gone horribly awry. He remembered how delighted he had been when the fabulously wealthy and terminally-ill Lady Paulet grudgingly accepted his offer of marriage, a union which, he calculated on the best of evidence, would last a maximum of six months before she passed away and left him her fortune. However, once the nuptials were completed, his new wife, far from fading away towards an imminent death seemed, against all expectations and previous expert medical prognoses, to acquire a fresh lease of energy. Indeed, she had become the life and soul of the regular parties held at Seaton Delaval Hall, drinking copious amounts of champagne, forcing Sir Stanhope to dance with her until he almost dropped down with exhaustion and then dragging him off to her bedchamber for hours of such tempestuous lovemaking that the poor fellow wondered whether *he* would be able to survive more than six months.

Now, there was even talk from Lady Paulet's physician of her living to a ripe old age and surpassing all previous records for the County, a prospect which filled Sir Stanhope with dread but which, upon his seeking in desperation to obtain a second opinion, was confirmed by another doctor. 'But she was supposed to last for no more than six months.' He almost pleaded with the doctor to amend his prognosis. 'And now it's almost twelve!'

With increasing regularity Sir Stanhope asked himself how much longer he could allow the situation to continue and whether he would have to think earnestly about adding Lady Paulet to the collection in his icehouse.

In the meantime, he needed to request a small loan from a wealthy business associate.

37

Perlee Parker pronounced himself far from disappointed with his first visit to the Flying Horse Tavern in the company of Ralph and myself. Indeed, there was no shortage of characters to whet his appetite in his quest for fascinating subjects whose image he could consign to canvass. Once again, Hell's Kitchen was noisy, smoky, crowded and rumbustious but, despite the apparent lack of order there, the atmosphere bore no hint of menace or trouble.

I spotted a number of signs on display which I did not recall having seen before. One warned *No animals allowed in the netty,* another cautioned *Street girls must not parade their wares on these premises,* a third stated *In order to prevent outrageous behaviour, absolutely no politics whatsoever to be discussed in this establishment.* I assumed that His Satanic Majesty alternated his notices frequently in keeping with the frivolous spirit of the place. That practice did not, however, detract from his determination to require strict adherence to his instructions and to take to task anyone who failed to obey them.

I recognised several of our fellow-customers from my previous visits and guessed that they must be regulars at the taproom. Captain Starkey was regaling his company with stories of his fratch with Monsieur Bonaparte's fleet at the Battle of the Nile where he served under Rear-Admiral Sir Horatio Nelson. In the far corner, Blind Willy was playing his fiddle and singing one of his songs to a sizeable audience, many of whom were joining in the choruses. The elderly crone was there with her scruffy little dog which barked noisily at a sign which decreed that *Dogs and women must be kept under control at all times,* as if it had miraculously acquired the ability to read. There were some unfamiliar faces too, including a one-eyed man, whom I assumed to be some kind of fortune teller, surrounded by a group of people as he examined what looked like a pack of tarot cards.

The pipe-smoking woman was there, still in her usual place leaning against the glass case containing a stuffed badger, this time with an empty creel slung over her shoulder. Even at a distance, I could detect a strong smell of the sea on her and was debating with myself the reason for this when someone nudged me sharply in the ribs and muttered, 'Dolly Peel,' in my ear.

'I beg your pardon?' I said, turning to find a man of medium height with a thin, long, pimpled visage and a pale, rather melancholy expression. He wore a long black coat over a waistcoat and red neckerchief, with thick brown leather trousers adorned (if that is the correct word) with various patches, tears and holes. His lank black hair was tucked under a broad-brimmed hat which rested upon a pair of disproportionately large ears. He carried a small white terrier under his arm.

'Dolly Peel,' he repeated, pointing to the pipe-smoking woman. 'Aa saw ye looking at yon fish-lass. That's her name. Walks from Cullercoats to Newcastle market every day to sell her fish. And not only fish, so they say. After the market closes, she comes in here to wet her whistle, then walks back again. It's a canny hike, ye knaa. Ten miles each way. Heart of gold, but ye divvent wanna cross her, marra. She can fight like a man. Her husband's away at sea, press-ganged he was, but she can look after her sel, no doubt about it.'

'Thank you, I'll make sure I keep on the right side of the lady,' I rejoined, thinking that was the end of the conversation. Dolly Peel certainly looked a formidable character. She had a large domed head, the shape of which was accentuated by her receding hair and the defiant way she stacked the remains of it in a pronounced wave commencing in the middle of her crown and sweeping back beyond the nape of her neck. Her face, bronzed by sun and wind, bore an expression which somehow managed to combine a defiant self-confidence with a humanitarian sensitivity. Her hands were bruised, blistered, chapped and patterned with cuts, presumably a testimony to the demands of her work which involved baiting fishhooks, cleaning and gutting fish and mending nets. Her habitual carriage and gait resembled that of a cat stalking its prey, her head held still and straight, her eyes intently fixed on her destination – her quarry, you might say – her body poised, her legs comfortably bent and ready to spring. Had she whiskers, they would indubitably have twitched. One was almost led to wonder whether, once she had gained the sparse shelter of the Cullercoats hovel in which she lived, she licked her body all over in feline fashion – or, at least, those parts of it she could reach without overcontorting herself.

As I considered these thoughts, I felt another sharp nudge in the ribs.

'Bogie Theobald,' he muttered.

'What?' I said, slightly irritated because of the abruptness of his tone and the soreness of my ribs.

'Bogie Theobald,' he repeated. 'That's my name. Best ratcatcher on Tyneside.'

At that point, Perlee Parker who must have been watching our exchange, interrupted us (an intrusion for which, I confess, I was most grateful) to introduce himself to my new-found 'friend' and immediately offered to buy the man a quart of ale, which he readily accepted, whereupon the two fell into an animated discussion while I left them to it and rejoined Ralph, who was standing near the bar-counter.

'You'll never guess who just came in,' he said.

'I don't suppose I will,' I replied, hoping to avoid a long drawn-out game of conjecture.

'One of your former colleagues from the Barber-Surgeons' Hall. Look over there. You can't miss him.'

And indeed, I couldn't. My eyes followed Ralph's pointing finger across the room and there, towering above the other customers was none other than Bold Archy. Since my recent dismissal from my apprenticeship, I had often wondered how the giant man had fared now that Doctor Stickler, for whom he worked most of the time, had been removed from the premises and - for all I knew - was still languishing in the cells of Newgate Gaol. I felt an urgent desire to satisfy myself on this point and, with Ralph in my wake, made my way through the throng towards Archy. When I reached him, I saw that he was accompanied by an old woman, whom I took to be his mother, the Widow Henderson. She was unremarkable, except for her heavily-rouged face, and it was difficult to reconcile her compact size with her son's extraordinary dimensions. With them was another woman, the dwarf who, on a previous occasion, I had seen in Hells' Kitchen dressed as a little girl but was now wearing a more adult outfit. The huge man and the tiny dwarf made a very curious pair.

I was not certain that Archy would remember me but as soon as he saw me, his expression bore the unmistakeable signs of recognition and to my immense gratification the words, 'Master James,' escaped his lips.

'You must be a friend of Archibald's,' Widow Henderson said, with a smile. 'He never forgets a face, you know. You may not realise it but, although he has lost many of his other faculties, his memory is as good as it ever was.'

I explained to her that I had spent many months at the Barber-Surgeons' Hall as an apprentice under the same master as Archy.

'Ah, you mean Doctor Stickler,' she said, shaking her head sadly. 'He's been sent back to Scotland and now Archibald assists Mister Ingham. He's a good man, you know, and Archibald is very happy there.'

I told her that I too had found Mister Ingham a good man during my time there, at which she replied, 'Of course, Doctor Stickler was a good man too. He thought the world of Archibald. He told me so himself on many occasions.'

I wondered briefly whether I should appraise the Widow Henderson of the true nature of the man and the plans which he entertained in respect of her son, but quickly dismissed the idea. I saw no point in disabusing her of the fond impression she had gained of Doctor Stickler, since their paths were unlikely ever to cross again.

*

It had been a most unhappy couple of weeks for Felix Brandling MP and his mood was as black as the skies from which torrential rain had been falling for some days. Firstly, of course, there was the unfortunate business at Emanuel Mordue's cockpit when that interfering rapscallion of a street artist had eavesdropped on his conversation – his *private* conversation – and then, with his knacky-kneed pal, had the temerity to denounce him to Alderman Applegarth as a cheat.

'A *cheat* he called me,' Brandling fumed to nobody in particular, as he sat alone in his study at Gosforth House. 'Damnable cheek. How dare the lower classes seek to insult their superiors. Never let me forget that I am an important man,' he reminded himself. 'A *very* important man.'

Then, a day or so later, he had received an unannounced visit from Alderman Applegarth which sent him off into an almost unstoppable bout of flatulence requiring the immediate and thorough fumigation of his drawing-room. It had taken Brandling an uncomfortable discussion with the Alderman to resolve the misunderstanding over the cockfight. Plus, the transfer from him to the other of one thousand pounds (as a penance, Applegarth had called it) as well as an additional one hundred pounds (being the value of the prize money fraudulently obtained by the subterfuge). Plus a humiliating apology, the like of which has rarely been extracted from a man of such importance. After all, he is a Member of Parliament, he confirmed to his inner self. And it is not in the nature of Members of Parliament to apologise for their actions. Why should they, for God's sake? Following which, both men agreed that it was a principle of great substance that those who occupied the upper echelons of society should demonstrate a united front in the face an attempt by lesser mortals to undermine their superiority and, therefore, that it was essential to deny any claims that division or animosity could possibly exist between themselves. And, of course, neither man would want a little disagreement to jeopardise the highly profitable 'enterprise' which they operated jointly in connection with the valuable items which could be found in the Council Chamber and adjacent rooms of the Guild Hall, as well as in other public buildings of the town.

Now that he had put that 'misunderstanding' over the cockfight to one side, he had hoped to be able to return to a more equable state of mind. It was not to be, however, because try as he might, he could not forget the threat which still hung over him in the form of the letter pushed under the door of Gosforth House. He turned those words over and over again in his mind. *Before the year is done ye must be deed.* There could surely be no doubt about what that meant. It meant that whoever wrote that letter was predicting his murder. Perhaps the writer and the potential murderer were one and the same person.

Being threatened was unpleasant enough. Being threatened by someone whose identity was unknown was doubly unpleasant. He realised, of course, that he had plenty of enemies. After all, he had made a successful calling in both business and politics and nobody could achieve that without upsetting a lot of people. However, the style in which the letter was written and its reference to the keelmen made it fairly clear where the threat was coming from. The long dispute, with its attendant rancour, had only served to aggravate the already troubled relationship between the keelmen and their masters. And, although it had been settled eventually, there would be many among the strikers who felt that they had been bullied into submission and wanted revenge. They had gained far less than the increase of four shillings demanded in the letter.

Another thought crossed Brandling's mind about the threat to his life. Was it just a fluke that the upstart artist who dared to draw a picture of him had made what sounded like a similar threat. *Before this year is out, I will see you hang,* is what he said. Could *he* have any connection with the anonymous letter, Brandling conjectured. If not, it was a huge coincidence. Perhaps he had been looking in the wrong place for the culprit by blaming somebody linked to the keelmen. On further reflection, however, he dismissed the possibility for two reasons. Firstly, the artist did not speak the Newcastle dialect and was unlikely to have used the expression *ye must be deed.* Secondly, the incident at the cockfight which was, so far as he could remember, the first occasion he had set eyes on the man, took place *after* the delivery of the letter.

There was another aspect of the letter which puzzled him, namely its reference to *a plague about your house.* What could that possibly signify? When people talked about the plague they normally meant the Black Death which was carried by rats and devastated the country hundreds of years before. It didn't make any sense that such a thing could return to Newcastle at the beginning of the nineteenth century. No sense at all. He couldn't make head nor tail of that idea.

He was still contemplating the likelihood that he would be unable to rest until the mystery correspondent had been unearthed when a distraught housekeeper interrupted him with more bad news.

'Beggin' yer pardon, sir,' she shrieked hysterically. 'They're all ower the place.'

'What are you talking about?' Brandling asked, irritated by having his peace disturbed.

'They're everywhere, sir, beggin' yer pardon, sir. In the scullery, in the parlour, in the …'

'Calm yourself, woman,' bellowed Brandling. 'I don't know what you're talking about.'

'Rats.'

'Rats?'

'Big black ones, beggin' yer pardon, sir. Huge black things. Aa canna gan back in there. Aa'm bound to get bit.'

So that was it! A plague of rats! So, one of the predictions in the letter had come true.

Felix Brandling sized up the situation and barked out an order to his housekeeper. 'Send for a rat-catcher straightaway. I want the best rat-catcher in the County.'

38

Perlee Parker first mentioned the idea of the painting at around the time that Ralph moved to London to take up employment as a cashier at the Charing Cross branch of Drummonds Bank, a respectable institution which numbered King George III among its honoured account-holders. I bade Ralph farewell at five o'clock one cold morning as he boarded the Royal Telegraph Post Coach from the Turk's Head and I made him promise to send me a letter as he soon as he arrived at his destination. Indeed, it may have been that very evening as we walked the short distance between the Flying Horse Tavern and his lodging-house in the Darn Crook that Perlee said, 'You know, James, I've found just what I've been looking for.' His face almost glowed with happiness.

Before I could ask exactly what he meant by that, he launched into an animated explication. 'So many *characters*,' he purred. 'And all of them together in one room. Hell's Kitchen is a veritable goldmine of characters. Without you, James – that is to say, without your kind invitation to accompany you there – I would never have come across them. And now, I would like to beg another favour of you.'

'I will certainly oblige if it is within my power to do so,' I replied, feeling flattered by his remarks.

'I am exceedingly grateful to you, James, and, with your indulgence, I will shortly explain what I have in mind. But first, I have a question which I would like to put to you. Have you, by any chance, heard of The Last Supper?'

I was somewhat taken aback by this and could not imagine how to respond until I recalled something of the kind being mentioned by Mister Hadwen Bragg during one of his Bible readings to which Bella and I used to listen when we resided at

Number 264 Spital Tongues. 'I do believe,' I said after some consideration, 'that it was the meal taken by Jesus and his apostles on the night before his crucifixion.'

'Ah!' said Perlee. 'You are quite correct, James. However, when I talk about The Last Supper, I refer not to the event itself but to the painting in tempera created by Leonardo di ser Pierro da Vinci which depicts that event and is displayed in the monastery of Santa Maria delle Grazie in Milan.'

'Well?' I asked, perplexed. 'What of it?'

'Ha! What of it, you say. Well, James, I will tell you. What we see in The Last Supper – the painting I mean – is a group of men sitting at a long table. Jesus has just announced to his twelve companions that one of them will betray him on the morrow. The artist has captured their different reactions to this revelation. For example, John looks as though he is about to swoon at the news. Andrew gazes in disbelief at his brother, Simon Peter, whose face is contorted with anger. Bartholomew and Matthew are both in great distress, the latter in tears. Thomas appears incredulous. Phillip has his hands aloft and a stunned expression on his face. Judas Iscariot appears rigid with apprehension at the discovery of his treachery and lowers his head, perhaps through shame or in the hope that his reaction will not be noticed by the others. And so on. In short, James, the painting contains a group of people who are all *characters.* Each one has been endowed by the artist with some particular trait which seems individualistic and interesting. And this has given me an idea for a scene which I would like to paint.'

'And what is the favour you wanted to ask?' I pressed him.

'Oh, yes, of course. I'd quite forgotten. Well, James, the scene which I would like to paint is of a collection of characters from Hell's Kitchen. Just imagine them gathered around a long table, each with their own individualistic and interesting trait:

Bold Archy and Kitty Dace – the giant and the dwarf – Blind Willie with his fiddle, Bogie Theobald the rat-catcher and his dog, Dolly Peel with her pipe and creel, the Captain, the one-eyed fortune teller, yourself, of course, James, and maybe I could also include Auld Judy. And I'm sure that Mister Elias Tobin would not want to be left out. What a splendid array of characters that would be!'

'Do you think of me as a character too, then, Perlee,' I asked, 'because of my knacky knees?'

'I think of you as a character, James, because of your kind and generous nature.'

'Thank you,' I said, 'but I am still no better informed about this favour you mentioned.'

'The favour is this,' he told me at last. 'I would like you, my friend, to assist me in persuading these characters to agree to be portrayed in my painting. You see, James, I predict that some of them at least will, through suspicion, fear or embarrassment, be reluctant to have their portrait painted. Therefore, I need you, since you are familiar with some of my previous efforts, to reassure them that I will, to the best of my ability, depict them with sympathy, sensitivity and affection.'

'I will certainly do as you ask, Perlee,' I rejoined, 'but I cannot believe that many of them will sit comfortably for hours while you attend to your work.'

'You are quite right, James. It is a matter to which I have already given some consideration. Consequently, what I propose to do is this. His Satanic Majesty, as we are pleased to call our esteemed host, has a suitable room on the premises which he has kindly consented to place at my disposal. It is a spacious attic enjoying good light and contains a table which, although not large, is sufficient for my purpose. I would like my assortment of characters to assemble there one morning for one hour while I determine how to marshal them to best effect and then produce a rough sketch of their disposition. Once I have transferred this to a canvass in my studio in the manner which I have previously demonstrated to you, I will if necessary supplement any images in my head with additional details gained through my observations of the individuals while they are going about their normal business in the Flying Horse Tavern. In that way, I will be of no further inconvenience to them.'

'And when you have completed the painting,' I asked, 'what, pray, do you intend to do with it?'

'That, James, I will guard as a secret for the time being except to tell you that its resting-place will be worthy of the fine figures it will portray.'

*

As he said so himself, Bogie Theobald was undoubtedly the most accomplished rat-catcher in the whole of Tyneside and, quite possibly, the whole of the County. He was never seen without at least one of his three Rothbury terriers, whether he was visiting a customer who wanted to rid his house of vermin or passing an evening in the taproom of the Flying Horse Tavern. He eschewed the fatal poison which almost all of his competitors employed, knowing that a rat which was killed by such a method would probably die in some inaccessible spot underneath the floor, thereby creating a most disgusting stench which the occupant was likely to find more intolerable than the original infestation. He also knew that, as well as dispatching its intended victim, the poison often had a deleterious effect on the health of his client or even the rat-catcher himself who might, after several months of its use, begin each day by vomiting blood immediately upon waking and eventually discharge it from all his other orifices, until he eventually experienced a slow and painful descent towards a ghastly death.

Instead, Bogie preferred to catch the rats in steel traps (or sometimes, in nets) and to transfer those which he found still alive into a strong metal cage. In this way, not only was he able to collect his fee of fourpence for each rat he removed from the premises of his client (or more, if they looked wealthy and willing enough to have a higher price extracted from them) but he could also sell the surviving specimens for five shillings a dozen to the owner of the Gallowgate rat-pit for use in the fortnightly events which alternated there with cockfights. Often, he would even manage to derive a third strand of income from the same source when he was engaged to officiate at a rat coursing. This was an onerous if well-paid task which required him to weigh and handicap the dogs, referee the contests and, on occasion, fight off the attacks of disgruntled owners who disagreed with his decision as to which combatant was to be awarded the victory.

He had just returned from a completing an errand at a house in Forth-bank where, a few days earlier, a child which had been left in a cradle was attacked by two or three rats. According to the tenant's account of the story, the family were not immediately alarmed when hearing the cries as they were accustomed to such sounds emanating from the infant and did not consider them untoward. Later, however, they discovered that the forehead of the child had been torn in several places and immediately summoned a surgeon, thanks to whose assiduous and expert attention a full recovery of the patient was contemplated. Because of the family's anguish at the child's suffering and their determination to ensure that there would be no repetition of the unfortunate occurrence, they had commissioned the services of Bogie Theobald to exterminate the vermin responsible, a undertaking which he accomplished with commendable proficiency and alacrity.

No sooner had he completed that task than he was approached by a woman who claimed to be a housekeeper in the employ of a Mister Felix Brandling, a person of whom Bogie was unacquainted but who, according to the housekeeper in question, was a very important man who wished to have his residence, namely Gosforth House, cleared of a plague (as she described it) of rats. Hearing of the importance of this putative customer and calculating from the name and location of the abode that he must be a man of some means, Bogie saw an opportunity to obtain a lucrative commission and judged that it might be possible to achieve a fee as high as sixpence per rat.

He loaded his nets, traps, cages and other tools of his trade onto his pony cart, spurred his cuddy into action and headed for his destination, a little way north of Bulmer Village. He presented himself, together with his favourite of the three Rothbury terriers which took turns to accompany him on his rounds, at Gosforth House, a splendid country mansion built of sandstone ashlar in the Palladian style. He was ushered by the housekeeper into the malodorous presence of a repulsively obese man who, without bidding him a civil 'Good Day', gruffly demanded to know the cost of having the plague (as he described it) eradicated from the premises. Even from the rudimentary assessment which he was able to make on his approach to the main entrance to the premises, it was immediately clear to a man of Bogie's experience that the vermin problem probably resulted from the inundation of the drains after recent heavy rain which had forced a colony of sewer rats to evacuate their normal hiding place in favour of the interior of the house. These were almost certain to be black rats, a particularly ferocious strain of the rodent.

Bogie did not answer straightaway but feigned concentration as if he were calculating the extent and complexity of the task before him. Then he replied, 'Aa would normally charge ye as little as ten pence for every little beggar Aa catch. That's providing they are of the brown rat variety. But if Aa should happen on any black rats – which Aa must tell ye are very vicious - then Aa would charge ye as little as a shilling each.'

'Ha! I can see that you're a businessman,' Brandling said. 'Ten pence, you say …'

'Ten for brown rats, twelve for black,' Bogie interrupted. 'The black ones are very vicious, as Aa've said. And clever. Take a lot more catching, they do. Gotta be care they divvent nip ye, 'cos if they do, they spread disease … '

'Disease? Like the Black Death, you mean?' asked Brandling nervously.

'Worse,' replied Bogie. 'Much worse.'

Felix Brandling knew everything there is to know about the price of coal, the tonnage output of all the collieries on Tyneside, the cost of transporting slaves and the likelihood of their surviving the voyage, the yield of sugar plantations in the Americas and the value of the commissions that could be extracted from commercial enterprises in return for the patronage of a Member of Parliament, but he was surprisingly poorly informed about the going rate of remuneration of rat catchers. However, despite the fellow's dire warnings about the threats offered by the rats, Brandling thought that ten pence for catching one seemed rather a lot of money, merely on the basis that, should the presence of say, twenty, of the creatures be discovered, it would cost him not far short of seventeen shillings. And, of course, if the damned things turned out to be Black Rats, that was a whole pound! He decided to offer half of the asking price.

'I'll pay you five pence for the browns and six for the blacks.'

Bogie once again went into an apparently intense deliberation with himself before emerging to affirm with great reluctance his acceptance of the extremely hard bargain which had been forced upon him. Then he unloaded his cart and set to work.

39

It did not take more than a few visits to the Flying Horse Tavern for me to recognise that His Satanic Majesty, Mister Elias Tobin, despite his somewhat gruff manner and strict disciplinarianism, was most sympathetic and accommodating towards those in impoverished circumstances or upon whom life had, in different ways, looked unkindly. He was inclined to allow beggars, trampers, travelling salesmen and other mendicants to enter the taproom so long as they did not attempt to overwhelm the premises with their collective presence or browbeat the customers into purchasing their tawdry wares or provoke a commotion or beg too aggressively. On occasion, he would even oblige such persons with a small measure of gin or ale without requiring a corresponding disbursement. Consequently, there tended to be a procession of vagrants who, through some apparently communal prearrangement, had conspired to limit their number to the extent permissible - or, perhaps, tolerable - in order to elicit from the regular clientele a modest donation towards their living expenses.

Blind Willie, whom I had first encountered in the All Saints' Poorhouse, was a frequent performer there. His cheerful disposition and entertaining ditties made him something of a favourite among customers in the taproom and his appreciative audience responded generously with alms. Despite his blindness, he was somehow able to detect the value of coins by the sound they made as they were dropped into his fiddle case and he would often surprise donors by calling out, 'God bless ye for that farthing,' or 'God bless ye very much for that ha'penny,' or 'God bless ye very much indeed for that penny.' When he had exhausted both his repertoire and himself, he would slump into a seat and declare loudly, 'Aa could manage a bonny one, ye knaa,' to nobody in particular, at which point he would invariably be brought a pint of beer.

The majority of those to whom I have referred above were of an advanced age, either in their fifties or even more elderly (such as Blind Willie). Occasionally, their number included a member of the fairer sex who had somehow failed in fulfilling successfully her station as a wife and grandmother or who had experienced the misfortune of discovering herself in the state of widowhood without the concomitant financial and familial support which one hopes that such forlorn creatures would deserve and receive.

One evening, shortly after I had attained the age of twenty-one and arrived at man's estate, I entered Hell's Kitchen, treated myself to the purchase of a quart of Mister Tobin's best ale (now guaranteed to be embittered with hops rather than camomile flowers) and found a vacant seat in the corner from where I could observe and listen to the comings and goings and intercourse of my fellow customers. Not long afterwards, my ears were assaulted - it is not too inappropriate a description to apply to the effect on my aural senses – by the high-pitched song of a salesgirl broadcasting details of her merchandise.

> *Silk shoe ties, a penny a pair*
> *Buy 'em and try 'em and see hoo they wear.*

To me, that voice was unmistakeable. Although many months had passed since I had last heard it, there could be no doubt. None at all. That squeaky, shrill timbre could belong to only one person. Indeed, as I observed when its owner came into view, it belonged to a young lady in her late teens, one whom I recognised immediately despite the changes which had taken place in her appearance. No longer was she a skinny waif, but now her sonsy body was filled out with womanly curves which put me in mind of a figurine of the goddess Athena which stood on a shelf in the study of Number 264 Spital Tongues, the place in which I had last seen her.

She was as surprised and delighted to see me as I was to see her and we laughed and hugged and cried until the tears streamed down our faces, while many of the customers looked on in wonder at what felicitous event could produce such an exhibition of rejoicing. I was, of course, most concerned to learn by what stroke of fate she had become reduced to selling shoe-ties, particularly since when I last took my leave of her she was flourishing within the comfort and safety of the Bragg house-hold. However, she insisted on first hearing an account of my own fortunes since I left there to take up my position with Mister Abel Grope, Undertaker and Coffin-maker. I complied with her directive in as brief a manner as I could without appearing tactless or ill-mannered, since it was *her* story which I desperately wanted to hear.

When it came to Bella's turn to fill in the missing details, she had a far more harrowing tale than mine to tell. She explained how, after she had been staying with Mister and Mistress Bragg for nearly six years, she happened one day to spot a notice in the *Newcastle Courant* seeking, as it said, a respectable young lady to take up a respectable position as maidservant at a respectable address in Benwell Village. As a young girl, she had always assumed that she would eventually be engaged as a la-bourer to a slater or a bricklayer and spend her working days crawling across the roofs of houses or climbing ladders. But see-ing this advertisement opened up in Bella's mind the possibility of entering domestic service, a calling at which she believed she could excel, thanks to the experience she had gained in the

Bragg household. Although reluctant to forsake the comfortable surroundings and lifestyle she currently enjoyed, she communicated her intention to Mistress Bragg, fervently hoping it would not in any way be construed as a indication of displeasure at her treatment at Number 264 Spital Tongues. In the event, Mistress Bragg was most considerate and understanding and kindly consented to provide a written unexceptionable character which in due course Bella presented to her prospective new employer and was taken on.

At first, she was very happy with her new position. Her mistress, a lady by the name of Eustacia Fenwick whose husband, Humphrey, was overseas on business, was a most kind-hearted person. She dressed Bella in a stylish outfit consisting of a black dress trimmed with a furbelow, a white ruffled half-apron and white lace headpiece and ensured that she was provided with whatever personal items she needed in order to feel at home. Bella's duties included cooking, cleaning the house, lighting fires and washing clothes, chores which she found a little tedious but not particularly onerous, as well as those which gave her enormous pleasure – looking after the three-year-old twin girls, shopping for groceries and taking the family dog for a walk every morning, whatever the weather. And in the evening, after Bella had finished her work for the day, Mrs Fenwick would invite her into the music room to listen while she played the pianoforte and sang or, on occasions, the two of them would sit and chat together almost as mother and daughter, rather than mistress and servant.

The situation changed for the worst, however, on the return from Spain of Mister Humphrey Fenwick a year or so later. He was much older than his wife, displayed little affection for her or their children and shared neither her genial nature nor her contentment with Bella's presence in the family home. Indeed, he often seemed distinctly hostile to, and resentful of, Bella and she rapidly came to the conclusion that the purpose of her employment had been as much to provide company for Mrs Fenwick as to perform household chores.

Then, a month or two after his return, Mister Fenwick's demeanour towards Bella changed suddenly. Instead of treating her in an offhand and dismissive manner he became what could only be described as over-familiar, displaying a degree of intimacy which Bella considered most improper. He began to comment favourably on her appearance, bombarded her with questions designed to elicit details of any previous love affairs (she had had none but declined to answer him on this subject) and even tried to persuade her to accompany him on a ride into the countryside in his chaise. It was noticeable to Bella that these approaches always took place when his wife was not present. When she refused to indulge him, he feigned wounded feelings. 'Why are you so unwilling to become my friend?' he asked. 'I'm handsome enough, am I not?' He was, Bella acknowledged to herself, a man who took pride in his appearance. He always wore good quality, well-tailored clothes. He had a fine set of teeth which, so far as she could tell without approaching them too closely, were original. He kept his hair neatly powdered. He was a little stout but less so than most men of his age and social class. In summary, he might have been a good proposition for an older woman who did not care about a man's character. But he was of no interest whatsoever to Bella and when, eventually, she summoned up the courage to make this fact as plain to him as it could possibly be, he struck her hard across the face. Then, grasping her tightly by the hair, he dragged her along to the sitting-room where his wife was engaged in a little embroidery and informed Eustacia that Bella had attempted to seduce him.

The immediate outcome of this episode was that Bella's employment was summarily terminated and she was thrown out on the street with no money or possessions beyond the clothes in which she stood. She was, in essence, confronted with the same circumstances which some years previously had forced Bella and myself to scrape a living for ourselves by begging and pilfering on the Keyside before we were rescued by Mister Hadwen Bragg. This time, however, she was not fortunate enough to come to the attention of that most benevolent man and, instead, had to rely on her wits and the meagre charity of others in order to survive. For several nights she was reduced to scouring the gutters for discarded fish trimmings and sleeping on the sawdust of a joiner's shop in Sandgate. Then one day, her throat wracked with thirst, she took a tin bottle down to the edge of the quay to obtain a drink of water and, either through negligence or intent, fell into the river. She would surely have perished had it not been for the vigilance of a fish-wife who happened to be on the bank nearby in the process of carrying the day's catch to market and saw Bella's predicament. The woman raised the alarm, alerting no lesser a person than Cuckoo Jack who managed to retrieve the poor girl just before she was about to expire. Once her saviours had resuscitated Bella with brandy and kindness and given her the first solid meal she had eaten for days, they took her across the river to St Mary's Church in Pipewellgate, where they left her in the care of Reverend Collinson, the rector of that parish. This was still her home – temporarily, or so she hoped, pleasant and welcoming though it was - and she now made a modest living by selling all kinds of ornaments, trinkets and other knick-knacks, laying out the goods for sale on the pavement during the daytime and hawking them around the town's taverns in the evening.

It was at this point in her explanation that Bella looked up, gave a whoop of delight and exclaimed, 'That's her.' I followed her gaze and my eyes alighted upon the figure of Dolly Peel who was standing in her customary place, smoking her trademark pipe and holding a glass of what I assumed to be Hollands. 'That's her,' Bella repeated, this time even more shrilly. 'She's the one who saw me fall in the river and called for help. She saved my life.'

I guess that the volume of her cry must have been audible above the hubbub of the room because Dolly turned in the direction of its source and, judging from the expression of pleasure which cast itself over those hardened features, immediately recognised the author. Whereupon, she left her position next to the glass case containing the stuffed badger and approached us.

'This is my dearest friend,' Bella told her, pointing to me. I was greatly surprised and not a little flattered by both the substantive and the epithet. 'His name is James.'

Dolly looked perplexed and shook her head. 'No, that's Knacky-kneed Mack,' she said, at which I had to acknowledge – not, I confess, without some embarrassment - the nickname with which I had first been christened by Belcher and Jago, my disgraced fellow workers at Mister Grope's business, but which had since become current among my fellow imbibers in the Flying Horse Tavern.

Dolly was curious about how the two of us had become acquainted and Bella explained that we had both been indentured as apprentice climbing-'boys' to Jeram Boag, Esquire, Master Sweep. Then, upon further probing from Dolly, she was compelled to recount for the second time that evening the treatment she suffered at the hands of Humphrey Fenwick which led to her destitution in the chares of Sandgate and, almost, to her demise in the cold waters of the Tyne.

'Aa've heard of him, that Humphrey Fenwick,' Dolly said angrily, when she had listened to the sorry tale. 'He's one of them aldermen, if Aa'm not mistook, who think they're superior to the rest of us. Well, Aa'm telling ye, Bella, Aa nivvor let a man get away wi'it if he's tret a lass or a bairn badly. And Aa divvent intend to let this Mister Fenwick get away wi' how he tret ye neither.'

'What do you mean?' asked Bella, flattered to know that Dolly wanted to take up the fight on her behalf but mystified as to how on earth she could hope to get the better a man of such wealth and high standing in the town.

'Nivvor ye mind,' Dolly replied. 'Aa tell ye, Aa've taken on tougher men than him and Aa'm yet to be beaten. So Aa just need ye to show me where this Humphrey Fenwick lives.'

40

A comeuppance for Humphrey Fenwick! And what a comeuppance!

What started out as Dolly Peel's plan to teach Bella's tormentor a salutary lesson ended up as sweet vengeance not just for Bella but, in a totally unexpected twist of fate and to my great surprise, vengeance for me as well. On the evening after Bella first appeared in the Flying Horse Tavern, she accompanied Dolly and me to Benwell Village to point out the address where Humphrey Fenwick lived. It was an imposing, ivy-covered mansion set in a tree-lined mews on a height overlooking the river, with a long drive and spacious grounds of manicured lawns and densely-planted shrubberies which betokened the presence of a full-time gardener. In front of the house stood a fine-looking two-wheeled chaise and a fine-looking chestnut cuddy, which I thought I may have seen somewhere before but could not recall the circumstances. Once Dolly was satisfied that she could retrace her way there, she instructed us to return at nine o'clock on the morning after next and to keep out of sight.

On the appointed day and at the appointed hour, Bella and I had concealed ourselves behind a hedge a few yards from the gate when Dolly arrived with three companions, all hardened women who stank of fish and (as she told us) harboured a love of revenge and a hatred of overbearing men. After we had all waited there about half-an-hour, the front door of the mansion opened and a gentleman whom Bella identified as Humphrey Fenwick emerged from the house, climbed onto the seat of the chaise, spurred his pony into action and headed down the drive towards us. As he approached our hiding place I could see him plainly and immediately recognised him as the man who had accosted me on the Keyside several years ago after my parents' deaths had left me impoverished, pretended to befriend me, taken me to Westgate-street and sold me (as I believed) to Mister Boag, the Master Sweep.

He reached the end of the drive and descended from the chaise in order to open the gate. As he did so, Dolly and her friends, like the Avenging Furies of Greek mythology, rushed forward with blood-curdling shrieks and seized him, stifling his cries of surprise and anguish with several pieces of sacking. They bundled him back onto his seat and Dolly took the reins while the other three sat on him, rendering him undetectable and immobile so that even if a constable should happen to pass by at that moment he would see nothing which might suggest that an abduction was in progress.

'To the river,' Dolly cried, and off they trotted down the long slope to the spot on the bank just below the Benwell staithes, while Bella and I followed slowly (on account of my knees) on foot. By the time we had caught up with them, Humphrey Fenwick had already been carried aboard a keel whose owner had been persuaded by Dolly to allow the boat to be used to transport the hostage to their planned destination. Once he had been securely confined in the huddock under the close watch of the three fish-lasses, the keelman used his pole to manoeuvre the boat out of the shallows and they headed downstream towards the coast some ten miles away. Meanwhile, Bella and I clambered into the chaise, Dolly took up the driver's seat again and off we went with a view (as we were to learn) to reaching Cullercoats in time to form a reception party for our honoured guest. During our journey to the coast from Benwell, past the lead-works, potteries, iron foundries, tan-yards, skinneries, tobacco and snuff manufactory and other industrial sites which belched their smoke and fumes across the river, we tried to elicit some indication of what Dolly and her friends were planning to do with Humphrey Fenwick. But all she would say on that subject was, 'Ye'll find out soon enough and Aa'll promise ye that ye'll nivvor forget it. And neither will that scoundrel. Aa've had my fratches with many a better man than him and won.'

Thanks to a propitious ebb tide on the Tyne, the keel and its passengers duly arrived later that afternoon at the harbour adjoining the little sandy bay just north of the mouth of the river, where they were greeted by a gathering of what appeared to be every fish-lass within a radius of five miles. It was here that the women usually waited for the men folk to return from their fishing expedition before they set to work emptying the catch from the nets and gutting and cleaning the fish ready for market. At the top of the strand, above the point where the tide normally reaches, it was their practice to excavate a deep pit in the sand where they threw discarded fish bones, innards, scales and eyes. The occasional high tide would reach as far as the pit, emptying it of its contents and washing them out to sea, whereupon a fresh one was dug and the process commenced all over again.

Dolly's three friends unloaded their human cargo from the keel and carried him up the beach, struggling and hurling abuse at his captors but to no avail. No sooner had they set him down on the sand than several of the spectators, who had all been informed at length by Dolly about his misdemeanours, fell upon him, striking him with their fists, feet and staves and tearing off his clothes. Within a few minutes he had been entirely divested of his beaver-felt hat, fine morning-coat, corded breeches, frilled shirt, neck-cloth, blue stockings, two sets of corsets, half-boots and underclothes and he stood naked, bruised and bleeding before the jeering crowd, his humiliation made complete by the removal of his wig, exposing a bald pate covered by pustulating sores. If he imagined that this was to be the nadir of his degradation, he was to be disappointed. A group of women seized him and carried him to edge of the pit containing the fish waste. There had not been a tide high enough to reach it for at least a fortnight so it was by now nearly brim-full with its foul-smelling contents, their condition made even worse by the recent spell of hot weather and the thick, dark clouds of bluebottles which swarmed noisily over them. To my nose the stench was unbearable, whereas Dolly and her fellow fish-lasses seemed completely immune to it. Into this mephitic cesspool, to a great cheer from the spectators, they launched Humphrey Fenwick, followed closely by the remnants of his clothes, which some of the women had shredded with their hooked gutting-knives. There was a loud squelching sound as he sunk slowly into the rotting mass and disappeared from sight, while, at the same time, several large rats jumped out and scurried away.

I am certain that he would have been left to drown or suffocate in a piscatorial grave had he not, through an extraordinary effort born of terror and desperation, somehow managed to find the strength to heave himself out of this quagmire at the fourth or fifth attempt, by which time his body was covered in a thick and slimy layer of rancid filth which adhered to his skin. As he stood on the sand, almost exhausted by the exertion, he looked less like a human being than a creature from a child's worst nightmare.

'Dinaa stand there much langer or we'll hoy ye back into the pit again,' Dolly roared at him. 'Gan on yer way back to Newcastle. It's only ten miles, Aa walk there every day me sel. If a low-class fish-lass like me can do it, Aa'm sure an important man like ye can.'

I never did find out how Humphrey Fenwick, covered in rotting fish waste and without clothes, money or means of transport, managed to get back to his mansion in Benwell Village. My only regret was that Perlee Parker had not been at Cullercoats with his sketchpad that day to record the event for posterity.

*

In accordance with Perlee Parker's injunction, I invested a great deal of time and effort during the days that followed in requesting, appealing, cajoling, inveigling, coaxing, persuading and even begging in order to gain the assent of those he had designated as *characters* and wished to appear in his painting.

Some of the transactions were relatively straightforward. Blind Willie readily agreed to take part so long as he was allowed to bring his fiddle, a proviso which it seemed to me entirely reasonable to accept. Bogie Theobald was initially too embarrassed by the proposition but reluctantly acquiesced, on condition (also granted) that one of his dogs could accompany him. Blackie Johnson, however, refused to commit himself unequivocally to be present on the appointed day, saying that he would first have to consult the tarot cards to establish whether the timing was auspicious or whether his attendance would instead lead to some unfavourable outcome.

When I explained to Dolly Peel that Perlee Parker wanted to paint her, she refused outright to countenance the idea, scowling, 'Aa suppose ye want me to tak off aal me claes, is that yer little plan?' Even when I was able to convince her that it would be quite unnecessary to divest herself and that Perlee's intentions were honourable, she again declined, this time on the grounds that she might be spotted and tracked down by the constables with whom she had endured many fratches. Eventually, after several more attempts on my part to persuade her, bolstered by the personal intervention and assurances of Perlee Parker himself, she reluctantly consented to participate.

In order to arrange for Bold Archy to take part, I had to seek approval from the Widow Henderson, who readily gave her permission on behalf of her son but insisted that she should come along too. That had not been Perlee's original intention because, as he told me privately, for all her qualities the Widow Henderson was not, strictly speaking, a *character*. However, it was obvious that without *her* presence (upon which her authorisation was conditional) it would not be possible to include Archy. And without Archy it would not be possible to include Kitty (without whom, the Widow Henderson insisted, Archy would refuse to come, which saved me the trouble of having to persuade *her*). 'I suppose we'd better let the Widow come, then,' Perlee said, resignedly. 'I can always omit her from the final portrait.'

My conversation with Captain Starkey was rather more complicated and lengthy, since I had to endure the usual rigmarole of a round of formal introductions, conducted as though we had never met before, followed by an account of his incident-filled voyage to New South Wales and his role in the campaign to pacify the Aboriginal tribesmen who were attacking the convicts. Eventually, he consented to becoming one of Perlee's subjects, although I confess to serious doubts as to whether he really understood the nature of the assignment, since he kept asking for reassurances that any prisoners-of-war would be treated humanely and not shot out of hand unless they attempted to escape.

Of course, since Perlee had first suggested the idea of the painting, Bella had turned up in Hells' Kitchen and, as he had no hesitation in describing *her* as a character, I explained that I would regard it as great favour if she appeared alongside me in the portrait, which she agreed to do.

His Satanic Majesty needed no persuasion. On the contrary, when I raised the matter with him he responded in terms which implied that since it was he who, as publican of the Flying Horse Tavern, was the person providing the venue, he expected to be depicted as the central figure in the portrait.

Auld Judy, Keeper of the Town Hutch, was the last person on Perlee's list with whom I needed to make contact. I found her in her customary location at the front of the Guild Hall, engaged in her customary activity of guarding the building against the attempted entry of any undesirables and potential trouble-makers as well as chasing away delinquent children. Fortunately, I encountered no resistance from this quarter. She had already sat once as the subject of a portrait by Perlee, as I knew, and she was rather flattered to be approached again.

So that was it. Bold Archy and Kitty and the Widow Henderson. Blind Willie. Blackie Johnson. Captain Starkey. Bogie Theobald. Dolly Peel. Auld Judy. Bella. His Satanic Majesty. And myself, of course. Quite a group. And, according to Perlee Parker, (almost) every single one of us a *character*.

41

Jasper Scuffins was becoming very impatient, the reasons for which were two-fold.

In the first place, Aeneas Snitterby, although having insisted that he was a man of his word, appeared to be extremely tardy in fulfilling his commitment to allow Scuffins to commence employment as an off-putter on the Benwell staithes, where he expected to spend the remainder of his working days in something approaching lucrative indolence. In the meantime, he was obliged to continue to heave coals on his keel while being subjected to the mistrust and opprobrium of many of his colleagues, who accused him of betraying their cause by persuading them to end their strike without achieving any of the objectives which he himself had once championed so vociferously.

The second cause of his impatience concerned the dog he had captured which, he had since been informed, was of a type known as a Dalmatian Coach Dog. He demanded that Kitty Dace regularly scoured the columns of the *Newcastle Courant* in search of an announcement which would reveal the identity and address of the dog's owner and confirm that the finder would become the recipient of a substantial reward (which, of course, Scuffins himself intended to claim). Unfortunately, however, she searched in vain. She was even made to check the *Newcastle Weekly Examiner* too but neither did this newspaper contain any reference to a missing Dalmatian Coach Dog. Meanwhile, Scuffins had to suffer the inconvenience of accommodating the creature in his Sandgate home, feeding it on food which he could ill afford and enduring its constant homesick whining. This couldn't go on much longer.

Then he had an idea. If he was unable to discover from the newspapers where the owner lived, perhaps the dog itself would lead him to its master's house - which, he surmised, was likely to be near the place where he kidnapped the animal. Then he could explain how he had found the stray near the Keyside and had looked after it and fed it for days while tramping all over the town in the hope that it might recognise its home and could be returned there safely. Such an act of altruism would, he imagined, surely merit a handsome reward.

And so, just as he had done some days before, he set off from Sandgate and headed to the suburb of Spital Tongues, this time accompanied by the Dalmatian Coach Dog. Once he had passed the St Mary Magdalene Hospital, the animal became more and more animated, as if it recognised the neighbourhood and sensed an imminent homecoming. Indeed, so excited was it, that it began to tug at its harness with such vigour that Scuffins was scarcely able to hold on to the leather strap attached to its collar.

They had almost reached the spot where Scuffins had originally snatched the dog, when it suddenly gave a tremendous jerk, wrenched the harness from his grip and raced off at such a speed that the keelman had no chance of catching up with it. He realised immediately that his gambit had failed and that no reward for his selflessness would be forthcoming.

*

As the Newcastle Society for Effecting the Abolition of the Slave Trade, as well as similar organisations in other towns and cities throughout the kingdom, became more voluble in ensuring that the increasingly horrific accounts of the slaves' maltreatment reached the ears of all sections of their community, the pro-slavery lobby did not continue always to get its own way. Gradually, more and more of those who were previously minded to support or, at least, abide the existence of the slave trade, came to question its morality. Eventually, to the incandescent fury of Felix Brandling, the town's MP and a lifelong supporter and beneficiary of the abhorrent business, the Newcastle Common Council passed a resolution calling on Parliament to conduct an urgent enquiry into the slave trade. When the motion was subsequently debated in the House of Commons, it was only an impassioned speech by the same Felix Brandling which ensured that the appeal was rejected.

At that point, Mister Hadwen Bragg, whose determination to rid the world of what he described as 'this despicable trafficking and exploitation of human beings' was matched only by his unwavering dedication to the rule of law, realised that, if the Newcastle Society for Effecting the Abolition of the Slave Trade was to stand any chance of achieving its ultimate aim, it would have to use every legitimate means at its disposal, however controversial that may be, to promote its cause. Shortly after the setback which the abolitionists' cause had experienced in the Palace of Westminster, he addressed a small gathering of the Society's most influential members who had assembled at his clothing emporium in Pilgrim-street to plan their next campaign.

His eyes still retained their customary twinkle, despite the gravity of his subject matter, but there was a great sadness in his voice as he spoke.

'We have organised petitions in our town just as other Societies like ours have done in Liverpool, Bristol, London, Glasgow and elsewhere and there are now well over two hundred thousand worthy folk who have added their name to our cause. It saddens me, however, to remark that our own Member of Parliament, the man who represents us in the House of Commons where laws are enacted and standards of acceptable be-haviour are defined, cannot by any measure be said to reflect, on the subject of the slave trade, the views of those of us who believe that it is an abomination in the eyes of God. Not only that, but he is himself mired in the guilt which falls upon those who participate in or profit from this despicable industry. He has refused to present or even accept our petition, signed by ten thousand principled Geordies, because it conflicts with his own corrupt interests.

'It behoves us to do everything in our power within the law to bring pressure, together with common sense and humanity, to bear upon those who govern us in order to turn their minds away from their present course and to convert them to the just and honourable cause which we espouse.'

'Everything within the law, you say?' interrupted the Vicar of Heddon-on-the-Wall. 'Haven't we already tried that and failed?'

'We must continue to obey the law, Reverend,' Hadwen Bragg rejoined emphatically. 'Any society which is not founded upon law will crumble. But, for my own part, I would, within these constraints, support any measure targeted directly against Felix Brandling in person. Although the man is a creature of God, as are we all, his well-being must, if necessary, be regarded as subordinate to the interests of the greater good. And the greater good is the abolition of the slave trade.'

As he resumed his seat to a smattering of applause from the rest of the group, he had no idea, despite his stirring words, what action could possibly force Felix Brandling to disavow his opposition to their campaign.

The opportunity was to arrive sooner than he could have imagined.

*

It was quite by chance that I renewed my acquaintance with an old friend I had not seen these past five years – a happy coincidence which indirectly advanced the interests of both my current and former hosts in their dealings with Felix Brandling MP.

Word had reached Perlee Parker of the existence to the west of the town of a curious five-sailed structure known as a smock mill, apparently the only one of its kind in the whole of the kingdom. He determined to visit this location for the purpose of sketching the unique edifice and, one morning, informed me of his intention and suggested that I might care to accompany him. I accepted the invitation for no better reasons than that it was a fine, bright day and I thought the walk, so long as if was not excessively energetic, would provide a beneficial exercise for my crippled knees.

We made our way along Westgate-street and had almost reached the lunatic asylum near the Leazes when a dog came bounding up to me, barking excitedly and even attempting to nuzzle its snout against my leg. At first I was somewhat discomfited by such an unambiguous show of affection and it took me a few moments to identify the creature, which was a little less sleek and glossy than on the last occasion I had seen it, but still recognisable. Perlee looked bemused at the sudden arrival of the dog and the undue attention it was paying me. 'It's Hamlet,' I explained. 'He belongs to Mister Hadwen Bragg and his wife.' This name was familiar to Perlee, whom I had often regaled with accounts of my time with that most hospitable family.

It struck me as odd that Hamlet should be at large on the streets of the town, since its owners had, according to my memory, always taken care not to allow it to roam alone beyond the confines of their home. He was wearing the same leather leash which Bella and I used to attach to his collar whenever we took him for a walk. I speculated that he had run away, a possibility which, on reflection, seemed out of character for such a docile and dutiful pet. Then a darker thought entered my mind and I wondered whether some harm might have befallen Mister or Mistress Bragg and rendered Hamlet a stray. When I expressed my concern to Perlee, he suggested that we should make a temporary diversion from our intended route in order to take the dog back to the Braggs' residence, a mile or so away, and to satisfy ourselves of their well-being.

I need not have worried.

On arrival at Number 264 Spital Tongues, we found its occupants in fine health and spirits, their mood lifted by their patent delight at welcoming myself once more to their home and at making Perlee's acquaintance and, in no small measure, by their relief at the safe return of Hamlet who, they said, had gone unaccountably missing several days before and had been greatly missed. Mister Bragg's head was even shinier than I had remembered it, while his whiskers had, to my mind, almost doubled in volume and his bright-blue eyes still twinkled cheerfully. Mistress Bragg, despite the passage of years, still retained her youthful attractiveness and natural exuberance. She insisted upon our staying for refreshment and laid before us an excellent pigeon-pie and a selection of her home-made preserves. No sooner had we finished these delights than Mister Bragg prevailed upon me to describe the course which my life had followed since the day I had set off to take up my position in the employ of Abel Grope, Undertaker and Coffin-maker. I attempted to convey the facts truthfully while omitting any reference to the reprehensible exploits of Belcher and Jago, my unfortunate encounters with Septimus Grymm, my discovery of Doctor Stickler's shadowy activities, or the recent deception perpetrated on Perlee and myself at the Guild Hall.

Then Mister Bragg begged to hear an account of Perlee's provenance and calling. Unlike me, my friend did not desist from relating the story of our fratch with Alderman Applegarth and Felix Brandling. At the mention of the latter's name, Mister Bragg bridled visibly and it was obvious to us from his reaction that he too had suffered at the MP's hands. Pressed to explain, he placed before us a number of pamphlets produced by the Newcastle Society for Effecting the Abolition of the Slave Trade and allowed us some minutes to acquaint ourselves with the horrors suffered by the wretches abducted from their villages in Africa, taken halfway across the world in the most foul conditions which a fifth of them failed to survive, then forced to endure a life of gruelling work under fear of the lash, all for the benefit of a group of merchants and plantation owners who cared only for their profits and nothing for the victims of their enterprise.

'Our Society has been campaigning for years to bring these facts to the attention of the public and to persuade the Government to introduce legislation banning this vile commerce,' Mister Bragg said gravely. 'But Felix Brandling has done everything within his power to obstruct us and to oppose any suggestion that slavery is something which should be proscribed by law.'

'The fellow is totally lacking in humanity,' Perlee commented. 'All he seems to care about is his own importance.'

'Not only that,' Mister Bragg continued. 'He is *personally* involved in the trade. He owns sugar plantations in the West Indies which rely wholly upon slave labour. He has business interests in the shipping companies which transport slaves from Africa and then return laden with the sugar they help to produce. His mansion in Bulmer Village is paid for with the blood and sweat of the enslaved. As a Quaker, it is not in my nature to denounce a fellow human, but I cannot in all conscience dissuade myself from condemning from the core of my being everything which that person stands for.'

He looked embarrassed at how robustly he had expressed himself and the intensity of emotions which his words had conveyed. For our part, Perlee and I were deeply touched by what he had said and by the images portrayed in the pamphlets he had shown us.

The three of us remained silent for a while, not knowing how to continue the conversation. At length, Perlee spoke. 'Mister Bragg,' he said gently, 'I have for some time now been considering how best I might cultivate my relationship with Felix Brandling in order to regain some of the ground he has taken from me, so to speak. In the light of what you have just said, I believe that some collaboration between us could achieve an outcome which would act to our mutual benefit as well as promoting our respective causes in relation to the man. What do you say to that, sir?'

Mister Bragg did not answer straightaway but sat quietly, contemplating Perlee's statement and balancing one thought against another. Then he said, 'Only last night, I was with a number of my fellow abolitionists - as we are described in the columns of the newspapers - discussing how we could overcome the obstacles which Felix Brandling has placed in our way. I vowed that I would do everything in my power, however controversial it was and so long as it does not involve breaking the law, to undermine the corrupt influence wielded by that man.' He leaned forward towards Perlee, his eyes twinkling and his mouth curved in a smile amongst his bushy whiskers. 'I would very much like to hear what thee has to say on this matter, Mister Parker.'

As Perlee eagerly outlined his plan, all thought of the smock mill was relegated to the back of his mind.

42

It had taken Bogie Theobald and his Rothbury terrier the best part of a day and a night to round up the rodents which infested Felix Brandling's residence and, when the rat-catcher inspected the row of cages lined up on the terrace in front of Gosforth House and counted their contents, he reached a total of seventy-two. Every one a black rat. Not a single brown rat among them. It had proved to be a lucrative commission and Bogie, whose prowess in arithmetic almost matched his prowess in rat-catching, calculated his earnings at thirty-six shillings. This, of course, did not include the thirty shillings he would receive from the owner of the rat-pit in Gallowgate, who would be particularly pleased to be provided with black rats as they proved more doughty opponents for the dogs that their brown counterparts and therefore made for a livelier contest. He loaded up his traps and nets on to his pony cart and presented himself at the tradesmen's entrance of the House, ready to show his catch to the owner and collect his money.

Felix Brandling was shocked to see how many rats had been found on his premises and even more shocked at how vicious and repugnant they appeared, with their hideous yellow fangs, ghastly pink eyes and grotesque tails. He was horrified to think of these loathsome creatures running around his drawing-room, his study, his kitchen … even his bedroom, carrying some awful virus that might infect him with a disease which would cause fever, nausea, suppurating sores and vomiting blood before an agonising and undignified death quite inappropriate for such a very important man.

'If ye would be kind enough to pay me my fee now, sir, Aa'll be on my way,' Bogie said, doffing his broad-brimmed hat.

Felix Brandling looked rather uncomfortable at the prospect of parting with his money. 'I didn't realise that you would find so many rats,' he said. Then, suspecting that a swindle was being perpetrated on him, he added, 'Are you sure that you caught all of them in *my* house?'

'Every single one of them, sir. Every single one.'

'You didn't bring them with you, then?'

'No, sir, and if ye would pay me my fee now, sir, Aa'll be on my way.'

Felix Brandling fumbled in his pockets and pulled out a handful of coins. He selected a guinea and proffered it in Bogie's direction.

'It's thirty-six shillings, if ye please, sir.'

'Thirty-six shillings? What do you take me for, you impudent wretch? Here, take this guinea and be off with you.'

'It's thirty-six shillings ye owe me, sir.'

'How dare you! I won't be defrauded by a hired hand. I am a very important person, you know.'

'Ye agreed to pay me sixpence for each black rat Aa caught,' said Bogie levelly. 'Aa've caught seventy-two, sir. So that makes a total of thirty-six shillings, sir, by my reckoning.'

'You have the nerve to accuse me of going back on my promise, do you? I am a very important man, I'll have you know. Now… take this guinea and get off my land or I'll call the constables to chase you away.'

'If that's yer last word, sir, Aa'll collect my cages and go.'

'And good riddance to you, you jackanapes.'

Bogie picked up his terrier, placed it in the pony cart and walked over to the terrace. He had been cheated before and he knew how to deal with such situations. It was the work of only a few moments for him, with practised ease, to open the doors of all eight cages. Almost at once, six dozen rats escaped from their prisons and poured in a squealing black tide across the courtyard and into Gosforth House where they soon occupied every room and, incensed at having earlier been captured and confined, began to take out their fury on the furniture, the drapes, the books, the letters, the food, the clothes in the wardrobes - indeed any item which yielded to their razor-sharp fangs.

Felix Brandling was in a state of utter panic. He stood rooted to the spot, shaking from head to foot, gasping for breath, his heart racing, his normally flushed face pale, drawn, stained with tears and dripping with sweat, his bowels protesting loudly. 'Do something!' he screamed as the rat-catcher climbed onto the seat of his pony cart and prepared to leave. 'Can't you do something?' he pleaded.

Bogie smiled, shook his head and began to untether his cuddy.

Brandling shouted at him again, his voice one of utter desperation. 'Please, get them out of my house,' he begged. 'I'll pay you *anything*. Anything you ask. But just get them out of my house.'

Bogie let go of the rope by which his cuddy was hitched to the gatepost and said, 'Ye'll pay me anything, eh?'

'Please,' implored Brandling, 'Just name your price and I'll pay it.'

'Ha!' Bogie sneered. 'If a man tries to double-cross me like ye did, Aa canna trust him a second time.'

'I'm sorry,' snivelled Brandling. 'I won't let you down again, I promise.'

Bogie knew that he had the upper hand on the man – the man who considered himself very important – and he revelled in the feeling of dominance over him. He intended to press home his advantage. Opportunities like these did not present themselves very often. 'Aa'll tell ye what Aa'm prepared to do, marra … (He no longer regarded the man as worthy of being addressed as 'sir') … Aa'm willing to catch them rats again – seventy-two Aa mean, and not a single one more – but it'll cost ye ten guineas.'

'Ten guineas!' Brandling howled, 'Ten guineas!'

'Correct,' said Bogie. 'Ten guineas is my price.'

Brandling had been party to enough shady business deals in the past to know when he was well and truly beaten. 'Alright,' he said resignedly, 'I'll pay you ten guineas as soon as you've finished. But please, just get on with your work before those creatures destroy my house.'

'Aa'll start when Aa'm good and ready,' Bogie countered. 'And Aa won't be ready until Aa've been given my ten guineas.'

'What? You want your money *now*?' Brandling asked, almost incredulous at the man's effrontery.

'That's what Aa said. We've already established that ye canna be trusted to honour yer word.'

'You mean to say that you're not prepared to take the word of a Member of Parliament?'

'A Member of Parliament is probably the last person whose word Aa'd trust. Now, let me remind ye that while ye are standing here delaying me, them rats are probably breeding away inside. And divvent forget that Aa'm only ganna catch six dozen of them beggars for ye. So ye better hurry and decide if ye're ganna pay me or not. 'Cos if ye're not, Aa'm ganning on me way directly.'

*

It took Perlee Parker several trips to the Fleshmarket before he was able to track down the man who had conducted the sale which he had sketched some months ago. He eventually spotted him still plying his trade, this time engaged in the more customary process of auctioning livestock rather than human merchandise. After the day's lots had been disposed of and the auction came to an end, Perlee contrived to fall into conversation with him and when he had aroused the fellow's interest in the scheme he had conceived over many weeks, he invited him back to the lodging-house to inspect the painting which he knew would capture his attention.

The auctioneer, a Romany by the name of Wildblood, was most flattered by Perlee's depiction of him, the more so since he had, until that very morning, been completely unaware that he had the honour to be the subject of an oil-painting. 'I thought it was only famous people who got themselves painted,' he said. 'You know, kings and queens and dukes and sirs. Not gypsies like me.'

'You'd be surprised,' Perlee told him. 'And, if you like the picture and are willing to do me a small favour, it would give me great pleasure to present it to you as a gift.'

'A gift?' Wildblood exclaimed in delight. Then, more guardedly, 'A favour? What favour?'

Perlee realised that, in order for the plan to succeed, he would have to take Wildblood completely into his confidence. 'The purpose of my stratagem,' he told the auctioneer, 'is to exact retribution upon a particular member of the town's aristocracy, someone who considers himself to be very important and who, although an advocate and guardian of the law, is far from being an adherent of it himself. He is a man whom it would give me great pleasure to bring down to size and to force to suffer the indignities which he is content to visit upon those among our fellow citizens whom he regards as lower mortals undeserving of consideration. To wit, Felix Brandling, our esteemed – I employ this epithet ironically – Member of Parliament, an institution packed with men whose guiding principles are self-interest, self-aggrandisement, self-enrichment and pharisaical affectation.'

When Wildblood heard this, he smiled quizzically. 'Nothing would amuse or delight me more than to be your accomplice in this venture,' he said. 'You see, my friend, I too have been badly done to by those who claim to act in the best interests of all and to apply the law even-handedly, only to treat their subordinates like animals. I know what it is like to be pursued as an outcast and a criminal as I strive to make an honest living. How many times have I been brought before the magistrates, charged as a vagrant and fined! A vagrant! I have been accused of not having a place to live. I have been accused of being unable to give a good account of myself. I have even been accused of pretending to be a gypsy. Pretending! I *am* a gypsy, why should I pretend to be one?'

'I can see that you have been dealt with badly,' Perlee said, sympathetically. 'So how is it that you came by your profession as an auctioneer?'

'I fathomed that it was a calling that would not lead to my arrest,' Wildblood replied. 'I'd already tried the rest. I've been a hawker, a street peddler, a chapman. I've been an entertainer of all sorts – a juggler, a tumbler, a minstrel – I even had a dancing bear once. But I was constantly being picked up by the constables as a vagrant. Then, one day, I saw a man holding an auction in the market-place in Durham Town and I thought to myself, *I* could do that. After all, all you need is a clever turn of phrase, an ability to talk at speed in order to generate some excitement among your punters and make sure they don't have much time to think before making a bid. And, I suppose, you have to have a quick brain for arithmetic to magnify the value of the goods in the mind of the buyer so that they bid higher and still think they have a bargain.'

By the time that they had been talking together for half-an-hour or more, Perlee had formed the view that Wildblood was a man whom he could trust, whereupon he outlined his plan and the part which he wanted the man to play in it. 'So, as you see,' he said, concluding his explanation, 'if all goes well, you will not only end up with your painting but you will also receive a commission of five per cent of the sale, which in this case is likely to be a considerable sum.'

'Five per cent, you say? I normally charge five guineas,' Wildblood ventured.

'You shall have your five guineas, my good man,' Perlee assured him. 'And maybe a lot more besides. Well, what do you say to my proposal?'

43

Felix Brandling had only just finished a modest repast of leg of mutton stuffed with oysters. Although he was well aware of the uncomfortable fact that any kind of seafood was likely to play havoc with his digestive system, he was unable to resist the exquisitely satisfying sensation of the creatures slithering down his gullet. On this occasion, however, he pushed the plate away with almost three-quarters of the meal untouched. In truth, he had little appetite since being overwhelmed with self-pity by the recent experience of having his house swarming with rats and then being bamboozled by the rat-catcher into parting with ten guineas. He was about to reach for the decanter of port when he heard the sound of a carriage coming up the drive and, a few minutes later, his housekeeper announced the arrival of Sir Stanhope Delaval.

'What are you doing here?' he greeted his visitor, brusquely. 'I'm not expecting you, am I?'

'No, Brandling, I thought I'd surprise you,' Delaval replied, his good eye fixed on the MP while the groggy one roved at large around the room, alighting on paintings by Joseph Wright, Joshua Reynolds, Lillian Heaven and George Stubbs which, he vaguely recalled, were remarkably similar to ones he had previously seen hanging in the Guild Hall or the Mansion House or, possibly, the Assembly Rooms.

'I wish you hadn't. I've had quite enough surprises for one day. Just had an infestation of rats.'

'Rats, you say?'

'Yes. I hate the filthy animals. In fact, I have a dreadful fear of rats.' He was never sure when speaking to Delaval which one of the man's eyes he should look at. It was impossible to look at both of them at the same time. 'Makes me come out in a rash and gives me awful stomach cramps. It must be some kind of disease. I think there's a word for it.'

'I don't doubt it, Brandling. There's a word for most things.'

'Quite so. Anyway, what do you want, Delaval?'

'Er … I saw the report in the Courant about your anonymous letter and I've been meaning to come round and offer my sympathies to you.'

'Took your time about it then, didn't you?'

'Well … yes … actually, I've been somewhat preoccupied with a few problems of my own, I'm afraid.'

'Is that so? Well, you can keep your problems to yourself, Delaval. I don't want to hear about them.'

'Ah! In that case …' Stanhope quickly realised that it would be injudicious at that juncture to mention the real purpose of his visit. Instead, he decided to play safe for the time being and returned to the subject of the letter. 'Do you have any clues yet as to who sent it, Brandling?'

'Not so far as I know. The constable who looked at it says he thinks it was written by a woman.'

'A woman? How on earth would he know that?'

'Your guess is as good as mine. Here, you can take a look for yourself, Delaval.' He pulled open the drawer of the bureau, reached inside and handed his visitor the sheet of paper containing the anonymous threat.

Delaval studied it for a few minutes then exclaimed, 'Well, I'll be damned if it *isn't* a woman's work!'

'What? What's that you say?'

'I recognise the author of this.'

'Do you indeed?' Brandling said, disbelievingly. 'And who might that be, I wonder?'

'You remember the dwarf I used to bring to the Hoastmen's meeting to take a record for me?'

'The midget?'

'That's her. Her name is Miss Kitty Dace. Well, I'm certain that this is her handwriting. I've seen enough of it, after all.'

'In that case, Delaval, you'd better get hold of her and find out what the hell she thinks she's doing, threatening a very important person such as myself.'

'That's not so easy as you think, Brandling. I haven't seen her since I was ambushed by those highwaymen on my way here some weeks ago. Either she ran off or they took her with them.'

'Ha! I remember. You never made it here that night, did you? … So, do you have any idea where this midget is now?'

'None at all. But now that we know who wrote the letter we can set the Town Guard after her. Shouldn't take too long to find her.'

'Of course, she might not be *that* easy to spot …'

A sudden thought occurred to Delaval, prompted by his recollection of the newspaper article. 'By the way, Brandling, wasn't there something in the Courant about a reward for catching the culprit? A hundred guineas, if I'm not mistaken?'

'Er … yes,' Brandling confirmed unenthusiastically before adding, more eagerly, 'but of course it is not to be paid out until after the culprit is convicted. Anyway, what of it?'

'Well … to be honest, I'm a bit short of money at the moment. A temporary state of affairs. The truth is, Brandling, I need a short-term loan and I hoped that, as an old friend, you might oblige me. So now I'm wondering whether you would advance me a few guineas … maybe twenty or thirty or even, perhaps, forty … you know, on account, as it were. Then you can deduct what I owe you from my reward when you eventually hand it over.'

Brandling lapsed into a brooding silence, interrupted only by the ominous rumbling of his innards. Having already been relieved of ten guineas by the rat-catcher that day, he was in no mood to hand over any more money.

'I'll tell you what I'll do, Delaval,' he said after some deliberation. 'When you have tracked down Miss Kitty Dace and informed the constables of her whereabouts, I'll advance you five guineas.'

*

The day was all set for the big occasion.

The *characters* - all eleven of us, together with the Widow Henderson - who had been selected and agreed to be sketched for Perlee Parker's portrait gathered in the attic room of the Flying Horse Tavern. Even Blackie Johnson - who was the one doubt - turned up, having drawn from his tarot pack (I am not sure whether this was by accident or sleight of hand) the Ace of Pentacles, the Two of Cups and the Page of Swords, three cards which he judged to constitute a favourable combination.

Perlee thanked us all profusely for coming and explained that he would first arrange us in the way in which he considered most conducive to our collective appearance. Then he would ask us to stay in those positions and to remain as motionless as our circumstances would permit while he composed a pencil drawing of us which would serve as his outline for the oil painting to be completed in his studio. (I noticed that he persisted in applying this term to the cramped garret at the top of his lodging house.) He emphasised that we had been chosen by him because he recognised something unique and interesting about each and every individual among us. (For practical or diplomatic reasons, he did not except the Widow Henderson from this description.)

Having completed his introduction, which left all of us in a very happy frame of mind, Perlee lined us up in the manner which he judged most apposite, mixing tall and short characters, keeping Bogie's dog away from the women (who, he assumed, would be fearful of having such a creature in their vicinity), getting Kitty to stand on a chair between Bold Archy and his mother, placing Blind Willie where his fiddle could be accommodated without imposing upon his neighbours, ensuring that His Satanic Majesty was prominently situated in the foreground, and so on.

Once we had all been allocated our respective positions, Perlee began to sketch us, presumably hoping to complete the task without further adjustment to our disposition. He had not, however, reckoned with the idiosyncrasies of some of those present. After a few minutes of disciplined silence, a commotion occurred when Bogie's terrier spotted a rat across the room, decided to chase it and, in the course of its pursuit, inadvertently nipped Captain Starkey on the leg, whereupon the latter seized upon the opportunity to declaim to everyone the story of how he was attacked by a rabid dog in Pondicherry during his time as an officer in the Duke of Wellington's army which led the expedition against Tipu Sultan.

Calm had only just been restored when there was a brief disturbance as Dolly Peel rounded on Blind Willie, accusing him of staring at her. It quickly subsided when His Satanic Majesty assured her that Blind Willie had not been capable of seeing anything at all since the day of his birth, more than seventy years ago. 'He's not staring at you, hinny,' he explained, comfortingly. 'He's just wondering where the smell of fish is coming from.'

During the course of the next hour, Perlee had to reposition one or more of our number in the interests of good posture or to avoid further disruption to the proceedings. Once, he made the mistake of asking Captain Starkey to move to his left by a small matter of two or three feet, a request which prompted the Captain to introduce himself all over again and then to recount the tale of how Major General George Walpole had sought his personal involvement against some Jamaican rebels whom he subsequently helped to defeat in the Second Maroon War.

Eventually, Perlee seemed satisfied with his sketch and once again thanked us all profusely for coming. 'Ladies and gentlemen, I aim to have completed my painting by the end of the fortnight,' he announced to spontaneous applause.

'And where's it ganna gan?' Dolly Peel demanded suspiciously.

'Ah,' said Perlee, looking in the direction of His Satanic Majesty with a knowing look which suggested that he had anticipated that question. 'Our host, Mister Elias Tobin, had kindly consented to allow me to display it in Hell's Kitchen for the time being.'

'What d'ye mean, *for the time being*?' Dolly demanded even more suspiciously. 'Where's it ganna gan after that?'

'Well now,' said Perlee. 'That rather depends on who buys it. But I have a plan which I am very confident will result in the painting being displayed in a prominent position in one of the most prestigious buildings of our town. A place in which I am sure you will all be very proud to appear.'

'Where is this building?' This time it was the Widow Henderson whose curiosity had been aroused.

'Until I have hatched my little plan,' Perlee replied, 'I regret that I am not at liberty to disclose that information. But, trust me, you will not be disappointed.'

There were several murmurs of dissatisfaction with this response and Perlee recognised that he needed to say something positive to placate the group. 'There are two more pieces of information I would like you to know, ladies and gentlemen,' he said, certain that his next remark would be well-received.

'What's that, then?' Bogie Theobald muttered sceptically.

'Firstly, if my plan succeeds – which I am most confident will indeed be the case – I expect to achieve a good price for the painting. And when I do, my friends, I intend to share it with you. Each one of you will receive one-twelfth of the whole proceeds of the sale.'

A collective gasp of delight indicated that Perlee's words had shocked and pleased his audience in equal measure. No one spoke for a while. Then Blind Willie, who had an uncanny ability to perceive things which escaped the notice of his sighted fellows, said, 'There'll be twelve of us in the painting. Are ye not keeping anything for yer sel?'

'No,' rejoined Perlee. 'I'll be selling another painting alongside the one of you which should earn me enough to live on for a while.'

'What's the second thing?' It was the first time that Auld Judy had spoken.

'Well now,' replied Perlee. 'I thought that it would be a good idea to give you all a name, a name that I could use as the title of my painting. I've noticed that famous paintings always have a name. Leonardo di ser Piero da Vinci said that a good painting is always enhanced by a good name …'

'… So what are ye ganna call us?' Auld Judy interrupted impatiently.

'I'm going to call you the Newcastle Eccentrics,' Perlee told her. He waited for a reaction but none came immediately, so he repeated the phrase. 'The Newcastle Eccentrics.'

Then a tiny voice piped up. 'I think that sounds canny,' Bella squeaked. 'But what does it mean?'

'We aal knaa what *Newcastle* means. It's the toon where we live,' said Auld Judy. 'But *Eccentrics*, what does *that* mean?'

'It means people who are a bit different from others,' Perlee said. 'A bit special. People who are interesting in their own way. It's a term of affection. I think you're unique, that's why I chose the name. And as I told you earlier, that's why I chose you all to be in the painting.'

Again, there was a brief hiatus in the conversation as Perlee's audience took in his explanation. It was Dolly Peel who broke the silence. 'Aa divvent really understand what ye said then, Mister Perlee, but Aa think it sounds canny.'

Dolly's endorsement seemed to reflect the mood of the others and several shouts of support were heard.

'Aa think we should aal gan alang with Perlee's idea.'

'Who cares if we dinaa knaa what it means?'

'Aa like it.'

'Eccentrics. It's a good name, aal reet.'

'So, it's agreed then.' Perlee looked pleased that his suggestion had won general approval. And he was hopeful that everyone would like the final result when they saw it hanging in the taproom in a couple of weeks' time.

After that, he would put the rest of his plan into action.

44

Sir Stanhope Delaval decided that the time had come for decisive action. After all, he reflected miserably, every single day that Lady Paulet managed to survive represented one day subtracted from his own prospective lifespan as a fabulously wealthy widower. He borrowed some old clothes from one of his gardeners in order to disguise himself as an impoverished wretch and set off for Newcastle.

The Dispensary was founded for the benefit of the poor of the town who could not afford the cost of treatment by travelling surgeons or by doctors at the hospital. It had been relocated to premises in High Friar Chare a few years ago in the face of opposition from the trustees of the Infirmary who judged that the Dispensary was likely to attract a coterie of undesirable clients whose presence would, in their words, 'pollute the atmosphere of the neighbourhood to the detriment of respectable hospital patients'.

Delaval waited outside the building for several minutes until he was quite sure that there were no other customers inside. Then, he entered cautiously, pulling his cap down over his face as far as he dared without causing himself to stumble into unseen obstacles. The oily fellow behind the counter greeted him in a condescending tone. 'Good morning, sir. And what little problem do we have today?'

Delaval took an instant dislike to the man but knew nevertheless that it would be unwise not to treat him civilly if he was to achieve his purpose in coming. 'Good day to you, sir,' he said, in as pleasant a voice as he could muster. 'I have what I believe you will find to be a singularly unusual request.'

'An unusual request?' mimicked the apothecary. 'You need not feel embarrassed, sir. I can assure you that I have been asked for every possible kind of medication to treat every possible kind of condition under the sun. Customers seeking cures for the most extraordinary ailments imaginable. Customers with continuous hiccups. Customers addicted to parsnips. Customers with moss growing on the backs of their hands. Customers allergic to their wife. Customers with hair that can't be combed. Oh no, sir, you would not credit the strange requests I have received. And, happily, I have managed to satisfy each and every one of them. So please tell me, sir, how can I assist your good self?'

'I need something guaranteed to kill a horse,' said Delaval.

'Guaranteed to kill a horse, you say?' Septimus Grymm sensed that he had become the target of a joke - one which was in extremely poor taste. He responded with fury. 'What you need is a horse-doctor, not an apothecary!' he roared.

Delaval was thrown off balance by the ferocity of the man's reaction and sought to pacify him. 'No, no, you don't understand,' he countered. 'A horse-doctor would tell me to shoot it.'

'Wise advice,' said Grymm, still angry. 'You should take it.'

'Please, let me explain,' implored Delaval. 'You see, if I shoot my horse, it will die immediately. But I want to kill it gradually so that it doesn't notice the deterioration in its condition. So what I need is some kind of slow-acting poison. Something that might take a week or two to kill her.'

'Her?' Grymm queried.

'Er … yes …' Delaval tried to recover from his slip of the tongue. 'The horse … it's … er … I mean she … is a filly.'

'A filly, eh?'

'Well … more of a mare, I suppose.'

Grymm felt that he had been placed in something of a dilemma. He had never before been asked to prescribe medication for such a purpose. Customers normally wanted some potion or pill to achieve a cure or an improvement in health, rather than the opposite. Furthermore, his previous subjects had always been human, but now he was being asked to prescribe for an animal. On the other hand, he was conscious of the fact that he had earlier claimed to be able to meet any request, however unusual, and was reluctant to suffer the humiliation of being proved wrong on this occasion. While he deliberated how best to respond, he happened to notice his customer's shoes, which he recognised as being of the finest quality. From this observation, combined with the enormous girth of the man's stomach which signified a rich and plentiful consumption of food, he deduced that the man, who was otherwise dressed in cheap, shoddy garments and concealed most of his face, was attempting to disguise the fact that he was far from impoverished. No doubt, thought Grymm, he was aiming to obtain the prescription he sought from what he probably regarded as a source of dubious standing not normally accessible to a person of his means. The situation therefore offered a lucrative opportunity, as Grymm saw it, to extract a high price for satisfying the customer's strange request.

'Very well, sir, I will do my best to help you,' Grymm said at length. 'So, let us recapitulate on your requirements. You would like some medication which will kill a horse ... '

'Correct,' Delaval confirmed.

'In small doses so that it … she … doesn't notice.'

'Yes.'

'Something that causes a slow death.'

'Not too slow.'

'Anything else?'

'It mustn't leave any trace …' Delaval insisted. Then he added quickly, 'You know, just so that the meat is not spoilt.'

'Oh?' Grymm frowned slightly at this additional qualification. In truth, he was struggling to think of a suitable concoction to sell to the customer. He cast his eyes along the shelves stacked with bottles and boxes and they came to rest on a jar of Congreve's Petroleum Pills. Grymm was well aware that, according to the advertising material distributed with this particular product, it was claimed to be effective in curing numerous ailments, including indigestion, gout, headache, tremors and palpitations, worms, hysteric diseases, rheumatism, consumption, stomach and bowel spasms, uropsical swellings of the legs, despondency, costiveness, female complaints, cholera morbus, languor and consumption. In fact, it appeared that there was almost nothing that Congreve's Petroleum Pills would not treat successfully. Therefore, Grymm told himself, since they were so universally effective there was surely no reason why they should not also produce the outcome desired by this latest customer.

'Yes, I have just the thing for you, Mister …?'

'I beg your pardon?'

'I was asking for your name, sir, as an esteemed customer.'

'Why do you need my name?'

'It's just that we like to know our customers personally so we can address them by name and give them a personal service. My name, for example, is Grymm. Grymm by name, but not Grymm by nature. Now, would you perhaps favour me by telling me yours?'

Delaval hesitated. He certainly did not want to reveal his true identity and knew that he would have to invent a fictitious one. An image suddenly came into his mind's eye of the plaque above the entrance to Seaton Delaval Hall, which was dedicated to the architect of that building. This gave him an idea. 'Oh, very well,' he said. 'I suppose there's no harm in it. The name's Vanbrugh.'

'Vanbrugh? An unusual name, wouldn't you say? How do you spell that, Mister Vanbrugh.'

At that point, Delaval wished that he had invented a simpler pseudonym. Preferably one which he could spell. He gave up after three attempts.

Grymm chose to ignore the customer's discomfiture, which only served to confirm his own earlier suspicion about the man's duplicity. 'Would you care to take a dozen of these pills for your horse, sir?' he asked.

Delaval replied with another question. 'Will that be enough to kill her?'

'I suppose it depends how big she is,' Grymm suggested.

'Oh, small, very small,' Delaval said, hoping to restrict the cost of the prescription. 'I'll just take a dozen, then.'

'A very small horse, eh?' Grymm was hoping the man might have been tempted to buy a double quantity and was a little disappointed at the size of the sale.

'How much will that cost?' Delaval asked guardedly, having absolutely no idea of the price of such items.

Grymm, suspecting that the man (who, he was now certain, was deliberately attempting to conceal his affluence) had absolutely no idea of the price of such items, decided that it would be quite inappropriate to charge him the normal sum of four shillings and sixpence. 'Since this is your first visit to our Dispensary, sir, and I would fervently hope to retain you as a valued customer, I am willing to let you have these pills at the greatly reduced price of three guineas.'

'Three guineas?' howled the valued customer, throwing his head back in astonishment and, in the process, knocking off his cap to reveal dark features, a cock-eye and a Roman nose. 'Three guineas?' he repeated, louder this time, meanwhile replacing his cap.

'A small price for killing a horse,' Grymm reminded him. 'Even a very small horse.'

At that moment, two women entered the Dispensary, presumably to purchase some cure or other. Their arrival placed Delaval in a particular quandary. He was outraged by the sum demanded by the apothecary for the pills but dared not start an argument or make a scene which would attract the attention of others and perhaps lead to his recognition and exposure as a potential murderer. In truth, he mused, he had little choice but to pay up and console himself with the thought that three guineas *was* a small price to pay for his imminent and eagerly awaited bereavement and subsequent inheritance of Lady Paulet's estate.

'I'll take them, Mister Grymm,' he said.

*

Perlee Parker was as good as his word. Before a fortnight had passed, he turned up at the Flying Horse Tavern one evening carrying not one but two packages wrapped in cloths and laid them carefully on a trestle-table which His Satanic Majesty had thoughtfully set up for that purpose against the rear wall of Hell's Kitchen. Most of those who, nearly two weeks earlier, had gathered in the attic room at Perlee's invitation (and, if I may claim a little credit for their attendance, in response to my own urgent promptings) were also present and crowded boisterously around the table in enthusiastic anticipation of seeing themselves captured in oils and in an attempt to obtain the best possible view.

Perlee waited until everyone had ceased their pushing and shoving and beseeched them in anxious terms not to press further forward or to touch the painting. Then he began to unwrap the smaller of the two packages, peeling back the layers of cloth slowly and methodically as if to heighten the drama and suspense of the moment. At last, the final layer was removed and the picture was revealed. It was rectangular in shape, around twenty-eight inches wide and twenty inches high and set in a satinwood frame, along the lower edge of which the title *The Newcastle Eccentrics in Hell's Kitchen* was engraved in gold lettering. There was a collective intake of breath as the on-lookers were confronted with the sight of themselves in the portrait, the figures immobile and at the same time animated, as captured by the artist's skilled brushwork.

As first impressions passed and each person began to ponder their own likeness more intently, they gave voice to their reactions, which were divided among those who felt flattered by the way in which they had been represented, those who believed themselves more alluring than Perlee Parker perceived them to be and those who considered that he had been too generous in his depiction of others in the group.

'Aa nivvor knew Aa was such a beauty,' Dolly Peel asseverated, with a hint of what I took to be irony, but which may in fact have been sarcasm (though I am not absolutely sure of the difference between the two).

'Aa've aalways thought ye looked bonny,' Bogie Theobald reassured her. 'Especially up against that stuffed badger,' he added, inadvertently diluting the impact of the original compliment.

'Enough of yer sawder,' Dolly retorted.

The Widow Henderson, whom Perlee had decided after all not to leave out of the portrait on the grounds that to have done so might have been perceived by her as an affront and, consequently, provoked the rescinding of her permission for Bold

Archy's inclusion (which would also have brought about Kitty's withdrawal), pronounced herself well pleased.

Curiously, even Blind Willie professed himself delighted with the result, whereupon he picked up his fiddle and began to perform a ditty while Bogie Theobald's little terrier yapped and barked and raced in circles around his feet.

Tarum tickle, tan dum. Tarum tickle, tan dum.
Tarum tickle, tan dum. Tarum tickle, tan dum.

For my own part, I was more than adequately satisfied with the manner in which I was portrayed, particularly since Perlee had omitted any indication of the parlous state of my knees. Captain Starkey, however, appeared not to recognise any of the individuals in the painting, including himself, or even to realise that it portrayed the group which Perlee Parker had sketched less than two weeks ago. 'These must be the prisoners we captured when the Irish rebels attacked our garrison at Newtonbarry,' he explained to the artist, after introducing himself.

The clear verdict of those present was one of contentment with the handiwork of the artist and pride at the prospect of their likenesses being displayed in Hell's Kitchen, as Perlee had previously intimated. The only slightly sour note was struck by Blackie Johnson who commented that the juxtaposition in the painting of Auld Judy and His Satanic Majesty imitated the inauspicious pairing of the High Priestess with the Fool in a pack of tarot cards.

'What's in that one?' Auld Judy demanded to know, pointing at the second package. 'Ye haven't done another picture of us?'

'No,' Perlee replied, 'but you might know who this is, Judy.' He removed the wrapping, with significantly less theatricality than he had employed with the first painting, to reveal a portrait containing two figures. The person on the left was an exceedingly fat man with sagging jowls and flecks of spittle on one of his chins. There was a label on his surtout which, on very close examination, could be seen to bear the initials FBMP. He was passing a handful of coins in a secretive manner to the man on the right, whose face was contorted into an expression suggesting that his nose was being assaulted by a foul stench. The title engraved along the bottom of the frame read *A Very Self-Important Man Bribes An Accomplice To Cheat His Best Friend.*

'Of course Aa know him,' Judy confirmed. 'Aa see the scoundrel most weeks when he calls in to the Guild Hall to parley with Alderman Applegarth aboot their little dodges. Aa dinaa knaa the other gagdie, though.'

'You think it's a good likeness of him, then?' Perlee pressed her for an opinion.

'Aa'd know him anywhere, even wi'oot the initials,' she said. 'What are ye ganna do wi'it?'

'I'm going to hang it in here with the other painting. One on either side of the fireplace.'

'Ha! Old Brandling would get the scunners if he knew aboot that, ye knaa.'

'I am well aware of that. In fact, Judy, I will be most grateful if you would assist me in bringing to his attention the information that his picture is displayed in the taproom of the Flying Horse Tavern.'

'What?' she exclaimed. 'Ye're not afeard of what he'll do to ye if he finds oot?'

'On the contrary, it's very important to the execution of my plan that he *does* find out.' Perlee gave a conspiratorial wink which Judy took to indicate that she should carry out his wish and not ask any more questions about his intentions.

45

Felix Brandling tore open the envelope that had been left for him in the lobby of the Guild Hall and read the letter inside, which gave no indication of its author.

The illegal exploits which you have been carrying out with that rascal Applegarth have finally been laid bare. What is more, you are currently the subject of mockery and ridicule within the walls of the Flying Horse Tavern. You will readily discover this, should you care to visit that place of refreshment.

The first thing which crossed his mind was to wonder which particular illegal exploits it referred to. There were so many of them. His second thought was how disgraceful it was for a man as important as himself to be the butt of derision, if indeed that part of the message was correct. Wary though he was, after his previous experience, of anonymous letters, he decided that he had better go and see for himself whether there was any truth in it.

Before setting off from his mansion, he attempted to disguise himself, not wishing to be recognised in somewhere as disreputable as a public drinking-house, a place which was presumably patronised by the lower classes. Such an undertaking was formidable, it must be stated. He wrapped a muffler around his neck, put on the wide-brimmed hat which he normally wore to ward off the scorching rays of the sun when visiting his estates in the Caribbean and turned up the collar of his surtout. These devices, however, did little to conceal his facial features or the rest of his considerable bulk.

Not having previously deigned to visit establishments of the like of the Flying Horse Tavern, he was at a loss to know which part of the building to enter and, by chance, happened to choose the door marked *Taproom*. His Satanic Majesty had been alerted to the likelihood that the MP would be coming to Hell's Kitchen and had posted an apposite notice near the entrance. As Felix Brandling made his way inside he was greeted by a sign which read, *Members of Parliament are welcome here on condition that during their stay they desist from their customary mendaciousness.*

He had never in all his life been in such a dingy, run-down dive. In fact, he could hardly believe that he had come at all. He cast around the room and could only wonder at the collection of weird, grotesque, low life congregated therein – the dregs of society, he reflected. Eventually, his eyes fell upon a painting hanging high up on the wall beside the fireplace. It depicted a group of people – a dozen or so - who appeared as odd as those who currently surrounded him. As he looked closer at the portrayed figures, the truth slowly dawned upon him. First, he recognised the fiddle-player as the same man he could see at that very moment sitting in the corner of the room and making a fearsome din with his voice and his instrument. And there was that huge fellow who towered over the other customers. Next to him in the picture was a dwarf. *The* dwarf! It was surely Delaval's little secretary, Miss Kitty Dace, whom Delaval himself had revealed to be the writer of the anonymous threatening letter. And there she was across the room in conversation with the huge fellow. So that was it! All the characters in the painting were to be found in the very place in which their portrait hung.

Brandling's surprise at this discovery was complemented immediately by his realisation that by establishing where Miss

Kitty Dace could be tracked down and arrested by the constables, he had just saved himself having to pay out the hundred guinea reward for bringing the culprit to justice. While he was feeling rather pleased with himself on both counts, his eyes wandered further along the wall towards another painting, one which set his heart racing, his blood boiling and his bowels trumpeting. For this was a picture of *himself* – there could be no doubt about that, the artist had captured him perfectly – together with his fellow conspirator at Emanuel Mordue's cockpit. And, to add insult to injury, the title of this outrageous slight on his good name was emblazoned across the edge of the frame. *A Very Self-Important Man Bribes An Accomplice To Cheat His Best Friend.* As he stood gawping in anger at it, he gradually became aware that people nearby were staring at him, pointing at him, laughing at him and several were holding their noses. They had clearly made the connection between the Very Self-Important Man in the painting and the figure presently standing in their midst. Furious, he turned tail and made to leave the room as quickly as his vast bulk, his gasping lungs and the density of the throng around him would permit, vowing to himself that he would make sure that whoever was responsible for this outrage would suffer severely for their actions. Then, just as he reached the door, he was confronted by the impertinent wretch who had sketched his picture at the cockpit and denounced him to Alderman Applegarth.

The impertinent wretch smiled at him and said, 'Good evening to you, Mister Brandling. Didn't I promise that I would see you hang before the year was out?'

'Get out of my way,' Felix Brandling roared, attempting to shove the man aside with his walking-stick. 'I never give place to fools.'

'But I do,' Perlee Parker replied, bowing and stepping to his left to allow the MP to pass.

*

The constable made his way cautiously among the throng of customers, peering this way and that through the taproom smoke as if seeking out a particular individual. He soon spotted Bold Archy – not a major achievement, given that the person of that name towered high above his fellows – and he headed towards the corner where Archy stood in conversation with his mother and Kitty Dace. When he reached the group, he removed from the inside pocket of his navy-blue uniform jacket what appeared to be an officially-headed document and, in a meek, apologetic tone, said, 'Pardon me, ladies and pardon me, sir, but I have a warrant here to serve on a Miss Kitty Dace.' Clearing his throat, he added, 'In connection with a threatening letter and treacherous public notices.'

The Widow Henderson was the first to react. 'A warrant, you say? For Miss Kitty? To arrest her, you mean?'

'I'm afraid to say that I do, madam. Would that be yourself, may I enquire?'

At that, Kitty burst into tears, let out a loud shriek, howled, 'No, that's me!' and, as if she had taken a fit, stamped on the floor as hard as she was able (which, in truth, was not particularly hard but, nevertheless, gave an impression of great distress).

'Oh!' said the constable, looking surprised that such a small woman could be guilty of the offences of which she was accused.

Dolly Peel, who was not far away, leaning against the glass case containing the stuffed badger, heard the commotion and came over to investigate. 'What's ganning on here then, constable?' she demanded to know, observing Kitty Dace's lachrymose and hysterical state, at which the constable explained that he was obliged by dint of his office to take the young lady into custody pending her appearance on the morrow before the town magistrate on serious charges.

'On what charges, may Aa ask ye?' Dolly demanded further and the constable reiterated what he had told the Widow Henderson moments earlier.

'And what manner of man has laid these charges against a person as innocent and defenceless as yon lass?'

'I am not at liberty to disclose that information,' the constable replied pompously, before adding, 'even if I knew it myself.'

'So ye're ganning to throw my little friend here into Newgate Gaol to spend the night with aal the rogues and ruffians of the toon before ye drag her alang to the Guild Hall? Is that what ye're saying, constable?' Dolly Peel removed the pipe from between her teeth, pushed her face close to his and gave him a blast of acrid smoke.

'That is precisely the task which my duty requires me to carry out, madam,' he said with a splutter and a bow, trying to preserve as much dignity as possible in the circumstances.

Dolly Peel glanced at Kitty, whose anguish had hardly subsided, thought for a moment, then said, 'Aa divvent believe for one moment that Kitty here is guilty of any wrongdoing, let alone the crimes ye have mentioned. So what Aa propose to do is to gan alang to the court in the morning with the lass to speak up in her defence and put the beak reet about her. Aa guarantee to bring her to the Guild Hall at ten of the clock. And ye, marra, will desist from any further attempt to detain her. Is that understood? Otherwise, with one click of my fingers, Aa could summon twenty folk this very minute to take ye outside, give ye a good braying, divest ye of yer uniform and send ye packing stark naked back to where ye came from.'

Discretion being the better part of valour, the constable weighed up the alternatives open to him with rapid contemplation, replaced the warrant in his pocket and said, with as much authority as he could muster, 'Your proposal seems quite satisfactory, madam. Tomorrow at ten, then.'

He doffed his cap and hurried off.

*

'I tell you, Applegarth, they were mocking me. Can you believe such a thing? They were making fun of me. *Me*! Felix Brandling, Member of Parliament for Newcastle-on-Tyne. They appeared not to know just how important I am.'

'Hard to believe,' Applegarth muttered noncommittally.

'There was my portrait in full view of the whole room with its scandalous title which accused me of bribing an accomplice to cheat my best friend ...'

'*Best* friend?' Applegarth interrupted him. 'Since when have *I* been your best friend?'

'Never mind that. The thing was that everybody saw it and everybody knew it was me ...'

'... Must have been a very good likeness of you, then ...'

'Yes, it was. And, as a consequence, I have never been so humiliated.'

'Really, Brandling? You surprise me,' Applegarth said sympathetically.

'So what am I going to do about it? I cannot allow my picture to continue to be displayed in this manner in public, can

I? Word of it is bound to spread fast. It could even come to the attention of the editor of the Courant, God forbid!'

'You could ask the mayor to close the place down.'

'Close it down? On what grounds?'

'Well … I'm sure you could come up with some excuse. Public hygiene, for example. I'm sure there'll be plenty of rats there.'

'Uh! Don't talk about rats, Applegarth. The mere mention of the word makes me feel quite ill. Anyway, closing the place will provoke an outcry. A riot even – and we've had enough of those recently.'

'You could demand the removal of the painting,' Applegarth suggested. 'Tell the publican that it's an insult to a very important person. Such as yourself, for example.'

'So you mean I'd have to admit that *I'm* the person in the painting? The one who's cheating his friend. His *best* friend, no less.'

'Mmm … yes … I see your problem. Maybe you should buy the damn thing.'

'And then burn it, you mean?'

'Well, I suppose so. Or perhaps you could display it in the lobby of the Guild Hall … you know, in the space that was left when we sold the Gainsborough.'

'I hope that's a joke, Applegarth.'

'Sorry, Brandling, I forgot that you don't have a sense of humour.'

'Well, that *was* in rather bad taste, was it not? Anyway, how do I know that the owner would be willing to sell it?'

'You don't need to worry about that, Brandling. Look at this.' Applegarth passed him the copy of the *Newcastle Courant* he had been reading and tapped his finger on an advertisement half-way down the front page.

SALE BY AUCTION

By Order of the Assignee
On the Premises, on Monday the 23rd of March,
punctually at Eleven o'clock, of the Flying Horse
Tavern, Groatmarket, Newcastle-on-Tyne

Two items as described below, to be sold (with Reserve) **AS A SINGLE LOT**, both being the work of the Artist, Mister Perlee Parker, formerly of Plymouth Dock in the County of Devon and now resident in Newcastle-on-Tyne:

1. An oil painting on canvass in a satinwood frame measuring 28 inches by 20 inches and entitled 'The Newcastle Eccentrics in Hell's Kitchen'
2. An oil painting on canvass in a satinwood frame measuring 36 inches by 24 inches and entitled 'A Very Self-Important Man Bribes An Accomplice To Cheat His Best Friend.'

The Sale items may be viewed on Friday next, the 20th of March, and until the Sale, in the taproom of the above Premises. They will be delivered to the successful bidder seven days after Completion of the Sale.

STRICTLY NO SURROGATES. BIDDERS MUST ATTEND IN PERSON.

Brandling studied the advertisement carefully for several minutes, muttering angrily to himself before launching into a fit of coughing, accompanied by a detonation of ill winds. Applegarth waited for these to subside before asking, 'Well, what do you think?'

'There are a few things about this that puzzle me,' Brandling replied. 'For a start, I would have to buy *both* paintings, from what I read, and not merely the one I want to get my hands on. What the hell would I want with the other one? It's just a picture of the rabble who spend their time drinking in that pigsty.'

'You could burn that one, too.'

'Huh! And another thing. What's this about bidders being compelled to attend in person? It means that I'd have to go back to that God-forsaken place again, rather than sending along someone to bid on my behalf. Why on earth can't they hold the auction somewhere more salubrious?'

'Like your place in Bulman Village, you mean? Maybe they're scared that your rats will gnaw the canvasses.'

'That's the second offensive remark you've made in the last ten minutes, Applegarth. I'm really not amused by your attempts at humour, you know.'

'I'm just trying to cheer you up, old chap.'

'Well, your frivolity is having the opposite effect upon me. Anyway, I don't suppose that I have a great deal of choice in the matter, do I? Unfortunately, important as I am, it behoves me to go in person and ensure that I get the accursed picture in the auction. I can't risk it passing into the possession of someone else who might be tempted to use it to make a bigger fool of me, can I?'

'Who else would want to buy it, do you suppose? Surely you don't have any enemies, do you?' Applegarth smirked, thoroughly enjoying Brandling's discomfiture, since he had not forgiven the man for the disloyal deed he had perpetrated at the cock-pit and which had been captured by the artist.

'Which great person does not have enemies, Applegarth? There are bound to be people who are envious of my achievements, my wealth, my importance, my intelligence, my popularity ...'

' ... Your humility, Brandling?'

'Ha! Humility, you say? Humility is a vice practised only by those who have plenty to be humble about. It does not apply to people such as myself. Nor even to *you*, Applegarth, I dare say.'

'Thank you for the compliment, if indeed that is what it was intended to be.'

46

It looked like it was going to be a busy day at the Magistrates Court. Although there was still an hour to go before the first hearing, the line of those summoned to attend already snaked down the stairs, out of the door of the Guild Hall and on to Sandhill. Inside, the Sitting Magistrate, Aeneas Snitterby JP, was going through the case lists with his clerk and constable in preparation for the day's session.

'There's a lot of lawsuits today, Your Worship,' the clerk explained.

'Well, that's a pity because I'm in rather a hurry,' Snitterby told them. 'Hoastmen business, you know.'

The clerk and the constable nodded dutifully.

'So I want you to get them through as quickly as you can,' he continued.

'Judging by the charge sheet,' the clerk informed him, 'almost all of the defendants are from the lower orders. So they're probably guilty as far as we can tell, Your Worship.'

'I'm sure that's the case. But for the sake of appearances, we have to go through the motions. I appreciate that it's all a bit of a charade – not to mention a complete waste of my valuable time - but you know what they say. Justice has to be seen to be done.'

The clerk and the constable nodded dutifully again.

'Right, constable, I'm ready now. Go and call the first defendant.' Snitterby said instructed him.

As he approached the waiting queue, the constable was bombarded with questions. 'Who is the Sitting Magistrate today?' (Some magistrates were notorious for sentencing more harshly than others.) 'What sort of mood is he in?' (They knew that a bad mood equalled harsh sentencing.) 'Is he in a hurry?'

(They knew that this too equalled harsh sentencing.) And so on.

Aeneas Snitterby JP, conscious of the huge workload which he faced and the early afternoon business appointment which he intended to keep, dealt with the first batch of cases in record time and with minimal clemency. Two thieves were to be transported for seven years for stealing a sack and a chicken respectively. Another received six months hard labour in the House of Correction for a larceny. A woman was fined nine pence and sentenced to be imprisoned in gaol for three months for assaulting a constable in the execution of his duty. Another woman (a vicar's wife, no less!) was fined four shillings and sixpence for urinating copiously in Charlotte-square. Two men, a tall one and a short one, were fined five shillings each for removing corpses from the morgue of the General Infirmary without a licence. Another was sent into solitary confinement for fourteen days for purporting to exercise the trade of a baker without having served an apprenticeship. A septuagenarian raff-merchant, arraigned by the Tyneside Association for the Prosecution of Felons for stealing two pots of forced rhubarb from a neighbour's garden, was ordered to be placed in the stocks at Sandhill for two days (a seemingly harsh punishment for such an elderly person until you realised that the neighbour in question was none other than Aeneas Snitterby himself).

'Call the next defendant and read out the charge,' instructed the magistrate.

'A Miss Kitty Dace, Your Worship. Charged with issuing a threat to kill a Member of Parliament and publishing treacherous public notices in support of the keelmen,' the constable announced with an officious intonation.

'Very well, constable. Put the defendant in the dock.'

'She's already there, Your Worship.'

'What? Is this some kind of joke, constable?'

'No, Your Worship. She's in the dock, but she's very small, Your Worship.'

'Well then, get her a chair to stand on. I need to see her before I sentence her.'

'Do you mean if you find her guilty first, Your Worship?' the constable asked nervously, as if conscious of the correct procedure but not wishing to complicate matters unduly.

'Er ... yes ... that's exactly what I meant.'

The court clerk produced a chair and Kitty Dace stood on it, enabling her to see over the side of the dock by peering through the row of curved iron spikes which were intended to prevent her improbable escape from justice.

'Good gracious,' cried the magistrate. 'My, my, I do believe it's Stanhope Delaval's little note-taker, if I'm not very much mistaken. He brought you to the meeting of the Company of Hoastmen, didn't he?'

'Yes, sir,' said Kitty. 'But then Aa got kidnapped when the master was attacked by highwaymen.'

'There's a ... er ... lady here to support Miss Dace, Your Worship,' the constable announced. (He gave a little cough before uttering the word *lady*.) 'Does she have your permission to do so, Your Worship?'

Before Aeneas Snitterby JP had a chance to respond, Dolly Peel marched across the courtroom and positioned herself beside the dock. She cut a daunting figure as she glared menacingly at the constable and the magistrate. 'Aa'm speaking up in her defence,' she said.

The magistrate felt slightly intimidated by the woman and decided not to object to her presence, despite the strong smell of fish which pervaded the courtroom as a result. 'Very well, madam,' he told her, 'but I'll thank you to put out that pipe, if you don't mind.'

She glared again and reluctantly removed the pipe from between her teeth before tapping ash from its bowl onto the courtroom floor.

The constable read out details of the letter which was delivered to Gosforth House.

> *Felix brandling if ye divvent give the keelmen a rise of four shillings a tide as sure as hell is hot but o a plague about your house for that o and worse than that before the year is done ye must be deed o ye and yer friends have been the worst gaffers to us that have ever came here and we will take care of some more ye may depend on it*

'Ha! Not exactly Shakespeare, is it?' the magistrate said, chuckling at his own witticism. Then, turning to Kitty, he asked, 'Did you write this letter?'

'Yes, sir, Aa did.'

'And what about those public notices in connection with the keelmen's strike?'

'Yes, sir, Aa wrote them too.'

The constable and the clerk were shocked at this brazen admission and both smiled broadly at the speed with which the case had been decided. They waited to hear the number of years for which the convicted prisoner would be transported. However, they had not reckoned on Dolly Peel's intervention.

'Aa've got something to say aboot this,' she declared. 'My friend might have written them, but that dinaa make her guilty.'

'How can that be?' asked the magistrate, humouring her a little.

'She was forced to write them. She would have been brayed if she refused. Brayed or even worse.'

'Is this true?' the magistrate asked Kitty.

'Yes, sir,' Kitty replied.

'And who is the person that forced you to write the letter and the notices?'

'Aa canna tell ye, sir.'

'You can't tell me, eh? Why not? Because you made up this story, is that it?'

'No, sir. If Aa tell ye, he'll be sure to bray me, sir.'

'Ha! Would you rather be sent to Australia, then?'

'No, sir, but Aa gave me word not to tell, sir. Aa'm sworn to secrecy. He made me swear on the Bible, sir.'

'*Aa* know his name,' Dolly Peel interjected. 'Kitty canna tell ye because she's too honest to break her promise. But *Aa* haven't made any promises so *Aa*'m free to speak.' She took out a small decorative tin box from her pocket and opened the lid.

'No snuff allowed in the courtroom,' the constable reprimanded her.

'Keep yer lang neb oot of this,' she rasped. 'It's for me health.' Ignoring the reproach, she placed a pinch of the tobacco on the back of her hand and insufflated the powder into one nostril with a loud sniff, then into the other with an even louder sniff. Even her sniffs seemed to bear a hint of impudence.

'Well, you'd better reveal the name of this person,' the magistrate instructed. He was becoming impatient at the length of time this case was taking.

'Before Aa do, Aa've got a question for ye.' Dolly Peel held up a copy of the *Newcastle Courant* which carried the report of the threatening letter. 'It says here that there's a reward of a hundred guineas from this MP gadgie for catching the culprit. So, if Aa tell ye who it is, do Aa get to pick up the money?'

The magistrate had never before been asked such a question and he was at a loss to know how to reply. He looked at the clerk for guidance, but the clerk, who was similarly nonplussed, shrugged his shoulders and looked at the constable to provide the answer. The constable, who was the least knowledgeable of the three on the subject of court procedure, indicated with a curious gesture involving a puff of his cheeks that he was completely the wrong person to whom to address such enquiries and looked back at the magistrate. The magistrate, realising from this procession of glances that it was he who must settle the issue, and still feeling somewhat intimidated by Dolly Peel, scratched his head a few times to give the impression that he was giving the matter his serious consideration and said at last, rather reluctantly, 'Well, yes, madam, I suppose you would be entitled to receive the reward.'

'Ha!' Dolly Peel whooped. 'Aa'll be ganning round to get me money directly.'

'Not yet, you won't,' the magistrate corrected her. 'Not before the person who forced the prisoner to write the letter has been named by you *and has been convicted.*'

'What? Ye mean Aa'm ganna have to wait?'

'Exactly.' Aeneas Snitterby was by now beginning to lose his patience. 'Now, before any more of the court's time is wasted on this case, I order you to disclose the name of this person whom you claim to be the guilty party. Otherwise, I will convict your little friend in the dock.'

'Aa'll tell ye reet enough,' retorted Dolly Peel. 'And there's nae need to get so narkt.' She pulled a small flask from her pocket and took a swig.

'There's no drink allowed in here,' shouted the constable.

She took another swig before replying, 'Ye mentioned snuff before but ye nivvor said nowt aboot gin, did ye?'

'This is your last chance, madam,' roared the magistrate.

'His name is Scuffins,' she roared back.

'Scuffins?' the magistrate asked, as though he either hadn't heard properly or he *had* heard but couldn't believe his ears. 'Do you mean *Jasper* Scuffins?'

'Aye. Ye'll find him in some tavern in Sandgate or on the river. Otherwise, he'll be in the Keelmen's Hospital.'

The magistrate's face was wreathed in a huge smile as he barked out his instructions. 'Constable, I want you to arrest this fellow Jasper Scuffins and bring him here for me to deal with. And you can release the prisoner in the dock.'

47

Perlee Parker decided that it would be fitting for the auction of the two paintings to take place in the same spacious attic room of the Flying Horse Tavern where, a few weeks before, he had sketched the collection of characters which he christened the Newcastle Eccentrics. And indeed, with the exception of Bogie Theobald, who had a prior appointment with some rats in the Mansion House, and Dolly Peel, who had a bumper catch of fish to sell at market, all of the characters turned up to see how much their painting would fetch.

There appeared, however, to be surprisingly few bidders. There was a dealer from Durham, a private art collector from Hexham and a rag-and-bone man from Morpeth. Felix Brandling was there, of course, still with the muffler and wide-brimmed hat designed to disguise himself. Hadwen Bragg was there too and greeted the MP loudly by name, so that if anyone present was initially unaware of the latter's identity, they would no longer be in any doubt about it.

Brandling glared back with unconcealed hatred. 'What are you doing in a place like this, Bragg?' he shouted. 'Given up your teetotalism have you?'

'I have come to buy some paintings, my friend,' Bragg riposted. 'Why else would I be here?'

On the stroke of eleven o'clock, the auctioneer, Wildblood, splendidly decked out in a scarlet waistcoat and grey pantaloons thanks to the generosity of the clothing emporium of *Bragg and Company*, entered, took up his place at the front of the assembled bidders and spectators and banged his gavel on the table several times in order to demand silence. Then, clearing his throat loudly, he addressed his audience in a strong, authoritative voice. 'Ladies and gentlemen, I bid you all a very good morning. Today, I am auctioning a single lot consisting of two splendid portraits in oil, both painted by the artist, Mister Perlee Parker, who we are honoured to have here with us.'

Perlee moved forward to reveal himself, bowed formally and received a polite round of applause in return.

'You will see the paintings displayed here,' Wildblood continued, indicating the two hanging on the wall behind him. This one …' – he pointed to *The Newcastle Eccentrics in Hell's Kitchen* - portrays a group of a dozen people, several of whom I detect among you now, and you may notice that the setting for the painting is this very room. It is a beautifully observed portrait with many fine details and I am sure that you will agree with the artist's opinion that everyone on this canvass is a character, in the sense that he or she appears to have a fascinating, individual quality which, I should say, Mister Parker has captured most skilfully. The second one is intriguingly entitled *A Very Self-Important Man Bribes An Accomplice To Cheat His Best Friend* … It appears to show a couple of rogues in the process of hatching a mischievous plot which involves the payment of money – a bribe, according to the title of the painting – in return, no doubt, for some favour of dubious legality. I understand that it is based upon a real scene which was observed locally and I imagine that it is intended as a depiction of the low life that one occasionally comes into contact with, even in such a fair and welcoming town as Newcastle.'

At this last comment, Brandling almost exploded with fury and would probably have done so, had he not realised that to raise a commotion would merely draw to the attention of everyone in the room that one of the so-called rogues was none other than himself.

Meanwhile, Wildblood made a convincing pretence of failing to notice any resemblance between the obese figure in the painting and the obese figure standing a few feet away. He continued with his introduction. 'On the instructions of the vendor, these paintings are to be sold together as a single lot and, for the purpose of determining their notional value, the worth of each will be deemed to be one half of the total of the successful bid. For example, if the sale price is, shall we say, twenty guineas, then the notional value of each painting will be ten guineas. The paintings will be delivered to the successful bidder one week from today, after their bill of exchange has been presented to and cleared at the Tyne Bank. Is that plain to everyone?'

'What if I only want to buy one of them?' bellowed Brandling, accidentally dislodging his hat and muffler in the process and revealing features which bore a remarkable similarity to those displayed on the wall at the front of the room.

'Quite simple, sir,' Wildblood replied. 'All you need to do is to submit the winning bid for the pair of them. Then you can donate the one you don't want to the Poorhouse or some other deserving cause and keep the one you want.' This prompted laughter from several of those present, while Brandling flushed with embarrassment and anger at what he saw as the auctioneer's attempt to make a fool of him.

Wildblood waited until the laughter had subsided and was about to resume when Brandling roared, 'I have never heard anything so preposterous in all my life. I *demand* that you sell the paintings separately.'

'You are in no position to demand anything, sir,' Wildblood countered coolly. 'I have explained the rules by which this auction is to be conducted. They were, I beg to remind you, set out clearly in the official notice published in the *Newcastle Courant*. I regret to say that if you continue with your tirade I will have you removed from these premises.' As he issued this threat, Wildblood looked across meaningfully at Bold Archy. Brandling's eyes followed the auctioneer's gaze, understood its significance and decided that he would probably be wise not to pursue his point any further.

'So, ladies and gentlemen, if there are no more questions, let us get down to business.' Wildblood paused and banged his gavel loudly on the table a few times for no other apparent reason than to test its efficacy. Having satisfied himself of that, he invited an opening bid, at which the rag-and-bone-man called out, 'Aa'll tak them off yer hands fer a half-guinea.'

'That's very civil of you, sir,' Wildblood told him, 'but there is a reserve price on the goods, which I am not at liberty to divulge except to reveal that it greatly exceeds the amount of your bid.'

The dealer from Durham, a scrawny fellow with a hunched back and broken spectacles, stepped forward and offered a guinea.

'Thank you, sir,' said Wildblood, 'but still nowhere near the reserve price, I'm afraid.'

Then it was the turn of the private art collector from Hexham, a tall, thin man who exuded a sophisticated air and spoke in genteel tones, albeit with a pronounced lisp. 'In my *professional* opinion,' he said, placing much emphasis upon the word *professional,* (although experiencing some difficulty at pronouncing some of the consonants) these paintings *do* have some merit. However, their value is no greater than ten guineas and, therefore, ten guineas is my final bid.'

'Ten guineas!' the rag-and-bone man cried out. 'Ten guineas, ye say? In that case, Aa'll be ganning on me way. Aa canna compete wi' aal ye rich gadgies.' He picked up his grubby sack, slung it over his shoulder, pushed his way irately through a group of onlookers to the top of the staircase and disappeared from view.

Wildblood shrugged his shoulders sympathetically as he watched the man leave, then said, 'Ladies and gentlemen, I have a bid of ten guineas. Do I hear twenty?'

For a while, nobody spoke and it seemed that the bidding might have come to an end. At last, Felix Brandling called out a bid of fifteen guineas, to which the private art collector immediately countered with one of twenty.

'I thought you said *ten* was your final bid,' the MP yelled, turning angrily on the tall, thin man. 'Now you're bidding *twenty*.'

'And *I* thought you said you only wanted to buy *one* of the paintings,' the tall, thin man retorted, coolly. 'Now you're bidding for them *both*.'

'Gentlemen,' Wildblood interrupted. 'Please can we dispense with the private conversation and get on with the bidding. Now, there is a bid of twenty guineas on the table.'

'I'll bid twenty-five,' declared Brandling, expecting that to silence his rival once and for all.

'Thirty,' the tall, thin man called out, much to Brandling's surprise.

'Thirty-five,' declared Brandling, stubbornly.

'Forty,' the tall, thin man called out, much to Brandling's irritation.

'Forty-five,' declared Brandling, determinedly.

'Fifty,' the tall, thin man called out, much to Brandling's exasperation.

'Fifty-one,' declared Brandling, slightly less resolutely.

'Fifty-five,' the tall, thin man called out.

'Why you are so keen to get your hands on these paintings?' Brandling shouted to him, feeling highly suspicious of the man's motives.

'I am a collector of fine art,' the tall, thin man replied, snootily. 'Have you finished bidding?'

Brandling fixed him with a glare and called out, 'Fifty-nine guineas.' It sounded like a taunt, rather than a bid.

There was a nervous tension in the room as everyone waited to hear how the tall, thin man's lisp would cope with the next round of bidding and its concomitant sibilants. But he disappointed them by shaking his head in a gesture of defeat and signally to the auctioneer that he had reached his limit and would now withdraw. Brandling smiled haughtily, pleased that he had come out on top.

'So, ladies and gentlemen, fifty-nine guineas has it at the moment,' Wildblood announced. 'Are there any further bids before I close the sale?'

No one spoke. He allowed a brief pause to elapse, then raised the gavel and was about to bring it crashing down on the table to signal the end of the auction, when a gentle but distinctive voice emerged from the back of the room.

'Five hundred guineas.'

There was a collective intake of breath as all eyes turned to detect the source of this remarkable bid. They alighted upon a gentlemen who sported luxuriant white whiskers and beneath whose shiny, bald head a pair of blue eyes twinkled. Wildblood contrived to react with shock and asked, 'Did I hear you correctly, sir? Please, could you repeat your bid?'

'Five hundred guineas.'

This confirmation elicited another gasp from many of the on-lookers and produced a startling effect upon Brandling whose features, now stripped of their previous concealments, became contorted with rage. His cheeks flushed and bulged, his jowls shuddered and juddered, his lips trembled and emitted large flecks of spittle and he began to cough, at first a mere tickle, then a wheeze, then a more violent hacking noise and, finally, a racking paroxysm which appeared to make his whole body vibrate and was accompanied by a thunderous emission of noxious fumes which caused those around him to retreat as far as the cramped space would permit. In that instant, the realisation dawned on him that, unless he was willing to spend a far larger sum than he had anticipated, Hadwen Bragg would inevitably become the owner of a painting which he could then display in his clothing emporium (or elsewhere, if the man were so minded) to be seen by his wealthy clients and make *him* - Felix Brandling, a very important person, Member of Parliament no less – a laughing stock throughout the town. So, he thought, he would have to pay out a small fortune (*very* small by his standards, it was true) or risk total humiliation. Meanwhile, the Eccentrics who were present in the room were swept along by a wave of excitement as they recalled Perlee Parker's promise to share with them the proceeds of the sale and realised that the amount involved could indeed be substantial.

'Was that another bid I heard from you, sir?' Wildblood enquired as Brandling struggled to regain a semblance of composure.

After a long, sullen silence - though not quite long enough to allow the auctioneer to bring down his gavel - Brandling muttered grudgingly, 'Very well then. I'll say five hundred and ten guineas.'

Hadwen Bragg remained completely impassive as though he had confidently expected Brandling to match his figure and was quite prepared to raise the stakes even higher. But if the

Quaker's first bid surprised everyone, his next move astounded them. 'Two thousand guineas,' he said, calmly.

The colour drained from Felix Brandling's face. In an instant, his complexion took on the pallid hue of a cadaver's. His lips trembled, just as they had done in response to Hadwen Bragg's previous bid, but this time the quivering was the precursor not to a bout of coughing but rather to an outbreak of weeping. 'Two thousand guineas!' he bawled, his voice breaking into a series of loud sobs as the tears ran down his cheeks, while those among the Eccentrics with some capacity for basic arithmetic attempted to calculate their potential dividend from the auction. Wildblood waited patiently while Brandling unwound his muffler and dried his face. 'Would you like to make another bid, sir?' he asked.

The MP looked across to Hadwen Bragg, trying to judge from the man's demeanour whether he intended to continue the round of bidding until the final figure had reached an even more outrageous level. If there was one thing of which Brandling was absolutely certain, it was that under no circumstances could he allow the sale to end without acquiring ownership of the paintings. The thought of his rival taking possession of them was unthinkable. Hadwen Bragg's deadpan expression, however, betrayed no indication of his intentions.

And then he did something quite unexpected.

Turning to Felix Brandling, he said, in a manner which sounded both compassionate and commanding, 'I would not wish to bankrupt thee, even if I was capable of such a thing, which I am not. So, if thee would care to trump my last bid, I will not press thee further and the paintings will fall into thy hands.'

Brandling took a few moments to absorb the implications of this statement and then rejoined, less than graciously, 'Well then, Bragg, if you are not going to outdo me, withdraw your last bid and let me have the paintings for five hundred and ten guineas ...'

Wildblood interrupted him in officious tones. 'The bid of two thousand guineas has been legally made and cannot therefore be withdrawn,' he asserted. 'So, should you wish to win the auction, sir, you must submit a higher bid.'

Brandling glared at the auctioneer, then at Hadwen Bragg. His bid, whispered in a voice laden with resentment, was scarcely audible. 'Two thousand guineas and a ha'penny piece.'

'Two thousand guineas and a ha'penny piece, did I hear you say, sir?' Wildblood shouted, keen to receive confirmation of the man's bid as well as to ensure that everybody else in the room was able to follow the proceedings.

Brandling nodded his assent bitterly and an expression of delight lit up the face of every Eccentric in the room at their unexpected acquisition of such untold riches.

'Are there any further bids, then?' Observing Hadwen Bragg's firm shake of the head, the auctioneer banged his gavel loudly on the table four or five times, the first to signal the end of the sale and the rest for dramatic effect. 'I declare the gentleman on my right to be the winner. Congratulations, sir, the paintings are yours for the sum of two thousand guineas and a ha'penny which, if my calculation serves me correctly, means that each has a notional value of one thousand guineas and one farthing. If you would be kind enough to let me have your details and a bill of exchange, I will ensure that the goods are delivered to you within the week.'

48

The Eccentrics who stayed behind in Hell's Kitchen after the auction were celebrating their new-found wealth by imbibing several quarts of hop-flavoured beverages, provided free on this occasion by His Satanic Majesty. Perlee Parker had reaffirmed his promise – not that anyone ever doubted his sincerity – to share the proceeds of one thousand guineas and one farthing among the eleven *characters* (plus the Widow Henderson) who appeared in the portrait.

A chastened Felix Brandling had gone off to reflect upon his bruising experience and to await the delivery of the paintings for which he had successfully bid and, presumably, to plan the destruction of at least one of them and, quite possibly, the other - unless he believed he could sell it or, perhaps, that he ought to retain it in order to savour its artistic merit (the latter prospect being most unlikely in such an inveterate philistine).

For my part, I was intrigued at the resourceful manner in which Wildblood, the auctioneer, played his role in the scheme Perlee had devised where Hadwen Bragg undertook to outbid Brandling until the bidding reached the predetermined figure, at which point he withdrew, leaving the latter as the victor but at a significant cost. 'How did you know that Brandling would be prepared to pay two thousand guineas?' I asked Perlee, as we returned to his garret that evening.

'I couldn't know for sure,' he said, 'but I was as certain as I could be that he would do everything in his power to prevent somebody else outbidding him in order to buy that painting. I gambled on the likelihood that such a self-important man would not countenance the possibility of another person – and, in particular, Hadwen Bragg – getting their hands on it. Otherwise, he would run the risk of complete degradation and disgrace. It is one thing for his portrait to be displayed in Hell's Kitchen where it is seen only by those whom he regards as inferior beings, but it would be quite another matter for the well-to-do customers of *Bragg and Company* to be confronted with the sight of their Member of Parliament labelled as a cheat and the betrayer of his best friend. He probably reckoned that this kind of exposure would mean the end of his career in public office. And the only way he could guarantee to avoid such a state of affairs would be to outbid everyone else at the auction, gain ownership of the painting and then ensure that it never again saw the light of day. Two thousand guineas is a lot of money, but Brandling can afford it.'

'But what if you had miscalculated?' I pressed him. 'What if Brandling decided after all not to make the final bid at the auction, leaving Hadwen Bragg to pay two thousand guineas?'

'Mister Bragg told me that he was willing to take that chance,' Perlee replied. 'But it was a calculated risk which came off.'

'So in the end, everyone has got what they wanted although Brandling may not have been too pleased at what it cost him,' I summed up cheerfully. 'You must be hoping that you never see that man again.'

'That's where you're wrong, James.' Perlee smiled conspiratorially. 'Revenge is sweet, as the saying has it, and today we obtained some measure of retribution. But I haven't finished with Felix Brandling yet. Not by a long way. Nor with his partner-in-crime.'

*

Jasper Scuffins was most aggrieved that his slack time in the company of fellow keelmen (or, at least, those few who still deigned to associate with him since he had spoken out in favour of calling off their strike) had been disturbed by the arrival of a posse of constables from the Town Guard who burst into the snug-room of the Three Indian Kings Tavern. He was outraged when they told him that he was under arrest. He was incandescent with fury when they announced that they were taking him directly to the courtroom on the orders of the Sitting Magistrate.

His anger abated when he discovered that the magistrate presiding over the court on that day was none other than Aeneas Snitterby, with whom he had secretly collaborated to bring about an end to the keelmen's dispute with the Hoastmen and who was shortly to become his new employer. He was quite certain that the man would treat him leniently and that in a few short weeks he would, as arranged, take up his sinecure as the off-putter on the Benwell staithes, an easy job with good pay and plenty of opportunity for supplementing it with illicit 'extras'.

'Put him in the dock,' the magistrate instructed the constable.

'With pleasure, Your Worship,' the constable replied deferentially before shoving the prisoner roughly into the same tiny wooden cubicle topped with curved iron spikes which, not long ago, had been occupied by Miss Kitty Dace.

With a dramatic gesture, Aeneas Snitterby held up a number of sheets of paper. Looking in the direction of the public gallery, which was nearly half-full with students of law, interested citizens, interfering busybodies and Geordies at large, together with a few down-and-outs who had come into the building in order to shelter from the rain, he declared solemnly, 'It is a very serious crime to issue threats against another person. In this case, a very important person.' Then, turning to the prisoner in the dock, he said, 'Now, Scuffins, I am told that you are responsible for this letter threatening our esteemed Member of Parliament as well as for various notices which contain malicious statements against the Company of Hoastmen and which urge people to commit treason. Is that correct?'

Jasper Scuffins was slightly surprised at the aggressive tone in Aeneas Snitterby's voice but had no doubt that this performance was for the benefit of the members of the public who looked on. He assumed that the magistrate would feel obliged, for the sake of appearances, to make a show of treating the trial seriously before announcing his verdict that the accused was innocent of all charges and would leave the court completely exonerated and without a single blemish on his character.

'No, sir, not me, sir,' he replied, with a surreptitious wink at the magistrate. 'Aa nivvor wrote no letter nor nothing else. In fact, sir, Aa canna write much. Only me name and a few other words. So Aa canna be guilty, sir.' That defence, he thought, should be sufficiently persuasive to enable Aeneas Snitterby to dismiss the charges without further argument.

'You may not have written the documents personally,' said the magistrate, apparently not yet quite ready to bring the proceedings to a conclusion, 'but did you ask somebody else to write them?'

Jasper Scuffins hesitated. Aeneas Snitterby seemed – inadvertently, no doubt - to be dragging things out unnecessarily and even, perhaps, opening up a line of questioning which could become a little complicated and make it more difficult for the magistrate to absolve him of any blame. 'Aa canna *make* somebody write anything, sir,' he said, not at all comfortable about the direction in which the exchange was heading.

'Well, did you *force* somebody to write them by threatening them with violence?' Snitterby demanded angrily.

The man is definitely over-acting, Jasper Scuffins thought, anxiously. He didn't know how to answer the last question except with a flat denial which would, he hoped, give the magistrate the opportunity to rule that he believed the defendant's evidence and would consequently acquit him. 'Definitely not, sir,' he said. 'Most definitely not.'

'But you forced a young lady to write this letter. You told her what to write and threatened to beat her if she refused. Isn't that the truth, Scuffins?' The magistrate's face gave no clue at all that he was acting out a pretence.

Jasper Scuffins was rapidly becoming very concerned and began to wonder whether he might have totally misjudged the situation and that Aeneas Snitterby was actually going to treat him like a real criminal. He was lost for words.

It was the magistrate who filled the silence. 'Jasper Scuffins,' he announced, 'I find you guilty beyond all reasonable doubt of the felonies with which you are charged. Beyond *any* doubt at all, I should make clear. Therefore, I have decided after lengthy consideration …' – he smirked at this point – '… to treat you to a long sea voyage at the expense of the Government.'

By now, Jasper Scuffins was completely alarmed at the turn which events had taken and was about to cry out in protest when the constable grabbed him around the head and prevented him from making any sound. Aeneas Snitterby, employing the customary expression which he adopted when dispatching the guilty to the penal colony in the Antipodes, declared gravely, 'I regret to inform you, Mister Scuffins, that your transport will definitely *not* be one of delight.' He could see that the subtlety of this witticism was wasted on the prisoner before him, so he continued, 'I have considered carefully …' – another smirk – ' … to which convict settlement you would be best suited. I have heard from the most reliable of sources that Norfolk Island is a particularly unpleasant place. A hell on earth, so they say. I trust that you may care to use your good offices to render it a more amenable environment during your extended stay there.'

Jasper Scuffins was still not absolutely sure whether the magistrate's verdict was a put-up job for public consumption and even now he held on tenuously to the slimmest of hopes that shortly he would be invited into the Mayor's Parlour by Aeneas Snitterby and the two of them would share a joke together about the charade over a glass of good quality wine. Any remaining doubts that he entertained had all but dissipated by the time he was marched down the wooden staircase leading from the dock and into the long, dark, damp, dank tunnel which took him directly to the Keyside and on to the prison hulk waiting there to transport him to the other side of the world.

49

It is a curious but well-observed phenomenon that some members of the ruling classes, particularly those who regard their perceived superiority as a God-given status, frequently pay no heed whatsoever to any lesser mortals who happen to be in their presence, even to the extent of appearing to assume that such wretched creatures are incapable of possessing any human faculties. Thus it was then, that Auld Judy, by keeping her ears and eyes alert and her wits constantly about her, was able to piece together a record of the nefarious undertakings of Alderman Applegarth and Felix Brandling MP, who often discussed their affairs quite openly in front of her without realising that the Keeper of the Town Hutch was a shrewd and meticulous listener and observer.

She had already played her part in Perlee Parker's plan by arranging the delivery to Felix Brandling of the message which provoked his furious trip to the Flying Horse Tavern where he discovered his less-than-flattering portrait displayed for all to see. Now, with her further assistance, Perlee drew up an inventory of the articles removed illicitly from the town's public buildings over a period of many months by Brandling and his partner-in-crime. It was an impressive list, and one which he incorporated into the letter addressed to the gentlemen in question.

STOLEN FROM THE GUILD HALL:

1. *Paintings by George Morland entitled 'The Anglers' Repast' and 'The Old Water Mill'*

2.   Prints by Thomas Bewick of 'A Squirrel' and 'A Heron', together with a number of his miniature woodcuts
3.   Portrait by Sir Joshua Reynolds of 'Sir James Hodges'
4.   Portrait by Jonathan Richardson of 'The Artist's Son, Jonathan Richardson the Younger, in his Study'
5.   Portrait by Thomas Gainsborough of 'Lady Georgiana Cavendish, Duchess of Devonshire' (subsequently auctioned at Sotheby's for 500 guineas)
6.   First edition copy (1797) of 'A History of British Birds' by Thomas Bewick

STOLEN FROM THE MANSION HOUSE:

1.   Portrait by William Hogarth of 'The Distressed Poet'
2.   Painting by Andrea Soldi entitled 'Portrait of a Gentleman'
3.   Painting by Joseph Wright of Derby entitled 'Matlock Tour'
4.   Painting by George Stubbs entitled 'Mares and Foals in a Landscape'
5.   Various items of silverware, including a 72 piece dinner service, 4 candlesticks, 2 candelabras, a water pitcher and a basin
6.   A queer-cased year-clock
7.   Various items of Newcastle glassware, including wine goblets, dram glasses, rummers, engraved mugs and decanters

STOLEN FROM THE ASSEMBLY ROOMS:

1.   Two glass chandeliers previously hanging in the Great Ballroom
2.   A mirror previously occupying the wall of the Saloon

3. *Painting by Lillian Heaven entitled 'Girl Drinking from a Fountain'*
4. *Painting by John Downman entitled 'Sir John Falstaff, Mrs Ford and others'.*

On the afternoon of the day following the auction which took place in the attic room of the Flying Horse tavern, Perlee Parker presented himself at the Guild Hall, armed with a large envelope and the knowledge that the two men were currently together in the Robing Room. He handed the doorman the envelope containing what he described as an urgent communication, with a request for it to be conveyed immediately to its intended recipients, and awaited the expected summons to their presence, which arrived within minutes.

Once they had overcome the shock of discovering the identity of their accuser and recognising him as the same fellow who had had the temerity to label Brandling as a cheat and then expose him to public ridicule by making him the subject of an oil painting, they were markedly less dismissive of Perlee Parker than they had been on his previous visit to the Guild Hall. Nevertheless, while their demeanour suggested a degree of trepidation at the detection of their crimes, they were brazen enough to feign innocence of any wrongdoing and to attempt to browbeat Perlee into believing that he had completely misunderstood the motives behind, and the implications of, their actions.

'What is the meaning of this piece of fiction?' blustered Alderman Applegarth, trying desperately to display a modicum of composure.

'Fiction, you say?' returned Perlee Parker, sinking uninvited into one of the leather-clad armchairs, which he selected because of its distance from Felix Brandling and the latter's booming eruptions. 'Perhaps we should send the Town Marshal and a few of his Serjeants and ranzelmen to your private residences to see whether they can recover any of the paintings and the rest of the stolen goods,' he suggested. 'Apart from the ones which you've sold off or auctioned, I mean. What do you think to that, gentlemen?'

For a while, neither Alderman Applegarth nor Felix Brandling could summon up a satisfactory response. At last, the latter said, unconvincingly, 'I trust, sir, that you are not imputing any misconduct on our parts?'

'Are you so blinded by your self-importance, sir, that you no longer consider the theft of public property to fall within that definition?'

'Damn your impertinence, sir,' replied Brandling, slightly emboldened by his third glass of port. 'In the first place, I *am* an important person, I'll have you know. A *very* important person, as I happen to be. A Member of Parliament, no less. And one can hardly be much more important than *that*, can one? And, secondly, the fact that both Alderman Applegarth and I have, quite altruistically and without a second thought for our own inconvenience, taken it upon ourselves to offer our personal guardianship for such prized public assets is something which should be greatly admired, rather than disparaged, as you are seeking to do.'

'Ha!' scoffed Perlee Parker. 'I have it on very good authority that some of these *prized public assets,* as you've described them are, far from being protected, currently housed in premises such as Gosforth House which are so disgustingly insanitary as to be infested by more rats than would be tolerated in a Sandgate brothel.' As he delivered this broadside, he reached over to a conveniently adjacent table, again uninvited, and selected the fattest cigar available while his two reluctant hosts seethed silently with scarcely contained rage. Next, picking up a wooden spill, he pushed it into the centre of the coals which blazed away in the fireplace and used the flame to light the tip of the tobacco leaf. Then, sinking back into the capacious armchair, he drew in a deep lungful of smoke and savoured it briefly before blowing it out disdainfully towards Applegarth's head, wreathing its owner in a cloud of acrid fumes. He waited for the Alderman's coughing fit to subside before commenting, 'I wonder what other tricks you pair are planning.'

The pair in question looked at one another guiltily, each with a pained expression which betrayed an apprehension that their recent conversation might have been overheard. Perhaps by coincidence or, more likely, because they regularly discussed topics of this nature, Alderman Applegarth and Felix Brandling had that very morning been contemplating the practicability of removing the large carved wooden frieze, with its representations of the Judgement of Solomon and the Miraculous Draught of Fishes, which decorated the chimney-mantel of the Merchants Court. Applegarth had also made the outrageous suggestion that they should appropriate the remains of the wombat and duck-billed platypus, both preserved in spirit, which had recently been donated to the town's Literary and Philosophical Society by the Governor of New South Wales, a proposition which found no favour whatsoever with Brandling, who fostered a loathing of all members of the animal kingdom except racehorses - a loathing which had been intensified by his latest encounter with rats.

Before either of them could decide how to respond, Perlee Parker spoke again. 'I would like you to be aware, gentlemen, that a copy of this *piece of fiction*, as you call it,' he said, pointing to the letter, which now lay next to Brandling's empty port sipper, 'is currently in the hands of Mister Hadwen Bragg, who will shortly have the opportunity, should he wish to avail himself of it, of sharing the contents with other members of the Newcastle Society for Effecting the Abolition of the Slave Trade, his numerous colleagues among the town's traders and the editor of the *Newcastle Courant* as well, of course, as His Worship the Mayor, who I am sure will be greatly vexed to learn that his official residence has been looted by common thieves …'

'*Common* thieves!' Brandling exploded. 'How dare you call us common, sir. I have never …'

He was interrupted by Alderman Applegarth, who placed a restraining hand on Brandling's arm and said, 'I believe that our young friend may be about to present a proposal to us. I think we had better hear what he has to say.' Brandling stifled a further tirade and, despite an angry glare at his colleague, took the latter's advice and subsided grudgingly into silence.

'You are quite correct,' Perlee Parker said. 'I will tell you plainly what you have to do in order to atone for your reprehensible actions and to prevent a full exposure of them, not just throughout this town but wider afield too. And certainly reaching the hallowed precincts of the Houses of Parliament. You will undoubtedly find this expiation painful but I believe that, on reflection, you will judge that the particular course of action I have in mind is far preferable to the alternative.'

'Spit it out, sir,' Brandling fumed impatiently, unable to hold his peace any longer and bridling at the unaccustomed experience of being dictated to by an inferior. 'What is it that you want from us?'

'There are a number of penances which you must carry out …'

'Penances? You talk as though you were my parish priest. You are not suggesting we put on sackcloth and ashes?'

'Don't worry, the reparations I have in mind have none of the trappings of the confessional. Think of them more as the labours of Heracles.'

'The man is talking in tongues,' Applegarth muttered loudly to Brandling. 'I can't make head nor tail of him.'

'The first thing you must do …' Perlee Parker declared, in a voice that brooked no rebuttal, '… is to restore to their original locations everything you have pilfered from this building as well as from the Mansion House and the Assembly Rooms. You have three days to comply with this requirement.'

There was a long silence as the condemned miscreants contemplated their fate.

'How are we going to explain the sudden return of the missing articles?' Applegarth asked at last.

'That's your problem. You will have to use your ingenuity, just as you did when you sought to explain their disappearance. Given your well-practised ability to dissemble, it should not cause you too much difficulty.'

'There's one thing at least on this list which we can't get back,' Brandling chipped in. 'The Gainsborough was sold to an American and is probably now hanging in some mansion in New York.'

'I've thought about that,' Perlee replied. 'And since you received five hundred guineas as the proceeds of the sale, I have decided that it would be appropriate for you to repay that sum to the public treasury. Plus interest, of course. Shall we say an additional one hundred percent?'

'One hundred percent? Are you mad, sir? Not even the most extortionate usurer charges that rate of interest.'

'You are quite right, of course. Perhaps we should ask His Worship the Mayor to determine what figure would be a fitting one.' Perlee Parker waited in vain for a response to his suggestion before continuing. 'Ha! I see you have no alternative to put forward. One hundred percent it is then. Anyway, gentlemen, there are two more tasks which must be carried out in order to earn a reprieve from the retribution which otherwise awaits you. The first of these will require your joint enterprise upon the arrival of the … er … works of art, may I humbly call them? … for which you, Brandling, bid successfully in yesterday's auction and which will be delivered to you within the week. The second wholly concerns you …' Again, he addressed Brandling directly at this point.

'Me? Why me?' Brandling protested.

'That will become clear when I explain the precise nature of the assignment,' Perlee replied. 'In the meantime, you can console yourself with my assurance that it is one which requires the agency of a person of great importance.'

50

'There's a … er … lady to see you, sir, beggin' yer pardon, sir,' Felix Brandling's housekeeper announced.

'Tell her to go away,' her employer commanded, sipping his port.

'Aa've aalready told her, beggin' yer pardon, sir. But she divvent tak nee notice.'

'Tell her again.'

The housekeeper returned a few minutes later. 'Beggin' yer pardon, sir, Aa told her to gan away but she still she divvent tak nee notice.'

'What does she want?'

'Aa dinaa knaa, beggin' yer pardon, sir. But by the smell of her and the canny big creel she's carrying, Aa think she's selling fish.'

'Fish, you say? Well, tell her I don't buy fish from hawkers. Nor anything else, for that matter.'

The housekeeper returned once again a few minutes later. 'Beggin' yer pardon, sir, but she won't gan away unless she speaks to ye first …'

He was about to dismiss the housekeeper for a third time when he saw that the visitor had forced herself through the door and into the lounge where he sat. She was a formidable looking woman with a domed head, weather-beaten features and hands which bore witness to a lifetime of tough manual labour. She clenched a briar pipe in her teeth.

'What is the meaning of this intrusion?' Brandling demanded angrily, thinking that the woman looked vaguely familiar.

'Aa've come to collect my reward,' said Dolly Peel.

'Reward? What reward, woman?'

'A hundred guineas.'

'A hundred guineas? Are you mad?'

'Aa will be if Aa dinaa get it, marra. Aa'm the one what's responsible for having that gadgie found guilty of sending ye a threatening letter. He'll be on his way to New South Wales now, poor divil.'

Brandling had received word earlier that day from Aeneas Snitterby of the transportation of Jasper Scuffins and, while delighted at the news, had tried to put to the back of his mind his promise of a reward. However, now that Scuffins had been convicted, he realised that he had no option but to pay up.

'I'll prepare you a bill of exchange,' he said grudgingly.

'Aa dinaa want no bill of exchange,' the woman retorted. 'Aa've larned nivvor to trust a gadgie that wears garters. Aa'll tak yer hard cash and nowt else.'

Brandling was reluctant to part with any cash, although he had plenty of it. He sensed, however, that he wouldn't get rid of the woman until she had her money and he knew that if she stayed much longer, he would have to have the place fumigated once more, this time to get rid of the stink of fish.

'Wait outside a few minutes while I go to my safe and fetch the cash,' he said reluctantly.

'Ye can tak yer time. Aa'm quite comfortable enough here, thanking ye,' she replied, dumping her basket down on the carpet next to the fireplace and, to Brandling's horror, sinking into one of his George II mahogany library armchairs.

He returned with the money in double-quick order and the woman counted it three times before pronouncing herself satisfied that he had handed over the correct sum.

'So you'll be on your way now then,' Brandling said. It was part assertion and part question.

'Oh, that's not aal Aa came fer. Aa have something for ye too,' she told him. She plunged a scarred hand inside her bodice and retrieved an envelope which she proffered in Brandling's direction. 'These are your instructions from Mister Hadwen Bragg. I believe ye knaa what ye need to do with 'em.'

Then he remembered where he had seen her before. She was one of the group of lower orders portrayed in that ghastly picture that he'd been forced by that gypsy auctioneer to buy alongside the one he'd really wanted.

After he had finally got rid of the woman (but not before she had finished off the contents of the port sipper which stood three-quarters full on the mantelshelf), Brandling opened the envelope and read through the sheaf of papers inside. As he did so, he sighed deeply several times. In normal circumstances, he greatly enjoyed the feeling of self-importance which he experienced whenever he made a speech from the benches of the House of Commons, particularly when it addressed one of his favourite topics, such as the Atlantic trade in slaves.

He was quite sure, however, that he would not be deriving any pleasure from the speech which he was due to make in the forthcoming debate on that very matter.

*

Newcastle Courant

SLAVERY ABOLISHED BY PARLIAMENT

On Friday of last Week, Parliament voted to abolish the International Trade in Slaves and to enforce the

---

Prohibition of this Commerce through the Application of our Nation's maritime Power.

The decisive Vote in the House of Commons followed an impassioned Speech during the Debate by Felix Brandling, the Member for Newcastle-on-Tyne, who had previously been a strong Advocate of the Slave Trade but who, inexplicably, came to the Abolitionists' Cause on this Occasion with a rousing Condemnation of the Horrors suffered by its African Victims and the Inhumanity demonstrated by those who participated in or profited from what he described as 'this despicable Trafficking and Exploitation of human Beings'.

We reproduce below some Extracts of the Speech, during which the MP appeared to be overcome with Emotion on several Occasions, paused frequently to fight back his Tears and was observed a number of Times to bite his Lip.

'I declare with absolute Certainty that there is not a single Soul here present whose Heart would not be overwhelmed with Pity at the Sight of six or seven hundred miserable Africans, Men and Women without Distinction or Separation, crammed together in the stifling Hold of a Slave Ship, surrounded by the most nauseous Stench and utmost Filth and Squalor, their Limbs manacled one to another, their Bodies rampant with Hunger, Thirst and Disease so that those fifteen or twenty percent who perish on-Board without being able to experience the Torments which await them upon Arrival at their

Destination are deemed to be the most fortunate among them...

'In the Plantations of the Americas, these Wretches are forced by their Terror of the Lash to labour naked all Day under the burning Sun like Beasts of Burden, weighted down by Chains or Neck-yokes or Leg-irons and mercilessly flogged should they dare to desist from their Toil for a Moment, so that many expire from their Stripes...

'The Men are worked until Death or, if judged not to be sound in Wind and Limb, are thrown into Cesspits or on to Dunghills and left there to die. The Women are savagely and repeatedly ravished and, unless they succumb to the Perils of Labour or the Pangs of Childbirth, are compelled to bear the Bastards of their Masters ...

'I vow never to rest until I have seen the Abolition of this iniquitous and inhuman Trade, a Trade which dishonours this great Nation of ours as well as every Individual who fails to denounce the Evil perpetrated against those African Wretches or who dares to claim that it is an Enterprise necessary to the economic Well-being of our beloved Country ...'

Delighted members of the Newcastle Society for Effecting the Abolition of the Slave Trade, who observed the debate from the packed public Gallery, were heard to comment afterwards that Felix Brandling's Speech could almost have been written by their Chairman, Mister Hadwen Bragg, a local Philanthropist and the Owner of a Clothing Emporium in the Town, so closely did the Sentiments expressed therein resemble his own.

*

Felix Brandling had carried out one part of his penance to the complete and obvious satisfaction of Mister Hadwen Bragg and, no doubt, of others in the Newcastle Society for Effecting the Abolition of the Slave Trade. Now, it was time for him to perform his remaining acts of atonement, in conjunction with his partner-in-crime, as Perlee Parker had branded Alderman Applegarth.

Over the next few days, a number of items which had been absent for some time from their original locations reappeared in various places within the Mansion House, the Guild Hall and the Assembly Rooms, presumably having been returned by those who had assumed temporary custody of them for the purposes of repair and restoration or by the chancellors of universities to which they had been loaned. It was also verified by the Keeper of the Town Hutch (a certain Judy Dowling, also known as Auld Judy) that a considerable sum of money – reputed to be one thousand guineas – had been contributed anonymously to the civic treasury, presumably by some charitable or public-spirited philanthropist.

In the heady hours following the distribution by Perlee Parker of the Eccentrics' share of the proceeds of the sale of their portrait, Bold Archy and Kitty Dace made the unexpected announcement that they had decided to join one another in marriage. This was on the face of it a curious union, with one partner being well in excess of six-and-three-quarter feet tall while the other failed to achieve even four. Nevertheless, it was perhaps no more curious than many others. I have, for example, heard of a man who married his pet dog and another who was so narcissistic that he married himself, although I must allow that these instances may be apocryphal.

Their betrothal was celebrated by a party held, at the kind invitation of His Satanic Majesty, in Hell's Kitchen, which was in full swing when a wayward spark from Dolly Peel's pipe accidentally set fire to the stuffed badger. The room had to be temporarily evacuated while the flames were doused and, when the merry-makers returned, they found that the badger had lost most of its bristles, shrunk in size and its limbs were partly fused together by the heat. Captain Starkey immediately identified it as the young sea-lion he had brought back from New South Wales, having fended off a brutal attack from the creature and being awarded it by his commanding officer as a trophy to mark his bravery. It was on that same evening that Bella and I (who had, during our time together at Number 264 Spital Tongues, become almost like brother and sister) came to realise that our mutual regard went far beyond the natural fondness which siblings share and that we were in fact greatly affectionated to one another.

There was still one more piece needed to complete the jigsaw …

'What makes you quite so sure that Brandling and Applegarth will keep to the last part of the bargain?' I asked Perlee Parker, whom I was helping to move his belongings into the fine apartment in Pilgrim-street which he could now afford to rent, thanks to the generous sum which remained after he had paid Wildblood his commission from the sale of the portrait depicting Brandling conspiring with the Setter-on outside Mordue's cockpit.

'You remember, James, when Applegarth tore up the sketch I had made?'

'Of course I remember,' I replied. 'I couldn't understand why you didn't seem annoyed until you showed me that you had copied it on to a canvass so that you could turn it into an oil painting. I hadn't realised how cautious you had been.'

'Well now, I am even more cautious than you imagined. Or perhaps even less trusting of some of my fellow men. Especially if they are unelected holders of public office.'

'I don't follow you, Perlee.'

'It's quite simple. I think that I must have had a premonition that at some time in the future I might have another reason to insure myself against some possible act of betrayal. So, just as a precaution, I made a *second* copy of the sketch. And I still have it. If necessary – for example, if our friends fail to honour their covenant - I can readily convert it into another painting, identical to the original of *A Very Self-Important Man Bribes An Accomplice To Cheat His Best Friend*. And, of course, I will then also be free to bring to the attention of the authorities the small matter of the extensive pilfering of public assets by those trusted to protect them.'

'Do Brandling and Applegarth know about this?'

'Certainly. I deigned to share this information with them. So, they can be under no illusion about what will happen should our work of art unaccountably vanish from its setting.'

*

I should explain to those not familiar with the geography of our town that, if a visitor to Newcastle follows the main road in from the western suburbs and descends the steep incline termed the Side, or (if he happens to travel in from the east and does not begrudge the inconvenience) comes along the Keyside from Sandgate, he will reach a fine open triangular space known as the Sandhill, which is generally agreed to mark the centre of the town. It is normally buzzing with the to-ings and fro-ings of traders going about their business, barrow boys trundling their wares to market, children playing hopscotch and rolling hoops, courting couples taking the air near the river, beggars pestering whomsoever crosses their path and all manner of entertainers and street performers, including buskers, clowns, escapologists and jugglers. Here, on two sides of the Sandhill, he will discover rows of lofty buildings which were once owned by wealthy merchants and which still bear vestiges of their former grandeur, together with several open-fronted shops and various dwelling houses adorned with diamond-paned lattice windows. He may even catch a glimpse, among those who have come to inspect or purchase the merchandise on display, of the recently-wedded pawnbroker, Walter Humble, together with his smiling wife Martha (formerly Scuffins), who will almost certainly be pushing a very young child in a wicker perambulator while an older boy skips merrily alongside.

The third side of the Sandhill is occupied by the Guild Hall, a handsome edifice built in a combination of Italian and Gothic styles, its façade embellished by the town's coat of arms with the motto *Fortiter Defendit Triumphans.* If the visitor approaches the public entrance, he is likely to be confronted by an old woman, possibly wielding a stout stick, and he should not make the error of imagining that her maturity renders her incapable of defending the place against those whose admittance she deems inappropriate. Assuming that he harbours no ill-intent and is allowed to cross the threshold, he will find himself in a large lobby area, thickly carpeted and well-appointed with various statuettes, wall-hangings and comfortable armchairs and benches in which those with business there may await their turn until their appointments with members of the Common Council or other dignitaries are due.

Should he cast his eyes around the walls of the lobby, his gaze is likely to be drawn almost magnetically to a space – the most prestigious in the whole building, it is said - which was once occupied by Thomas Gainsborough's painting of Lady Georgiana Cavendish, Duchess of Devonshire and, later, left vacant for some time. In its place is now displayed a magnificent portrait, much admired and talked about throughout the town, entitled *The Newcastle Eccentrics in Hell's Kitchen,* a work by the artist Mister Perlee Parker, whose signature appears in the lower right-hand corner of this masterpiece.

The painting depicts a group of a dozen Geordies (as we locals are widely known) and is set in the taproom of a nearby hostelry called the Flying Horse Tavern. Since it was given pride of place in the Guild Hall, on the insistence of Mister Felix Brandling, Member of Parliament for the town, and Alderman Applegarth, a leading member of the Common Council, those whom it portrays have become household names in Newcastle. Bold Archy, Kitty Dace and the Widow Henderson. Blind Willie. Blackie Johnson. Captain Starkey. Bogie Theobald. Dolly Peel. Auld Judy. Bella. His Satanic Majesty. And myself, of course, James Maclachlan.

Quite an assortment. And, according to Perlee Parker, (almost) every single one of us a *character*.

51

Newcastle Courant   5 January 1822

DISASTROUS FIRE, OWNER MISSING

On the Evening of Thursday last, the Mansion House known as Seaton Delaval Hall suffered considerable Damage as the Result of being consumed by a devastating Conflagration. By sheer good Fortune, coupled with the exemplary and courageous Applications and Energies of the Workers of the Household, together with many Volunteers from local Villages, several Sections of the Building were saved. These include the East Wing, which houses the magnificent Stables with their unique and distinctive Stalls constructed in Stone, and the West Wing which contains the Great Kitchen and several Servants' Quarters.

At this Moment, it is conjectured (without conclusive Verification having been so far obtained) that the Conflagration was activated by the fortuitous Ignition of a Jackdaw's nest situated in the Flue of a Chimney adjacent to a wooden Roof Joist. Once the Flames had spread from the Source of the Fire, they increased with such Speed, Intensity and Fury that all Efforts to quell the Blaze were rendered futile. Witnesses claimed to have observed the Glass in the Windows and the Lead in the Roof melting before their Eyes due to the Potency of the Inferno.

The Hall, which was designed by the Architect Sir John Vanbrugh and completed around the Year of Our Lord 1730, was noted as among the most magnificent and sumptuous Buildings in the North East of the Country.

Several Hours after the Fire had been extinguished, a human Body, unidentifiable due to the advanced Extent of the Burns it had suffered, was found in the Mahogany Room which served as the Study of Sir Stanhope Delaval who resided at Seaton Delaval Hall with his wife, Lady Isabell Paulet.

Household Servants reported that Sir Stanhope had not been seen for some Days before the Tragedy. Lady Paulet, now well into her tenth Decade and reputedly one of the oldest surviving Persons in the North of England but still a Woman of considerable Activity and Well-being, is reported to have informed the Constables that the Corpse probably belonged to a Gentleman of the Road who had somehow managed to insinuate himself into the Building unobserved in order to seek Shelter and had unfortunately become trapped and perished in the Blaze.

The Constables are attempting urgently to make Contact with Sir Stanhope. Lady Paulet stated that her Husband is somewhere overseas on Business but was unable to specify exactly in which Country he is currently situated.

AUTHOR'S NOTE

The Newcastle Eccentrics were a group of people, also called the Props or the Worthies, who frequented the town around the beginning of the 19th century. They were portrayed by the artist Henry Perlee Parker in his oil painting entitled *Hell's Kitchen* (dated around 1817), which was set in a room of the Flying Horse Tavern in the Groatmarket. A number of those portrayed are referred to in *Newcassel Props*, a 19th century Geordie folksong. The original painting is depicted on the cover of this book. An engraving of it known as *Eccentric characters of Newcastle upon Tyne*, by George Armstrong and published in 1820, also survives.

Some of the characters in this novel are based to a greater or lesser extent on members of the Newcastle Eccentrics and others who lived in the town around that time.